Christmas at Cedarwood Lodge

Rebecca Raisin

ONE PLACE. MANY STORIES

HQ

An imprint of HarperCollins*Publishers* Ltd
1 London Bridge Street
London SE1 9GF

This paperback edition 2018

1

First published in Great Britain as *Celebrations and Confetti, Brides and Bouquets, Midnight and Mistletoe* by HQ, an imprint of HarperCollins*Publishers* Ltd 2016

ISBN: 9780263275315

MIX
Paper from
responsible sources
FSC™ C007454

This book is produced from independently certified FSC™ paper to ensure responsible forest management.
For more information visit: www.harpercollins.co.uk/green

Printed and bound in Great Britain by
CPI Group, Croydon CR0 4YY

REBECC[...]e of books morph[...]She's been widely [...]ogies, and in fiction magazines, and is now focusing on writing romance. The only downfall about writing about gorgeous men who have brains as well as brawn is falling in love with them – just as well they're fictional. Rebecca aims to write characters you can see yourself being friends with. People with big hearts who care about relationships, and, most importantly, believe in true, once-in-a-lifetime love.

Follow her on Twitter @jaxandwillsmum

Facebook https://www.facebook.com/RebeccaRaisinAuthor

Website rebeccaraisin.com

Also by Rebecca Raisin

Cedarwood Lodge Novellas

Celebrations & Confetti at Cedarwood Lodge

Brides & Bouquets at Cedarwood Lodge

Midnight & Mistletoe at Cedarwood Lodge

Once in a Lifetime Series

The Gingerbread Café trilogy

Christmas at the Gingerbread Café

Chocolate Dreams at the Gingerbread Café

Christmas Wedding at the Gingerbread Café

The Bookshop on the Corner

Secrets at Maple Syrup Farm

The Little Paris Collection

The Little Bookshop on the Seine

The Little Antique Shop under the Eiffel Tower

The Little Perfume Shop off the Champs-Élyséesh

Thank you to my bookish pals for your friendship.

Writing would be a lonely job without you.

For Marie Webdale whose friendship spans the oceans that separate us

Chapter One

Staring up at the imposing structure with its weathered façade, I had a terrible premonition that I'd made a mistake. A huge one. But, I reasoned, clawing back rising panic, I had *always* wanted to buy the hundred-year-old abandoned lodge. It had been put up for sale recently, and I'd jumped at the chance. The old place had good sturdy bones; it was solid, despite the desertion of its caretakers eons ago.

Even though I'd always dreamed about owning Cedarwood Lodge I hadn't expected for it to happen so soon. But it had, and I'd fallen madly in love with the place as it stood, shutters broken, doors in need of paint, ivy creeping through broken panes of glass, and cascading roses growing wild and free around the porch balustrades. Here was a place untouched for decades and I had a chance to bring it back to its former glory.

The September sky shifted from foggy wisps of gray to country blue as dawn arrived in the small New Hampshire town of Evergreen. A sputtering car swung into the long, winding driveway and I turned to watch my oldest friend, Micah, leap from his battered hatchback.

We'd been best friends since childhood and, though we'd drifted apart as adults, he was the first person I called when I bought Cedarwood Lodge – I offered him the job of maintenance manager, which he'd accepted with a '*Hell, yeah.*'

"You look exactly the same, Micah," I said, reaching up for a hug. "You haven't aged a bit." He'd filled out, no longer the lanky teenager I'd left behind, but aside from that he was the same old Micah with the same affable smile.

1

"It's the daily hikes up the bluff. That thin mountain air does wonders for my skin." He waggled his eyebrows. "We've got a lot of catching up to do. I almost fell over when you called. Lucky for you I was between jobs..."

"Lucky for me, all right."

I couldn't believe it'd been so long – when was the last time we had properly caught up? Five years ago, six? Time had ticked by so fast while I'd been away.

"You're different," he said, gesturing to my outfit and my usual flyaway curls restrained with a clip. "A little more polished."

I grinned. "Denim cut-offs and messy hair didn't quite cut it in Manhattan."

"What? Crazy city folk." He clucked his tongue.

"Right?" I joked. "How's Veronica?" I expected him to gush about his long-term girlfriend. Instead, his lips turned down for the briefest second, before he masked it with a smile.

"Veronica? There's a blast from the past. I haven't seen her for two and a bit years now. She was like you, Clio, left town and didn't look back."

Surprise knocked me sideways that she'd left town, left Micah.

"Sorry, Micah. I thought..." *Way to go, Clio!*

He touched my shoulder, giving me time to wrench the metaphorical foot from my mouth. "It's OK." He let out a half-laugh. "One day she just decided this place was too small for her big dreams. This town, it isn't for everyone."

An awkward silence hung between us. What kind of friend had I been to him? If I'd known, I would have come home for a visit to comfort him, make sure he was OK, like he would have done for me. Shame colored my cheeks, because I realized if he had called me I probably would have played the *too busy* card.

I knew Micah inside out – or at least I had at one point in my life – and I sensed he was downplaying the split. But I could see by the set of his jaw that the conversation was over. A part of me deflated – if they couldn't make it, what hope did any of us have? They'd been *the* perfect couple.

I tried desperately to think of a subject that would get us back on an even keel. "Look at that view, Micah. Tell me I'm not imagining it – this place *is* magical, right?"

"Magic to its very core." He flashed a grin, reminding me of the playful guy he'd been in high school. The one who transcended cliques and was friends with everyone. "And soon you'll have the banging of hammers and the whine of drills to contend with, so soak up the serenity while you can."

Work was set to start today – with plumbers, electricians, glaziers and carpenters arriving. Once they'd completed their jobs, painters would come in to pretty the place up. A project manager called Kai would be here soon to oversee it all while I concentrated on building the business and events side of things. Micah would float between us all and make sure things ran smoothly.

"Who'd have thought I'd end up back here, the proud and slightly nervous owner of Cedarwood Lodge?" I scrunched up my nose, my earlier doubts creeping back in. What had I done? I planned *parties*, not renovations! I *hired* places for events, I didn't buy them! Sometimes my audacity at buying Cedarwood Lodge scared me silly. It was such a huge gamble.

With a smile Micah said softly, "Never in a million years would I have thought you'd come back from the bright lights of the big city. Seems once people get a taste for it, Evergreen pales into insignificance. But I'm so glad you did. Remember when we were kids and hung out here? Even back then you talked about the parties you'd host, colors you'd paint the place. Ten years old and you predicted Cedarwood would be yours, *and* you were right."

The memories brought out a rash of goose bumps.

Cedarwood had been our own private playground. We had run breathless through the overgrown grounds, peeked into dusty windows and imagined the scenes that might have taken place there before it was abandoned.

The lodge had been closed ever since we could remember, and though stories had been whispered around town about the previous owners, we'd been too young to understand.

3

"It feels good to be home," I said, meaning it. At that moment Manhattan seemed light years away. "I didn't realize how much I missed you until I saw your goofy face."

"Oh, that hurt, that hurt a lot. *Goofy?* Don't think that just because *you've* come back all New York-ified that I've forgotten the girl with the uneven pigtails and mouth full of metal! The one who wore leg warmers as a fashion statement!" He raised a brow, challenging me.

I stifled a laugh. He was right. I had been a fashion *don't* when I was a teenager, but things quickly changed when I met Amory – my best friend in New York – who showed me how to dress to impress.

Would I regress, being back home? Go back to sweats and trainers? In my tailored suits and perilously high heels, I felt as though I had slipped on a different persona.

In the so-called 'city that never sleeps' it had been crucial to be assertive, ambitious, and one step ahead of the game. It had taken me years to build up my client list and I'd worked so damn hard for it. Maybe the old adage was true: you can take the girl out of Evergreen but you can't take Evergreen out of the girl, because here I was, home again.

I shielded my eyes from the rising sun. In the distance the mountain range was a riot of autumnal color: reds, ochres, dusty orange, and saffron yellow – the leaves on the hardwood trees clinging on for one more day.

"I hope I don't mess things up, Micah. This is my last chance. So many things could go wrong," I said seriously. I could lose everything. The place could remain silent, might never be filled with the tapping of high-heel shoes, the popping of champagne corks and peals of laughter. I couldn't go back to Manhattan; that door was firmly closed. "What if, after all the work is done, no one hires the place?"

"Hey…" he said, gently rubbing my arm. "That's not the Clio I know. Where's the girl who left town screeching about setting the world ablaze?" He gave me a playful shove. "Where's she gone?"

4

Up until a few months ago I'd been brimming with confidence, sure of my place in the world. But then I'd messed up – been too honest with a bride, misunderstanding her nerves for something else entirely. It had shaken me up, and made me question myself and my ambitions. Maybe I'd just been lucky before, but that bride kicked my legs out from under me, and I hadn't quite managed to get back up yet.

"She's. Right. Here." I rallied, pasting on a smile.

"Is that supposed to be a smile or a grimace?"

I flashed a sillier grin, reverting back to my teenage self and finding it refreshing. "God, it's good to see you, Micah." He was the one person I could be myself with. There was no point pretending because he knew the real me.

"Evergreen was never quite the same without you."

During our teenage years we'd spent weekends dreaming of a life outside of here. I guess we'd always thought the grass was greener elsewhere and, for a small-town girl, it was. It was so damn green it glowed, and I wished things had turned out differently there. At least I had Cedarwood as a consolation prize.

Micah grinned. "Hey…" He checked his watch. "Where's your mom? I thought she'd be here."

I shrugged. "I have no idea. When I rang again she made some flimsy excuse. I honestly thought she'd be bursting to see the inside of the lodge after all these years. But I guess she'll get here when she gets here."

My first day back in Evergreen I had driven straight to Mom's place to surprise her with the news about buying Cedarwood Lodge. It had been almost impossible to keep it secret but I'd wanted to tell her face to face and had guilelessly expected shrieks of joy. Instead she paled to a ghostly white, as if I had told her something shocking. We'd never been super-close, but still, I'd expected a smile, a word of encouragement, a hug that said *welcome home*.

Up until last winter Mom had owned an inn in the center of Evergreen, so I'd also been hoping for a bit of guidance. In my heart of hearts I hoped buying the lodge would bring us closer together, but I guessed hoping didn't make it so.

Micah smiled but it didn't reach his eyes. "She's probably just tying things up so she can concentrate properly once she gets here." He pulled me into one of his breath-stealing bear hugs to comfort me, because we both knew it was more than that.

"Yeah," I said. Mom was retired now, so it wasn't as if she had anything keeping her busy per se. Maybe she just needed to get used to the idea that her taking-the-world-by-storm daughter was back home… *without* actually having taken the world by storm. Was she disappointed in me? It was hard to tell.

"First things first," Micah said, dragging me back to reality. "Let's check out your bedroom and see if I can make it a little more comfortable like you asked."

Stepping into the warmth of the lodge, I snuck a glance over my shoulder to watch Micah's reaction, and sure enough he was wide-eyed, just like I'd been at seeing the place for the first time. Faded sunlight caught the crystals in the chandeliers and cast prisms of color around the room. I breathed in the scent of long-forgotten memories before leading Micah up the spiral stairs to the suite that was to be my home for the foreseeable future.

I swung open the heavy oak door. The suite needed a little TLC, though the stone fireplace and view to the mountains made up for it.

"Right," he said, surveying the scene. "This shouldn't take too long; just needs a few nips and tucks and a lick of paint here and there."

I smiled at Micah's assurances that it wasn't a big job, as I was eager to make the suite my own, and snuggle in bed with the mountains a stunning backdrop to my dreams. In the basement I'd found an antique bed with an elaborate bedhead, which I'd repainted champagne-white. Dragging it upstairs had been a feat, but one I managed with only a few scrapes and bruises. Once the room had a facelift with paint, some luxurious bedding, and new décor, it would feel more like me, more like home.

He opened the creaky bathroom door, exposing the old claw-foot tub and a marble vanity – the perfect room to relax in with a book and a rose-scented bubble bath after a long day.

"I can fix the broken tiles, and redo the grout."

I nodded eagerly. While the lodge was ancient, the bathrooms were still functional, and would only need some modern accoutrements to get them up to code. Some proper exhaust fans, and new lighting, maybe heat lights for winter... my list kept on growing. "Great!"

I grabbed Micah's arm, eager to show him the view from the landing at the top of the stairs and ask his advice on what to do with the space. The mountain range was visible from every window on the east side of the lodge and I wanted people to be able to soak it up in comfort. The reflection of the trees shimmered on the surface of the lake, and it was easy to lose an hour staring outside at such elemental beauty – it was spellbinding.

Our tour was interrupted by the rumble of engines roaring along the main road.

"Can you hear that?" I asked, dropping his arm and dashing closer to the window to get a glimpse of them arriving.

"That, my friend, is the sound of progress. Time to get your overalls on, Clio!" He gave my high heels a pointed look and was rewarded with an eye-roll. "Let's meet them out front!"

We flew down the stairs and on to the porch to watch the procession arrive. Cars and trucks turned into the driveway in convoy. Some were loaded with supplies, others were bare except for hard-hatted drivers with determined expressions.

Anticipation sizzled through me. It was really happening! This beautiful, timeworn lodge was about to be transformed back into its glorious self.

7

My old life was behind me. Here – in the town where I grew up, in the abandoned lodge I'd played by as a child – people would fall in love, they'd marry, they'd have families, and then they'd return to Cedarwood and celebrate once more...

Chapter Two

A few weeks later, ignoring a head throb from the ever-present noise, I gave myself a silent pep talk. *You can do this! All you have to do is paint them a charming picture of what will be.* I buttoned up my navy-blue blazer, straightened the seam of my crisp linen trousers and slipped on red heels, the ones Micah teased me relentlessly over.

With the buzz of a drill nearby, I picked up my paperwork and iPad, which had a 3D presentation loaded and ready to play. Eventually I'd have an office in a suite off the lobby, but right now it was still too frenetic with workers for me to concentrate, so in the interim I'd set up a temporary office in the front parlor, a room once used for pre-dinner aperitifs.

The couple's car churned up the gravel and my heart rate increased. They'd called the night before and enquired about hiring the ballroom for their fiftieth wedding anniversary. It had taken all of my might to keep my voice level and act like I'd hired out the ballroom a hundred times already. But it boded well, having interest in Cedarwood at this early stage.

I peeked out of the newly replaced window and watched Edgar help his wife Imelda into a wheelchair. *Damn it!* There were no ramps in place. I made a mental note to check we had mobility aids on the list. Cedarwood had to be accessible to everyone.

With a broad smile in place, I hurried outside to greet them.

"Welcome to Cedarwood!" I said, too brightly, my nerves jangling to the surface. I was half-jogging toward them, mentally assessing the area for a plank of wood, or something to use as a ramp... when the heel of my stiletto got caught in a hole in the deck. With a calm smile that belied the drumming of my heart, I attempted to wrench my heel out, trying to appear casual, but it wouldn't budge. Damn it! With one last heave, the heel came free but momentum sent me flying forward with a screech. *Oh, God!* I flew precariously into the air, taking great leaps to avoid a tray of paint and a scattering of drill bits. *Please*, I silently willed the universe, *don't let me upend the paint all over her!* With a hop, skip, and a jump to avoid everything, I ended up on my knees by the woman's lap, my pulse thrumming in my ears.

Note to self: make sure walkways are cleared at all times.

Sweat broke out on my forehead despite the chilly autumn day. Red-faced and righting myself, I held out a hand and said breezily, "I'm Clio. And as you can see, I've been falling over myself to meet you." *Kill me.* Thank God I hadn't taken her out. I could already imagine the story getting Chinese-whispered around town: *Did you hear Clio Winters tried to murder her first client, and it was little old Imelda no less!*

Imelda chuckled and shook my hand. "Aren't you as pretty as a picture? I hope you didn't ruin those heels. Do you think they come in my size? My life flashed before my eyes but all I could think was, I need a pair of those dancing shoes for the party..." Her eyes twinkled mischievously.

Admonishing myself silently for being a klutz, I dared a quick peek at my trousers; they had somehow remained intact – however, from the pain radiating upwards, my knees hadn't fared as well. "I'm sure they'd have your size and I think the leopard-print ones would suit you..."

She cocked her head as if contemplating. "I might just have to find some for the party. What do you say, Edgar?" She craned her neck and smiled benignly at her husband.

"They most certainly *look* like dancing shoes... Could be a new type of workboot, but what would I know?" He glanced at the hole in the deck and then my heels, and raised his

10

eyes to the heavens. I tried to hide a smile and remain professional, but a giggle escaped. It couldn't be helped – I liked them both instantly.

I stepped forward and shook Edgar's hand. The speech I'd prepared had flown straight out of my head as I'd toppled into Imelda's personal space, but I sensed my spiel would have been too formal, too stuffy for these people. Game face on, I cleared my throat and tried to regroup.

Right. *Explain yourself, and don't fall over!* "As you can see, Cedarwood is getting a bit of a makeover. It's a work site at the moment, but soon…"

"It's just as gorgeous as ever," Imelda said, her eyes shining. "Can we take a look through?"

"It's a little noisy what with the—"

"Noise schmoise," she said, waving me away. "We don't mind that, do we Edgar?"

I gulped. What if something fell on them, or Edgar tripped and broke a leg? I'd planned on showing them the ballroom from the adjoining outdoor deck and showing my presentation. Not opening myself up for a health and safety lawsuit on the first day.

"We're as tough as old boots, even if we look a little fragile. Don't you worry about us," Imelda said.

If we walked slowly, and carefully, surely it would be OK for a few minutes? Though I'd managed to fall over already…

"So sorry that we're not fully equipped at the moment. Let me help you lift the chair," I said, praying I didn't get a finger caught in the wheel spokes and drop her, or something equally idiotic.

"Help with the chair would be mighty kind," Edgar said, moving to one side while I took the other. We hefted the surprisingly light Imelda up.

With my back holding open the oak door, Edgar wheeled Imelda into the lobby, the scent of wet paint heavy in the air. Drop sheets were scattered across the floor to catch spills, and the sounds of work echoed around the lodge.

"It might look like a big mess at the moment, but trust me, there's a method to the madness. We have a strict schedule in place." It was hard to envisage what the lodge *would* look like with groups of laborers in clusters, drilling, hammering, filing, and edging. Tools were scattered, buckets were littered here and there. Bags of rubbish sat awaiting removal. The couple followed my noisy tread, the wood underfoot making a weird kind of song depending on where we stepped. *Squeak, ping, pop, ahh.*

Imelda shook her head as if she was mesmerized. "I'm sure you've got a handle on it all." We continued through the expanse of the lobby with its thick American oak pillars, and dusty chandeliers swaying in the breeze, their crystals clinking gently like a song, prisms of colored light dancing on the walls. The mantle of the stone fireplace was missing and it needed a little love, but a fire crackled in the grate, adding to the ambience.

Firelight flickered across the room. Even in its disorderly state the lodge radiated a type of warmth, a feeling of relaxation and expectation of what might be...

"As you can see, I'm trying to keep as much of it original as I can." I wanted the lodge to keep its old-world charm. "The overall look will remain as it was all those years ago."

"That's music to my ears," Imelda said, beaming. "We worried the lodge might've been purchased by a huge consortium and turned into some modern monolith. I'm so glad that's not the case."

We continued to a small salon where I narrowly avoided kicking over a bucketful of cleaning equipment. The room was musty, with old brocade curtains clinging to their rusty rails. "Edgar, don't you remember, we used to play charades in here," Imelda said, reaching up to grasp her husband's hand.

"You've stayed here before?" I asked, a shiver of excitement running through me. They'd stayed at Cedarwood in its heyday? No one I'd known had actually been *inside* the lodge, as it had been closed for so long.

Edgar turned Imelda's chair to face me. "We got married here," she said dreamily.

I gasped. "You did? That's incredible!" No wonder they'd been so eager to see the place as it was – warts and all – and could imagine what it would look like in the future.

Her face broke into a smile and I could see the bright-eyed young girl she'd been. "Coming up to fifty years ago I was a blushing bride of twenty-five years old. Edgar was twenty-six. We found each other late in life, or what was deemed late back then. All our friends were already married and had a bunch of babies. We fell in love but there were only a few weeks before Edgar was shipped off to the war."

"I can't believe this!" My pulse thrummed, knowing their story ended in Happy Ever After, because here they stood. "What a story, and to have you return to the lodge…" I wanted to hug them, but held myself in check. "How long were you away, Edgar?" I asked, thinking of the young man – as he had been then – being thrust into such a dangerous wartime situation.

He gave Imelda a meaningful glance and said, "Two years, four months, and one day." He blushed. "Or thereabouts. Thankfully, or not so thankfully depending how you see it, I was shot in the foot and sent home. Never ended up making it back to my platoon, though…"

A ray of sunlight landed on Imelda like a soft spotlight. "Yes, I was lucky and got to keep him safe at home with me."

They recollected the war, and how they'd missed each other fiercely for the two and a bit years he was away. They talked about the letters they wrote and all the promises they vowed to keep as soon as he returned home.

"Did you keep those promises?" I asked.

"We did," he said. "You just don't have an inkling when you're young how fast those years flick by. Though I'm sure there've been plenty of days Imelda has wanted to walk off into the sunset with someone else," he laughed.

Imelda considered it. "Once or twice I wanted to put your head in the oven, I can't lie."

He nodded. "See? Luckily our oven is electric. And we made it through fifty years with lots of talking, lots of *communicating* as you young folks call it." He chortled. "When we heard this place had itself a new owner, we knew it was a chance to throw one hell of a party. We like the idea of coming back to where we began."

They exchanged a glance, a private message in their rheumy eyes. Whatever happened in my life, I vowed right then to wait for the perfect man. I wouldn't compromise. I wanted the fairy tale that I saw before me. Even if I ran into my old gang of friends in Evergreen and was the only one still single, still utterly without *The One* at thirty-three. Now was not the time to dwell on it. It didn't matter. Love couldn't be rushed. *Focus, Clio, this isn't about you.*

"I promise if you have the party at Cedarwood there'll be lots of celebrations, and confetti. It will be an ode to your life together, the love you share. I'll make it as special as it so deserves to be."

Imelda gestured for me to lean close and gave me a tight hug. "What do you mean *if*…We came here to tell you to get the ball rolling. We aren't spring chickens any more. The only problem I envisage is time. You see, we want to celebrate on our wedding day. Makes sense of course, but that's only six weeks away… Do you think you can do it?" She gazed around the lodge, like she was imagining the place as it once was.

Could we get the ballroom and entrance done in six short weeks? There was the garden to consider, guest bathrooms, safety measures… But their faces – they looked so awed by the lodge, how could I say no? "Sure," I said, voice brimming with confidence for the first time since I'd arrived. "We can do it."

She gave me a grateful smile. "I'd better find those high heels then. Maybe I'll get the leopard-print *and* the red. You just never know when a gal might need a pair of fancy shoes."

"It pays to be organized." I winked. "And I'm truly honored you're going to have the party here." My mind spun with ideas, questions, solutions, and we hadn't even started yet.

"It's like the circle of life. We started here, and it will end here…" Imelda was a romantic, and I sensed a like-minded soul.

I said, "Would you like to continue to the ballroom?"

Edgar pushed the wheelchair slowly forward. "Sure, let's see it."

Imelda smiled, and fussed with a rug on her lap. "If I close my eyes I can still recall the excitement in that young girl's heart, feel the butterflies floating in her belly at the thought of how that handsome young man was going to be her husband. I really didn't believe you'd show up, Edgar. Isn't that the silliest thing?"

Edgar went to reply but stopped as Imelda's hand went to her throat, and her face paled. She let out a small groan, and scrunched her eyes closed.

I dropped to my knees and gazed into her face, but her eyes stayed tightly shut, screwed up in pain. "Imelda? Are you OK?" Panic seized me, but Edgar appeared resigned but calm.

Edgar rubbed her shoulder. "She's OK. She'll be right in a moment." His voice was soft with acceptance at whatever it was causing her pain. He opened a bag hanging on the back of the wheelchair and rummaged around, taking out a pillbox and a bottle of water. "We fought a war, financial troubles, and everything in between, but we can't fight time," he said, sadly.

It was a full minute before Imelda returned to us, "Sorry," she said, giving my hand a pat. "Another spell, I take it?"

Edgar stooped forward and handed her two pills and the bottle of water. She took them with trembling hands and drank, before saying, "The mind is willing, but the body just won't listen sometimes. Don't you worry, pet. It's OK. Nothing is going to stop me from having a party at Cedarwood Lodge. Nothing." She stuck her chin forward, resolute.

15

Once Imelda's color returned to normal they peeked into the ballroom with cries of delight. "I'm so glad you're not fussing with it," she said. "It's like something out of an F. Scott Fitzgerald novel."

"Isn't it?" I said, her description apt. "Have you thought about themes, colors? Cuisines? I can show you—"

She cut me off. "You're the expert. All I ask is that the room is bright and cheerful; think colorful bunting, and streamers cascading down. I know it doesn't sound like much, but I'd love for it to look just like we had it all those years ago."

An hour later, after firming up more details, we said our goodbyes and I told them to visit any time so they could see the lodge being shaped back into the beauty of its halcyon days.

Hopefully it would return them to their wedding night and their hearts and souls would be young again, with their whole lives together ahead of them.

I couldn't wait to call my best friend, Amory, and tell her every little thing. And to see if my name was still making the gossip page...

Chapter Three

"Clio, they sound amazing! So they've booked the party?" Amory shrieked as I sat down with a laugh at my desk, ignoring piles of invoices that needed to be paid and filed away.

"They did! And get this: they didn't want to see color swatches and menus, or a song list. They said I was the expert and just to make it bright and colorful. Only kicker is I have to get everything finished and organized in six weeks."

"You can do it, that's what you're good at. Deadlines." She let out a laugh. "You lucky thing not having to consult with them every five minutes – why can't they all be like that?"

Our clients in New York were pernickety to say the least. Bridezillas were plentiful, and the women weren't opposed to throwing tantrums a five-year-old would be proud of, but I always rolled with it. It came with the territory to receive phone calls at two a.m. from a blushing bride-to-be, sobbing about centerpieces or tiaras. That's what separated the good party planners from the bad. My job was to say *yes*, always.

I could fix anything, especially under pressure.

But then I had opened my big mouth.

Shaking myself out of reverie I said, "I'm sure the next clients won't be so easy." In the background phones buzzed and drawers banged. Office life. I felt a pang for it. We lapsed into silence as I debated whether to ask.

"Darling, about…" She hesitated and I steeled myself. Amory always knew what I was thinking without me having to say a word.

"Don't tell me. They're still talking about it? *Still?*" It had been months. Months since I'd packed up my desk and hidden in my shoebox-sized apartment until the sale of Cedarwood had settled. Surely they'd moved on to newer scandals by now? I'd been avoiding the online gossip sites for months in case I saw my own name trapped in a headline once more.

The previous headlines were still burned into my retinas: *Party planner to the A-listers tells reality-star bride to run from celebrity groom!*

Amory let out a nervous laugh. "Well…"

I groaned and cupped my face. "Tell me. I can handle it."

She took an audible intake of breath before launching into the whole sorry story. "It seems it's ramping up. She's saying you had a thing for the groom, and that's why you did what you did. Because you were after him and his… money."

I let out a squeal of protest. "*She didn't!*"

"She did."

"But that's not true!" I wailed. Outside the sun sank low, coloring the sky saffron.

Her voice came back a hissed whisper. "*I* know it's not true. But you've really underestimated her. She's set on ruining your reputation to save hers."

"But my reputation is *already* ruined! Why does she have to continue with it?" The whole sordid thing was so unfair, and I kicked myself for believing in the blushing bride-to-be when she'd poured her heart out to me minutes before she was supposed to walk down the aisle. I'd been appalled by her confession – how could she marry someone she didn't love when her heart belonged to another? With the clock ticking, I'd advised her to run, get out of that church before she made a huge mistake, because I believed her tale of woe and didn't want to see her waste her life with the wrong man! And it had turned out to be the stupidest thing I'd ever done.

Really, I should have known. It was Dealing with Brides 101. Never, *ever* advise them. Wedding-day jitters and cold feet can make a person say the craziest things. It was my job to reassure them, not tell them to run! And these were not your average Manhattanites. He was a millionaire movie star, for God's sake.

"She's vindictive."

"I can understand why she'd try to save face. What she told me was pretty damning, but to turn it around like that…" I was bewildered by it. I had only met the groom twice and one of those times was on the aborted wedding day when I had to tell him she'd taken flight. *Because of my advice… stupid, stupid, stupid.*

Amory clucked her tongue. "It's a simple case of *you know too much.* She's got to make you the villain, so nothing rubs off on her. It wouldn't take a genius to unearth her real story… but it's juicier with you cast as the crazed, infatuated wedding planner."

It was so damn ridiculous I could only sigh. Something like this would only happen in New York. "She's so bloody cunning. I wish I'd shared my side of the story earlier. But it's too late; no one would believe me now."

"She's called Flirty McFlirtison for a reason," Amory said sadly.

I couldn't help but giggle. Amory had disliked the reality-star bride Monica intensely and given her the nickname. It had been tricky to mask our true feelings around her because she'd been the client from hell, unless a man happened to walk by, and then she'd bat her lashes, leaving us shaking our heads.

I should have known never to trust her. The day after the wedding, Flirty started doing some major damage control and piling the blame on me. Once the news broke, no bride would go near me with a ten-foot pole.

"Jesus, Amory, I thought it would've all blown over now," I said, slumping in my chair and gazing out at the beautiful explosion of color as the sun sank below the mountains.

"Here's an interesting twist… it's come out that he had her sign a watertight pre-nup the night *before* the wedding,

19

so that's why she did a runner. You were just the perfect scapegoat. She's denying that, of course."

I groaned. "Celebrities. I will never understand them."

Still, even after all the A-list weddings I'd planned, I believed true love conquered all. Nothing would take away the pleasure I got out of organizing nuptials between two people who were *truly* smitten, even if they were on the never-heard-of-you list. Monica was driven by greed – she was just a reality-TV starlet whose show was cancelled after one season, but she still craved the limelight and would do anything she could to get tabloid attention. I'd been unlucky to get caught up in her schemes.

"Celebrities," she agreed. "You don't know how lucky you are, Clio. Granted, it wasn't an ideal exit from the agency, but look where it's taken you! I'm *wildly* envious. In time you'll see it was the best decision you've ever made, and you'll think of us scrabbling after every high-profile party with pity."

This was Amory's way, to line every cloud in silver. "I hope you're right. Otherwise I've bought a lodge on a whim because of what happened. In Evergreen. A town with a population of five hundred and three people!"

"That's the spirit!" she shouted, and I could just see her swinging in her office chair, tapping her pen, as if I was sitting across from her. "Now turn off Bonnie Tyler, please – I can almost hear your sobs from here. Leave Bonnie for the broken-hearted. And get back to work. You're the boss now, darling, so square those shoulders and own it."

She knew me so well, even what my choice of music meant.

Once I hung up, I turned the volume up and listened to Bonnie's gravelly voice, not sobbing… not quite.

After all, what did *I* have to cry about? My reputation in New York was ruined. I'd invested every last dollar into a rundown lodge in a small town. There was nothing to worry about!

When I did something, like mess up my life, I did it right. And that included listening to music and crying like it was an Olympic sport. Who cared if everyone was saying

20

I loved some random celebrity and had ruined his marriage? It would be yesterday's news eventually, right? And being blacklisted by every New York event-planning agency? Pffft. Big deal. I'd make my own success. In a town with five-oh-three people. Easy.

Oh, God, what had I done?

Chapter Four

"Is that Kai?" Micah asked, as we watched the new arrival jump down as deftly as a dancer from the cab of his truck. Even in the shadows, Kai stood out – with his wavy, sun-bleached hair and surfer's body. I hadn't expected that. Builders were weathered, ruddy men who wore expressions of weariness from overwork, weren't they? Kai looked more like a pro surfer than someone who did manual labor. Golly, if Amory was here, she'd be elbowing me forward by now.

"Yes, Kai, the project manager," I stage-whispered. "He had to finish up his last contract but he's here for good now… well, at least until the lodge is done." I adopted a disinterested expression and hoped Micah hadn't caught my moment of surprise when I clapped eyes on Kai.

Micah smiled, and waggled his brows, insinuating something untoward.

"And what does that eyebrow jiggle mean?" I asked, crossing my arms and staring him down. Even after all these years I could still interpret Micah's body language, though it wasn't hard when he was being so obvious about it.

"It *means* you hired some surfer god and…"

I poked him in the ribs to be quiet and hissed, "Oh, jeez, Micah, I didn't know he was…" What was he? "…He was… a surfer," I finished lamely, watching Kai, who was rummaging in his truck for something.

He did resemble the perfect leading man in a romantic comedy, a polar opposite to the heroine... wait, what was I even thinking? Did I picture myself as the leading lady? Ridiculous! My heart was a no-go zone for the foreseeable future. My one true love at this point had to be Cedarwood Lodge.

"We've only spoken on the phone. And, for the record, I wouldn't date anyone who worked here out of principle." There, that sounded believable.

Micah went to retort but was called over by one of the painters. "Saved by the bell," he joked before jogging off.

"Morning," I said to Kai, hoping I wasn't blushing after Micah practically accused me of hiring someone for their looks! It was absurd. But those eyes... mesmerizing.

"Hey," he responded with a bright smile. His blond hair was mussed, windblown.

I shaded my face as the fall sun climbed higher and warmth seeped into my bones. Kai's arrival meant I could knuckle down and focus on building marketing campaigns and our social media pages, spreading the word about the lodge while he instructed the team.

"You look familiar," he said, narrowing his eyes. "I know we've had a hundred conversations on the phone, but..." He surveyed me, and I blushed under his scrutiny. Damn it to hell and back. Had he read about me in the paper or on one of those dodgy online gossip sites?

I gritted my teeth so tight I almost gave myself lockjaw. Managing to prise my mouth open a notch I said, as casually as I could, "Where did you say your last job was?"

Please, do not say New York or any of its boroughs!

He cocked his head, scrutinizing me as if we were long-lost cousins or something. "Georgia."

I almost collapsed in relief. "Georgia. I hear it's pretty this time of year."

"It's pretty," he agreed. "But not as pretty as here." He stretched and his shirt rode up, exposing toned, tanned skin. I tried so hard not to eye the ripple of his muscles, or imagine how they'd feel under my hand. I wasn't used to seeing men *sans* suits, and it gave me a jolt. Surely, as a boss, I shouldn't even be thinking in such a way? But I was merely admiring the newcomer for his sporting prowess. Over the phone I'd got to know him – he was one of those keen athletic types. Surfing and hiking and all the exercise he did sculpted him, and we all knew a healthy body led to a healthy mind. I made a promise to myself to run some laps of the lodge later. It wouldn't hurt to get in shape, would it?

"So," I said, businesslike, casting my gaze away from his exposed skin and back to his face. "I'll show you where you can stash your things."

"Perfect." He bent to the cab and picked up a leather tool belt and satchel full of paperwork. The nuts and bolts of code and health and safety missives hurt my brain and I was glad I had someone professional to oversee it all. While Kai had been finishing up on another building site, he'd also been choreographing behind the scenes with the tradespeople at Cedarwood via phone and email and checking in with me at the end of each day. Having him here in the flesh would be even better.

Micah wandered outside with one of the painters, pointing and gesticulating to the eaves above the lodge, which had been painted the wrong color. I waved him over, and he excused himself and jogged the short distance so I could make the introductions.

They shook hands the way men do, hard fast pumps. "We've got Isla arriving today," I said. "And she'll…"

Before I could finish, a motorbike came careening around the corner and into the driveway. Isla? On the phone she'd sounded chirpy and enthusiastic.

I'd hired her instantly because of her knowledge about garden design and her clear vision for Cedarwood, which matched my own. Her résumé was impressive for her age, mid-twenties, and I liked the fact she had a flair for topiary.

A cloud of dust rose up as Isla stepped off the bike and handled her helmet. Strawberry-blonde hair fell around her shoulders in waves, and her light-blue eyes shone with eagerness. Freckles spotted the bridge of her nose like constellations. Holding out a hand, she said, "You must be Clio."

"Yes. Nice bike," I said, grinning. "Great timing, Isla. This is Micah and Kai. We're going to go for a tour. Join us?"

Isla gave me a wide smile, shook hands with Kai and Micah, and turned in an arc to survey the grounds. There was an energy radiating off her that was impossible to miss, as though she couldn't wait to grab her secateurs and start pruning.

I went to ask Micah about the painters and their roof folly only to see him staring at Isla slack-jawed. Lifting a finger to his chin, I shut his mouth so it wasn't as obvious to Isla as it was to me.

He gazed at Isla, goggle-eyed, lost in a daydream before eventually coming back to reality.

Isla swiveled back to us. "This is like something out of a Grimms' fairy tale," she exclaimed, motioning to the overgrown gardens. "I can't wait to get started!"

Shading my eyes once more, I flashed her a smile. I had this sudden sense that the trio in front of me would shape Cedarwood into something great again. Between us, we'd give it the kiss of life, and resurrect it from its somnambulant state. Along the way, maybe a love affair would blossom... On this estate where vibrant mountains watched over us, where the lake glistened in the distance, maybe Cupid sat on a branch, hidden by a leafy canopy, his bow stretched taut, before shooting his arrow, straight into the heart of the next perfect couple.

I grinned at Micah, who was fidgeting with his folder, his cheeks ablaze. Isla was watching him with a frown, trying to gauge his inability to make eye contact with her.

"Well," I said, clapping my hands for their attention. "Let's give you guys the tour, and then we can get to work!"

Ringing Amory later that night with my daily update, I pulled a blanket over my knees and munched on buttery microwave popcorn. I'd have to shop properly and stop eating like a college student, but time had a habit of running away from me, and at night, with the draught leeching in, all I wanted to do was rug up, eat junk food and drink cocoa.

"Hello, sunshine!" Amory's tinny voice echoed around my bedroom, making it feel homelier – as if she was here with me.

I pushed the popcorn to one side. "So, today's news... Kai the builder arrived and also the landscaper Isla, so it feels like we're making real progress!" I stopped to wipe crumbs from the bed. "But no matter how much work we put in, I just can't shake the feeling that it won't be enough... What if no one comes?"

"OK, look, the lodge *will* happen because you're a gun at what you do. I have absolute faith people will flock in droves to Cedarwood. You know that! No one can win against you when you wow them with your vision and paint the pictures you do just with words – I mean, that's a gift that can't be taught. What you *need* is romance to distract you."

I groaned. "Romance? That's the last thing I want. And which bit of me moving to a town of five hundred and three people did you not remember? There's no one suitable. Besides, I wouldn't have time. I have this overwhelming fear that if I take my eyes off of the project, it'll tumble down like a house of cards. I don't have a plan B any more, this *is* plan B. I can't afford to get starry-eyed and lose focus. There's the—"

She interjected. "And that's exactly why you need the distraction of a man! That worry will eat you up, just like it did here. You were on the path to burnout, and without me there to fishhook you out at night, what will you do? Worry, that's what. Life is all about light and shade, work and play. You just have to find the right balance. Think of snuggling up at night with some bronzed, buff guy who will take your mind off your woes."

I choked on a popcorn kernel, thinking of Kai. "Bronzed, buff guy in Evergreen?" I managed. "You're dreaming. Men here don't take weekends in Cabo to work on their tan, I'm sure of it."

"OK, maybe they don't go to Cabo, but you can renegotiate with yourself about what exactly you want in a man. Surely there's someone there who'll do for now. What about old flames? A boy-next-door type? Someone who'll happily sweep you off your feet."

Old flames… There *was* Timothy. I'd only thought about him in passing since I'd returned.

"What?" Amory said, breaking my reverie. "I'm right, aren't I? There's some unfinished business with a guy there? Tell me I'm right!"

Was there? I really didn't think so. And what was I even having this conversation for? Amory was trying to distract me from the real issues in my life by wooing me with the idea of romance. "No, no… there isn't unfinished business. Nothing of the sort. I see what you're doing, you know."

"But…?" she said, ignoring the fact I'd caught her out.

There was no hiding from Amory once she clued on to something. She was FBI grade when it came to interrogating someone and sensed any weakness. "*But nothing.*"

"Don't tell me… He was your first love. Right? That guy who broke it off with you when you left Evergreen?"

"So? It's not like I've been pining for him or anything. Timothy was a million years ago. I bet he's married and has five kids and a house with a picket fence and a dog called Buster. A nice handicap at golf, and a wife with a blonde bob and bright-blue eyes who bakes cookies. *From scratch*." I could see him having that kind of perfect American life, with his perfectly white teeth and perfect children with their perfect manners. *Perfect, perfect, perfect.*

Amory gave me one of her overly dramatic world-weary sighs. "Not that you're into stereotyping or anything! Darling, I'm not asking you to marry him, I'm only saying that I think you need some balance. If I don't lecture you, you'll spend every waking hour crunching numbers and making those ridiculous pie charts before ending the night planning your dream wedding on Pinterest. And soon enough you'll be a shriveled-up old maid in some windy, creaky lodge with a menagerie of animals who share your bed."

I guffawed. "As if! I don't even use Pinterest any more!"

"Liar. You forgot to make your dream-wedding board secret. I like the pearl wedding dress the best, the backless gown... stunning."

I wanted to dissolve into the floorboards. How could I have forgotten to make it secret! I'd been planning my own wedding since I could talk, but what was wrong with that? I just really liked weddings. Was that a crime?

"Your romantic side is what makes you shine so brightly. Promise me you'll find Timothy and go for coffee. And if he's married, then don't kiss him. Simple. But on the other hand, if he's single... well, first love rekindled. God, I'd pay to see that."

She was incorrigible. And if I didn't nip this in the bud she'd get carried away, and start pinning her *own* suggestions to my dream-wedding board. "Amory, my life isn't a romantic comedy. First love rekindled? That only happens in movies. Fiction!"

"And where do they get their inspiration from, huh? Real life, that's where! Non-fiction!"

Amory was a bulldozer when it came to pushing me out of my comfort zone. But she really didn't understand the complexities of finding love in a small town. Again, I realized she'd jabbed me into a corner with all this nonsense about love.

"I actually phoned you to talk about the new members of staff who arrived…"

"Don't try and change the subject. Your mission is to have coffee with the Matt Damon lookalike, and report back."

"Oh my God, Amory. Wait. How do you know what he looks like?" Timothy did bear an uncanny resemblance to the actor Matt Damon, and I knew he still looked just the same because I'd stalked his Facebook profile once. OK, maybe twice, but I'd had a few cocktails and didn't everyone do that anyway? There wasn't much to see because it was locked up tight, which left me with just his profile picture.

"I found your yearbook and saw all the scribbled love hearts around the photo of him. Seriously, you were the sweetest thing, weren't you?"

I blushed, grateful she couldn't see me. "Before you corrupted me."

"Which was so much fun! I have to go into a dinner meeting, which fills me with joy, so call me and tell me everything, just as soon as you've done it. Deal?"

I avoided the demand and said, "Don't let them cold-shoulder you because of me."

She let out an evil chuckle. "Don't you worry, darling. They've tried that, but then I got the go-ahead from you-know-who's squad, to organize her surprise birthday party – so I'm quite the flavor of the month. You know what these agency backstabbers are like. Fickle."

Sadly I did know, all too well, how the tide could turn in an instant at the agency. "You're a superstar. I wish I was there to see it."

"One celeb party is the same as the next, no matter how we dress it up. You're not missing out."

"I guess. Wait, before you go, how are things with Cruz?" While Amory made a show of behaving like some kind of man-eater, I knew she had deep feelings for the mysterious Cruz, who hailed from Ecuador and was all intense with deep, smoldering eyes.

"The same," she sighed. "You know men in Manhattan. Can't really commit to anything except their gym routines. And I'm crazy busy myself, so we'll have to wait and see. We're meeting for cocktails tonight, and then a show on Friday, so two dates in one week... a miracle in these parts."

Amory would never fully admit how she felt about a guy; it was like some protective instinct in her. And she'd been equally blasé about most guys up until now. Cruz was different, and I hoped she'd open up to him. "He really likes you, Amory, you can tell, so I hope you don't act indifferent with him."

"Darling, I don't act indifferent, I *am* indifferent. Because most of the guys I've dated have been total bores. There's no point hiding the fact they sent me into a slumber. Cruz is the first guy I haven't had to fake it with... and I'm not only talking sex," she laughed. "But I won't pin my hopes on him, not just yet. There's a definite sizzle of attraction, but what if it fades?"

"That first overwhelming *can't eat, can't sleep, can't stop thinking of you* stage of love might fade away but it'll be replaced with more enduring emotions like comfort and stability." What the hell did I know? I couldn't even remember the last time I'd been on a date... still, it seemed like sound advice.

"Boring! I want the sparks."

I laughed, knowing Amory wouldn't settle for mundane, ever.

"Oh, God, please tell me that's *not* Bonnie Tyler warbling in the background again?"

I froze.

"Darling, when you play 'Total Eclipse of the Heart' I know things are grim. Please, turn it off and listen to something more upbeat?"

"It's… the radio!" I lied.

After ending the call, I leaned back and smiled. Amory always knew just what to say to perk me up, even if it was to rekindle a pretty dull flame from my past… Turning up 'Total Eclipse of the Heart' I thought about my best friend's advice. Believing that true love was out there was easy; I just couldn't quite believe it was going to be found in the tiny town of Evergreen.

Chapter Five

The evenings grew longer and winter crept closer, bringing moody gray skies and the promise of cooler months to come. Under such solemn light, I felt the space between me and Mom yawn wider. She still hadn't appeared and I knew something was up. I dialed her number again and was rewarded with the robotic voice: *the number you have dialed...* I hung up. Enough was enough.

At the lodge, things were progressing hectically and only just behind schedule, and I supposed the world wouldn't fall down around me if I took one night off from the endless paperwork and reconciling the figures. There was just so much to do, but I wasn't concentrating properly with Mom's absence on my mind.

The wind keened like a lost soul as I locked the front door of the lodge. Kai was wandering around the grounds so I set off and found him peering into the window of one of the chalets near the lake.

"I'm going out," I said. "Are you OK to lock the front gate?" He always stayed behind, his work days longer than anyone else's, as though he couldn't fully relax until he'd checked every single job.

"Sure," he said, trying to make out the chalet room configurations in the encroaching darkness.

I buttoned up my coat as the bracing winds took hold. Kai looked downright spellbound. Surely it wasn't just the chalets prompting such a reaction? "What is it?" I asked. "You look like you've found Wonderland."

"I have found Wonderland. I had no idea the chalets were so well appointed. I guess I expected them to be derelict. It won't take much to get them ready for guests, just the usual safety checks, and a few modernizations."

With twenty chalets on the property, it wasn't viable for me right then, as much as I wanted them to be rejuvenated. There was new bedding to consider, mattresses, linen, and décor, as well as the TLC they needed. It would have to wait.

"I know," I said with a sigh, wishing my funds could stretch that tiny bit further but knowing I couldn't risk it yet. "There's also the old stone chapel to do. It's got the most glorious stained-glass windows that funnel in breathtaking kaleidoscopic colors. It would be perfect for weddings. But for now I have to focus on the lodge itself..."

"When word spreads you'll be busy here, Clio. This place has a bygone-era feel to it. I've traveled a lot, and I haven't seen anything like this."

I crossed my fingers, hoping he was right. "I've bet my entire fortune that people will want holidays where they learn to tango, take up life drawing, sling on backpacks full of gourmet picnic food supplied by us and hike up into the foothills."

It was as though I could visualize them: groups huddled by the fire playing cards, mahjongg, bridge, and charades.

"No shopping malls, no tearing around trying to see every single tourist attraction. I think you're on to something here."

"I hope guests see it that way. Without sounding like a disgruntled grandparent, I want to go back to a time where people made their own fun. Let's pray I'm not the only one who thinks it's a good idea."

He ran a hand through his tangled, too-long hair. "I'd put money on it but I'm not a gambling type."

Cedarwood *had* to offer something unique to draw people to such a small town, and I banked on old-school

33

fun and frivolity. Dances, trekking, water sports on the lake, and games, canasta, bingo nights, pottery in the west wing, and still-life drawing in the east. Language lessons, cooking classes, and singing and theater for those who wanted to perform. Chalets with reinvigorated claw-foot baths and a wall of books for those who wanted peace and quiet. But I needed the numbers in order to hire the staff...

I wanted to recreate that time, that *feeling*, when holidays were about relaxation, or being awed by the natural beauty of the elements. Having a place where you could do as much or as little as you liked. The entire train of thought made me realize again just how much work I had to do on the marketing front. I took my phone from my pocket and snapped a picture of Kai standing by the front door of the chalet. Social media would eat him up. "Mind if I post this online?" I indicated to the photo.

"Sure, go ahead."

With deft fingers I posted the pic with the description: Our project manager Kai at one of the #CedarwoodLodgeChalets before renovations.

"Why did the lodge close?" he asked, arms folded as he leaned against the balustrade.

I lifted a shoulder. "As far as I can tell, they struggled through wartime, and recessions, and I guess they never really recovered financially. The husband left first and then the wife, for reasons unknown, and not long after she closed the place down."

"Why'd he leave her?"

I clucked my tongue. "That part is a little hazy. I was too young to understand."

"It's a shame when they had all of this." I might have mistaken it, but I was sure I caught a glimpse of longing in his eyes. Like he had fallen under Cedarwood's spell.

"The thing is, it's not a broken heart. We can fix this," I said, smiling up at him.

He faced me, and the full force of his gaze hit me. I envied the girl who'd lose her heart to Kai. Loving him would be like tumbling into an abyss – he had a depth, a magnetism, that was compelling.

"Cedarwood has a murky past, but it's being reborn and I have this idea that it'll be a place where people fall in love, and lives will be changed for the better." Too whimsical? I had to remind myself I wasn't in an office full of women who planned weddings for a living any more.

He took an age to reply, like he was absorbing my words, pondering his answer. "There *is* something special about this place. It's not just you who feels it." A blush crept up his skin.

While his words were innocent, my heart knocked a little harder. I fumbled with a response before sticking to the rudimentary. "So... don't forget to lock the gate. I'll see you tomorrow." Kai stared at me so intently, I blinked and walked away, unsure of what exactly had happened, and why I felt a charge in the air.

Twenty minutes later I pulled into Mom's driveway, my thoughts inexplicably fuzzy. I took a deep breath and focused my mind on Mom, reminding myself not to push too hard; not to say anything I'd regret. If I did, she'd shut down and I'd never get to the bottom of what was bothering her. My mom, despite having run an inn where she dealt with guests for most of her adult life, was insular. She didn't socialize, her only real friend was my Aunt Bessie, my father's sister. Aunt Bessie was so full of life that no one could avoid being swept into her world, so I'm sure my mom just gave in to it.

I killed the engine, and gazed up. The kitchen curtain shivered, alerting me to Mom's presence.

Donning a friendly smile, I went to the door and knocked, waiting an age for her to open it, as if she was trying to decide whether to pretend to be out or not. How had we come to this?

Finally the door swung open and she feigned surprise. "Clio! I wasn't expecting you."

I held out a bag of groceries I'd stopped off to buy. "Thought we could rustle up some dinner, what do you say?" I held back the real words that threatened to pour from my lips: *Why haven't you come to see me?*

She darted a quick peep behind her.

"Is someone here?" I ventured. Mom hadn't dated after Dad died. Did she have someone special now, and that was what was distracting her? At least that would be progress.

"No, no. It's fine. Come in."

I held in a sigh. "I thought we could make lasagna and roast vegetables. Are you hungry?" Mom had lost weight, too much weight. She'd always been whisper-thin, but now she was almost invisible.

"My favorite," she said, attempting a smile.

The cottage was immaculate, not a cushion out of place. Mom had always been tidy but this was the next level. The small living room sat solemnly; the kitchen was pristine and smelled of cleaning agents, not a place where food was made.

"Help me peel the vegetables?" I stood at the sink and washed my hands.

She did as instructed, and worry hit me anew, watching her tiny frame move around the kitchen. I should have come over sooner. I debated whether to ask her outright what was wrong, but she fixed me with her Mona Lisa smile, so I let it go, hoping she'd eventually soften and confide in me. *There's a first time for everything… right, Clio?*

"Where's Aunt Bessie? I thought she would have called in at the lodge. I've called her a few times but got the machine."

Mom washed potatoes and carrots and placed them on a tea towel. "You know Bessie – she's desperate to see you but she's on a cruise with her book club. When she phoned I told her all about your homecoming and how you turned up unannounced." There was a light rebuke to her voice, and I realized that no matter how I approached my mom, it would never be the right way. "She gets home soon and, whirlwind that she is, will no doubt come straight to you."

As if visiting me first up was out of the ordinary. I was grateful for Aunt Bessie in my life. She'd always been there for me, and made up the shortfall my mother had left.

She owned a gourmet donut shop in town called Puft. My aunt took the basic donut and transformed it into a sweet-lover's delight. Big, custard-filled donuts balanced precariously on a cloud of Chantilly cream on top of thick chocolatey shakes. Donuts were stacked like the leaning tower of Pisa, each with different fillings – from passion-fruit curd to chocolate hazelnut custard, hand-spun candyfloss on top. Or for those wanting simpler fare there were mini pistachio and honey rings, or lemon-flavored churros with orange sauce. My Aunt Bessie always emailed me the menu to proofread and it was torture not being able to taste the words.

Once she was back from her cruise I planned to go in and roll out, having my fill of her delectable treats.

She was a cuddly, bubbly person and had been a refuge in my formative years. Aunt Bessie was the type of person people confided in, and she welcomed them in to her open arms. Along with confidentiality, she also provided advice, hugs, and donuts. *So many donuts.*

"You should come by the lodge with her, Mom. We had a slight issue with the plumbing, but thankfully it didn't blow the budget." She turned away, but I kept on, hoping it would sway her. "The electrics have been fixed. The wainscoting has been replaced but still needs painting. The floors need to be sanded and polished, but we had a problem with a patch of rotted wood in the—"

"Do you want me to chop and fry garlic?"

Was I speaking too softly? "Sure. Did you hear me, Mom? About the lodge?"

Her hands fell to her sides and she stared out the window as if debating what to say. She'd gone so pale,

I worried I'd pushed her over some invisible precipice. "I heard."

"Well?" I asked softly.

"Well, what?" When she turned to me her eyes were bright with tears. What could have provoked such a thing?

"What is it, Mom? Why are you so upset?" I moved to hug her but she stiffened at the sight of my outstretched arms.

She shrugged. "What do you want me to say? That I'm happy for you? OK, I'm happy for you. Is that enough?" Her voice was almost inaudible.

"Aren't you glad I'm home?" I swallowed a lump in my throat. It hurt the way she froze me out. No wonder New York had been a haven for me; it was easier to ignore this *strangeness* when I was away.

"I'm glad you're here." She motioned to where I stood.

"Here? But not at Cedarwood?" I leaned casually against the counter, and tried to keep the conversation light despite the tense atmosphere.

She turned back to the chopping board. "Look, can we just make dinner and talk about other things?"

"Other than the lodge, you mean?" What was it about Cedarwood that upset her so? Outside, stars twinkled in the inky night, as if urging me on.

"Yes, other than the lodge. I'm tired of hearing about it." Garlic skin coated her fingers as she peeled and chopped. "I know that sounds harsh, and I don't mean it to be."

"OK," I said. "But I'm a little confused as to how you could be tired of hearing about it, when we haven't really spoken." God, sometimes I wanted to shake the woman. Why wouldn't she want to hear about the biggest gamble of my life? The very place I'd always dreamed of owning. It didn't make sense, but Mom's moods had never been easy to translate.

"I hear about it in town. That's enough. I want to talk to you, just not about that."

38

I remained silent, and we prepped the dinner that way, both mired in our own thoughts. With the white noise of TV in the background, it was enough to pretend we were listening to that.

Sitting down at the table, I took the spatula and served Mom a generous slice, hoping she'd eat with gusto. "It's good to have dinner together again. I've missed it."

"Me too," she said.

"We could make it a regular thing. Maybe Friday nights? And I can give you a rundown about what stage I'm at with the lodge?" I hadn't meant to bring it up again, but really, it was all I had these days and it wasn't like I was discussing something scandalous.

She sighed and placed her napkin on the table. "Clio, I'm just… confused. You were doing *so* well in New York. Why would you give it all up to come back here? That place…" She grimaced. "…It's a money pit. What if you lose everything?"

With a deep breath I said, "It's a risk, a big one. But to be honest, Mom…" I stalled. Would telling her the truth help or hinder? "I couldn't stay there. I had an incident with a bride, and I got fired. It was a big misunderstanding, but the press got hold of the story and it gathered momentum, giving me no choice but to leave. I was basically blacklisted by every agency in and around New York. And then when Cedarwood came up for sale… it seemed like fate, a lifeline."

Her face pinched. "I'm sorry to hear about your job. I know how much you loved it. It just seems like a step backwards coming home. There's nothing here for you."

I worked my jaw, fighting back tears. I felt so goddamn sorry for her, for myself. We were back to the same pattern of the past.

"Mom, *you're* here." When my dad died, part of her did too, but I'd always hoped it was just a phase, just part of the grieving process. Instead of pulling me close, she pushed me away. As the years passed she'd folded in on herself even more until all I had left was a shell of what she had been. Even Aunt Bessie hadn't been able to pull her out of the funk she was in, though she never gave up trying.

She pushed her plate away. "What if you lose all that money, Clio? Your father's money?"

Ah. "Is that what this… silence is about? You're worried about my inheritance money?"

She had the grace to blush. "Well, it's a lot of money."

My shoulders drooped like I carried a lead weight. I'd never given much thought to her feelings about the legacy my father had left me. I presumed he'd left her a share too. It had been invested for me until I turned twenty-one and then I had reinvested it in a risky start-up and tripled the money. It was beginner's luck and I knew it, but I'd done it out of spite – Mom had given me such a lecture about that money when I took charge of it so I did the exact opposite of what she advised. And luckily for me it had paid off; I took the money and ran, knowing it could have easily gone the other way. Much later I'd withdrawn the money to buy Cedarwood, and at the time it had felt right – like his legacy was always meant to bring me home.

"It *is* a lot of money. I've gambled, there's no question about it. But if I host one large function a month, I can make it work. Then there's the chalets, the chapel for weddings, and renting the rooms in the lodge. I want to market it as *the* holiday destination in New Hampshire. I can't say for sure, but I think Dad would be proud."

She sighed. "It's too late now, Clio. It's done, so you have to make the best of it. You could have gone anywhere in the world with that money, and you chose to come here. It's mind-bending, that's all."

"I've always loved Cedarwood Lodge. You know that. And I guess I hoped we'd be closer, not just in terms of distance…" My voice trailed off.

I wished so much we could be the sitcom mother and daughter. The ones who knew each other inside out and didn't have to guess at moods, or whims. The ones who met

40

for coffee and cake and a shopping expedition; swapped novels we loved. But it would never happen. She was damaged somehow, and it was up to me to be there for her, no matter how hard it was. At the moment, though, it was hard to accept this was my lot.

"Eat," she said. "It's going cold." But she didn't lift her fork again.

Chapter Six

"Micah!" I half-screamed, half-choked as I tried desperately to stop the water spurting from the kitchen faucet. "*Micah!*" He finally caught my eye, frowned, raced over and leap-frogged through the open window as I frantically threw my body in the way of the streaming water. "Shut the water off," I shouted. He pulled a face and leaped back outside.

After a minute or two the water stopped and I sank to the floor with relief, soaked through and shivering, but not quite drowned – which I counted as a win. Micah's quick footsteps sounded back through the hallway as he returned, towel in hand. "You'll do anything for attention."

"Right!" I said, swatting at him and reaching for the towel. "Give me that!"

As I began to wring myself out, he offered me a hand up and we slipped and slid over the wet floor like we were roller-skating, before sinking into the safety of the kitchen chairs and falling about laughing.

"It's rusted through," said Micah, who had managed to compose himself and was peering into the old spout. The kitchen was yet to be renovated, but must have last been replaced sometime in the fifties. It was lovely as it stood, with duck-egg-blue cabinetry and aubergine benchtops with chrome molding, but it was ratty around the edges, and needed to be updated with modern appliances. Still, it was like stepping back in time, and I half expected an apron-clad housewife from the fifties to appear brandishing a tray of prawn cocktails and devilled eggs.

Having to be budget-conscious, I hoped the rest of the plumbing was in better shape – already we'd had an issue with the main guest bathroom in the lobby and we'd be stretched for cash if we kept having nasty surprises like that. "Can you rig something up for now? When the new kitchen is installed we'll have all new tapware so there's no point getting anything fancy to replace it."

"We've got a bunch of odds and ends in the storeroom. I'll see what I can do."

I surveyed him from the corner of my eye. Micah was always a ball of energy, the type of person who couldn't sit still, but he was more jumpy than usual.

"You go clean yourself up, I'll deal with this." He motioned to the wet floor.

"Thanks, Micah, but I can do it. Before you go, anything you want to discuss?" *Smooth, Clio.*

He was practically itching to chat but, being male, tried to pretend otherwise. But he had forgotten how well I could read him. He made a show of scratching his chin, and thinking hard about what I could possibly mean. "Nope. Can't think of a single thing."

The cold air was taking my breath away, leaving a trail of goose bumps in its wake, but the damn man was going to confide in me, even if my lips went blue while I waited to go upstairs and change. I'd witnessed love at first sight and I wanted information!

"Nope, you say? Well, let me tell you what I observed and see if it rings any bells. *L.O.V.E.*" I sang the letters. It was in my nature to tease him. And we hadn't had five minutes together alone for me to ask him outright.

He guffawed. "You're such a child."

"Shall I continue?" I sang a song about kissing.

43

He held his hands up. "OK, OK. For the love of God, don't sing. So, Isla may have taken me by surprise, but it doesn't mean anything."

I huffed and puffed in disbelief. "It was love at first sight, that's what it was." I hugged myself tight, imagining Micah as the hero of the first love affair at Cedarwood, and Isla his stunning heroine. Would I plan their wedding? Their baby shower? I couldn't help it, it was inbuilt in me to think of every stage as an event to celebrate.

"*Love* is too hard," he said gruffly, wearing a dark expression, which I knew meant *leave it alone*.

But he should have known me better than that. "Micah, no! Love isn't too hard. Is this because of Ronnie?"

He sighed and folded his arms. "It's not because of Ronnie. Well… maybe in part," he admitted with a shrug. "The split with Ronnie taught me love is totally unrealistic. Because you place all these expectations on one person – of course it's destined to fail! Eventually that person won't make you smile any more. They'll be the cause of the tightness in your chest, the reason you can't sleep at night."

I frowned. It was unlike Micah to talk so pessimistically. "What expectations? Love can be as simple or as difficult as you want it to be."

He ran a hand through his hair. "There's always expectations. The expectation you'll follow them anywhere, you'll forgo your dreams for them, and then they just leave anyway, even though you sacrificed it all."

"So, don't have any expectations, and then you've got nothing to lose, right?"

The kettle I'd been waiting for when the tap exploded suddenly screeched and I poured water into two cups, motioning for him to sit at the trestle table. While he ruminated I added a log of wood to the cast-iron potbelly stove and stood with my back to it, warming myself.

He sighed and his mouth became a tight line. "I admit, it was nice to have that heady, heart-thumping feeling about someone again."

My damp clothes shrank against the heat, biting against my legs as they warmed. "So, that's a good thing, Micah! What happened with Ronnie was obviously devastating, but that doesn't mean you can't start over with someone new."

The way his eyes filled with pain was enough to make me regret bringing Ronnie into the conversation again.

"I didn't see it coming." He rubbed at his face. "It blindsided me. And I want to avoid ever feeling that way again."

"What exactly happened?" The hurt on his face was evident.

The whine of a chainsaw buzzed outside. Isla was trimming something back in a frenzy. "That's the thing," he said. "She just drifted away like it was nothing. Like what we had was nothing."

"Really?"

"She breezily announced that she was off to LA for a job interview. *Los Angeles?* A job interview? It was the first I'd heard of it. She'd been working at the bank for ever, and I thought she loved it there." He shook his head. "I offered to join her there after work on Friday and stay for the weekend but she wanted to go alone. Suffice to say she never came back. Wound up working in some cocktail bar. Was it always that bad here?" he asked, confusion lining his face.

"It wasn't you, Micah. It was something in her." In my heart of hearts, I wasn't surprised Ronnie might've got itchy feet at some point; she was one of those people always looking for more. Still, I hadn't thought she'd leave Micah. They'd been joined at the hip and I'd always hoped to find a love like theirs. How could she have been so callous to Micah, the person who loved her more than life itself?

"There was no malice in it. In her mind we'd come to the end of the road. And what could I do? I couldn't force her to love me. So I let her go, and wished her well. Told her I was here if she needed me."

A *pah* of surprise escaped me. "I don't think many people would have been so understanding, Micah."

With a half-smile he waved me away. "It hurt, no two ways about it. Without her I didn't know who I was any more."

Admittedly, I felt a wave of anger toward Ronnie, despite Micah's assurances it wasn't her fault. "I'm annoyed that you gave up your own dreams of studying medicine to stay here like she wanted and then in the end she left anyway. You could have lived near me in New York, like we'd always planned."

"Doesn't matter now. Truly, it doesn't," he said, seeing the concern on my face. "I made my choices; it's not her fault. I enjoy what I do. So what, I fix things, instead of people?" Micah tried for that impish smile of his.

"There's still time, you know." I could picture Micah wearing a white coat and making rounds of the local hospital. He'd be the type that patients felt comfortable around, with an impeccable bedside manner.

He lifted a shoulder. "I'm OK, I've got Cedarwood now, right? But can you see my point, about trusting someone again? I don't want to be swept away, because I know, when I fall in love, I fall hard, and where does that leave me? On a precipice, alone. Nope, I'll never put myself in that position again."

Surely if he felt that frisson he should follow his heart. "So you haven't had a relationship since Ronnie left?"

"Nope. None. A casual date here and there, which was more for companionship. Then, when I'd resigned myself to being single for ever, someone walks into my world, and I get this *zap*. I honestly thought I'd never feel that ever again after Ronnie."

"Micah, you can't live like a hermit your whole life."

"I'm just happy to know my heart isn't frozen solid. And I'm not a hermit – I go out, I see friends. I'm happy, really."

I frowned. "Ronnie isn't coming back, Micah. You don't have to follow anyone to the ends of the earth; you can set some boundaries…" I felt like an agony aunt doling out clichéd advice, but I didn't know how else to make him see that love was *always* worth it.

"I know she isn't…" The buzz of the chainsaw mercifully ceased and Micah adjusted his voice accordingly. "And even if she did, I'd never contemplate reconciling. She's shacked up with some guy in LA, and they've had a baby." He paused at the mention of the baby. For as long as I could remember Micah had talked of the family he'd have. "Anyway, I don't want to make Isla uncomfortable. What if she doesn't like me the same way? How awkward would that be? God, I sound like I'm back in high school."

I laughed. "You do. Anyway, all you have to do is ask her to go for coffee! It's not like you're asking her to marry you." Even though I was already mentally assessing color combinations for the wedding centerpieces…

He grinned and color flooded his cheeks. "You said yourself not to mix business with pleasure."

I guffawed as the potbelly coughed and spluttered behind me. "Since when did you ever listen to me? What the hell would *I* know?"

Outside, the symphony of work started in earnest: chainsaw, hammers, and a lawn mower. Isla must have roped in some extra hands to help.

"Since always. You've steered me straight since we were kids."

With one last attempt, I gave Micah a hard stare. "*I've* steered you straight, you say?" I didn't wait for a response. "Then you have to listen to me – give the *idea* of love a chance. Just entertain the idea and ask Isla for coffee."

"No, Clio. I'd hate to make her feel uncomfortable."

"Jeez, Micah, so much for steering you straight." I lifted a palm in surrender.

"Don't you dare play matchmaker."

I pretended to be outraged. "Me? As if I have time to meddle with your nonexistent love life," I lied.

If Cupid needed a helping hand, who better to do that than me?

Chapter Seven

With things somewhat under control at the lodge, I dressed warmly for town, and slipped into high-heeled boots. I needed to collect some supplies and wanted to drop in on Imelda and Edgar for an impromptu meeting to firm up numbers, and show them some pictures of the ballroom renovation. It dawned on me that, after their party, it wouldn't be long until I could start preparing for Christmas, and the thought of decorating the lodge for the festivities had me in paroxysms of delight. A winter wonderland wedding would be perfect, but I needed to show off the venue to attract brides. A wedding expo would be ideal, and I made notes about what I'd need to do in order to achieve it, feeling a pang for Amory, wishing she was here to share the joy of winter and all it entailed.

Tying my scarf as I went, I found Kai in the ballroom, grinning up at the ceiling. "The electricians have just left. They've replaced the old insulation and fitted downlights so it's not as gloomy with only the two chandeliers at each end of the room. What do you think?"

I surveyed the new lighting. "It makes the space appear even bigger. The downlights were a good choice, Kai." They sent out little stars of radiance which helped brighten the room. I'd been wary when it came to adding such modern features in the traditional ballroom, but they fit seamlessly.

"Won't be long until it's finished and ready for the party. Mind if I hitch a ride to town with you? I need to meet with Walter at the hardware shop."

"Sure," I said. "Let's tell Micah to keep an eye on things."

We found Micah halfway up a ladder in the abandoned library. The room was the stuff of every bibliophile's dream. Deep, dark mahogany shelves recessed into all four walls. Ladders were still attached, which slid across like something from the 1800s. It was bereft of novels and I couldn't wait to go book shopping and fill the room with old tomes whose perfume would scent the air. With a fire crackling, and the teapot steaming, I was sure we could host book clubs here. Author events. Writing retreats.

"We're going into town, Micah. Keep an ear out in case anyone needs a hand?"

A fine layer of wood dust coated him, as he sanded back one of the rippled and cracked water-damaged shelves. "Sure. But only if you bring me back a donut from Puft."

"Deal," I said, grinning.

When we parked in front of Puft, Kai jumped out, ear pressed against his phone. From what I could gather it was his boss, and there was a new job on the horizon once Cedarwood Lodge was finished. Soon he'd leave, and I wasn't sure how I felt. Would I be lost without his easy-going guidance, his calming influence on me? Only time would tell, but I wasn't looking forward to losing him.

It was warmer in town without the cold gust of wind drifting off the surface of the lake.

My aunt's donut store was doing a roaring trade with tables out front full of lunchtime patrons. I pushed my face up against the glass and searched for her, but saw only faces I didn't recognize behind the counter. As I turned I tripped over the foot of a chair, and landed smack-bang into the arms of someone walking the other way. We thumped foreheads, and tears stung my eyes. What was it about this place that made me so clumsy all of a sudden? High heels and Evergreen were a veritable deathtrap. An apology fell from my lips as I blinked hastily to correct my blurry vision. Just what I needed, a big black eye to greet potential clients.

"I'm sorry, I'm such an…" *Oh, God.* The words froze on my tongue.

"Clio?"

I nodded dumbly as I stared into the deep hazel eyes of Timothy. The first person to break my heart – a very handsome man with powerful shoulders that suggested time spent at the gym and a smile that would make many a woman melt.

"Hey." *Smooth, Clio.*

In the filmy light of midday his lips twitched as he rubbed the soft spot above his eyebrow where we'd bumped heads. "I heard you were back in town. I've been meaning to come out to Cedarwood and say hi."

"You should." I'd forgotten how modulated his voice was, every word measured and thoughtful. Maybe it was concussion, but his mouth, the way his lips twitched, held a whole host of memories for me; suddenly I was back in his parents' basement with him, listening to pop music and stealing kisses. My turncoat gaze darted to his ring finger and found it bare.

"How is it going at Cedarwood? From what I hear around town you're not far away from being able to open."

I swallowed hard and willed my voice box to engage. "Yeah, it's going well. No great disasters as yet. But there's still time." How could I say something so opposite to what I was thinking? *You're thirty-three, Clio, not thirteen.* Somehow the gangly, brace-face teen had returned uninvited. I coughed and recovered, summoning a voice I used on my most famous clients, one that hid how starstruck I was.

"How're things with you, Timothy? I thought you'd be married and have about a hundred babies by now." I left out the part about the picket fence, the cookie-baking wife, the fluffy dog called Buster…

Just then a squeal rang out as two children ran from the bakery holding chocolate-iced donuts. They laced their free hands around his legs. *I knew it!* I bet they had perfect manners too. And dabbed daintily at their mouths with napkins after they ate their bounty.

51

He wobbled as they took hold. "Clio, I'd like you to meet Scarlett and Zander. Haven't quite made it to a hundred kids yet, but these two have the energy of fifty at least." He held back laughter, and glanced down at them with such fondness in his eyes that my heart just about stopped.

I won't lie. A part of me, that teeny, tiny, hopeless romantic part of me, died. *He had made children!* Actual living, breathing little humans. And not just your standard cute ones; really gorgeous, impish ones.

"Nice to meet you, Scarlett and Zander. You chose well. I happen to know those donuts are the best in the world."

Scarlett narrowed her eyes, held the donut tighter, and shot a glance up to her father for... what? Reassurance? Even the... what... five-, six-year-old – she could have been two, three, for all I knew – could see straight through me, like I was wearing a flashing sign: FRAUD, beware! If I hadn't already felt like a member of the secret group *Being Left Behind*, I did now.

They could have been *my* children, if things had been different. And if they had been, surely they wouldn't clam up like that? Scarlett was so cold she was practically frosty, an icy wind radiating from her. And the little boy wasn't much better. Zander glared at me and tugged his dad's jean-clad leg. Although maybe it was a stranger danger thing, and in that case, they were pretty perfect, just as expected. *Damn it.*

"Anyway," I said, ignoring the death stares. "I must dash, I've got paint that needs... painting, and all sorts of very important jobs that need doing." *Kill me.*

Timothy gave me a slow, saucy smile that provoked a jelly-legged reaction. What was happening to me? Had I made a mistake leaving town to follow my dreams? For the briefest moment in time I pictured myself as a wife, a mother. I shook the insanity away before I lapsed into an existential crisis about lost loves, and sliding-door scenarios. I pulled the strap of my bag tight, and went to step off the curb with an awkward backwards wave.

Timothy grabbed my arm. "Wait," he said. "A few of the old gang are getting together next week. They'd love to see you. Micah will be there."

"Umm, yeah..." I said distractedly as Scarlett, the girl with the most angelic cherubic face, stood behind her father dragging her index finger along her throat. Was she warning me to say no? What *was* that? I had zero clue about children, but it did intimidate me. She who could handle the worst Bridezillas was scared of a five-year-old!

Tim, oblivious to my hesitation, said, "So it's a date! See you at Shakin' Shack. Micah knows the details." He bent to kiss my cheek as I mumbled about confirming closer to the day.

They walked away hand in hand as Scarlett turned once more to glare at me. What had I just agreed to?

Really, though, it would be good to see the gang again. Over time, we'd lost contact, but I often thought about them. Would I be the only one who was still trying to make sense of her life? Timothy radiated a cool, calm vibe like he was exactly where he was meant to be, and I was his polar opposite, fumbling with making basic conversation. The collected Manhattanite in me had vanished and was replaced with the former version of myself. Imagine if they knew I'd been fired and shunned in New York. Would they secretly think I deserved it for being ambitious when I left Evergreen? Only to return home, tail between my legs, buying the lodge on a whim, and claiming I'd make it something great?

With a deep, steadying breath I gave myself a pep talk, and tried to quash any crisis of confidence. Further ahead, Kai was leaning against the wall, his arms folded across his chest, like he was in contemplation.

"There you are."

Kai had one leg against the wall, soft sunlight making him sleepy-eyed. "Sorry, I had to take that call. It was about another job. Looks like it'll be Christmas in San Francisco for me."

San Francisco… the other side of the country. My heart dropped at knowing Kai wouldn't be around for the renovation of the chapel or the chalets. I felt a pang of sorrow that he'd be elsewhere, and for Christmas Day too. I always knew he'd be leaving, but a part of me wanted to host a Christmas Day party for the staff who were away from family, and make it special. And Kai had become part of the Cedarwood family – that was why I particularly wanted him to be here.

"Who was that guy?" he asked.

"Oh…" I waved him away. "Just an old friend."

Kai raised a sardonic brow. "Cute kids."

I laughed. "Yeah, *cute*. Let's go to the hardware store. I need to find Imelda." Angst sat heavy in my belly and I had the overwhelming sensation I'd let life pass me by while trying to reach the unattainable in my career. Was I doing it again, setting myself up for failure? What would I have left this time if Cedarwood didn't work out?

Kai put his hands on my shoulders. "Breathe. Your shoulders are up around your ears."

I wriggled from his grasp, but he held me firm. "Take a *deep* breath, and count to five…" Kai was often mystical, like some kind of surfer yogi, and I just didn't understand it. How would holding my breath for five seconds achieve anything? Even being rewarded by staring into the ocean blue of his calming gaze wasn't enough to make me believe.

"I'm fine, Kai. Really. I'll count to ten later to make up for it. Let's go."

With one of his penetrating looks he said, "Clio, seriously, you hold so much stress in your body, it's toxic. Just chill for five seconds."

I willed my eyes not to roll, but he was so sure it would fix everything I didn't have the heart to ignore him again. "Fine. One, two, *threefourfive*. There. I'm cured." I grabbed his hand and dragged him across the road, surprised to feel a tingle racing up my arm from his touch. Kai had the sort of hands that were made for holding, I guess. Strong, warm hands.

Walter, Imelda's son, was standing by the cash register, spooling a ream of escaped receipt paper.

"Well, hello, Clio. Would have recognized you anywhere after Mom's description of you – Carrie Bradshaw hair indeed. Though don't tell anyone I know who Carrie Bradshaw is – I'd never live it down." Walter had a ruddy complexion and deep-set eyes, just like his father. He wore a checked shirt and suspenders, which somehow suited him, being holed up in a hardware store, which was ripe with the scent of old motor oil and dust.

I winked. "Your secret is safe with me. Is Imelda here?" Even though they claimed they'd retired years ago, Imelda was often found here according to Micah. He said she couldn't quite let go of her working life. Edgar tinkered around with tools as well, and swept up the workshop, their days too long without something to keep their heads and hands busy.

"Mom's out back in the office." He jerked his thumb in that direction. "Says she had to tidy up some paperwork, even though my wife does it these days." He shrugged. "What she means is, she's double-checking the figures because she can't grasp that anyone else could do it right. Who am I to argue?" There was no malice in his voice, just deep-seated admiration.

"They need to find a hobby, maybe?" I smiled and then dropped my voice. "While I've got you, can I ask a favor?"

He nodded.

"I want to do a slide show of photos that we can play before the speeches. Set to music, maybe songs they've loved over the years? A photo montage of their love through each decade."

Walter grinned. "Now you're talking! Mom and Dad would love that."

"But let's keep it between us?"

"Your secret is safe with me." He repeated my earlier sentiment.

I smiled. "Can you get hold of some photos without them knowing?"

Walter thumbed his chin. "It wasn't long ago that Dad had all his photos scanned and saved in the cloud – that was a fun day explaining what the cloud was. How about I copy the photos onto a USB and you can choose which suit?"

"That'd be perfect. And what about music? Any chance you can take a flick through their albums and let me know what stands out, what songs you remember hearing?"

At that he rolled his eyes dramatically. "I wouldn't even have to look. Dad serenaded Mom with Percy Sledge's *When a Man Loves a Woman* at their wedding, and then every year since, but Dad can't sing a jot, and he's so out of tune it's actually painful to hear. Mom seems to like it, though."

I let out a burble of laughter, imagining Edgar warbling to Imelda in spite of being tone deaf. "Gosh, they're adorable. OK, so that can be the first song, and can you email me the titles of any others that mean something to them?"

"Sure." His face broke into a huge grin, making the resemblance between him and Edgar more obvious. "They're really excited about the party, Clio. And what you're doing will thrill them, it really will. I can sneak over to their house this afternoon for a recon mission and send it all to you."

Kai wandered over, his basket full of pipes and tubes and God knows what.

"I'll leave you to it," I said, grinning at the huge smile on his face. Men and hardware stores! Even the surfer yogi wasn't immune. "I'm going to have a quick chat with Imelda and then I'll meet you at Puft later?" Kai nodded as they fell into serious conversation about amps of drills and which battery had the longest life.

Imelda's office was meticulously tidy, with stacks of yellowing paperwork in neat straight piles and a scented candle flickering on the table.

"Hello, pretty girl!" Her face crinkled into a smile. "What's been happening at the lodge?"

I detailed the progress we'd made and where I was at in terms of the preparations. "What about a dance, Imelda? I know you're wheelchair-bound, but you can still share a moment, right? Your favorite song, you two on the dance floor?"

Her face brightened. "Oh, that's a great idea! With Edgar propping me up I can stand for a little while, at least... How about a love song, and me and Edgar standing in each other's arms for as long as we can?"

"Yes! Let me find a special song." I would dim the lights, and it would be so romantic. There wouldn't be a dry eye in the house.

After discussing the party with Imelda, who exclaimed over every tidbit with glee, I headed to Puft and crossed my fingers my aunt was in. From the gaggle of customers still queuing, I doubted she'd had time to do anything except work since returning from her cruise, but I was eager to see her.

As I squinted through the glass the front door burst open, bells jangling noisily together. "Well, there you are! I'd recognize those curls at fifty paces!" Aunt Bessie's husky voice boomed, startling me.

"Aunt Bessie, you look amazing!" With a full face of heavy makeup, and bleached-blonde teased-up hair, Aunt Bessie hadn't changed one iota. There was no evidence of a single laugh line and I expected she'd had some cosmetic help. She wore a tight-fitting sweater that accentuated her big bust, and tight jeans that exposed her curves – she was simply larger than life.

"Well, shucks. It's the eight glasses of water I drink a day, you know." She winked comically. "I expected to see you in overalls but I should've known the big city would change my girl!" She let out a cackle that drew the attention of her customers. "Tell me what's been going on over at Cedarwood. I've spent the better part of the morning trying to escape this place to visit you but these people had other ideas." She gestured at the patrons filling almost every table.

Aunt Bessie motioned to a table, and told the young girl behind the counter to bring us coffee and a serving of cookies-and-cream donuts with an extra helping of chocolate sauce.

I raised a brow.

"You'll work it off running around that lodge of yours. Now tell me everything." Aunt Bessie was a breath of fresh air, and I felt like I could do anything, *be* anything, with her on my side. I waxed lyrical about the renovations, Edgar and Imelda's party, and my plans to meet with the old gang. I managed to gloss over the reasons for leaving New York and thankfully she was too eager to hear about the lodge and didn't notice.

She raised her eyebrows. "The old gang? Does that include *Timothy*?" His name came out sing-songy, and I could see where I got the same urge to tease Micah.

I studied my nails to buy time. "It does, as well you know. Stop fishing."

She feigned surprise, putting a hand on her bust. "*Me*? Fishing? I was merely asking about one of your oldest friends." The gleam in her eye suggested otherwise.

Expertly, I changed the subject and focused on Micah's reluctance regarding romance and how obvious it was he and Isla were perfect for each other. "Sounds like we need to meddle," she said.

"I think you're right." I clasped my fingers, plotting. "How about I invite Isla here for coffee and I also invite Micah, but then, *dang*, I can't make it…"

Her heavily made-up eyes widened. "And I'm here to pass on the message: *Look, kids, why don't you sit together. Clio says everything is under control and you might as well take an hour to relax… How does that sound?"*

Only my aunt would understand my motivations and back me up. "Sounds like love is in the air…"

We gossiped about every little thing, and Aunt Bessie promised to visit once she had caught up at Puft. It wasn't until I was back at the lodge that I realized she hadn't mentioned my mom and her radio silence. Maybe Aunt Bessie wanted to see Mom in person first before making excuses for her?

Back at the lodge that afternoon I was sitting at the trestle table in the kitchen when Isla walked in. I made a show of shuffling paperwork and letting out loud sighs of frustration.

"You need a hand?" she asked.

I fumbled some more, and tried my best to look piqued. "What I need is some time away from all of this." I gestured to my notebook, which was filled with loping red scribbles.

She gave me a sympathetic arm-squeeze. "Why don't you take some time off tomorrow? I'm sure we can cover for you."

Dang it. "Erm. Maybe. What about you, Isla? I've been so busy I haven't even asked how *you're* feeling. How are you settling in here?"

She flicked the kettle on. "I'm great. Beat, you know, but that's part of the job. It's a good kind of tired. The garden is really taking shape." She flashed a smile and pottered about making coffee, grabbing a tin of biscuits.

I leaned back, rocking on my chair. "And what about the other staff? No problems with anyone?" Gosh, I couldn't work out how to bring the conversation around to Micah without making it blindingly obvious. Was I losing my touch as matchmaker?

"Everyone's been great, really friendly and supportive." She held up an empty cup toward me and I nodded yes for coffee.

"If you need an extra pair of hands, let me know. With the party deadline, I know I've put you under pressure and I'm sure Micah can help you."

At the mention of his name she flushed scarlet. "Oh... yes. About that." She chewed her lip while she pondered.

"What is it?" I urged her on.

Her gaze darted over my shoulder to the hallway, and as she turned back she dropped her voice to a whisper. "Can I ask you something... and I hope you won't take it the wrong way?" She fidgeted with the handle of her cup.

"Sure."

"Are you and Micah... like, together?" She looked downright mortified at her question.

I furrowed my brow. "A couple?"

She nodded. "Sorry if it's too personal, I just wondered... you seem to be so in tune."

I shook my head, and laughed. "No, no, he's like the brother I never had. Just best friends. And we're in tune because we've known each other for a million years. Why do you ask?" I tried not to grin, but my lips twitched in spite of it. *She liked him!*

Her face flushed a deeper shade of scarlet, bringing out her freckles. "Sorry, I just wondered. I'm not interested in him or anything like that." A nervous, high-pitched giggle escaped.

Sure.

I kept my mouth shut and hoped she'd explain herself to break the silence.

"It's only... I just thought, well, urgh..." She played with the length of her ponytail and tried to compose herself. "He just seems like a really amazing guy, and I thought there was no way he'd be single, and I was curious. *Just curious.*"

"He's single. *Totally* single." She wasn't paying attention; her eyes were glazed as if she was stuck in a daydream. Time to move on to Operation Cupid. "Hey, do you want to meet in town for lunch tomorrow? My aunt owns the Puft bakery and I've found the best way to recharge and re-energize is by stuffing my face full of sugary snacks. What do you say?"

With a few blinks she was back to me. "I'd love to. I've walked past it and been meaning to stop in."

"So, meet there at lunchtime?"

"Deal."

I picked up the paperwork, and my cup of coffee. "I'd better make some inroads then. See you tomorrow."

I went and found Micah and spun the same story. He eagerly accepted, though was concerned about the toll Cedarwood was taking on me. "I'm fine, Micah. Nothing an hour off with my best friend won't fix, right?" I gave him a dazzling smile, all the while wondering what kind of wedding dress would suit Isla. What flowers she'd choose for her bouquet...

"Right." He grinned, none the wiser. "So, lunchtime? We'll drive there together?"

Shoot! "If you don't mind, I'll meet you there. I've got some errands to run... erm... afterwards."

He was busy masking up the stairwell bannister for the painters, and nodded distractedly. "OK, sure, I'll drive myself there."

"Perfect. And my treat too."

He laughed. "Now you're talking."

Chapter Eight

"So, canapés, my darling!" Georges, the caterer, brandished a plate of tiny morsels that had my mouth watering. He was a big, round, jovial sort, with a shiny, bald head and a whopping great laugh. I'd known him ever since I was a little girl when he worked for Aunt Bessie before starting his own catering company. Unfortunately, his business was flailing, according to word around town. I felt for Georges – it would've been darn near impossible to make a living here catering. He traveled far and wide for clients out of necessity, but the costs were exorbitant and ate into his profit. Today he'd arrived with tasting plates for the canapés for Imelda's party and I hoped we'd be able to work together going forward.

"Georges, *wow*. I wasn't expecting anything so inventive! These look amazing! What's this?" I pointed to a shot glass filled with yellow soup, and topped with some kind of mini bread.

"That's a saffron and prawn bisque with shrimp toast. Very popular. And this..." He pointed to a Chinese soupspoon filled with fragrant meat and fresh herbs. "... Is Peking duck-inspired. All of these are miniature versions of gourmet meals. There's not a prawn cocktail or chicken skewer in sight!"

I let out a volley of laughter. Poor Georges – how I'd underestimated him. "Sorry, Georges. It was unforgiveable, what I said. I thought..."

"You thought because we live in a backwater my culinary skills were also stuck in the nineties. It's OK. I get it." His rotund body shimmied as he laughed. "Let's take a look at the kitchen," Georges said, bundling up our napkins.

I gathered up the tasting plates and followed behind.

"There's one problem, Georges. The kitchen is not exactly finished. Or…" I gulped. "…Even started yet. But it will be. Trust me, by party time you'll have yourself a shiny new spick-and-span space with all the modern gadgets you could ask for." I only hoped that was true. Our craftsman was dillydallying and time was running out. We wandered into the kitchen, Georges casting a keen eye over the old cooktop.

He folded his arms over his chef whites and his face paled to match. "When are they starting it?"

"Soon," I said. "Very soon."

Georges sighed good-naturedly and shook my hand, silently agreeing on a partnership I hoped would last us decades. "I can see this being the start of a beautiful friendship." He winked and laughed that deep, belly cackle of his. "Let's just hope I don't have to cook in this…"

The next day I bounced out of bed and went to my office, taking a pot of coffee big enough to drown in, planning to tick off my to-do list. I updated social media for the lodge, sharing more photos, and checking the insights to see how the pages were growing. I had an enquiry about a baby shower, which I replied to, sending examples of menus and room styles and sizes. I tried not to worry about the salons being finished on time, and instead focused on responding enthusiastically about Cedarwood's charms. It was only an enquiry, not a booking, so I could panic later if they wanted to go ahead.

Next on the list was gathering interest for the wedding expo. I uploaded some stunning black-and-white shots of the chapel from a distance. Its rustic façade would make a great backdrop for professional wedding photos. I searched for bridal websites and took out some paid advertisements, describing Cedarwood Lodge and its amenities. Perhaps the start of December would give me enough time to organize the expo? Would that be enough to get the chapel fixed, and furnished? I wrote furiously about all the things I'd need to do in order for it to happen. I paused again, wishing Amory was here to help. We usually worked together on weddings and big events, and I missed brainstorming with her. Whenever I erred on the side of caution, she pushed me over that precipice into believing I could do it.

Once notes were made, I designed an e-newsletter and sent it to my contact list with a subscription link to sign up.

There was a knock at the door, and Kai stuck his head in. "You're early," I said, stating the obvious – he was always ahead of schedule.

"I've always been an early riser, can't help it. Usually I go surfing before work, but there's no surf here, and the lake is a little flat... so here I am." His tousled hair was windblown, and not quite as blond without weeks of sunlight to bleach it.

"The lake?" I laughed, picturing Kai trying to surf on the still water on this chilly autumn morning. In summer it would be great for kayaks, paddle boarders, kids with boogie boards... It wouldn't be long now before it froze. Perhaps we'd need to invest in ice skates?

"Well, up you get!" he said.

"Up for what?" I pulled my jacket tightly around me as the draught blew in from the open doorway.

He tutted, but his eyes twinkled mischievously. The look spoke volumes. "Time to head up the mountain before the workday starts in earnest."

I furrowed my brow. "It's not even seven in the morning, Kai. It's freezing out." Winter was creeping closer every day, the sky dark, somber. And I did not climb mountains, not for anything. I was made for high heels not hiking boots.

"Then we'll walk faster. Come on..." He took my hand, leaving me no choice but to follow; he snagged my scarf from the hook and passed it back to me. Still, I tried to extricate myself with excuses.

"Kai, it's very sweet of you to invite me, but I'm not really a fan of exercise. You go, and I'll have a nice hot coffee ready for you when you return. I've got so much work to do!"

"No dice. Get going." He stood behind me with his palms against my back, pushing me like a child, before grabbing my hand and starting out in a jog. The shock of cold air on my face, and *running*, was almost too much to bear.

It wasn't until we were at the foot of the mountains that I noticed he still held my hand. For warmth, I surmised. Hailing from a sunny climate, he probably felt the cold more than me – and it was chilly so early in the morning.

"Nothing like starting the day with some blood-pumping activity. You're lucky to live here, Clio. This is my idea of heaven. The mountains, the lake, the steep bluff in the distance. So many adventures to be had." His voice carried up the mountain but it was all I could do to keep up. He dashed ahead and dragged me along.

My lungs burned following his hectic pace. "You're like a mountain goat!" My body was not made for running, had I mentioned that?

"Wait until you see the sun from up here. It'll be worth it."

"I much prefer the little glow of yellow from my office lamp." Why on earth did people do this? My calf muscles froze in protest.

"Didn't you ever head to the summit when you were younger?" He was annoyingly chipper. And wholly with breath. I pulled my hand from his grasp and doubled over, hands to hips. I was going to die, I was sure of it.

Once I'd caught some semblance of breath I said, "No, I didn't climb up to the summit! But I've seen the postcards, that's enough! Micah had his sporty friends for insane challenges like that, while I waited in the comfort of the living room with the heater on."

The earth was soft and velvety from dew, and the smell of ozone was thick in the air.

Kai grinned. "This is what you need, Clio. To save you from sleepless nights, and carrying around that anxiety you try your best to hide."

How did he know I couldn't sleep? "I don't know what you mean." I couldn't hide the haughtiness in my voice. "As if trudging up a wet and slippery mountain could ease any pain! It will cause more." What was with this guy, with his breathing techniques, extreme sports, and mumbo jumbo? And still he was Zen – as if he was exactly where he was meant to be.

"You'll see. Keep going, princess, we're almost there." Once again, he took my hand and hauled me the rest of the way. Once we reached the peak, he spun me around to check out the vista. I was dizzy with disorientation.

Arms crossed and disdain evident on my face, I was set to ridicule him, but the words froze on my tongue. Under the blanket of early-morning fog, the view was breathtaking, trees spanned for miles undulating on the landscape. Dark atmosphere and gray clouds sat heavily above, making the green of the ground more vivid. The sun splintered the sky, one lone ray landing on the earth like a spotlight.

I felt Kai's gaze on me. Damn it. It was spectacular and I'd wanted so much to tell him he was insane for making me do this.

"It's very… pretty," I managed.

"It sure is," he laughed, not taking his eyes from mine.

The air was heavy with words unspoken and for one lonely minute I pictured Kai kissing me. How had I gone from abject misery, climbing a steep range, to floaty desire? There was something so mystical about him, like he was at one with the earth, and soaked up the beauty of nature… and it was compelling. I shook the thoughts away and blamed it on lack of oxygen at this altitude.

"Next we'll try yoga. *At midnight*. I'll make you so relaxed you're floppy."

I went to argue, but couldn't form words. Midnight yoga?

***

Later that morning I was measuring up the ballroom for furniture placement, and also planning the table and chair combinations. In town, the local party store had furniture for hire; not the most modern or luxurious of options but it'd do for the interim. Eventually I'd buy my own to fill the ballroom, but that would depend on the budget and what was left after the renovations. My cellphone squawked, the alarm I'd set reminding me of my cunning plan. I shuffled my paperwork together and went to hide in my office until both Isla and Micah had left for Puft.

Safely ensconced with the door locked, I texted Aunt Bessie: *They're on route. xxx*

Thirty minutes later Aunt Bessie texted back:

Oh, they make the cutest couple! They were both a little bewildered when I said you'd been called back for an urgent meeting! So far they've spent a lot of time looking at the table. Will interfere if I need to xxx

Micah would see straight through my cancellation but that was OK. I'd just deny it – hopefully he'd be all starry-eyed and ready to give love a chance, and then he'd forget about that tiny detail. It could happen!

Let me know how it ends up. I'm not saying I expect a marriage proposal but a date would be nice. xxx

While I waited for news I punched purchase orders into the laptop. The paperwork side of the lodge was never-ending and we hadn't even opened yet. To keep track of what we were spending I entered it every day, but I knew I wouldn't be able to keep it up myself once we were busy with guests. With staff wages, purchases and invoicing, I'd need a full-time bookkeeper to keep things on track. The costs were mounting up with the renovations, but I did some quick breathing exercises to pull me from panic, and then stopped and laughed. Damn Kai and his mumbo jumbo...

An hour later my, email pinged. A bride-to-be had seen the chapel photos on Instagram and wanted to visit next month to survey it as a potential wedding venue. I could feel it in my bones that Cedarwood was going to be popular because of its unique appeal. Even with my amateur attempt at photography it was attracting enquiries. I emailed her back and told her about the bridal expo and held my breath as I sent it. There was no going back now. Well, why not! There'd be brides and bouquets as far as the eye could see at Cedarwood Lodge in December if I could pull it off. Who needed sleep anyway?

I jumped up to find Kai and see if he'd stay on and give the chapel the TLC it needed, but then the door swung open, catching me mid-flight.

"Kai, you won't believe..." My words dried up. "Micah, oh, hi. What is it?" He wore a look of mutiny and I knew damn well why. It was all I could do to stifle giggles and instead appear unruffled.

With folded arms he said, "The old set-them-up-and-don't-arrive trick? I really thought your matchmaking days were over, but I guess not." He stared me down and it was all I could do to keep a straight face. He couldn't actually prove I'd done it on purpose.

I put a hand to my chest. "Me? I did no such thing! As you can see..." I gestured to the multitude of paperwork scattered over the desk, notebooks filled with scrawls and laptop glinting with pictures of the lodge on a slideshow. "I've been *extremely* busy and an emergency cropped up. Anyway, how was it?"

He rolled his eyes dramatically. "When you use that chirpy voice it's even more obvious. It was a setup and Aunt

Bessie was in on it. She was one step away from lighting candles and serenading us."

Dang it! Aunt Bessie, like me, was a hopeless romantic, but wasn't exactly subtle at times. "Did Isla catch on?"

"I'm sure Isla thinks Aunt Bessie is great, if not a little zealous with customer service."

I laughed. "Well, look, you survived a real date!"

Groaning, he fell into a chair and rubbed his face. "She's great: funny, beautiful, and totally eccentric when she talks about flowers, which she does *a lot*, but she's leaving, right? When Cedarwood is finished. So what would be the point? Don't you see, I'm setting myself up for failure if I even consider it? We both know long-distance love doesn't work out. You tried it and failed, right?"

"It didn't work for me, but Timothy and I were so young! That was completely different. This is just another damn excuse from you. It baffles me, Micah!"

"I wish you'd focus on your own love life and leave me be. You're being the world's biggest hypocrite, you know." He ran a hand through his hair, and dropped his gaze like he was confused. Isla had ignited something in him and he just had to work through those feelings and leap!

"Did Cupid strike me with his bow and arrow?" I retorted. "No, he struck you! So don't try and turn this around on me."

"Yeah?" His lip twitched as if he knew a secret. "And you and Kai aren't spending any time alone together?"

I let out a scoff. "That's only by brute force. He's got it in his adrenaline-junkie head that climbing up mountains will help me sleep. And it does because my entire body aches afterwards and all I want to do is snooze so I can't feel the muscle pain."

He grumbled under his breath and I knew I'd won the battle.

Men. Love wasn't that complicated, surely? My mind drifted to Kai, and as I thought about him packing up his truck with all his tools, and driving off into the sunset, I understood Micah's worry a little better.

"Yeah, well, dating Isla isn't a good idea," he said. "She's great, but she's a nomad, going from job to job."

"Hmm," I mused. Really, anything could happen, right? Isla could fall in love with Cedarwood and want to stay on...

Had I broached that possibility with her?

Chapter Nine

"So, I'll organize someone to fix the stained-glass windows?" Kai leaned against the stone wall of the chapel, pad and pen in hand. It felt cooler inside since the thick limestone walls absorbed the frosty air.

"Yes... ideally I want to keep these windows if they can be restored, rather than replace them." Sun leached through the glass and colored the stone floor in prisms of light. The stained glass was circa 1920s and I didn't want to lose any of the heritage. Even if it cost more to find an artist to repair what remained, it would be a worthy investment. The designs were eye-catching – flowers and cherubs, a landscape made from glass – but they were also a marker of another time, and part of the history of Cedarwood.

He continued: "Before we do that, though, the beams have to be raised and the rot at the base fixed. Also, the vestibule is full of rising damp and some of the stones need to be replaced. Aside from that, the main issue is refurnishing it."

The pews still sat in solemn rows in front of the pulpit but the elements had ravaged them over the years, and sadly they weren't restorable.

"Could you make new pews?" I asked. "It's not as though they're complex, are they?" Kai hadn't signed on to renovate the chapel, and I wondered briefly if I was looking for an excuse for him to stay. Or was it that I relied on him, and knew he'd do the job properly, safely?

"I could knock some up. If we found some nice timber they'd last for ever. If the snow and rain hadn't seeped inside these would have too. Once the windows are fixed and the damp sorted the chapel will stay dry and the furniture will be safe all through the winter." His breath came out wispy with fog from the cold. "I'll get them done before I leave so you can go ahead with your bridal expo. I'll submit our plans to the council for approval, but you'll have to follow up on them once I'm gone. They can get lost sometimes unless you badger them."

I nodded, feeling a catch in my throat. Perhaps it was the chill of the room. "It'll be so strange without you here."

He gave me a weak smile. "No one will force you up the mountain."

"True. Small mercies and all that."

We lapsed into silence, as I fumbled for something to say. A knock at the door saved us, so Kai made his excuses and left.

"Have you got a minute?" Isla's forehead furrowed.

"Sure, what's up?"

"The grounds beyond the lake are a little unruly, and I wondered if you wanted me to work that far along. Or are we leaving it wilder?"

Beyond the lake was the entrance to one of the walking trails, and the land was overgrown and full of brambles. "We will need to tidy that area if guests wander that far, but it probably won't be an issue until spring. I think Kai and Micah are the only ones crazy enough to walk in lashing wind and rain at the moment."

"OK, well, I'll add it to the list and see how we go for time." She shuffled around like there was more she wanted to say.

"Anything else?" I asked, giving her a wide smile.

She chewed on her bottom lip before replying. "Clio, thanks for offering me the contract for Cedarwood. I know you would've had applicants with more experience." It struck me that the bubble we had was bursting. Everyone was thinking of their next job, of leaving Cedarwood for good. I'd miss them all, and what we shared here, and it was hard to believe I'd continue without them. Still, I wouldn't pine just yet. We had a few more weeks together.

"Your resume was best suited to us. There was no question about your being the right landscaper," I said, meaning it.

There were times Isla had a kind of solemnity, a heaviness, as though she carried a burden. When that passed she was energetic and lively, but when her guard fell, like now, it was obvious there was something wrong, always hovering just below the surface. I sensed she needed a confidante.

"That's nice of you to say." She fiddled with her gardening gloves and wouldn't meet my eye.

Rays of saffron sun shone through the stained-glass window. "Isla, what is it? You know you can talk to me as a friend."

"Do you have sisters?" she eventually asked.

I shook my head. "No, I'm an only child. What about you?"

"Same." She smiled. "With my job, I don't tend to have many friendships. They're a little hard to maintain when I pack up and leave all the time. Sometimes I wish I was more grounded, settled, you know?"

Outside, the rumble of a truck started, coughing and spluttering like it was on its last legs – I wouldn't miss the noise once the renovations were done. "It must be hard moving on all the time."

She dropped her gaze. "Yes."

"Well, how about you sit down for five and tell me what's really bothering you? Whatever you say stays here, in this chapel."

She gave me such a grateful look my heart nearly tore in two. Maybe that sadness she carried was pure loneliness and I understood that. I'd felt it often enough myself since returning home to Evergreen, but thankfully I had old friends to fall back on.

73

She moved from foot to foot, the room humming from the noise outside. "I feel like I'll drown in these feelings if I don't confide in someone."

I gestured for her to continue.

She blushed, bringing out the freckles on her nose. "He makes me forget there's anything in the world except him and we've barely even talked. I can't think straight when he looks at me. It's the strangest thing. I've never felt like that before, and I don't know what to do."

"With Micah?"

She nodded.

I hid a smile but inside I was jumping for joy. "Why not meet for a date and see what happens?" Micah had valid reasons for being wary about plunging into love again, but I couldn't see what was holding Isla back. Shyness, and what else?

"I doubt Micah even knows I'm alive! When we talk it's like this halting, awkward mess."

"Nerves, perhaps? On *both* your parts..." It wasn't my place to tell her how Micah felt but I was sorely tempted, and had to allude to it. Surely she could read the signs?

"Do you think he feels the same?"

I nodded. *Whoops.* What else could I do? Time was running out. Isla would leave soon unless something was done. "I think you're both struggling with the same feelings and how to act on them."

Her blush deepened. "Well, that throws up a whole new set of problems. Unrequited love was torment enough, but that is infinitely worse."

"Why?" I asked, confused.

"I worry..." Her face pinched. "...That Micah will see the *real* me, and it'll all be over and I'll have to leave Cedarwood early because it'll hurt too much to stay."

"What do you mean, the real you? Unless you're some kind of knife-wielding maniac in secret...?" I gave her a half-smile.

She laughed. "I can wield the secateurs fairly well, so unless you're a hedge you're safe. But it's more than that."

"OK... like I said, whatever you tell me stays in this room."

When she gazed up at me, my heart seized. She wore a look of abject grief, like she was one step away from dissolving into tears. What could make her so unhappy? I moved to embrace her. "Seriously, Isla, talk to me. It can't be that bad..."

After a deep, shuddery breath she said, "A few years ago I was visiting my parents' farm for the weekend. It'd been almost a year since I'd seen them. That night their house caught fire. We still don't know how it started, maybe faulty wiring, something shorted out. It spread so quickly, and it destroyed the house, and all of their farming equipment."

"Oh, Isla, that must have been terrifying. Were they OK?"

She nodded. "They got out just in time. But I went back in for the dog, Roxie. I couldn't let her suffer like that, knowing she was trapped and inhaling all that toxic smoke. I raced around the back and into the kitchen where she usually slept, and found her whimpering. As I went to pick her up a beam fell, blocking my path. Roxie scampered over it and out the door, but I got stuck, the smoke distorting my vision. The kitchen collapsed all at once, and I knew I had to clamber through the flames or I'd perish in there. It was the most terrifying thing ever, and I could hear my mom screaming my name. So I just reacted, and ran through the fire. I was burned down my body."

I let the story float, absorbing it all. "Isla, what a shocking thing to go through. I can only imagine how frightening it was for you and your family, but why would sharing that with Micah matter?"

"The burns." She swallowed hard. "I've never given the scarring much thought because I was so damn grateful to be alive. But now I wonder how they'll feel under his

75

touch, how they'll look… and I just want to retreat. What if it repulses him? Or the thought of it puts him off?"

I hadn't even thought of the scars. I'd only thought of her near-miss and how terrifying it must've been for her. "Oh, Isla. What a thing to worry about. Micah's…" I groped for something that wouldn't sound like platitudes, something that would convince her to take a chance. "If you knew him as well as I do, you'd know it would be a non-issue for him." I paused. "Unless it's upsetting for you, and then he'd be concerned. Out of all the men in the world, Micah would be the one to make you feel beautiful, because you are beautiful, and those scars, no matter how much you dislike them, are part of your story. They're part of who you are, and how you got to this point, and I'm sure Micah would say the same. It's a big ask, me telling you to trust in him, but I think you should."

Her eyes were glassy with tears. "You really think so, Clio?"

"I really do. You can hide away for ever, but what good would that do you? Why not risk it and see, and I bet you'll be surprised." I could only guess Micah would run his fingertips along them, and ask Isla about that night, and make her feel like the most beautiful woman on earth. When he fell in love he was lost to it, and scars or not, their romance would blossom if only they could move on from their pasts. They were utterly perfect for one another and I sent a prayer up to the universe to make it happen for my two friends.

"I guess I've built it up into this huge issue and I can't see past it. It's like I don't know who I am any more. I always have this instinct to run, so I never get close to anyone. I don't know, it's just easier that way."

"I can understand that, Isla. What you've been through is pretty huge. Have you thought about putting roots down? See what happens when you stay for a while? We'd love to have you full-time at Cedarwood. No pressure, but you'll always have a place here if you need it. What's the worst that can happen?"

76

Hope danced in her eyes. "Really? You want me to stay?'

"Of course! But there's plenty of time for you to decide. You do what's right for you."

"Thanks, Clio. Gosh, it's good to have another girl to talk to. I miss that."

"I do too. So let's make it a regular thing." I gave her arm a squeeze. Isla needed a friend – it was as obvious as the freckles dotting her nose – and I was more than happy to be that person. And I was glad she'd shared her secret with me. I'd tread gently with my two lovesick friends.

Chapter Ten

With two short weeks until the party, the lodge facelift was at full speed ahead. Kai and I had spent the better part of the day setting up the sound system in the ballroom, before working around the electricians who were fiddling with wires after the downlights had shorted, then blinked before going dead. In the end I gave up. "Kai, we're in their way, let's leave them to it?"

He nodded, and gave the guys a wave, before following me outside. "Let's head up the mountain," he said.

My eyebrows shot up. "We've lugged boxes all morning, and untangled five million cables, and you want to trudge up a huge mountain? You're crazy."

"I won't have much longer to do it. Come on, humor me," Kai said.

"OK," I said reluctantly. Despite my protests, a bit of space from the lodge was just what we both needed. We'd been working since sun up and hadn't stopped for lunch or an afternoon coffee break. "Where do you come from, Kai? Which part of Australia?" It struck me I could now walk and talk simultaneously up the mountain without my lungs burning.

He jogged up ahead, then spun to face me. "I'm from Bondi, a beachside city, which is always full of tourists. The faces always change with the seasons, but I'm betting that doesn't happen here."

"Why'd you leave?" My calf muscles began to protest as the climb steepened.

With hands on hips, he considered the question. "The coastline is beautiful, and Australian beaches are the best. Bright white sand, and the whole surf culture... But it wasn't enough. I figured I'd pack up and see a bit of the world. Maybe I'd stumble on something that made sense to me. I've always felt like there was something more for me than surfing all morning and fixing up other people's homes in the afternoon."

"Have you found that mysterious something?"

He laughed. "I'm still searching."

"And what do you think it is? Money? Waves? Lifestyle?"

He took an age to answer but finally said, "I think it's a feeling."

"A feeling?" I mused about what he could mean, ready to tease him, but then I realized we were both similar really...

I went to prod for details when something stopped me. Something was amiss, and it took me a good minute to comprehend it was the smell of smoke in the air. My heart stopped as I turned to face Cedarwood. Plumes of thick black smoke rose from the roof into the lilac sky. "Oh my God, Kai! It's on fire!"

I skidded forward to get a better look, but from our vantage point we couldn't see the front of the lodge, or whether everyone was out of harm's way. My heart raced and my breath grew short as fear seized me. This was my place. My life. Everything I had, all of my dreams were tied to the lodge and... I froze. Micah. Isla. The team.

"Quick..." Kai grabbed my clammy hand to steady me as my body turned liquid, seemingly unable to hold me up. "We have to get down there. We have to make sure everyone is OK."

"Yes!" I had to calm myself and get down there fast.

Running and skidding down the mountain, brambles ripped at my jacket and scratched my skin. But I couldn't stop. I couldn't stop until I knew Micah was OK. I couldn't lose him. He was like my brother. He knew me inside and out. I couldn't face this world without him and for some reason I had this overwhelming sense he was the person in danger. He'd protect Isla, I knew he would.

The descent was interminable, as my heart thundered in my chest. Cedarwood seemed to glow bright in the sky and, watching the dancing flames, my mind went to Isla and my blood ran cold. She'd be reliving her worst nightmare. I had to get to her. We tumbled to the bottom, muddy and red-faced, the acrid stench of the fire growing stronger as we neared the lodge. Kai was just ahead of me and I motioned for him to go on. The closer I got to the lodge, the more my fear choked me.

Breathless, I finally came to the front of the lodge, where a few men stood, eyes wide with shock watching orange flames lick the roof. "Where's Micah? And Isla?" I asked, my voice sharp and shrill with panic as I looked around, desperate for any sign of them. Kai ran around the side of the lodge calling up to see if anyone was inside.

Then, through the smoke, I saw them sitting on the grass out of harm's way. I scrambled over, my eyes stinging.

Micah was wrapped in a blanket, his face black with soot. Isla had a protective arm around him, her features lined with worry. Breathless, fearful, and about to sob, I fell at their feet. "Micah! Micah, oh my God, are you OK?" All I wanted to do was hug him, know he was safe, sure that no matter what happened to Cedarwood I would still have Micah. And beautiful Isla with her scared eyes, and ravaged heart.

He nodded and clutched my hands, giving me a reassuring smile. "I'm fine." Despite his assurance his hands shook and I held on tighter.

"Isla…" I turned to her, aware of how much this fire would have affected her.

She shook her head, as if to say *don't mention it*, so I stayed mute, while I tried to discreetly check Micah for any injuries. Was he burned? His hair was now cropped close to his head in messy tufts, but aside from that and black soot coating his skin, I couldn't see anything else.

A wail of sirens rang out. Fire engines careened into the driveway, followed closely by an ambulance. "Did you inhale much smoke, Micah?" While I was concerned about the lodge, seeing Micah's charred hair and blackened face scared me silly and all I could think of was his safety and that of everyone here.

"A little, but I got out quick. I'm really OK, Clio, but I've got some bad news."

"Shush, Micah. Let's worry about all of that later." I knew he meant the lodge, and the fact we'd have to start over, but right then all I cared about was them.

I turned to Isla again, unable to shake the feeling she was reliving a past nightmare all over again. "Are you really OK?"

She nodded, biting her lip against the tears that threatened to flow. "I'm fine. Everyone is. I couldn't find him, and I wanted to go in, but I... something stopped me, and it was like my feet were made of lead."

I wrapped my arms around her and whispered. "He got out. He's OK."

She swatted at her face with the back of her hand and nodded.

"Can you help him to the ambulance?" She needed to feel like she was helping, that she was there for him, or so I figured. I silently thanked the universe she hadn't raced into the lodge after him. Who knew what might have happened?

Her face pale with worry, she led him to the paramedic who was busy pulling supplies from the ambulance.

The paramedic sat Micah down and asked quick-fire questions, assessing him and dabbing on ointment, fixing on an oxygen mask. Firefighters lined up before running into Cedarwood, hoses clasped tight.

"Don't worry." Kai appeared, slightly breathless, at my side. "We'll fix it." I didn't know if he meant the lodge, my stuttering heart, or what.

I shivered, chilled to the bone despite the crackle and heat of the fire the firemen were frantically hosing down, bringing it slowly under control. Would it all go up? My dreams, gone in one big puff of smoke? Kai inched over and wrapped an arm around me. "You're shaking."

"Do they know where it started? How?"

"The ballroom," Kai said.

The ballroom! I sniffled, trying desperately to hide the shock clawing at me. "Is everyone else accounted for?"

Kai nodded. "Everyone's fine. Joe the carpenter was the only other person inside when it happened. We think it was the same downlights that shorted out before; they were set too close to the insulation. And when the electrician fixed the wiring, the heat from the lights set fire to the padding. We'll have to check once it's out. But Micah saved the room, pretty much, Clio. He got up there fast with a fire extinguisher and managed to put most of it out. Without his quick actions the whole place would have gone up. Joe got out, but when Micah didn't follow he went back in, and found him. He'd been overcome with smoke by then."

"He could have died in there." I shuddered at the thought. Micah would have been thinking only of me and Cedarwood, of the hopes I'd pinned on the place, and not his own life.

How close to disaster we'd come.

A fireman walked over and removed his mask. "It looks worse than it is," he said. "The room has sustained a lot of damage, and the floor above it, but it's mostly cosmetic. Close call, but your friend managed to keep it at bay."

I tried to respond but my voice caught. I tried to compose myself to speak. "Thank..." I swallowed hard as the actualization hit me anew. In the end I gave up and let the tears flow.

The fireman patted my shoulder and said to Kai, "It's shock. Better if you get Clio out of here for the night. Tell everyone to stay away. We'll keep a few guys here just in case. The paramedic is taking Micah and Joe to hospital for observation."

"Sure," he said. "I'll tell everyone to pack up and head home. Thanks for all of your help." The fireman nodded and went back to his team. Kai pulled me close, and I rested my head against his chest. The steady thrum of his heart was a comfort as I tried to think rationally.

Kai lifted a finger to my chin. "Are you going to be OK if I go chat with everyone? I'll only be a second."

I wiped at my face. "I should speak to them. I can…"

"Hey," he said. "You're upset. And rightly so. It's a big shock and no one is going to hold it against you if you sit for a while. I'll be right back."

Isla darted a glance to the firefighters before jogging to me. "I'm going to go with Micah. Just so he's got someone with him. OK? I'll report back as soon as we know anything. Will you be all right?"

"I'm totally fine. He'd love that. And please, call me as soon as they check him over." Micah was in good hands; he didn't need me hovering over him, wringing my hands and pacing. Still, it was hard to switch the worry off.

Isla gave me a quick hug and ran back to the ambulance, hoisting herself inside before they shut the double doors.

The tradespeople gathered their tools and gave me somber waves as they headed for their vehicles. I sucked in a breath of air, trying to steady my heartbeat. We'd been lucky, so very lucky. Thankfully Micah had installed fire extinguishers into every single room before anyone so much as picked up a hammer. And he was OK, wasn't he? He'd be OK. Sobs started anew as I imagined a very different scenario, a world without my friend. And I vowed we'd do another safety check before any work recommenced at Cedarwood.

Kai was staying in a motel the next town over, in a basic room with a tiny kitchenette and small bathroom. There was a double bed, a sofa, and an old box TV on a buffet. I was tucked up on his sofa, phone resting on the arm, waiting for any news about Micah.

"Thanks for the coffee," I said. "I should probably go. I don't want to intrude any more than I have."

Just then my phone buzzed, and I answered without looking at the display. "Isla?"

"Clio! Oh, thank God, are you OK?" My mom's desperate voice screeched down the line.

"I'm good, Mom. You heard about the fire, I take it?" My voice came out limp. I couldn't fake it with her today.

"Yes, why didn't you call? Are you sure you're OK?"

Kai motioned to the door, as if he understood the need to speak privately. I nodded thanks. "I was going to head over to you. I'm with Kai... I'm fine, Mom. I wasn't close when it broke out. But Micah was. He's in hospital under observation and so is one of the carpenters. We're worried about the amount of smoke inhalation at this stage."

"Poor Micah. I bet he was the hero, wasn't he?" Her voice was soft with pride. Mom had always liked him. The Micah effect – everyone did.

"If it wasn't for him there'd be no more Cedarwood. I owe him everything. But still, I wish he hadn't put himself in harm's way. I'd choose him over property any day of the week."

"That place, Clio..."

"What?"

"I think you should sell it. Get out, get away before something truly terrible happens."

I sighed. "It was an accident, Mom. There's bound to be accidents, no matter how much we try to prevent them. This was a one-off, an electrical issue that will be investigated to make sure it doesn't happen again. To advise me to sell seems a bit dramatic. Why do you hate the lodge so much, anyway?" Again, I had that overwhelming feeling it was about more than the bricks and mortar of the place, and right then I was tired of pussyfooting around her.

"I just don't like the idea of you in that big, old lodge alone."

"I won't be alone. Eventually I'll have guests staying in the rooms. You could always sell your cottage and live with me. There's plenty of room, you know."

She gasped as if that idea was preposterous. "That place is hexed, I'm telling you right now."

"What, Mom? What do you mean *it's hexed*?"

84

"Nothing. I didn't mean to say… that."

She was speaking Mom riddles again. "Can we stop sidestepping the real reason for once? Do you have some connection with the lodge I don't know about?" My mind reeled through possible reasons. The previous owners? "Did you know the woman who lived there? The one whose husband abandoned her and the business?"

There was a pause. My pulse sped up. Was Mom connected to the former owners? If so, why hadn't anyone breathed a word of it to me? Evergreen was a small town. Surely something would have got back to me after all these years, unless… it was something they all wanted to forget.

"No," she said, her voice tight. "If you're coming to stay here for the night, I'll leave the key out. I have to go to bed…"

"Actually, I think I'd better stay where I am and wait for news. I don't want to disturb you." In actual fact, I couldn't be bothered with Mom and her delicate moods. And I knew she was hiding something and I'd probably push her to breaking point trying to find out what it was.

"Pass on my love to Micah."

Did I imagine it, or was she rushing me off the phone, grateful for the reprieve?

"Bye, Mom."

I turned to Kai, who'd reappeared, frowning.

"Problem?" he asked.

I shrugged. "Nothing serious." It was too soon to confide my suspicions to anyone. Besides, I couldn't exactly explain it when I had no real information. "I think we should go visit Micah at the hospital. Isla hasn't called and I'm worried."

"Let's go." Nothing ruffled Kai. Maybe it was the Australian side of his nature – he was a laid-back, roll-with-the-punches kind of guy. I liked that he was still in control, but moved through life in a fluid, easy-going way.

At the hospital we found the nursing station and asked about Micah and Joe. With a smile, the young nurse pointed us to a room further along the corridor with assurances that Joe had been discharged and was totally fine, and that Micah was being observed overnight and would likely be discharged first thing in the morning. Relief flooded me, and I pulled Kai forward, counting room numbers.

We came to a single room, with the sound of a TV blaring some cops and robbers show. I was about to knock when I saw them and wrenched my hand back. Isla was on the small bed next to Micah, running the pad of her finger along his jawline, before kissing him softly on the lips and then murmuring quietly to him as he closed his eyes.

I nudged Kai, who stood behind me, and moved out of sight. Kai grinned, lacing his hand through mine to pull me away. Once we were out of earshot Kai said, "I think Micah is *totally* fine. And in good hands." He waggled his eyebrows just like Micah would do. My heart just about exploded with so many feelings – relief, awe, happiness... and hope that my two friends had opened their hearts to one another.

"Let's get out of here," I whispered, wanting to dance down the hushed, antiseptic-scented corridor. Micah deserved to tumble into love with someone gorgeous, bubbly, and free-spirited like Isla.

"The night is young. Should we get a bottle of wine and head to the lake at Cedarwood?"

I gasped. "The lake? Are you crazy? It'll be freezing!"

He shrugged. "We'll take a couple of blankets. When's the last time you switched off your phone, lay on your back and counted stars?"

"Counted stars?"

"Yeah," he laughed. "Soak up some of the moonlight – it's good for the soul, like midnight yoga... but I'll let you off that activity for tonight."

The autumnal sky was pitch-black, and there was a bite to the air. "OK, why not? But it'll be even colder by the lake, just so you know, you with your sensitive Australian skin."

"I can handle it," he laughed. "The view will be worth it."

I shook my head, bemused to be getting myself into such a situation. Even though we'd been told to stay away from Cedarwood, I felt like a worried parent, and I'd be glad to see the lodge for myself from a distance and make sure it was OK. I'm sure, deep down, Kai sensed that and had made up the counting stars idea to make me feel like I wasn't some needy parent, returning to the nest, when in fact I was.

We gathered wine and glasses from Kai's motel, pulled blankets from the bed, and drove back to Cedarwood, winding down the driveway past the lodge. It looked gloomy in its abandoned state, with the smell of smoke and sadness still heavy in the air. A part of me wanted to go inside and investigate, but we weren't cleared as yet to enter. The thought of the lodge sitting empty for a night hurt right down to my soul. Sentimental or not, it was part of me now.

"We were lucky today," Kai said, as if guessing my mood as he drove past the lodge and toward the lake.

"Damn lucky." No matter what happened once we investigated tomorrow, if our plans ground to a halt, I'd for ever be grateful that Micah, Isla, and Joe were safe.

"Once we have the report from the firefighters, we'll gear up to get the ballroom back into shape as quickly as we can. We can do it," Kai said, his voice resolute. "We'll just have to get everyone to help."

I searched his face. "You think so?"

He nodded, parked the truck under a copse of white cedar trees, and killed the engine. "I *know* so. It's important not only for your future but for morale. Everyone has worked so hard, and they want to see it finished. I didn't tell you before, but I've had calls from the previous laborers, and they've offered to come back if we need them."

Those weary tradespeople who'd left Cedarwood with tired faces after such long, hard days? "They'd come back and start over?"

"You treated everyone like they were part of the family, and they want to see this place done. Of course they will."

Something fluttered inside me, hope maybe. "Wow, OK." I shook away the worry and angst from the day, their compassion giving me a boost. "We can do it! No matter what we find tomorrow, there will be a solution so Imelda and Edgar can still have their party here." I was used to solving crises, right? That's what I was paid to do. Make it work, no matter what!

"That's the spirit!" He grinned, and my heart beat staccato. Kai was one of the good ones.

We laid our rug by the lake, the wind icy as it blew toward us. "We're going to catch our death here." I laughed and fell back, gazing up at the star-filled sky. The moon was a fuzzy yellow orb, illuminating the ripples on the water like diamonds.

"Do you think they'll end up together?" he asked.

"Isla and Micah... I don't know. He was with Veronica – Ronnie, we called her – for most of our teens, right up until a couple of years ago. I thought I'd come back to Evergreen and they'd be living the American dream. But she left, and it tore him up pretty bad. When I think of love, I always picture those two, the way they finished each other's sentences, cast these long looks that conveyed some private meaning, and sensed each other's needs on some deep level. He's adamant he doesn't want anything serious, but Isla is pretty damn amazing, and I think, despite being younger than him, she's mature and sensitive in a way that suits him." It still hurt the edge of my heart thinking that Ronnie had waltzed out of Micah's life in such a blasé fashion, so coldly, leaving such damage in her wake. Though I was one to talk. I'd left my best friend too and hadn't made a quarter as much effort at keeping in touch as I should have. Life had just got so busy...

"Some relationships are a warm-up for the real thing. Maybe the first one was just practice."

I turned to face him. "Do you really believe that?"

With his hands clasped across his belly, he said, "It makes sense, right? Do you think you're only allowed or allotted one love your entire life?"

"If I say yes does that make me seem naive?" I plowed on. "I guess I thought you'd recognize true love when you saw it. Like the world would flip over, colors would brighten, it would be like having your favorite song on repeat." Oh, God, had I really just said that to him?

But deep and meaningful Kai didn't laugh. Instead, he contemplated it before saying, "Maybe. Have you been in love before?"

I sighed. "You know that guy we saw in town? Timothy?" He nodded. "We were high-school sweethearts. I suppose a much more subdued version of Micah and Ronnie. But looking back I think it was puppy love. In New York I had lots of *first* dates, but work was hectic and I couldn't or wouldn't commit to men who counted three months as a long-term relationship. What about you?"

He pushed his hands under his head. "There was a girl back home. But when it came down to it, there wasn't enough between us for it to go anywhere. I felt a little like a cardboard cutout, going through the motions as if it was expected of me. Meet a girl, move in together, and eventually propose. But it never felt quite right. I left Australia, with no hard feelings between us, searching for something else. I don't know whether it's love or a different life, or something spiritual I want. All I know is that, if I'd stayed, suddenly I'd be sixty and looking back wondering why I felt so empty. I want more, as selfish as it sounds. Or if not more, something truer."

"Do you think the tiny town of Evergreen is the answer?"

He faced me, moonlight reflected in his eyes. "Could be. I have an affinity for this place. Like I belong. Maybe it's being so close to nature. I've always been happier in the wild than out with a bunch of people. Weird, huh?" He took a sip of wine and cupped his glass by his side.

89

"Not weird. Evergreen is the kind of place you can get lost in if you want. You've climbed the mountains, you know how easy it is to find solitude here."

"Until Cedarwood Lodge is alive and kicking."

"From your mouth to the universe's ears." I laughed.

A shooting star flashed across the sky leaving a phosphorous trail.

I made a wish. That Kai would find what he was searching for, and that he'd find it close to Evergreen.

Chapter Eleven

"So, hang on, let me get this straight. Micah, the best friend who happens to also be a super-hot male, has hooked up with the landscaper, Isla? And Kai, the Australian surfer god, is searching for something but doesn't know what? And there was a fire, *thank the lord you're all OK*, and your mom is acting weird?" Amory spoke at lightning speed and I had to pause a second to untangle her words.

"In a nutshell, yes. And the fire broke out in the ballroom ceiling, so we have to start the reno over and we've only got two weeks until the party."

She let out a *pah* of surprise. "You make New York look positively boring! I need to pull some vacay time and haul ass there."

Laughter burbled from me. "It does seem rather fraught on the retell, but it's mostly been lots of work. Cleaning, and painting, and paperwork. And now this drama…"

"Don't Negative Nelly me! You can still do this! And what about Timothy? That fine specimen of young love? Have you reconnected?"

I groaned. I'd forgotten her earlier directive about catching up with him for coffee. "Well, we're all supposed to be going out on Friday. But that's only because I literally bumped into him in town…"

She cut me off. "Bumped into him? Like meet-cute bumped into him? Like the beginning of every single decent romantic comedy?"

"If I eye-roll any harder I'll see my brain. Yes, but it wasn't like the movies at all. It was painful and all sorts of awkward because he had his two children with him, who were so frosty they were practically snowmen. The little girl made the finger-across-the-throat gesture behind his back. And she's only, like, four, or eight, or something!"

"OK, OK, that's interesting. We don't know enough about kids to translate the meaning. It could be anything! Did he say where their mom was?" Her voice rose with excitement and I knew I had to put a stop to her scheming. Before I could answer she was off again. "Was he wearing a wedding ring?"

I debated whether to lie, because if I told her the truth there'd be no going back.

"He wasn't, was he?" she said triumphantly.

Dang it! "No, he wasn't. But that doesn't mean anything! He could have been swimming, or at the gym and taken it off for safekeeping. *Besides*, I'm not interested in revisiting the past." I didn't know which way was up at the moment and definitely couldn't be trusted with matters of the heart unless they related to someone else's heart. Someone like Micah and Isla.

"Did you have butterfly belly? Yes or no?"

"Possibly, but I think that was because I had a traumatic bump to the head…"

"Yes or no?"

"It was more nerves…"

"So that's a yes. Did he give you that same special smile from back in the day?"

Damn it.

"I'll take your silence as an affirmative. And who invited who out? Actually, don't bother answering that – it was him." The clack of laptop keys clattered down the phone line.

"What are you doing?"

"Research."

"His Facebook page is locked down."

Her curse rang out and the keys clacked furiously once more.

"He doesn't use Twitter."

I was met with silence.

"Or Instagram."

"Are they so remote they can't communicate? I mean, how do these people survive?"

I giggled. "I think they meet face to face."

She gasped. "Bloody hell. OK, so if we can't stalk him online, I suppose you're going to have to do this the old-fashioned way."

"I'll go to the catch-up because I said I would, but that's it. I've got too much to do here, especially now, and Kai's making me do midnight yoga by the lake because apparently it's the only way to get the knots out of my shoulders and help me have a proper deep sleep. So, with all of those late nights and waking with the birds, I'm totally bushed. Maybe I'm getting..."

"Whoa, whoa, whoa. Kai's making you do midnight yoga by the lake? The downward dog, you say?"

"Can you get your mind out of the gutter?"

"Never. Love is what makes the world go around and I am your cheer squad."

"Riiight."

"So, you just happened to be together at midnight?"

"Well, we were climbing the mountain..."

"What for? To escape the fire?"

"No, for exercise."

"WHAT! You don't exercise!"

"I know, but Kai's really attuned to the earth and nature and he seems to have this kooky idea that I hold stress in my body and it's toxic and a spot of midnight yoga will ease all of that. And I must admit, I'm sleeping soundly at night. But yeah, it's pretty exhausting."

"But why midnight?"

"Something about the shift in ocean current or the moon, or something."

"Golly, and here I thought you'd be going to some little backwater with people who wore overalls and ate stalks of hay, and you're surrounded by all these potential husbands."

"They're not potential husbands! One of them might be married and the other one works for me! How do you twist something innocent into... matrimony?"

"Oh, please... don't tell me you haven't thought about it?"

It had crossed my mind about Kai, but only in that very blurry, 'I wonder where he'll end up' way. "No, I haven't. Not at all."

"You can't fool me, Miss Winters. But fine, keep your secrets."

"How're things there?"

"Fine. Fine."

"Oh no, what now? I know your fine does *not* mean fine. It means the exact opposite of fine."

Amory groaned. "You're the only one who can pick that up in my voice. It's quite a nuisance. I didn't want to tell you, because seriously it's just ridiculous. Have you had any calls, any requests for interviews?"

"You're the only one with my new number." When I left the agency, I'd had to hand in my phone like a naughty schoolgirl.

"Ah, of course. Well, yesterday your lovely face popped up on page two of the *Gazette*."

I frowned. "And?" They'd already found photos of me, and – I noted – always the ones where my hair was out-of-control curly or I wore some unflattering expression.

"I know it's probably innocent, but you're all over the groom!"

I gasped. "Did they Photoshop it? I haven't even..." Oh, God! "When I broke the news to him, his lip started to wobble – so I reached out to hug him! I was only comforting him! Who would've taken a photo of that precise moment? The vultures!"

"I know, and then they sold it. Surprised it's taken this long to make the papers, to be honest."

"Oh, Amory, this is a disaster! No one will ever trust me to host their weddings, even in deep, dark Evergreen."

She let out a long sigh. "I know. Maybe keep a low profile with your marketing for now. Don't go shouting about yourself, stick to advertising just about Cedarwood... but maybe keep your name out of it."

"I cannot believe this. I'd give anything to turn back time." I couldn't even see a way to spin the story in my favor. As the saying went, *any publicity is good publicity*... but even for a wedding planner in the arms of someone else's fiancé? Somehow I didn't think so.

"Don't be blue," Amory said, sensing my discomfort. "Sometimes I wish I could pack up and come and stay with you. I could hike or do Pilates in the stream at quarter to ten or something."

A giggle escaped me, picturing her doing just that. "You'd never make it up the bluff in those heels."

She laughed. "True, and I think I'd tumble forward if I wore flats. My body is used to be being artificially propped up six inches."

"I miss you."

"Don't go getting all soppy on me, my mascara isn't waterproof."

"Time for those eyelash extensions."

"I'll Snapchat you later."

"I love it when you talk tech."

"That's if you even get Wi-Fi *out there in them hills*." She adopted a hillbilly accent.

"I'll start my dial-up as soon as the homing pigeon brings your message."

She laughed uproariously. "Now, about the party, what theme are you going for?"

I sank back into the chair in the lobby as rain clouds gathered outside. "*A riot of color*. Imelda loves bright and pretty things so I want to make it an explosion of glamour – but bright and happy. Their son, Walter, gave me hundreds of pictures of them throughout their lives; half of them are black and white, so, with the backdrop of fuchsia and saffron and indigo, the photos will stand out. I've made a photo montage and coupled it with their favorite songs. Simple yet elegant. I want the focus to be on them and their family and friends, a celebration of two lives merged and what comes from that."

"That sounds amazing! I've got some frames here I could send."

"God no, then I'll be arrested for stealing or something."

"Good point. Well, let me know if I can find anything around town and ship it over."

"Thanks, Amory. Ship yourself here, that'd be good."

"Be careful what you wish for."

***

I'd left Kai in one of the upper rooms of the lodge, poring over the fire inspection report with promises to meet later to discuss it. It was good to be back inside, and as I walked sedately down the stairs I couldn't help but shiver at how close we had come to losing everything. Still, time marched invariably on and it was time to catch up with my old gang of friends.

Micah honked the horn and I went outside, shrinking as the cold hit my skin.

I figured I'd be subtle when I mentioned Isla. Take it slow and not scare him off. I jumped in the car and fastened my seatbelt. "So-o-o, anything you want to tell me?" *Whoops*. Perhaps subtle wasn't in my vocabulary. Micah had been discharged from the hospital early that morning, but I'd insisted he take the rest of the week off, no matter how much he protested, so now was my chance to grill him.

"Well, I'm glad you asked," he said, grinning, "This morning I had waffles for breakfast, with strawberries and cream, and I hiked up the bluff to work the sugar out of my system, since I'm banned from returning to work, when I am *perfectly* fine. That what you wanted to know?"

I slapped his arm playfully. "You know it isn't! I *was* going to tell you Isla was walking around Cedarwood all moony-eyed and dazed; if I didn't know better I'd say she was lovestruck but I won't bore you with any details..." I made a show of gazing at my nails like they were fascinating while Micah's driving became a little too erratic for my liking.

"She was? What did she say?"

I smiled. "Eyes on the road, Micah! She couldn't form words. Just mumbled and wandered around in circles, pruning, chopping, shaping plants, even though her mind was clearly elsewhere." Luckily for me, Isla worked at four times the speed of any normal person, so even in her love bubble she was still doing a great job.

"Maybe she's homesick?"

"Lovesick, more like. You can give up the act, Micah. I saw you at the hospital."

A blush crept up his cheeks. "Why didn't you say?"

I laughed. "It was fun to watch you squirm."

Micah shook his head, and grinned. "It was certainly unexpected. I..." He grappled with what to say. "I was lying there thanking God Cedarwood didn't burn down, and she walked in with coffee. I thought she'd come for the ambulance ride, to make sure I was OK, and then hightail it. But she stayed, and she kept giving me this look – like I was already gone. As if it was a much closer escape than it was. And the next minute she was kissing me. I didn't fight it."

"Aww, love after a near-miss is always more powerful. Makes you realize there's no time to waste. I *really* like her, Micah." His driving slowed back to a normal pace, just slightly over the speed limit.

"Me too," he said, his voice soft. "But this morning she pulled away from me. Like she's regretted acting on impulse or something."

Her past... maybe she was still scared about confiding in him? "It's been a big week for everyone, Micah. Don't read into it. There's no way in the world that girl is not smitten with you. She was probably zapped from no sleep. I told her to take some mornings off, but, like everyone else, she refused. You're a stubborn bunch."

"You're the stubborn one!" He tapped the steering wheel and seemed to ponder it all. "So, you ready for this, the grand old high-school reunion?"

"Sort of." What if we'd all changed so much I didn't know what to say? What if the conversation was stilted? "There'll only be the old gang, right?"

"Right. It'll be fun. Besides, you can wow them with stories about your fast life in New York, and all the celebs you rubbed shoulders with. They'll eat up every word."

"Yeah." God, I hoped New York didn't come into it. Imagine if they'd read stories about me? It didn't bear thinking about.

"Timothy's divorced, you know?"

"Oh look, we're here," I said, as Micah pulled into a car bay in front of Shakin' Shack, the local bar.

He didn't move to get out, just gave me one of those beseeching looks of his.

"And what's that face for?" I asked.

"I know there's a reason you came home – and it wasn't just to buy the lodge. I can tell by the way you purse your mouth when I mention New York. But I want you to know, you're not taking a step back coming home. Or taking a leap back if you choose to date someone from your past."

"Firstly, there was something, yes, but it's not the time or place to go into it. And secondly, I don't think it's a step back. I haven't acted like that, have I?"

He shrugged. Had I? Acted like some big-city upstart?

"I don't think I have, Micah. And Timothy could be married, divorced, gay, or straight and it wouldn't bother me one iota because I am not interested."

Micah put his palms up in surrender. "I was simply stating a fact. And that's a little hypocritical of you, since you were all set to play Cupid with me and Isla, were you not?"

He had me there. Still. "So?" I said, petulantly.

"So?"

"So what?" I said.

"So be that way. It's your life."

"Fine."

"Fine," he said, crossing his arms.

The ridiculousness of the conversation hit me, and I burst out laughing. "Oh, God, we've regressed back to high school."

Micah unfolded his arms and groaned. "You were even more stubborn then. This argument would have continued for a few hours at least."

"What are we even arguing about anyway?"

"I don't know. Maybe we're both scared of plunging into new lives… in your twenties, nothing really matters, but in your thirties, you suddenly feel the need to weigh up every choice. You ever feel that way?"

I sighed. "All the time. I thought I had life pretty well sorted out, but it turns out I didn't. Makes me wonder if I know myself at all sometimes."

"You know what we need?"

"What?"

"Beer."

"And lots of it."

We ambled inside. The dimly lit bar was almost empty, and a part of me hoped they'd cancelled and I could go home and do midnight yoga, and forget about it all… but then Timothy stood and waved us over to a corner booth.

"Hey," Timothy said, giving me a chaste kiss. "Micah. Like the new do." He pointed to Micah's closely shaved hair. Poor Micah hadn't had much choice after the fire had torched his locks.

Micah ran a hand over the stubble. "Yeah, you know me, always leading the way in the grooming department. Bet I wander into town next week and see clones everywhere." Everyone laughed and I hovered in Micah's shadow, unsure of which persona to be. The girl they used to know, or the one I was now… whoever that was.

99

Around the booth were a few old friends from our high-school days. And Timothy was *sans* children. Pasting on a confident smile, I sat beside Micah, who shuffled them along to make room.

Sherri – a girl I had done music and drama with a million years ago – gave me a hug, reaching over Micah's head to do it. At school she'd been the drama geek, and had gone on to make a few commercials, before deciding to concentrate on writing instead. I'd always liked her and I could tell she was that same quirky girl.

"Clio, you look great! New York agreed with you." She gave me an appraising once-over, and tutted. "I can't see your shoes but I bet they're fabulous." I'd swapped the jeans for a dress and a blazer and some kitten heels, lest I fall on my face again.

I laughed. "They're baby heels. I seem to find every groove in the wood, or hole in the ground here. And it only seems to happen when I can fall into the arms of a stranger and totally embarrass myself."

"I don't believe it for a second," Sherri said. "When I heard you'd bought the old lodge, I was sure it was some kind of myth. I honestly thought that place would stay locked up for ever. What made you decide to buy it?"

Running from a PR nightmare. "Oh, you know, I've always dreamed of being my own boss, doing parties for people my way. When it came up for sale after all these years, it seemed like a sign."

"Fate?"

"Kismet?" Timothy interjected.

I laughed. "Yes and yes."

Bennie waved across the table. He was another friend from high school, one of those guys who'd lived and breathed sports and hung out with me and Micah a lot back then. "Hey, Bennie. The years have been good to you as well."

He blushed. But really, he looked the same – they all did, except with some extra laugh lines, and fuller, more adult faces.

"I can't believe we're all together again, as if no time has passed at all. What have you been up to?" he said.

Everyone spoke at once and stopped and laughed. A silence filled the booth so Micah filled in the gaps. "Football jock Bennie went to college on a football scholarship, but busted up his knee, which put an end to his football career. Sad for Bennie, but great for us, because he came back to Evergreen and opened up a gym, which we frequent to pump iron and talk about what could have been. Sherri got married to said football jock, and they had twins, and then thought that was too easy so followed up with another little girl. This is their first night out since the baby was born."

"You got married?" My jaw fell open. Never in a million years would I have paired those two up, but I could see now how suited they were. They mirrored each other's hand gestures, and laughed at the same time. I'm sure at school they wouldn't have looked at each other twice; funny what growing up does to people.

"We did." Sherri giggled. "Once he stopped parading around like a beefcake I could see the appeal…"

Bennie pretended to be offended. "Beefcake? What am I *now*? Strawberry shortcake?"

Sherri puckered her lips and replied. "With a cherry on top."

Bennie grinned and took his wallet from a pocket, flipping open a compartment. "These are our girls. There's the twins, Izzy and Dell, and the baby, Eva. As you can see, they've got their mother's good looks."

Sherri beamed.

"They're gorgeous," I said, feeling a slight twinge in my lower gut. What on earth was that? A reminder from my biological clock? I ignored it, and studied the photo. They were sweet things with their mom's jet-black hair, and big dark eyes.

"I'm sorry about your football dreams, Bennie. But to think you're parents now, wow, I bet you feel complete." Where had that come from? Perhaps I was saying what they wanted to hear. But you could read it on them as surely as if it was tattooed how happy family life made them.

Bennie shrugged. "Football seems a lifetime ago. We're happy here. We are complete. Well... except for a little boy. Sherri isn't keen on trying again, but who knows, after a few glasses of wine maybe I can convince her." He gave her a look loaded with suggestion.

"Clamp that mouth of yours closed." She shook her head, and guzzled more wine. "He thinks you can put an order in, *one little boy please*, and once he's delivered our baby-making days will be over... but what if we have another set of twins? Golly, sleep is so underrated when you don't have kids."

"Sleep is for amateurs," Bennie said. "We can sleep when we're dead!"

Sherri eye-rolled. "Easy for you to say, mister. Don't think I don't know you nap at the gym. Micah told me!"

Bennie turned to at Micah. "You told her?"

Micah lifted his hands in surrender. "It was an accident. It slipped out."

Sherri stared her husband down. "*Sleep is for amateurs*, right?"

Bennie colored. "Right." The jukebox in the back played one of our high-school faves, a pop ballad we used to croon to. I caught Timothy's eye and smiled.

Micah slapped Bennie on the back. "My gym fees just went up, didn't they?"

"Tenfold," he laughed.

We lapsed into silence as a waitress walked over. "Can I get you drinks?" We ordered a bottle of wine, and some beers. It felt good to fall back into old routines. Jesting, joking, making light of every little thing, Bennie making us cackle with kid-wrangling tales, and Sherri telling us the truth after his exaggerations. Most of my friends in Manhattan were childless, and planned to stay that way, and I wondered if they'd regret it later. Would I? It wasn't too late, but with no relationship on the horizon, it didn't

102

seem like an option either. Their stories warmed me through, and part of me yearned for a family I didn't have.

More drinks were served and Timothy scooted around the table and sat beside me. "Tell us about the life you left behind…"

There was something in the way he said it, or the way he arranged the words, that gave me pause. Did he suspect something, what with my hasty arrival in town?

"Well…" I paused to work out which part to tell. "It truly is the city that never sleeps. Everyone works hard and plays hard too. Ambition is what drives the place, that and cocktail hour." I laughed, trying to appear relaxed and make light of it all. "It was fun, but not the kind of place you want to stay for ever." *But I had.* How I'd wanted to stay. I'd loved the high drama of New York, and the speed with which lives were lived. But maybe Amory was right and, if I'd stayed, I would have been heading for burnout. My sleeping patterns had been interrupted by hosting parties that carried over to the next day, and there was always the worry about the next one. Making it perfect. Keeping clients happy. Would Cedarwood be the same? Somehow I doubted it. While I'd still have a lot to do and organize, the pace would be different, I was certain of that.

"What about you?" I asked. "Your kids are like little rays of sunshine." *Sort of.*

He gave me that same smile, the one reserved only for me. Did he use that on his wife? Puppy love, I reminded myself. And a million years ago at that.

"They're going through a bit of a stage at the moment. Testing the boundaries and all that jazz. It's not their fault," he said, when I urged him on with a nod. "I've recently split with their mom, and it's been a big adjustment for them. For all of us."

At the bar the tender wiped down the bench, and looked around at the all-but-empty tables with a sigh of resignation. "I'm sorry it didn't work out." I was dying to prod him for answers, and wondered why… was I simply curious? Or was it something more?

"We tried to make it work for the kids' sake but we were just too different in the end. We were so young when we got married, *too* young, really, and it was never quite right, but we stuck at it until it was obvious we were making each other miserable. Melanie left, and it's been a trial."

Please, not *that* Melanie. "Melanie?"

"Melanie Locket. You know, dancer Melanie? We got married a year or so after you left."

I stiffened. So he had got married a mere *twelve months* after we broke up? There I was calling it puppy love between us, and he'd gone and walked down the aisle with *her*? Micah had certainly kept that on the down low. And no wonder. Melanie had been my nemesis at school. She'd bullied me and the other gangly girls at school. The archetypal blonde-haired, blue-eyed cheerleader with an added evil streak. How could he have married *her*?

"I see," I said lamely. "So…" Words escaped me. Had I really known him at all? How could he have married the girl who'd made my life hell at school? Many a night I'd lain sobbing in his arms, rehashing something she'd done that day to torment me. Thank God I wasn't that pushover type any more, the one who bruised easily.

He sipped his beer and then said, "Yeah, it all happened so fast. Driven by hormones, I suppose. Now Melanie's moved out of town, and I'm sole parent. You can see how the kids are struggling. They think they did something to warrant her leaving, but she moved away for work, and sees them every other weekend."

Was he still pining for Melanie? It was hard to tell, but I thought I could see a trace of hurt in his eyes.

I changed tack; I'd ruminate about it all later. "So what do you do for a job?" He'd been applying for colleges when I left, and had never been fully decided on what to be 'when he grew up', as he dubbed it.

"I'm a real-estate agent. I was kicking myself that I hadn't heard about Cedarwood being put up for sale. It was all done cloak and dagger, wasn't it?"

I settled back into my seat. The rest of the gang were joking around, playing rock, paper, scissors to settle an argument. "I did wonder why – after all this time lying vacant – it was finally offered for sale," I said. "What's the story with the previous owners? Does anyone remember?"

Timothy shrugged. "As far as I recall, the husband left and she stayed on, but closed the doors to guests. A few years later she moved on and it lay abandoned until you arrived."

"But what's the story behind that?"

Their faces were blank. Bennie said, "No idea. It's weird, isn't it, that no one mentions them?"

I hadn't found any of the former owners' personal belongings. There'd been not even a scrap of paper left behind, only some antique furniture – that was it. Odd, if they'd moved on so hastily. No books, no clothes, nothing. Maybe there was detritus in the basement. I'd have to have a more thorough search.

"Do you think the town is behind some kind of cover-up?" Micah asked, his voice jocular, but underneath I detected a hint of wonder. Was the tiny town of Evergreen hiding their secret? If so, why, since they weren't here any more? Why had we never questioned it as kids? It had been dubbed the abandoned lodge and that had been that in our eyes.

"Well, you have to admit it's strange for secrets to remain buried in Evergreen," said Sherri, playing with the stem of her wineglass.

"Perhaps we should do some digging?" I asked, and held my breath. They didn't need to know I suspected my mom had some tie with Cedarwood Lodge.

Bennie piped up, "My mom's still the head librarian. Want me to see if she can dig up any articles on the previous owners?"

That wouldn't hurt, surely? "Could you? It'd be great to have some background about them. I feel a little like I'm babysitting their child, sometimes. And that they'll come back, disappointed to see how I've changed it."

"Or maybe you'll uncover their secrets," Sherri said, pulling her eyebrows together. "Be careful…"

"Speaking of secrets," Timothy said. "Who was that guy you were in town with the other day?"

"What guy?"

"Tall, blond, surfer dude." He kept his voice light but I detected an undercurrent of something more. Was he jealous?

"Kai. He's the project manager."

Timothy raised his eyebrows. "Right. Good you've got some help." I might have mistaken it, but he seemed relieved. "We sure had some fun, didn't we?" he said, wistfully. "Are our love hearts still visible on the old chestnut tree?"

The bar was quiet, with only some soft notes drifting from the jukebox. I could easily have been a teenager again, just by swapping the bar scene for the diner down the road. It felt good to be back with my friends, knowing they hadn't changed. They were still the same big-hearted people… but I missed New York and I missed my old life. Part of me thought that would all become a distant memory as Evergreen swallowed me up. And I'd be all right with that, wouldn't I? Like Micah said, I wasn't taking a step back coming home, was I?

"Yep, our names are still carved on the trunk of the chestnut tree near the lake. First crushes, the stuff of legend."

"First *love*, don't you mean?" he said, his eyes twinkling. He was giving me the green light – I could read him like a book, but coming home didn't mean repeating the same old patterns. Not in this, anyway.

"It was a first, for sure," I said, remembering he had married Melanie practically five minutes after I left town. Melanie of all people! Had he broken up with me for *her*? Had he lied, all those years ago? I supposed it didn't matter now. But in some deep recess of my heart it stung a little, still. "We were so young."

Micah shot me a look, one I recognized so well – *do you need to be rescued?* He always had my back, and could read my nervous tics that no one else even noticed. I shook my head almost imperceptibly.

"Sherri, how's the writing going? Should I be stocking up the library room at Cedarwood with your novels?"

She flashed me a grin. "Well, at the moment I'm busy wallpapering my bathroom with rejection letters, but as soon as I get *The Call* I'll let you know, and you can stockpile my novels for your guests."

I laughed. A wall full of rejection letters: a nice, healthy, passive-aggressive way of dealing with the failure of something she'd obviously been working so hard for. "Are you still writing fantasy novels?"

She shook her head. "Nope, I'm writing romance. Bennie seems to think I base every hero on him, and wants to know if we should 'practice'…" She made air quotes. "…For a scene. The poor fool he is. My heroes would never let their wives do the midnight feed…"

We all laughed, and Bennie said, "What? I'm being a supportive husband!"

"Yeah, sure you are," she laughed. "I've just had a revise and resubmit, so fingers crossed my latest *heaving bosoms bonkbuster* gets a yes. Isn't that what you call my novels, Bennie?"

"I can't win." He grinned.

Later that night, with sore cheeks from laughter, we said our goodbyes with promises to catch up the following week. I was buzzing from the night and tipsy enough to know I'd sleep as soon as my head hit the pillow – with or without midnight yoga.

Inside Micah's car, with the heat blasting, I tried to make sense of my roiling emotions. Being home and seeing my old friends was like slotting back into a cozy pair of jeans. A comfy fit, tried and true. But that feeling of failure still haunted me. It was like part of me thought I had given up without a fight in New York, and that I'd regret it for ever. All those years of hard work, to end up back where I started.

"Timothy couldn't take his eyes off you," Micah said.

"I know, I felt it like a laser beam." Sure, my heart had skipped a beat seeing him and my pulse had jangled, but was it because of Timothy or because I was back with people I hadn't seen in so long, who made me feel good about myself?

"It was so good to see them. I'd never have guessed Ben and Sherri would have married!" I laughed, happy to be in the warmth of the car with my best friend.

"I wrote you about it. But you mustn't have got the letter. You were invited to their wedding." The words hung in the air.

Shame colored me scarlet. I remembered getting letters from Micah and putting them aside to read later, but later had never come; there had always been somewhere to be, someplace to get ready for. "I'm sorry, Micah. I should have made more time. I don't know what happened to me when I left. It was like I had blinkers on."

"Happens to the best of us." He shrugged. "You can't live in two worlds at the same time. We understood."

"I wish I'd been at their wedding." How could I have switched off friendships that meant a lot to me? In the early days they'd made efforts to stay in contact but I'd snubbed them, always excusing my behavior as a side effect of my job.

Stars twinkled overhead as we drove back to the lodge. The closer we got, the more I felt I was returning home, not in the literal sense – obviously the lodge was my actual home – but more in the sense that I was returning to where I was always meant to be. The thought was a comfort.

"It was a small wedding held at her parents' farm," Micah recalled. "They'd been strapped for cash because of his knee surgeries, but Ben insisted on getting married then and there despite their lack of funds. I did wonder at the time if Sherri was happy with such rushed nuptials. Doesn't every bride want all the bells and whistles?"

"Not always. I bet it was perfect. Hey, why didn't you invite Isla tonight?"

He tutted. "I was going to but then I thought about her sitting to one side not getting the jokes, or the references to our high-school days, and thought I'd rather save her from that."

"Yeah, good point."

"But she was a little standoffish, so I really don't know. I'm just going to keep my distance and see…"

Micah was such a gentle soul he'd never push a point with someone, but surely he could approach her and ask? "Why don't you talk to her about it?" I wanted to shake them both. I thought after the fire they'd jumped down the rabbit hole together and it would all fall into place.

He shrugged. "It's no big deal."

"But it is! You adore her."

With a long sigh he said, "Let's see what tomorrow brings."

Chapter Twelve

With just over a week until the party, things were looking grim at Cedarwood. Autumnal rains had made work slower, especially in the garden. Everyone had worked double time, pulling together, and they were bone-weary. The ballroom ceiling was still bare, replacement chandeliers hadn't arrived – they were lost in transit – and the overall feeling was of hopelessness. We'd got to the point of sheer exhaustion, despite our very best efforts. Instead, I worked on plan B, which was hosting the party in the lobby. It wouldn't have the grand exit to the deck, which we'd planned to string up with fairy lights, but it was still a beautiful space, and I could decorate it enough to pass muster.

Gripping my coffee mug tight, I went outside, hoping the view of the mountains would cheer me up, so I could try and rally the troops, and spur them on when they arrived.

My cellphone buzzed. Amory.

"And to what do I owe the pleasure?" I asked. Amory would be walking to work, sipping takeaway coffee from Starbucks, newspapers bundled under her arm.

"Clio, darling. Now don't be alarmed."

"Oh, this sounds ominous."

"There's an article in today's paper saying Flirty McFlirtison is considering suing you. I'm sure it's just an attempt to scare you into hiding further in the middle of nowhere to keep you quiet, but I thought you should know."

"What? They can't sue me! What for?" My heart raced so fast I thought my chest would explode. Could she sue me? Take Cedarwood?

"For damages. For the cost of the wedding and all the accoutrements."

"What? You're kidding!" Amory's early-morning phone call was enough to send me into a tailspin. I had so much to do at the lodge, and now this disaster to deal with.

She made soothing noises. "I know, I know, but she's filed a motion saying there were other costs. Emotional as well as financial. Their honeymoon, for example, and her mental health… there's doctors involved."

I cupped my head and wailed. "So, *she* is filing the suit against me, or they both are?"

"It doesn't say. Maybe you could call the fiancé, and find out? He could probably convince her to drop the charges if he wanted to."

Light rain sprinkled. "I don't have his number. Some stalker I am – allegedly. God…" I ran a hand over my face. "This couldn't come at a worse time."

"I've got his number. There's ways and means, if you know how… well, OK, I just opened up the database with their file, but I'll text it to you."

"What am I supposed to say?"

"Say you're sorry, you meant no harm. Mention you're practically living in the wilderness and they won't hear a peep out of you. And also say they can sue you but all you own is a rundown old lodge – no, say *cabin*, in said wilderness. They don't need to know the grand scale of Cedarwood. And I doubt they'll check."

I let out a half-wail, half-groan. "OK."

"Report back."

"Will do, love you."

"Kisses."

My phone pinged with a message containing the groom's number. Johnny was a ridiculously famous actor. Older now, but still working sporadically, and popular despite his

111

provocative not-so-private life. I'd spoken to him briefly at one of the planning meetings, and then woefully on the wedding night to tell him she'd gone.

Would he hold a grudge? Why *wouldn't* he! Run, I'd told his fiancée, *run!*

I dialed, hoping it would go to voicemail and I'd be given a stay of execution. And really, I hadn't prepared anything to say.

"Yeah?" A husky male voice answered.

"Johnny?"

"Do you know what time it is?" he grunted.

Celebrities and their beauty sleep! "I do, I'm sorry."

"If this is about the fireworks, it wasn't me."

Fireworks? "No, it's not about that. It's Clio. Your... wedding planner," I said, my toes curling.

"Oh. You."

The disdain in his voice was apparent.

"It's me. I'm so sorry to have woken you. But you see, this whole... saga, well I wanted to discuss it with you. I know I made a mistake, a huge mistake, but I was working off the information given to me at the time."

"You told my fiancée to run. To go marry some other guy!"

"Well, yes, and I can see how that might come across..."

"Come across? You can see, can you? I'm a laughing stock!"

I swallowed a lump in my throat. "I thought... she told me she loved someone else. So the romantic in me, the normal *sane person* in me, thought fleeing was the only option. You wouldn't have wanted to marry someone who didn't love you, surely?"

"None of them love me. They love the *idea* of me."

I reared back. "And that's enough?" Alarm bells clanged in my head – I was doing it again, saying things I shouldn't. But settling for someone who clearly didn't love you? It was outrageous.

"Listen here, I don't know why you think it's OK to call me after what you've done – you're either courageous or really,

really stupid. But I think we've covered all we need to, unless there was anything else? One last piece of advice?" he said, his voice heavy with sarcasm.

Why did I not just focus on the matter at hand? Now I'd upset him, and it would do my cause no good. "Flirty... I mean Monica... is threatening to sue me for damages, and I'd hoped you could convince her to drop the charges. I've left New York, I don't have a trust fund, or any real cash..."

He let out a belly laugh. "What's this got to do with me?"

"Could you call her? Tell her to stop all of this nonsense? I'm not in Manhattan, and I won't be back. I've lost my job, my life..." My voice broke. Some professional. But what if it did go to court and I lost the lodge?

He softened. "Look, it's a ploy, OK. You're an excuse to keep her face in the papers and, as an aside, it's managed to skyrocket my career again." He chuckled like it was nothing. "Everyone wants to hire the broken-hearted, washed-up movie star. Let it play out, and I promise you things will settle down."

"You ruined my career, my life, for publicity?" Was he for real?

"I didn't set out to do that. *You* told her to run, don't forget. It's just a lucky side effect that it's rekindled a career I thought was virtually over. Anyway, if Monica had stayed, our marriage would have lasted until the summer of next year, and that would have been that. It's the way it works in my world."

These people lived in a parallel universe, surely? How could that ever be acceptable? "What about real love? Finding someone who genuinely cares for you?"

"That stuff doesn't actually happen in real life when you're me."

I rolled my eyes. Movie stars, honestly. "It actually does, you know. I've planned weddings for celebrities just like you who've been in love – heart-stopping, can't-eat, can't-sleep love."

"And you're the expert, I take it? Have you been in heart-stopping, can't-eat, can't-sleep love recently?"

113

"Well…"

"Well, what?"

"Well, not exactly."

"Not exactly?" His voice was incredulous. "Yet you dole out advice like you know it all. You're one of those types who always plays Cupid, yet has never really been in love. Am I right?"

Was I? He had hit a nerve, as the truth of his statement struck me. All I did was focus on other people's love affairs, but that was my job, my passion… I swallowed hard and said haughtily, "I've seen it happen to those around me. And it's not something you can rush, it has to be the right person…"

"Fairy tales."

"What you need," I said, feeling bolder as the conversation went on, "is to find a person who isn't wowed by your celebrity status. A person who knows your profession is a one-way trip to ego land. A girl who won't kowtow to you or let you get away with any foolhardy behavior just because you can." Good advice, whether I was a meddler or not.

He let out a guttural laugh. "Yeah? She sounds peachy. And where would I find a girl like that?"

"Who knows, but isn't that the fun part? The anticipation?"

"Look, I'll talk to Monica's people about the lawsuit, OK? She doesn't have the money to actually fight you, so I wouldn't worry. It's all smoke and mirrors. But keep in touch, yeah?"

Oh, God, he did have a heart! Wait. "I'm not *that* girl, if that's what you're thinking." Had I given him the wrong impression? What was with the about-face?

He let out a bawdy laugh. "Well, that's good to know, Clio. Maybe I'll hire you again one of these days…"

Clutching my phone, I sat on the back porch of the lodge and watched the sun rise. I thought about all the things that had led me here, not just to Cedarwood but

114

to this point in my life. My focus had been on celebrating other people's love stories, making sure their weddings, anniversary parties, vow renewals went off without a hitch... but in the meantime I'd put my own love life to one side. Would I run out of time, if I didn't put myself first every now and then? But did I want love – messy and complicated and time-consuming, when the lodge was like an unruly child demanding my attention?

My mind drifted to Timothy and what he was left with. He had responsibilities now, real commitments, little people who needed him, trusted and relied on him. Even if I wanted to pursue something with him, it wouldn't be breezy. There'd always be little people to consider.

Kai's truck rumbled up the driveway, and he grinned at me through the windscreen before pulling up and jumping down from the cab.

"Morning, sunshine," he said. "What's with the long face?"

I gave him a slow smile, wondering how the man could be so happy so early in the morning. All that yoga, I guess. "Just thinking."

"That'll do it," he said, joining me on the porch. "Close your eyes."

I turned to him.

"Just close them."

I did as instructed. Tingles raced down my body as I tried to anticipate what he was up to. He didn't touch me, but I could feel his energy radiating over me somehow. My skin broke out in goose bumps. I was certain his hands hovered above, moving slowly over my head and down my chest. All my anxiety drifted away in a cloud, and I was left with a warm feeling of total contentment. I was so relaxed I was almost supine, as Kai stepped away, his footfalls squeaky on the deck.

"What *was* that?" I asked.

"Reiki." He smiled and ran a hand through his hair. "It's the best way to get rid of all those negative emotions that pull you down. It's one of those things people scoff at, but until you've tried it, you just don't know."

I couldn't speak. I was lost somewhere in the deep blue of his eyes.

I tried to blink the sudden attraction away, but all I could feel was his presence. Something deep inside me rose up, the tingle of expectation touching every nerve as it traveled the length of my body. In his eyes, I could see myself reflected. Before the moment could get any more awkward I stood, brushing the dust from my trousers.

"Well, I'd better…" we said in unison.

"Yeah," he laughed.

Chapter Thirteen

"Don't fidget!" Micah admonished me.

"Well, you've got your hand clamped over my eyes so tight I bet my eyelashes are going to snap clean off!" I laughed and took some ungainly shuffles forward.

"You can walk normally, you know, I've got you."

I tried to walk but, shrouded in darkness, I couldn't seem to remember how to do it, worried I'd trip on something.

"OK, you ready?"

"Ready," I said.

"One, two, three," he said, taking his palm from my eyes. "It's done! Again. And ready to decorate. So get your skates on and let's do this!"

I gasped, and put a hand to my mouth. "Micah! How did you get it done?" The ballroom stood empty before me. The ceilings had been redone, the new reproduction chandeliers hung. New downlights had been fitted, and the scorched smell had evaporated. The walls were fixed and painted. The ash and rubble had been removed, and the floors waxed to a shine, ready for the tap of dancing shoes.

"It wasn't me." He grinned. "Kai got everyone together, and with all hands on deck…"

"But yesterday… I just thought there was too much to be done." I guess I'd been the one who'd given up hope, and hadn't noticed they'd all pulled together one last time.

"Where is he?"

Micah pointed to the ceiling. "Upstairs. Mentioned something about measuring up the suites."

"You guys…" A group of the tradespeople had clustered by the doors. "…Are the *best*! We can get this party started now!"

They let out a cheer, and I hugged them one by one, promising them free holidays at the lodge with their families once we were open for guests. Tears stung my eyes as I realized my dreams were about to come true. Despite the fire, the setbacks, the fear, it was all going to be OK. We'd host our very first party at Cedarwood, on time, and on point.

Two days later, Kai sat beside me, going through paperwork, while I made a list of things that still had to be done. Micah walked in, arm wrapped around Isla, and I hid a grin. Isla winked at me, and I knew it meant they'd talked about her past, and Micah would love her all the more for it.

"Team meeting?" he said.

"Yup. We have exactly five days until the party and I want to make sure we're all aware of what needs to be done."

Kai shuffled his papers into a stack, and waited.

"Kai is double-checking the safety aspects and the mobility aids. We want to make sure Imelda can get around every inch of the lodge if she so desires."

"Got it," Micah said, scribbling notes.

"Isla, where are you at?"

The gardens were taking the longest to do because there was only Isla to do it, and the weather hadn't been ideal. Most days she sat out there in driving winds and sheeting rain, until I pulled her inside, and admonished her with the war cry, *you'll catch your death*. It reminded me of my mother – she used to do the same thing when I was younger, like she was doing some kind of penance weeding our garden in inclement weather.

Isla fidgeted with her hair. "There's so much to do, and I'm worried we'll run out of time. I've been concentrating on clearing the west side so at least it's tidy, but I was hoping to get some flowers planted and the fountain up and running. The grounds, though… well, they seem to go on for ever."

I gave her a reassuring smile. "You've done a great job, Isla. Seriously. I'll try to think of a way to get you some extra help. In terms of resources and equipment, just let me know what you need and we'll order it. If you concentrate on the immediate area around the lodge itself, that will be enough. But it would be great if the fountain did get finished."

Kai spoke up. "We have got a couple of people coming in for the fountain – someone to look at the electric water pump, and another guy to fix the render, and then Isla can plant the water lilies." We chatted for the next hour, our notepads filling with last-minute jobs. Stress tried to creep into my shoulders, but I pushed it away, giddy with the thought that we were almost there, if only we could work doubly hard once more. I only hoped we all had enough left in the tank to do it.

Everyone scurried away, ready to round up help and get the jobs done. Outside was a flurry of activity, men jostling as they went to and fro to the bins, some hooting and hollering about lending a hand.

With the furniture delivery imminent, I didn't have time to help Isla out in the garden – cleaning the lodge would take an age and we just didn't have the people power. I did the unthinkable and called Mom, hoping she'd be amenable to my request.

"Clio, hi," she said. "No more fires?"

I detected a touch of empathy in her voice. I double-checked the phone to make sure it was in fact my mother's number. "Not yet, but the day is young."

She tutted.

"Mom, I need your help. I know you're not keen on Cedarwood, for reasons I can't fathom, but will you come and trim the hedgerows? Our landscaper is swamped and we're running out of time. I can't really afford any more helpers."

"So you found it?" she said, her voice anxious.

"Umm?" The hedges surrounded the front of Cedarwood as a boundary line; they weren't exactly hidden.

"The maze."

"*The maze?* No!" Micah and I had played all over the grounds of Cedarwood as children and had never come across a maze. "Where's the maze?" And how on earth did she know about it?

"It's on the eastern side of the estate, near the lake."

"We haven't got that far back yet." There was a collection of chalets on the eastern border, more spacious, with extra bedrooms.

"Leave it hidden, *please.* I'll help you if you promise me that."

"Well…" Part of me wanted to drop the phone and run through the grounds to find it… first, though, I hoped Mom would explain herself. "Why?"

"I don't want to talk about it. But will you do me that one thing?" There was an edge to her voice, as if she was one step away from screaming.

I sidestepped her demand. "Did you used to work here?"

"A long time ago."

"And?"

"And then the doors were closed."

"Why, what happened?"

"It's such a long story, Clio, and I'd rather not get into it with you over the phone."

I tried to gauge every nuance in her voice for clues as to what had taken place. Did I detect a brief hint of guilt? I couldn't be sure. Not wanting her to shut down completely, I asked again, "So, Mom, I'm really in a bind, can you help with the hedges?" And hoped in person I'd get some answers.

"If you promise me you'll leave the maze hidden."

"I guess that leaves me no choice. OK, it'll stay hidden for now."

It was almost impossible not to yell *tell me your secrets!* But everything was baby steps with Mom. Her standing on Cedarwood soil was a start. A very promising one at that.

"Good, I'll come then."

The tradespeople who'd stayed around for the ballroom reveal said slow goodbyes as I enveloped them all in hugs and offered my thanks once more. They drifted to their vehicles. We waved to them as they drove away, their faces weary but triumphant. I hoped they'd take me up on the offer of returning with their families to holiday at Cedarwood over the summer. They'd worked so dang hard for me and words just weren't thanks enough.

There was only the four of us now, and whoever else I could rope in to help. And while I was happy we were getting closer to the result we wanted, I was still sad to see the tradespeople go. They'd given it their all, and wouldn't be here to see the finished product – the place dressed to impress for the party.

Isla cuddled up to Micah. She seemed a perfect fit, her body folded into the crook of him, her hand entwined with his. "I might go warm up in front of the fire," Isla said.

"Let's all go inside. I'll make cocoa."

We trampled inside, our boots dewy from the wet grass. Even I'd relegated my heels to the back of the wardrobe recently, not only because I tripped over anything and everything like some blustering fool, but because it was damn cold. We'd be in for a snowy, white Christmas if this kept up. The thought sent tingles of excitement through me, imagining decorating the lodge for the festive season, and the parties we could host here. But one step at a time...

Inside we gathered in the front parlor, a spacious room that was now furnished with sumptuous chairs with fat cushions. Micah added more wood to the fire, which shot up tiny sparks like fireworks.

I hurried to the newly installed kitchen, made a pot of cocoa and brought it back with mugs and marshmallows. The kitchen craftsman had finally answered the phone, and feeling sorry for us because of the fire, and our deadlines, had sent his entire team the day before to fit

121

it out. Everything was done by the skin of our teeth at Cedarwood, and I hoped in time we'd be more organized.

Isla helped me serve the warm drinks before we settled in to the soft cushions of the couches once more.

"So," Isla said, taking a sip of her hot drink, "did you wangle any help for the garden?"

I smiled, having completely forgotten to tell her about Mom, and her surprise knowledge. "Yes, my mom is coming." I went to tell her about the maze, but stopped, remembering my promise. "Just so you know, my mom – Annabelle – she can be a little… reserved. Don't take it the wrong way, she's just introverted."

Isla tilted her head. "Annabelle's your mom?"

I raised a brow. "Yes. Do you know her?"

"I've been having breakfast at Puft and I chat with her most mornings. She's always very interested to know what's going on here. I thought it was odd she hadn't visited you, but she said she was busy helping your Aunt Bessie in the kitchen at Puft…"

"She asked *you* about Cedarwood?" That was a very different spin to the one my mom had been giving me this entire time. She hadn't wanted to hear a word about the place when it was me talking. How odd.

"Every day."

"She'll be here soon, so if you can show her what you want her to do, that would be great."

So Mom wasn't as uninterested as she led me to believe. Why would she ask Isla about Cedarwood? And what had happened in that maze?

Chapter Fourteen

Mom and Aunt Bessie arrived wearing old clothes and workboots, ready to tackle the garden with Isla. I watched Mom's reaction as she wandered the grounds, her face pinched, her shoulders slumped. As soon as she was out of earshot I said to my aunt, "What happened in the maze?"

My aunt's mouth tightened. "It's a long story, and not mine to tell. But she has her reasons. She got the shock of her life when you turned up announcing yourself as the new owner of Cedarwood. We didn't see that coming! Tread carefully, Clio. This is a huge step for her, coming back here." Aunt Bessie's jovial nature was gone, replaced with quiet concern. But still, what was with all the secrecy?

"Why won't anyone tell me what happened? I'm not a little girl any more, I'm sure I can handle it."

She patted my hand. "It shaped her life, and it almost broke her. So let her tell you in good time, OK?"

"I don't see why she just can't confide in me." I tried not to be petulant, but really, what could be so bad?

Aunt Bessie shrugged. "You think she's aloof, cold, but she's not, not really. It's a way to protect herself, her heart. She loves you more than you could ever know…"

I frowned. "She's got a funny way of showing it."

"It's self-preservation."

I could read between the lines, and understand what my aunt meant, but sometimes it was hard not to be bitter about it all. I didn't see the need for secrets, for hiding behind smokescreens, but I guess it was Mom's way. That distance wasn't a new thing; she'd been like that my whole life.

My aunt gave me one of her face-splitting grins. "I promised your dad I'd always look out for you both. He'd have been really proud of you, you know."

I smiled, trying to conjure a memory of his face to mind, but only recalling a fuzzy picture of a man with a smile like my aunt's and the same big, blue eyes. "I hope so," I said. "Sometimes I feel like there's a presence next to me here. Just every so often, when I'm alone, the shadows deepen… I wonder if it's him?"

"Could be. When we were kids he always promised he'd haunt me if I didn't give him half my marbles. Of course, he was still alive back then so I paid him no mind…"

We laughed and continued into the lodge. "Let me show you around." Would the secret come out by itself? I wondered whether perhaps, if I found the maze, the secret would reveal itself to me, the mysterious event that happened there so many years ago and made my mom the person she was today.

***

I woke to the bleating of my alarm clock. I hit the buttons until the screeching stopped, and pulled the rugs back over me, settling down. Until I remembered. *The party!*

Today!

I threw the covers to the side, and raced to the shower. There was no time to fill the claw-foot bath for a proper soak, so I quickly scrubbed myself awake, eyeing the gold faucets, the regrouted tiles, and the ornate antique mirror hanging over the vanity. As I applied makeup, my phone pinged with a message from Amory: *Good luck for tonight, darling! Show them how it's done! xxx*

Her message gave me the boost I needed. I texted back: *Thanks, Amory, wish you were here xxx*

Ten minutes later, dried and dressed, I fluffed my *un*-Carrie Bradshaw curls, and took the stairs two at a time down to the lobby, almost taking out Kai, who stood at the foot, folder in hand.

"Whoa, where's the fire?"

"FIRE?" I screeched. "Not again!" Wild-eyed with terror, I sniffed the air, only detecting the scent of Kai. Woodsy, spicy, and manly.

He grabbed my hand. "It's just an expression... albeit a bad choice under the circumstances. I need you to breathe, to take five deep, centering breaths." His beautiful, serene lips twitched, like he was making a joke of his own foibles.

I kept my eyes on his and pecked him on his beautiful lips. He let out a little shocked gasp and I laughed. "Breathing, schmeathing." I was too excited to regulate anything except my caffeine intake and even that would have to wait. "Kai, let's breathe later. We have to dress the room, and about five million other things!" I pulled him by the arm into the ballroom. Had I just kissed him, even in jest? A tingle of belated longing raced through me, but Kai was right there once again, talking to me about something.

He tried to get me to focus on his face. "Clio, I get that you're excited. It's a big day for the lodge. But it's quarter past six in the morning. At least have a decent breakfast, some herbal tea, and then we can get moving. Definitely *do not* have any coffee. You're already wired."

A manic laugh escaped me. This was my favorite part of being an event planner. The day of. It's where everything (hopefully) came together, the room alive with decorations, the champagne glasses polished to a shine and waiting patiently to be filled. Fairy lights were strung, glittering in each window... but today was even more special, more sentimental than any party I'd done before, and I only hoped Edgar and Imelda loved every second of it.

"OK, yes. No coffee, good idea."

In the kitchen, Kai brewed a pot of tea, and I surveyed the newly installed kitchen, making sure it was spotless and ready for Georges. It was shiny and new but still I felt a twinge for the older kitchen, which was now relegated to the scrap heap.

It dawned on me how early Kai was. It was a record, even for him. "Why are you here already, Kai?"

"I wanted to go over everything, make sure it's right, in case we need to touch up paint or anything else before the party. I'm nervous too. I don't want anyone tripping over an uneven floorboard or brushing up against wet paint, if we retouch."

I nodded. "Yes, good idea. One last safety check. Though I moved all the tables and chairs into the ballroom last night."

He raised a brow. "You moved them all? By yourself?"

I laughed. My legs felt like lead today after all that heaving. I hadn't banked on them being solid oak. "I couldn't sleep. It was one less thing I'd have to do today. I meant to get them moved yesterday, but we ran out of time." I flexed my bicep, which was actually more concave than convex. "All part of the job," I said.

He shook his head. "You should have asked me, I'd have helped."

"It's OK. Let's go over our list."

An hour later, Micah and Isla found us in the ballroom, setting up the framed photos of Imelda and Edgar and their family and friends. Kai was placing them in a pattern along the walls, with temporary hooks. Their smiling faces buoyed me, as they stared from each grainy photo.

"That looks amazing," Isla said. "I love the different sizes." She walked up to survey the biggest photo, the one that took pride of place in the middle. "Is that their wedding day?" Imelda wore a simple shift dress and Edgar a suit with pant hems that sat just above his ankle, no doubt a borrowed suit in which he still managed to look debonair, despite its being stretched to fit over his lanky frame. It wasn't their clothes you focused on, it was the light in their eyes. Happiness radiated from the picture – it gave me goose bumps, trying to imagine that they'd shared fifty years of wedded bliss from that day forward. Their separation in the war only made their reunion sweeter, for how lucky they must have felt when Edgar made it home alive... unlike so many of his friends.

"Yes, they were married in the chapel at Cedarwood," I said. "See the lake in the distance?" I pointed to a patch of glittering water that was gray in the photo.

Isla's eyes filled with tears. "They still look the same," she said. "Sure, they've aged, but they've both still got those same smiles, like they're sharing a secret."

I slung an arm over her shoulder. Edgar and Imelda were firm favorites with everyone who worked here, not just for their graciousness in thanking everyone, and inviting them to their anniversary party, but because they were good, honest people, who made everyone feel like they mattered. "The secret is their love. Can you imagine knowing you've got someone on your side, no matter what, for the rest of your life?"

Micah stood just off to the side of Isla, and they exchanged a look, one of longing and hope. I moved away, not wanting to intrude on whatever was passing wordlessly between them. I could have been totally wrong, but I had a feeling there'd be another wedding at Cedarwood soon...

Kai sensed the moment too, and said, "Clio, could you help me in the lobby for a minute?"

Like children we dashed into the sumptuous room, and covered our mouths, giggling. Kai composed himself first. "Is there something in the water here?" he joked. "Sends everyone into a tizzy of romance?"

I nodded and said seriously, "Yes, I do a special love dance when there's a full moon, and Gemini is rising in Taurus. Seems to be working so far."

He shook his head and laughed. Gazing at Kai from under my lashes, my heartbeat sped up, but it was just the *idea* of love that caused it, the thought of having something like Imelda and Edgar. Or something like what was blossoming between Micah and Isla.

Maybe I was destined to be single? Perhaps the wedding planner who made other people's wedding days perfect – and had the biggest dream-wedding board on Pinterest – wasn't capable of love herself.

"I'm going to miss this place," he said.

Kai had got the call the day before – another job awaited him in Vermont. He was leaving the day after the party. And after the Vermont job he was heading to San Francisco for a job over the Christmas period. I wanted to say so many things, to beg him to stay and help renovate the chapel and make me climb the godforsaken mountain... But I didn't say a word, because what did we have? A friendship, and that was all. I had no claim on him and I couldn't stop him from taking good, paying work for a whim of mine, much as I wanted to.

"I wish you could stay."

He cast his eyes to the floor. "I'll be back one day to visit... and you won't remember me, you'll have so many faces passing through."

Silence filled the space. As if I'd ever forget Kai.

"Let's go back and hang the tulle from the ceiling," he said eventually, his eyes not shining the way they usually did.

Micah and Isla were unpacking boxes of candles, ready to adorn each table. Isla jumped up when she saw me and inched over to the door, motioning me to follow. "I told him a few days ago," she whispered. "You were right. About everything."

I gave her a hug, and resisted the urge to jump up and down. "I knew it!"

"You know the offer you made?"

"About staying on?"

She nodded. "I'd love to, if it still stands. And not only because of Micah. I don't want you to think I'm the type of person who clutches on to any man..."

I thought of her racing around the streets on her motorbike – she wasn't the type to let a man dominate her. "I know that."

"It's more that I finally feel like I fit. I can stop running for a while and make friendships that will last, you know?"

I smiled, understanding she'd found a place to put down roots, to make a life with people she trusted, who wanted so much to be there for her. "I totally get it, Isla. And I'm so glad you chose us."

"OK, I'd better get back to it." She couldn't hide her happiness; it radiated from her.

But it was all hands on deck inside, a flurry of activity, and I moved to help them, heart bursting for Micah and Isla.

I took the lengths of golden tulle from the trestle table; it was soft as silk in my hands. Kai carefully extended the ladder to the ceiling so he could bolt the fabric from the middle point, and we could drape it along sections of wall. Under the lights, it would shine luminously and break up the monotony of the wood, giving the room a touch of old Hollywood glamour.

I handed a section to Kai and he climbed up the ladder. "Here?" he asked, gathering the material.

"A little to the left... more... yes."

With quick steps, he was back down the ladder, attaching the bottom half to the wall above the pictures we'd hung.

After double-checking the preparations I sent everyone off to rest and get ready for the party, and headed to my suite.

Upstairs, I ran a bath, figuring I could steal ten extra minutes to soak the anxiety away as best I could, before a long night on my feet. Though my limbs were heavy, I was full of energy. All the hard work had been done – and in this case, renovating the lodge thrown into the mix – and now we could enjoy the fruits of our labors, by making sure Imelda and Edgar had one of the best nights of their lives.

I undressed and stepped into the rose-scented bath, trying my hardest to relax, but my body wouldn't cooperate, thinking of this and that I'd forgotten to do. Groaning, I climbed out, toweled myself dry and debated what to wear.

Eventually I decided on a navy-blue jersey dress that hugged my frame and gathered on one side. I stepped into a pair of wedges of the same hue, and applied makeup and a slick of gloss. I was eager to get downstairs, and didn't bother with any more primping and preening. It was almost as though I could hear Amory's voice. She'd be admonishing me for not making up my eyes, and fussing with my hair. I really missed her. We'd always hosted parties as a team, but I'd make her proud, doing this on my own in my dream location. My beautiful old lodge.

Chapter Fifteen

I gasped. Imelda was transformed, wearing a scarlet dress with a faux-fur wrap, and her shiny red heels. Her ash-gray hair had been set and fell in soft curls around her shoulders. Behind her, pushing the chair, Edgar was suited up, and this time I noted the hem of his pants covered his ankles.

I rushed to greet them. "You both look very dashing," I said. "Imelda, you're sparkling like a movie star."

"A very old one."

I bent to kiss her, and stood to shake Edgar's hand. He was cold, I noticed, his hand clammy. "I'll get the fires stoked up a little more. It's freezing out tonight."

"Thanks, dear. Now let us see the ballroom. I've heard it's as pretty as a picture."

Edgar remained silent, but gave me a smile. Maybe he was nervous. The entire town had heard about the party, and each day the numbers increased. I worried the costs would jump too high, but they assured me it was fine. They wanted to have the time of their lives no matter what.

The double doors of the ballroom were swung open, revealing the room in all its glory. Round tables were dressed with white tablecloths and adorned with candelabra and glittery white candles. Champagne flutes stood proud. The tulle ruffled slightly as we walked in, the gauzy material casting a shadowy hue over the room. Vases of bright, colorful blooms perfumed the air. The fire was crackling softly in the background, a nice soundtrack to the party.

"Oh, my lord. It's the most beautiful room ever. How on earth did you do this in such a short space of time, my dear? I was expecting... I don't know, just the bare minimum, but this... it's so *elegant*."

"I had a great team of people who helped every step of the way. Let me show you the photo wall." I took the handles of the wheelchair so Edgar could see them up close too.

Edgar shook his head, and took a handkerchief from his top pocket. "Remember that day, Mellie?" He pointed to a shot of the family sitting at the top of the Grand Canyon. "You thought we'd be able to climb down there, and got all uppity when that ranger told you off."

She laughed. "What was I thinking? Such a troublemaker back then."

When they came to their wedding photo, they clasped hands and remained silent, their eyes wandering slowly over it, taking in every detail.

"You both looked so happy," I said.

"We were, gosh, we really were. It's hard to believe it's almost over," Imelda said, her voice barely audible.

"We haven't even started yet," I said. "We've got the whole night." It struck me later she wasn't referring to the party.

***

The party was in full swing, music played from unseen speakers, and the tap of high heels could be heard all the way to the lobby. I'd got my wish: Cedarwood had been given the kiss of life once more, and I couldn't wipe the smile from my face.

I rushed back to the ballroom, champagne bottles clutched against my chest. Kai took the bottles from me, and stowed all but one behind the bar. He went around topping up glasses ready for the speeches. I motioned for Isla and Micah, who each grabbed another bottle and followed suit.

With a wink at Edgar, a sign for him to get ready, I fiddled with the microphone, adjusting the height for him.

I gave him a nod, and handed the microphone over, then tapped a champagne glass with a spoon in an effort to get everyone's attention.

Edgar stood tall and proud, and nodded to the guests. He cleared his throat, and said, "Bear with an old man tonight, folks... Allow me this moment. You know, not all of us are lucky in love. Some people find love but lose it, some only have an imitation of the real thing. Others search for it their whole lives, never quite catching it, but always believing it's there if only you try hard enough. Me and Mellie were part of that exclusive club of lucky ones. We knew it from the moment we laid eyes on each other, what we'd found, and we cherished that these last fifty years, trying not to take it for granted. There were times where our love dimmed, those periods in a marriage where things get hard, and the only reason the light didn't fade to black was because we worked on it. *We worked hard on it*, knowing that it was a rocky patch and that we could beat anything that tried to pull us apart. Our kids grew up, and moved out, and are a great source of pride to us – they're good people with big hearts, and that's all you can ask in a person. And then there's you. Those who've been with us since our marriage, and those we've only just met..." He nodded to me, smiling. "You've enriched our lives, and added to our story, and we want to thank you for that. Imelda and I wish you all lives filled with love and joy and happiness, and hope you find what you're looking for. If you'll indulge an old man once more, allow me to say this: life really is what you make it, so don't settle for second best. Grab hold of it and shake it up, follow your dreams – because one day you'll wake up, and if you're lucky enough you'll be seventy-six and standing where I am and wondering where on earth did all that time go? From the bottom of our hearts, thank you all for celebrating with us here tonight."

We clapped, the sound deafening as Edgar's words reverberated in our minds.

He waved, and hobbled back to Imelda, whose eyes were shiny with tears.

Georges entered the room with the cake aloft and everyone cheered once more. As Edgar pushed Imelda's wheelchair to the center of the room, guests threw heart-shaped confetti at her feet.

Georges presented Imelda with the cake to more gasps of delight. The couple radiated a type of joy I hadn't seen in such a long time. They appreciated every little thing, from the frames on each table, to the tulle draped above, and now the elaborately decorated, colorful cake. They cut the cake, both holding the knife before Imelda spoke a few words.

"My darlings, like Edgar said, we wanted to thank you all for making time for us tonight. And we wanted to say a special thank you to Clio and the team at Cedarwood for achieving the impossible to make sure we could celebrate here, back where it all began. I hope you'll all remember the lodge, and look after our newest Evergreen resident."

I blushed to the roots of my hair and mouthed thank you to Imelda.

Next came the slideshow, and Imelda and Edgar's family circled them as photos flashed from a drop-down screen. Their favorite songs played, and there was much crying and squeals of delight. I watched them for a beat, surrounded by their family, in their own little bubble of memory. While that played, I took a champagne flute and went outside on the deck for some fresh air, and to think about the night and the words that had been spoken. A lone tear escaped, part happiness, part sadness. I didn't want it to end, for people to leave the lodge, but I supposed what I really meant was Kai. He kept intruding on my mind, and I was sad that he was packing up and leaving Evergreen for good in the early hours of tomorrow morning. I wished I'd been truer, followed my heart more with him, but what did I want? There was an unmistakable spark there on my part, but it was too late. And really, what could happen? His job took him around America, and Evergreen would become a distant memory, so maybe it was for the best. The vague pang of desire I had was too indistinct to act on anyway.

I drank my champagne, toasting my new life at Cedarwood Lodge, knowing, even though I had a hard road ahead of me, I was in charge of my life for the first time ever. For now, it was time to serve the cake and start the cleanup.

Back inside, I watched everyone for a beat, and smiled to myself at the obvious joy on their faces. The first Cedarwood party had been a success, and not even the exhausted haze I was in could dampen my happiness.

Under the moonlight, after much kissing and hugging, the last guest finally left. I shut the main doors and leaned against them. Every muscle ached, and I could still hear the thump of music even though it had been silenced an hour ago. I took off my heels and limped into the kitchen where the team sat nursing cups of steaming-hot coffee.

I sat heavily, and let out a sigh of relief. "Thank you for tonight. You guys were totally amazing."

Micah and Isla were draped together, and Kai sat next to Georges, who snored softly, his arms resting over his chef whites.

Coffees were emptied and slowly everyone pulled themselves up and headed for the door. We'd made beds up in the suites so no one had to drive after such a manically long day. I'd promised them all a full breakfast in the morning, and only hoped they'd sleep in so I could too.

Georges tapped my shoulder. "Night."

"Night, Georges. Thanks for your help."

Micah's eyes were practically hanging out of his head. He took Isla's hand and led her away, with a backwards wave.

"S-o-o-o, then there were two." Kai looked alert, as if he'd already had eight hours' sleep, though I knew he'd been at it longer than anyone.

"Let's soak up the moonlight one last time," I said, pulling him up.

We retreated to the deck once more.

"You look beautiful under the stars," Kai said.

He was wearing a suit, and it fit him well, making him all the more handsome, like some billionaire playboy with his too-long locks and penetrating blue eyes.

"Thank you." I tucked a tendril of hair back. "You don't look so bad yourself." A sudden wave of shyness hit me. Hadn't I wished I had time to tell him how I felt, the inkling I had that there was a spark between us we hadn't acted on? I froze, unsure of my footing. Was there any point further complicating my life? Kai was leaving, and maybe that spark would fizzle out when we parted for good, because this was goodbye...

Kai watched me for a beat. "I'll miss this place."

A lone star streaked across the sky, stardust following in its wake. I took it as a sign: Kai wouldn't come back, so this was my chance. It was time to take a risk!

Standing on tiptoes, I acted before I could overthink it and quashed his farewells with a kiss. It was almost instantaneous – heat exploded through me as Kai leaned in, deepening the kiss, making me dizzy. After an age, he pulled away, but his hands slung low on my hips. All I could do was stare into his eyes, struck mute by desire. I'd never been kissed quite like *that* before.

"Cl-li-oh!" A voice emanated from the front hall, slowly reaching me as I came out of my daze.

I looked back at Kai, but I couldn't read his expression.

"Clio," he said, his voice soft. "I have an early start tomorrow so I... I'd better head in."

"Sure, go for it." I tried to sound blasé. So much remained unsaid, but what could I say now that someone was here? Would he just wake up and drive out of Cedarwood like nothing happened?

I took a step back from Kai. The moment to say anything had slipped away and my worry about what that kiss – *that kiss* – had meant settled in. "Cl-li-oh!" I turned toward the voice just in time to see Amory burst through the ballroom doors.

"Amory! What are you doing here?" My surprise rang out in the cool, autumnal air, but I glanced back over my shoulder to see Kai disappear through the back door.

"I couldn't let you throw your first party alone, could I?" Amory said as she strode across the floor in her six-inch heels and tight wrap dress, looking every inch the polished Manhattanite. "But where is everyone? It's only just after midnight!"

I laughed. "We're in Evergreen, not New York!" I gave her a huge hug, shocked she would come all this way just for me. But of course she would. She was Amory; it was just her style to arrive 'fashionably late'. And to interrupt…

I tried to compose myself so she wouldn't see my inner turmoil. Should I have told Kai I had feelings for him? But what exactly were they? They were too indistinct to act on. Surely he knew after the kiss?

"Seriously, Clio, where is everyone?" Amory said, spinning around on her heels as my head reeled with a jumble of emotions.

"No, really, Amory. Everyone went home. Parties in this neck of the woods tend to finish before the witching hour – all that fresh mountain air, you know. And tomorrow…" I took a deep breath. "…Most of the team are leaving, now the lodge is finished."

"Well, darling," she said, linking our arms and steering me down the steps to the lush gardens, the flowers a riot of color under the moonlight, "I'm here to stay."

I was giddy with the knowledge Amory wasn't leaving right away, but I knew there was another reason behind her sudden arrival. I could see it in the set of her jaw, the tenseness in her shoulders. Not wanting to ruin the moment, I decided to wait. She'd tell me when she was ready. Now wasn't the time to start pushing her over her secrets, especially when I had one of my own.

Stars twinkled in the inky night as we stared out at the place I called home, and I knew with a startling certainty that Kai would be gone when I woke up. But the thrill of that one kiss definitely wouldn't fade from my memory any time soon!

Chapter Sixteen

Blustery winds lashed at the windows, rattling the shutters, and a draught raced up the staircase in an eerie *woo*. December had well and truly arrived, bringing with it icy winds, sheeting rain and the urge to snuggle by the fire. But there was no time for that, with only a few days until our bridal expo, and Christmas to plan too.

"Tell me this place isn't haunted, Clio," a wide-eyed Amory said, clutching a loop of silver tinsel to her chest like a safety blanket.

"With the ghosts of boyfriends past?" I teased, warming my hands by the fire. It crackled and popped, a comforting soundtrack to frosty nights with us holed up in the lodge, working away in one room or another. While the main renovations had been done, there was always something else that needed some attention. From polishing paint-smudged, fingerprinted balustrades, to excavating the debris from a musty, unused cupboard we'd missed the first time around.

She grinned. "You wish."

"No, I do *not* wish. Men complicate everything!"

The creaks and moans of the lodge didn't bother me any more. I was used to the grand old dame making her presence felt in the whispers of wind, and shivers of brocade curtains. And if the ghosts made their presence felt, then who was I to judge? I hadn't mentioned it to anyone, but sometimes I awoke with a start, and had the feeling I wasn't alone, which was all sorts of crazy. I put it down to fatigue and erratic, dream-filled sleep.

139

"Speaking of men…" Amory said, falling into a plush, wingback chair we'd rescued from the basement and rejuvenated. "Correct me if I'm wrong, but I was thinking back to a few weeks ago – the night I arrived actually – and I *could* be mistaken, but did I interrupt you and Kai? I wasn't paying attention at the time, but I'm sure you two were in each other's arms like… lovers." Her eyes twinkled mischievously and it was all I could do to keep my expression neutral.

Damn it! I had tried very hard to forget all about Kai and the spontaneous kiss under the moonlight. He had left before I was up the next morning, and I hadn't heard a peep from him since. He'd probably forgotten all about me and Cedarwood by now, and thus there'd been no point confiding in Amory about our brief clinch. Without him here, the work days had lost some of their shine – for me anyway.

"In his arms?" I said doubtfully, as if she was silly to suggest such a thing. "God, no. We had been discussing the… the cleanup. Probably why he hotfooted out so early the next day." I lifted a shoulder as if it was nothing, but the mention of Kai and *that* kiss still had the ability to make me woozy. What could I say? It had been a long time since I'd been plagued with thoughts of a man in the romantic sense – it jolted me, these long-dormant feelings.

Not fooled, Amory narrowed her eyes and said breezily, "Oh, *my mistake*, this postcard must be for someone else then…" With a playful smile she waved the postcard in front of me.

With a shriek I snatched it from her, and held it to my chest. "Did you read it?"

She faux-gasped, "I would never do that!"

"You liar!" I laughed, and lobbed a cushion at her.

Even if Amory had read the postcard, which I had no doubt she had, I wanted to read it alone and savor it. I peeked at the festive picture on the front of a snow-covered park with a line saying: *Wish you were here*. Of course, I instantly read too much into it…

"Well, aren't you going to read it?"

"Later," I said. "It's probably just a polite reminder asking for his last invoice to be paid." Which I really needed to do. Was I subconsciously holding out so he'd call me? *No, no, no.* I was just time poor, that was all.

She rolled her eyes dramatically. "As if… Just read the damn thing. And then we can dissect every word for hidden meaning."

It was hard to hide anything from Amory, but I kept the farce up, not willing to give in so easily. "Can we get back to decorating?" I motioned to a box from which shiny baubles and sparkly tinsel spilled out, dusting the floorboards with glitter. "All we've done so far is make a mess."

"Fine." She grinned. "Let's throw some tinsel around while we talk."

She was incorrigible, and wouldn't give up until I'd read the damn card and deliberated over every single syllable with her.

Her innocent act didn't fool me, though – I wasn't the only one keeping secrets. She'd been at Cedarwood for a couple of weeks now, and her lips remained firmly clamped about why she'd hastily left Manhattan.

I hadn't pushed for details, hoping Amory would share when she was ready. I had a feeling it was something to do with Cruz, and not a problem at the agency, from the amount of work calls she was fielding, telling them with good grace that she was on a sabbatical.

I waggled my eyebrows, sensing an opportunity. "Fine, I'll tell if *you* will."

"Oh, you cunning little minx." She puckered her lips.

"Learned from the best." I winked.

"Fine."

"*Fine.*"

"You first."

I flipped the postcard over and read Kai's loping scrawls:

When the noise of the city gets too much, I think of Cedarwood. The silence, the stars, and being surrounded by the beauty of nature. What happened the night of the party?

Kai

Heat rose in my cheeks. What happened? A kiss happened, and not your run-of-the-mill kiss either: a knee-trembler, a time-stopper, a gasp-inducer, the type I'd only ever read about before, but was I alone in that thought? He hadn't called since, had he?

"Come on, the suspense is killing me!"

I handed the card to Amory and she pretended to read it for the first time. "I knew it! God, you must've been so annoyed when I stumbled in at that exact moment!"

I let out a nervous laugh. "The timing wasn't ideal, but I was happy to see you. Besides, as you can clearly see, it didn't mean anything to him. The poor guy got out of here as quick as he could so he wouldn't have to face me again."

A scoff escaped her pinked lips. "Where does it say that?" She made a show of rereading it, squinting at it up close.

Giving her a long look I quoted from memory: "*What happened the night of the party?* Not exactly a declaration of love, is it?" In my heart of hearts I hadn't expected anything more. So far my love life had been underwhelming. It wasn't that I didn't want romance, it was more that I hadn't found anyone who flipped my world upside down. And I was just too busy to waste time with Mr Right Nows.

Amory stared me down like I was an unruly child.

"What's that face supposed to mean?" I asked, folding my arms.

With a huff she said, "You're looking for a reason to cast him off before it's even started! If you read *between* the lines of what he wrote, he's saying he misses Cedarwood, which really means he's missing *you*, and he's asking if the kiss meant something to you, because it clearly did to him! Men don't send correspondence if they don't care, for God's sake."

It was my turn to scoff. "It doesn't mean that at all! If he was interested he wouldn't have left before the sun rose the next day, would he? It was like he couldn't get out

142

of here fast enough. The postcard is a reminder: *hey, pay your bills, lady.* Which I intend to do once we get all of this work done." I sighed. There was never enough time, and my nerves became more frayed the closer the bridal expo crept. Love would complicate things. Better instead if I focused on my friends, my brides, and my business. Just like usual: *work, work, work.*

I bent to the box of decorations, and busied myself rummaging.

In a softer tone Amory said, "Darling, he stayed on longer than he was contracted. *That* is saying in *invisible* letters – he's keen."

Who knew what anything meant when it came to men? Kai was more sensitive and quiet than I was used to and I didn't know how to read him, or his postcard. He was gone, and that was that.

Just then Micah wandered in, lugging another big box of Christmas decorations, and I was glad for the interruption. Having my easy-going best friend from Evergreen and my fashion-conscious best friend from Manhattan in one place might have proved tricky for some, but not for these two. They had gelled from the get-go and delighted in ganging up and teasing me good-naturedly, just as I would expect from both of them. Proof I had good taste in friends.

"Three more boxes to go. Jesus, Clio, when you decorate you don't go lightly, do you?" He wiped a layer of sheen from his brow.

I stared him down. "It's Christmas, Micah. And you of all people should know what that means." When I had lived in Evergreen as a teenager, Christmas had been left to me, and that meant Micah had been roped in to help, no matter how much he'd complained. From decorating the fir trees in the front yard, to hanging fairy lights in the window, he'd been part of every step, willing or not. Secretly, he adored Christmas but thought it unmanly to admit it. I'd been able to read that guy like a book back then, and nothing had changed.

"It means carols on a loop, eggnog for weeks, and lots of sparkly things, right?" he said, hands on jean-clad hips.

"Right! And that's just the beginning," I added, grinning. Christmas was my favorite time of year. And that meant any Grinches had to suffer in silence or face my steely-eyed glare. I had plans for an intimate Christmas Eve party, with all the trimmings. It didn't matter if I was hosting a party for four or four hundred – it had to be right. The lodge would shine so brightly you'd see it all the way from Australia if you squinted hard enough. So what if I liked Christmas? It was the one time of year when you could be sentimental and surround yourself with friends who were more like family. I loved every single part of it, including decorating like my life depended on it.

Amory held up two baubles to her ears like earrings. "We should get some tacky Christmas jewelry. You know, the type that flashes?" She swapped the baubles for a trio of star statues that she centered on the coffee table.

"We definitely should."

"Are you going to reply? I notice he's scrawled a return address on the card..." She took an ornate angel from the box and set it on the mantelpiece, casually bumping me out of the way with her hip as if I wouldn't notice she'd switched the conversation back to Kai.

I bent to the box and grabbed a length of golden glittery beads out, intending to wind them around the stairwell bannisters in the lobby. "I don't know. Anyway, what about you? Why'd you leave Manhattan?"

I propped the postcard on the mantel, near the rosy-red stockings hanging at an angle, waiting to be stuffed by Santa (a girl could still believe).

A gold Christmas candle threw light around the space, flickering festively. Amory nodded to Micah's bent head, as if to say *not in front of him*.

"Oh, don't mind Micah. He's used to doling out advice to women." Better if there were no secrets between us, then less chance I would talk out of turn. Besides, Micah was a good sounding board. He wasn't dismissive like some men could be. Still, Amory shrunk back as if she didn't want to share with him just yet.

Micah got the hint and said, "How about I make us some eggnog from my secret recipe?" He waggled his brows and I knew that meant he'd probably do his usual heavy-handed trick and add too much bourbon. He said it had to buzz on your tongue or it wasn't Christmas. *Yeah, right.* Micah just really liked bourbon.

"Bring back a plate of gingerbread men too!" I said. "The ones with the little snowflake scarves!" Something to soak up the alcohol…

"And grab some of those reindeer cookies Georges made!" Amory faced me, patting her belly. "Your chef will be my downfall, you know."

"Mine too. Let's worry about that next year."

She nodded. "Yeah, no one watches their weight over Christmas. That's just rude."

Micah shook his head ruefully as he wandered down the hallway. "Just yell out if I can do anything else, *princesses.*"

The Christmas carols had finished so I pressed the *go* button again, smiling as Dean Martin warbled 'Let it Snow'… Peeking outside, snowflakes seesawed down, blanketing the ground white; I couldn't wait for the brides to see Cedarwood in all its wintry glory, flashing festively and dusted with soft white snow. Who wouldn't want a winter wonderland wedding here?

It was Christmas-card perfect. Warm, welcoming and ready for guests.

"Anyway…" I dragged myself back to the decorations and took some reindeer bunting from the box. "What happened? Tell me everything…"

Amory fiddled with a big golden wreath for the front door, bending it back into shape and said, "It's a long story."

"We've got time." She'd try anything to avoid talking about it, and it was totally out of character for her. I'd left her to stew on it, thinking she'd confess when she was

145

ready, but now I felt like she needed a push. Besides, I was worried about her. She wasn't one to keep secrets.

She sighed. "You're going to think I'm slightly insane, really you will, so just pretend I'm not – OK? Keeping in mind I've been dating Cruz for just over a year, yeah? Not five years, not ten, not—"

"I get it," I interrupted solemnly, noting her downturned lips, the slight tremble in her hands. Amory would try to make the situation funny, or lighthearted; it was her way to downplay things, but I could see whatever it was had obviously affected her.

"So, Cruz invited me over for dinner. As you know, our dates went inexplicably from twice a week to almost every day – it was all getting very serious quite rapidly. After a month of that he was dropping hints about how settling down really appealed to him, babbling about friends of his who'd just had a baby who was as *cute-as-a-button*. He actually said *cute-as-a-button*…"

"Oh… a baby." I bit my lip to stop myself from saying anything more. Amory had zero inclination to have children. Less than zero. She was openly opposed to it and had told Cruz early on it was a deal breaker for her. He'd accepted that, not having the desire himself. They weren't that serious, anyway, or so I'd thought, according to Amory.

"Right!" She toyed with a length of tinsel. "So, I go there for this fancy, home-cooked meal, he's got this little table set for two, candles, flowers, soft music, the whole nine yards."

I turned the carols down slightly so I could concentrate. "OK, none of *that* screams weird to me, but keep going." I'd always liked Cruz – for a Manhattanite, he was more grounded than most, and didn't bother with the pretensions of big-city living. He was himself, always, a smoldering-eyed, nice guy who showed his love for Amory in little romantic ways all the time. He didn't get moody about girls' nights out and gave Amory space when she needed it without question, which she did oftentimes. He understood her work came first, and her friends were like family. When she was having a high-maintenance day, he rolled with it, rueful grin in place, mouth shut against her sudden diva demands. He was a keeper in my books.

"So I sat there sort of stiffly, feeling a little uncomfortable. The night reeked of change, and I wasn't sure why. But I could *feel* it in my bones. He popped the champagne cork and poured. I didn't even wait to clink, I guzzled it down. And then another."

I laughed, imagining her pinched face, her wide-eyed worry as she quaffed expensive champagne like it was water. "Classy."

"It gets worse," she groaned. "He pottered about making the entrée, a fancy ceviche dish that took an age to assemble—"

I interrupted. "Is he a good cook, though? That's the *big* question." Was I the only one who routinely set smoke alarms off by burning toast? I was easily distracted and the kitchen was a no-go zone for me if I could help it. The only times I tried out my culinary skills were with Mom, and that was only because she tended to avoid cooking altogether.

"Darling, don't you remember? Cruz was a chef before he moved to Manhattan. He worked under Jacques What's-His-Name for about a hundred years before he got dragged into finance by that boss of his with dollar signs for eyeballs – don't get me started on that guy. Anyway, Cruz was adding these micro herbs to the dish and telling me all about his parents and how much they wanted to meet me, and what did I think about a trip to South America to visit them?"

"Aw, that's so sweet, he wants to show you off! A trip to South America sounds totally amazing, Amory!" Cruz was a really nice guy in a sea of maybe-nots. Amory pretended it wasn't serious but it was obvious to me how much he adored her, and she kept him at bay for reasons I couldn't fathom. To protect her heart, I suspected.

She rubbed a hand over her face. "Don't you think it's a bit... heavy... meeting them?"

I frowned. "No, I don't think it's heavy! You've been dating Cruz for over a year now and that's a long time, especially in Manhattan minutes. It's the normal progression of things." It was exasperating at times being so utterly different to Amory. How could she not see this was a sign of commitment from Cruz? Surely that was a good thing?

Plumping a candy cane-festooned cushion she said, "Darling, that might be the normal progression of things for people who are willing to settle down, but that's not me! They'll expect some perfect Stepford type, won't they?"

"What do you care? You don't normally let anyone intimidate you." I had the sneaking suspicion she cared more than usual about what they'd think of her because she really did love Cruz, despite trying to act flippant about the whole relationship.

She folded her arms. "I'm not willing to pretend I'm ready for marriage *and* babies, just because I'm at the age where it's deemed I should be. Don't you see? He's expecting one thing to lead to the next, and I'm not interested in all of that. Next minute I'll be pregnant with triplets, and living in a cottage *without* Wi-Fi." She shuddered. Amory really didn't like being without the internet and I had to laugh.

"I'm sure it's not as bad as all that. It sounds romantic, like Cruz was trying to show you he's committed, and most men in New York would run a mile rather than do that. What happened next? Surely that isn't why you left town?"

She took a deep breath. "Well, then he circled the table, and bent down. *On one knee!*"

I dropped the reindeer bunting about the same time my jaw fell open. "Oh my God, he PROPOSED?"

Color rose up her cheeks and she averted her eyes. "Not exactly."

"What do you mean, *not exactly*?"

148

"Well…" She put the cushion in place on the chaise and then flopped beside it. "Obviously, I freaked out, didn't I? He knows I don't want the whole meet-the-parents, marriage-and-children, live-in-suburbia thing. I haven't kept it a secret!"

I held up a hand. "But did he or did he not say the words: *Will you marry me?*"

She let out a high-pitched squeal. "I don't know! I blinked rapidly, and pretended I had something in my eye! *An eyelash emergency…* I told him I'd be back in a minute – I just had to rinse my face…"

I cupped my mouth and said, "Oh, Amory! *You didn't!*"

"I *did*, and I went through the bedroom and plunged down the fire escape, and half-ran, half-hobbled off into the night."

"The fire escape!" I let out a groan. "Amory! But you're scared of heights!"

"I'm scared of marriage proposals more! And my poor Manolos will never be the same." She blinked back tears. I only hoped they weren't for her expensive designer heels, but for her predicament with Cruz.

"Forget about the Manolos. What did he do?"

"God, it was tragic. So, he leaned over the railing and called out, saying he just wanted to talk and why was I running, but by then I was breathing hard and quite wild-eyed with it all. You know I'm not much of runner, and I'd just plummeted down God knows how many stairs."

I flopped on the opposite chaise, truly stunned. Who'd run away from a guy like Cruz? It was mind-bending. But Amory was my best friend, so I was on her side, always. I did have to suppress a giggle at the picture she painted. "Have you spoken since then?"

She scrunched her eyes closed. "Only by text. I can't face a phone call. Firstly, I'm terrified of the whole potential proposal thing, and secondly, what if he thinks I'm a basket case for running?"

"You *are* a basket case for running! Maybe he was just going to… serenade you or something. And you, with your steely heart, threw yourself down the side of a building to get away?"

She covered her face and mumbled, "I know, I know. I wasn't thinking rationally at the time. The next day I finished up at work, and told them I was taking a sabbatical and then made my way here, all before I could change my mind. And then I thought about telling you and wanted to dissolve into the floor. So now you know." Her face paled at the recollections and I moved to hug her, silly girl that she was. All that fuss, just so she could avoid hearing someone declare their love.

"Shouldn't you at least talk to him? Put the poor guy out of his misery?"

She shook her head. "I texted him that I was here and taking a break."

"And what was his reply?"

"To take all the time I needed. He'd wait for me."

"Wow, what a monster," I said.

She lobbed an inflatable Santa at me, which bounced off and hit Micah as he walked back through the door holding a tray of steaming-hot eggnog and plates of Christmas cookies. "Whoa!" he said, just managing to right the mugs as they wobbled, eggnog splashing over the sides.

"Sorry," Amory said. "That was Santa's fault."

We sat and each took a drink, cradling the mugs for warmth, and then my phone pinged. I sighed, expecting it to be an anxious text from one of the brides attending the expo. Instead it was from Timothy: *Great to catch up the other night, would love to have dinner with you sometime this week? Timothy x*

My stomach flipped. I wasn't sure exactly how I felt about Timothy. There hadn't been time to really ruminate about it all. So I texted back quickly, shielding my phone from Amory's prying eyes: *Hey, Tim! The impromptu drinks were fab.*

I paused, weighing up what else to say. It wasn't as though we'd planned to meet, so technically it wasn't a date, more two old friends being at the same place at the same time.

150

Can I take a raincheck for dinner for some time after New Year? Hope the kids are well!

It wasn't that I didn't feel a frisson of something there; it was more he was a father and I had to tread carefully, realizing he was a package deal. And those kids weren't exactly amenable to some stranger wandering into their lives. I still hadn't recovered from Scarlett's slit-throat gesture... And my mind... well, it was on Kai. I mean, Amory, and her troubles. Not Kai. Kai was long gone.

Better to stick to other people's love lives for now. After a deep drink of eggnog, I said, "So what happens now?"

Amory took up a gingerbread man, biting his head off in one fell swoop. Between crunches she said, "Look, darling, there's no question I adore the man, but I want to move along on my terms. This may sound ironic coming from a girl who plans weddings for a living, but I just don't want to be told there's stages and like clockwork I have to tick them off, just because everyone else does."

Without the bedlam of the big city there was time to talk seriously about these big, life-changing things on a deeper level than we would have in Manhattan. Time moved at a slower pace at Cedarwood. We let ourselves relax, and confessions were mulled over, rather than responded to quickly and less thoughtfully between cocktails and pumping music as it had been in the past.

Micah sipped his eggnog, and hummed to the carols, contentment shining in his eyes – or more likely the bourbon was taking effect!

I debated whether to push Amory for a deeper truth. I didn't want her to think I wasn't supportive, but I also thought she might need a shove to be honest, even with herself. "Is it really that, though, Amory, or is it that you don't want to admit how you feel?"

"Don't Doctor Phil me, please, *oh psychobabbler*. I realize I've acted a little rashly, but imagine if he did propose? It would have been all sorts of awkward."

"Why? Would you have said no?"

"I wouldn't have said yes."

Micah piped up. "Hang on, hang on, so explain what happened." Amory nodded so I gave Micah a rundown of events. He murmured to himself before saying, "There's got to be a way you can meet in the middle. And what if he wasn't about to propose? He might have been about to tell you he's sorry but he's decided to become vegetarian."

Amory laughed. "But the ceviche, Micah. Ceviche is fish."

Micah steepled his fingers. "Maybe a pescatarian then?" He laughed. "But you see my point, right? It could have been a marriage proposal, but it also could have been, '*Hey, girl, you want to fly first class and meet my parents? Then I'll wine and dine you in Paris, how 'bout it?*'"

I let out a peal of laughter at Micah's attempted accent. It sounded more hillbilly than South American.

"Maybe," she said, giggling. "But on one knee? Don't men reserve that position for the proposal? Like, isn't it *hallowed*?"

Micah nodded. "Well, yeah, you'd hate to get a girl's hopes up if it wasn't the case. I think you should at least talk to Cruz, let him explain. He's probably out of his mind worrying about you." *Thank you, Micah!* She was more likely to listen to a third party than me, knowing I had a soft spot for Cruz.

"Yeah, I guess. I will, eventually. Let's get back to decorating. All this love talk gets too soppy after a while. Plus, we've got wreaths to hang on the doors, and stockings for the fireplaces in the suites upstairs. Fairy lights, and these things..." She lifted a row of jingly Christmas bells. "Micah, what about the trees? Did you tell Isla which ones we wanted?" Amory subject-changed like a pro.

At the mention of Isla's name Micah's face changed – it softened and his eyes glazed. Amory noticed it too and we exchanged a *proud parent* kind of smile.

"Yep, Isla's on to it. I'll help her bring them in tomorrow. Speaking of which, what would you buy a girl like Isla for

Christmas? She's not into fashion, or jewelry... but I want to get her something special, that shows her how much I love her. Amazing and unique, like Isla."

Isla, with her long strawberry-blonde hair, athletic physique and penchant for fast motorbikes, certainly wasn't your run-of-the-mill girl. She was fast becoming the sister I'd never had and deserved to be spoiled this Christmas.

"What about a book of poetry?" I said. Love poems, was there anything sweeter? "No," I said, changing my mind. "It's not quite right, is it?"

Amory wrinkled her nose in contemplation and then lifted her index finger. "Oh, I know the perfect gift! A star!"

Micah cocked his head. "A star?"

"You can buy a real-life star, and even name it if you want to. That way, when you're canoodling under the moonlight, you can point it out. Tell me that's not the most romantic thing ever!"

His face crinkled into a smile, and he said, almost to himself, "I'll buy her a whole constellation." He got that same dreamy, faraway look in his eyes again and I knew we'd lost him.

Amory sank back into the chaise, but I pulled her back up and said, "We've got decorating to do, Miss Jones."

Chapter Seventeen

With a few days to go until Cedarwood was overrun with blushing brides-to-be, I was overcome with the usual pre-event nerves. We had so many loose ends to tie up, including confirming all our vendors were on track and ready to wow our brides with their wares. Usually I thrived on the lead-up to any event, but because the bulk of my funds was invested in the expo it upped the ante, and made it all the more crucial that it go off without a hitch. It would be quite some time before I had enough of a financial buffer that I wouldn't have to worry about every last penny. Still, it would keep me sharp, and invested in Cedarwood, knowing I couldn't rest on my laurels.

Kai's postcard stared at me from its perch on the mantelpiece, and I smiled, remembering him. I could hear him in my mind, *Clio, take five deep breaths for me...* and before long I'd tumbled into a Kai daydream. The *what if* always lurked in my subconscious, floating to the fore every now and then. When I tried to think of the chapel, and what needed to be done for the expo, all I could think of was Kai as he'd been in there – leaning against the damp wall, his blond hair mussed and windblown...

Half dreamy, I still had this niggling feeling that I was forgetting something to do with the chapel but I just couldn't put my finger on it. I'd have to find my to-do list and check it over.

"Earth to Clio, Earth to Clio!" Amory waved a hand in front of me and laughed.

"What?" I said. "The gift bags and…"

She rolled her eyes. "You didn't hear a word I said, did you?' She searched her own list and said, "We have to make up the suites with the new linen, and yes, you're right, fill up the gift bags, choose napkin colors…"

"Knock, knock," Isla's voice rang out, only slightly muffled by the branches of a fir tree she was carting. "Where do you want it? Please don't say upstairs."

"Isla, God, why are you lugging that yourself! Micah said he'd help!" She was almost bent over backwards with the weight of the tree in her arms.

"He's lugging an even bigger one behind me somewhere. But it'd be good to put it down. *Any time soon.*"

I rushed forward to take some of the weight, fir needles poking me in the eye. "Argh!"

"Golly, and you call *me* a city girl!" Amory laughed. "Let's put the smaller one in the lobby and Micah can take the other to the ballroom, yeah, Clio?"

Blinking away the sting I said, "Yes, perfect!" Decorating the tree was the cherry on top when it came to Christmas, the scent of earth and pine heavy in the air, the unmistakable perfume of the festive season! Waking up on Christmas morning with the snow-covered mountains in the distance, and trudging downstairs to warm myself by an open fire, peeking in stockings, drinking a gingerbread coffee – it was all to come and I could hardly wait. In the coming years I imagined some grand festive seasons if only I could make it through these first frugal times…

For a moment all the stress about the bridal expo vanished, and the thought of spending Christmas with my friends and family in the place I'd always dreamed of living thrilled me. I was exactly where I was meant to be.

The only thing casting a pall over my new life was Mom. She had refused to come back to Cedarwood and wouldn't explain why. I knew she was somehow connected to the old owners who'd abandoned the lodge, and that she refused to talk about the overgrown maze hiding in the gardens, but she wouldn't say anything more, and her silence made it so much worse. As though she couldn't trust her own daughter with a secret. Those past hurts all resurfaced, as they tended to do at Christmastime.

Still, I was working hard on rebuilding our relationship, even though she made it difficult – I was seeing her once a week, having dinner, attempting to have that mother-daughter relationship I'd always dreamed of. I hoped to slip out the next day and visit her before we really knuckled down to the expo preparation. I also planned to swing by the Evergreen library to see if I could find any old articles about what exactly had taken place here all those years ago. There must have been something in the papers or at least a photo or two of the place in its heyday. I'd spent hours searching the web as well, but a place as small and out of the way as Evergreen didn't exactly have much of an online presence. I couldn't find anything that told me what had actually happened all those years ago.

When I mentioned the mystery to any Evergreen local, they were conspicuously vague. But I couldn't let it go. I had to find out what had happened. It was more than idle curiosity, it was a feeling that the future wouldn't be as bright until we'd dealt with the past, laid those old ghosts to rest.

Isla shuffled along, hefting the tree into a corner, her breathing heavy. Amory tried her best to help but toppled on heels she refused to stop wearing. I'd given up weeks ago, and was back to wearing ballet flats for comfort as well as safety with the amount of running about I did. Once the tree was in place we stood, hands on hips, and admired it. The green pop of color brought the lodge alive – I knew it was these touches that would make the brides coming next week sit up and take notice. Cedarwood Lodge was definitely a gorgeous place to spend time and, more importantly, get married!

"Let's decorate it!" Isla said, beaming, her freckled skin luminous with her efforts.

Even Amory was getting into the Christmas spirit, though she did her best to act indifferent. "I'll get the box of decorations."

Isla's cheeks were ruddy from the cold and her eyes twinkled with happiness, just like the constellation of stars Micah would buy for her. She'd fallen head over heels for him and things were going well for the lovebirds. They tried to hide their affections but didn't always succeed, I must have walked in on them kissing a hundred times since they started dating, and it always embarrassed them more than me. I *loved* love, and gave myself an imaginary pat on the back for playing Cupid with those two.

Covertly scrutinizing Isla, I did what I did best: I began planning a wedding. Imagining what color bouquet would suit her best (red and ginger bird of paradise flowers that would pop against her white dress, and complement her glorious red mane of hair), what song they'd choose for their first dance ('Come Away with Me' by Nora Jones). But I shook the mental preparation away, lest she see my eyes had glazed over and I was lost to the netherworld of wedding planning... Not to mention there'd been no actual proposal either. I was getting ahead of myself; it must've been the thought of all those brides about to descend. I had weddings on the brain and, seeing romance blossom before me, it was impossible not to plan their perfect happy ever after.

Micah trundled in with the second Christmas tree. Though it was twice the size of the other one, he had it over his shoulder like it weighed next to nothing, and I couldn't help but laugh as Isla gave him the goggle-eyes. "Where would you like this fine specimen?"

"The ballroom, please," I said, pointing the way, almost giddy over so much wonderful Christmas preparation.

When Amory came back with decorations, we bent to the box, pulling out lengths of tinsel and ornaments. Holding a delicate handmade porcelain angel in her hands Amory said, "I'm only helping if I get to put the angel on top."

I clucked my tongue as I weaved the tinsel over the tree. "You are such a child."

"You're only saying that because you wanted to do it."

"True," I laughed. "Lucky there's two trees."

"Before you start bickering about who does what, can we discuss the plan for the expo?" Isla joked, managing to drag her gaze away from Micah. "I want to double-check I haven't forgotten anything."

Amory hugged the angel tight and said, "Yes, let's. Team-meeting time."

Isla had been in the throes of landscaping the overgrown and forgotten tennis courts, but as winter blew in, she had shelved it for another time. There were also plans for volleyball by the lake – we were going to freight in some soft white beach sand, but again, winter had halted any of those ideas. Due to the arctic weather, and snowfall, Isla had taken on a more fluid role, and had agreed to be the recreation manager for our brides and any guests who might book in over winter.

"Let's make coffee and chat," I agreed as I turned on the dazzling twinkling lights and smiled at our barely dressed tree. There would be time for adding baubles and trinkets, but for now it sparkled with light and tinsel.

We ambled to the kitchen, calling out for Micah to join us. It was such a comforting space with its big old potbelly stove sitting in the corner like a long-lost uncle. I set about making drinks while the trio sat at the table, chatting about the expo and the odd jobs that still needed to be done. We'd been more organized this time, as I'd wanted to avoid any of the big setbacks we'd experienced with the anniversary party we'd planned last month. It was such a relief to be only a week away with most of the bigger jobs accomplished. Everything we needed – from Christmas decorations, to tubs of flour and sugar, right down to the Jingle Bells doormat – had been ordered ahead of schedule and delivered already.

I joined them and once again we tucked into Georges's festive treats. He was testing them out for the expo and I knew snowman cake pops would be a huge drawcard. Not only did they look utterly festive, they tasted delicious too. Any future Christmas wedding would be remiss not to include them!

"Right," said Isla as she took a notebook from her pocket. "So, what activities are we focusing on for the expo, and any guests who book in, bearing in mind it's freezing out?"

"Sledding," Amory piped up, cradling her coffee for warmth. "People love bundling up and heading outside and Walter from the hardware store gave the sleds we found in the storeroom the kiss of life."

Micah nodded. "They're painted rocket-red and will fly down the slope! I would have killed for one of those when I was a kid – hey, I'd love to go on one now!"

I grinned, but remembered that these great ideas all came with added admin. "Good idea, but I'd better check we're insured for that activity before we advertise it." I gulped. The paperwork never seemed to end and now I had to add liability insurance on top of the other costs. Safety was our first priority, but I still wanted our guests to have fun.

Isla read off her list. "What about a snowman competition…"

"I think snow-people is the correct term," Amory admonished with a sardonic smile.

Isla grinned and said in a faux-serious tone, "Snow-object building, in no particular shape, size, color or sexual orientation. And we will award the loser first place, just to be fair."

We all laughed and I was struck by how happy I was, here in the snug little kitchen, the snow falling outside, surrounded by friends – both old and new. I nodded for Isla to continue through her list of ideas. It was great she'd taken to the role of recreation manager of Cedarwood Lodge. She was full of initiative and we were lucky to have her.

"In the evenings we can light the campfire, toast marshmallows and sing songs." Isla held up a hand. "Before you call me lame, Clio expressly asked for old-school fun and frivolity and nothing screams that more than singing 'Kumbaya' and having melted, charred marshmallow scald the inside of your mouth. Right?"

There were murmurs of agreement.

"The ice skates we found in the basement were no good, but, again, Walter came to the party and found a supplier with some excess stock quite cheaply priced. We have to pick those up, and then we can offer skating on the lake. Plus we've got the indoor activities we'd planned: life drawing, charades, tango lessons... anything else?"

"The bridal fashion show, that's going to be spectacular, with bridal gowns, but also bridesmaids' dresses, and mother-of-the-bride ensembles. Aunt Bessie has so many donut wedding cake ideas, I really think they'll garner a lot of interest. There's also the florist demonstrating different bouquet ideas, and centerpieces for the table. He mentioned some of the blooms were exotic, and quite dazzling in their color palettes."

"I can't wait to see them." Amory shot a finger up. "Oh, Georges is doing cooking classes. But why don't we suggest a Christmas-themed class? Besides, I think we've eaten most of the Christmas cookies and can vouch for how good they are. What do you think, Clio?"

"Yes! Georges won't object to being surrounded by a bunch of giggling girls. We've got the library, the dance studio, the art room, and billiards in the games room – I think we're covered. All we really need to do is wow them with what *could be* if they hire the lodge for their weddings. Show them that their guests would have a fantastic time – that they'd rave about attending *the* wedding of the year. Really paint our brides a picture of the uniqueness of the lodge and surroundings and what we can offer; anything is possible, remember. The key word is... *yes*. If they ask you something outrageous, yes, sure, we can do it! We can do anything for a price." I gazed one by one into their fervent eyes and smiled. "Let's hope we get some wedding bookings." If we didn't, it was a lot of money to outlay, but I knew the old adage was true: you had to spend money to make it.

Isla beamed and scribbled some more notes onto her pad.

The potbelly belched and we huddled closer. Once again it occurred to me by how lucky I was to be surrounded by people who wanted Cedarwood to succeed as much as I did. As we chomped through Georges's Christmas cake pops, we made final plans for the expo and allocated jobs. I just hoped this bridal expo would go off without a hitch!

Chapter Eighteen

·

"Wake up! Wake up!" I dashed into Amory's suite and shook her awake.

"Oh my God, you witch," she groaned and pulled a pillow across her face. Amory was a fan of late nights and long sleep-ins, and generally needed two extra-shot lattes before she could converse with any sort of sense, but I'd grown to love the early mornings at Cedarwood, and was forcibly making her wake up and see what she was missing out on.

Seeing the sun rise so spectacularly above the mountain range, brightening the murky winter dawns, was something else – a glorious way to start the day and, much as she complained, Amory was slowly coming round to the routine too. I blamed Kai for my sudden need to be at one with nature... It was all his fault, showing me the beauty of a new dawn. God, I missed his Zen face, his presence around the lodge.

Today my aunt was joining us for breakfast to discuss her part in the expo and was waiting downstairs. Everyone in the baking business seemed to thrive on being up before the sun and my aunt was no different, arriving on our doorstep laden with boxes filled with tasty donut treats. The only problem was that Aunt Bessie wouldn't let me open them until Amory had joined us. Damn it.

As I glanced around Amory's room, it looked like she'd been burgled, the room ransacked. Clothes were draped over every surface, makeup was scattered over the desk and the top of the chest of drawers, and strewn high heels were death traps waiting for her to trip over.

"This room is a disgrace!" I picked up clothes, making a pile on the end of the bed. She had no respect for her things, mostly designer labels, and they were tossed on the floor like she thought nothing of them.

"Yes, *Mom*." She saluted with her eyes firmly closed. "I'll change my wicked ways when I'm dead."

"I can't actually be in here without tidying up. Maybe I'm more like my mom than I thought. Or maybe it's just that you're like a messy teenager and anyone would tidy lest they trip and fall out the window. *Death by mess*," I joked. Again, this was where we differed. I liked things neat and orderly, and Amory was more chaotic. I lined up her heels in the cupboard and folded her clothes away as I waited for her to wake up a little more before I accosted her again. "You'll thank me when you don't wear odd shoes by mistake. Seriously, how can you find anything?" For someone so put together, she was a closet slob.

"Listen, *fun police*, stop whining and tell me what time it is?" She rolled to her side, and finally opened her eyes.

"Six-thirty. Time enough to trudge up the mountain and take in the sunrise…" I hid a smile, knowing there was no way I'd ever go all the way back up that mountain without Kai forcing me. I missed him, and his philosophy, even if it meant exercise was involved. And there was no way Amory would either unless she needed to get a signal on her phone.

"The only thing *I* climb is the corporate ladder, so get out, unless you have coffee!"

I went to the bedside where I'd left a cup of steaming coffee, and brandished it to Her Majesty. She swiped it like I knew she would, and I laughed as she practically inhaled it in one gulp. "And… it's your lucky day. Aunt Bessie is here, and with her are some truly delectable donuts, so if you hurry there may be a couple left. But *only* if you hurry."

"Please tell me she has those cookies-and-cream donuts?" Amory said as she ripped the covers back. I had taken

Amory to Puft the first morning she was in Evergreen and ever since she'd been obsessed with the *party-in-your-mouth* morsels.

"I can't say what flavor, you'll have to drag your sorry self downstairs."

With my aunt visiting so early to chat about work it brought forward the pre-event buzz; I was a little hyper with excitement. I raced back downstairs to the warmth of the kitchen where she sat cradling a cup of coffee and munching her way through an almond cronut, her latest venture, a croissant-donut hybrid that sold out as quickly as she could bake them.

She flashed me a grin. "Did you convince her?"

"I think *you* convinced her. When she heard the word 'donut' things suddenly changed, and the coffee definitely helped."

Aunt Bessie laughed, and yet her face didn't wrinkle at all. Even at such an ungodly hour of the morning she was fully made up, her bleached-blonde hair set, and her body encased in her signature form-fitting ensemble. She was a breath of fresh air, and glamorous to boot.

I plucked a cronut from the pile, and bit into the pillowy softness. Between mouthfuls I said, "You all set for the expo? Do you need a hand with anything?"

"Nope, I'm all set. I've got my neighbor Miranda coming in to help me bake and a whole host of ideas for recreating those stuffy wedding cakes into delectable donut towers. Now, down to business. You know how glamorous dessert buffet tables can look? Well, I'm thinking of doing one of those. It's going to look spectacular. From Boston cremes, to French cullers, candy-cane flavored, and gingerbread custard, I'll have every base covered. Donuts can be gourmet, you know, and this is my chance to prove it."

"I know," I said, hiding a smile at her suddenly solemn tone. My aunt took her donuts very seriously indeed, and I knew the idea of a donut buffet instead of a formal dessert would be tempting for our brides-to-be. Everyone wanted something different and donuts were making a comeback; better, bigger and bolder than ever in the foodie world. Especially the creative samples my aunt baked. They were more like art on a plate, or in some cases on a milkshake – where she stacked donuts on top, layered with whipped cream and custard, and candyfloss to finish. Using vibrant icing, it was a kaleidoscope of colors, flavors, and textures. "Sounds like you have everything under control, Aunt Bessie."

The water pipes rattled upstairs, the usual accompaniment to Amory's morning shower and a sign I had my aunt alone for a few more minutes, at least.

I stood to refill our coffee cups and smiled. It was a comfort to have family around again. I'd missed it in New York. Mom hadn't visited me there, and Aunt Bessie had only come once, claiming the crush of people made her nervous. The big city was a huge culture shock when you came from a town as small as Evergreen.

Returning to my seat I reached out for her hand, "Thank you so much for helping out with the expo. I really appreciate all the time and effort you've had to put in. It means a lot to me."

Lifting a shoulder, Aunt Bessie squeezed my hand. "Well, of course... what's family for?"

Speaking of which... "Have you spoken to Mom lately?" I asked, hesitant to bring it up, but knowing I didn't have a choice if I wanted some answers. Aunt Bessie read Mom's moods better than anyone, and I knew they confided in one another.

My aunt's eyes shadowed. "Yeah, she told me you've been visiting. You're a good girl for that, Clio. I know it's not easy."

"I wish she'd respond to me. Talk to me, and not just because she has to." I struggled to find the words. "I feel like, since coming home, she's even further away from me. I don't know how to bridge the gap."

Her face fell, and all at once she looked every inch her age, as if the constant worrying about Mom pulled her down. "I shouldn't have forced her to come to Cedarwood to help out that day," she said, shame coloring her cheeks pink. "I had no idea it would be that difficult for her after all this time. I honestly thought it would be some sort of closure for her. That she'd see how much you've done with this place, that it was different now. But obviously she could only see it as it was back then. And those ghosts, they haunt her."

"What's with this running loop of secrecy about Cedarwood? Honestly, Aunt Bessie, I can't be much help if I don't know." Aunt Bessie was usually as straightforward as they came, but in this, she was a trapdoor, refusing to budge.

As usual the question was evaded. "She loves you, Clio, you know that, right?"

I nodded bleakly. Mom loved me as much as a houseplant as far as I could tell. "She does, *trust me*, that's why she's scared." Aunt Bessie slid her gaze away and dusted crumbs from the table into her palm.

No matter how old I got, I still pined for that mother-daughter relationship, knowing it'd probably never come to be. Still, I had Aunt Bessie, who was a wonderful, vivacious woman and mother-by-proxy in times like this.

Aunt Bessie played with the handle of her mug. "If only you knew her the way I do, the way I *did*. Some people are built differently, and a mistake can push them over the edge. She's spent this whole time clawing her way back up. There were times I didn't think she'd get there. So, please be patient. Better we have her like this than not at all."

Shivers coursed through me. I knew exactly what Aunt Bessie meant, and that was my biggest fear. That one day the business of living would all get too much for Mom. "Can't you just tell me, Aunt Bessie? What happened to her at Cedarwood? Maybe I can help."

She lifted her palms. "That's for her to tell you, baby girl. It really is. I'd love nothing more than to explain it to you so you understand, but I promised her, just like you did about keeping the maze secret."

Part of me realized that they'd kept the secret for good reason, and unearthing it could send my mom toppling back down the rabbit hole, but I just couldn't let it go. Who would I tell anyway? Surely they could trust me, of all people? It seemed half the town knew, so why not me? It hurt, not knowing.

"Was Dad involved?"

She shook her head. "No, honey, he wasn't in her life at that point. But in my opinion I think he rescued her from herself, and when he died, well… it started over again."

I only had blurry recollections of the man, a big, ruddy-faced guy with an amiable smile, who'd died when I was a child. I'd have given anything to remember him better, to have five more minutes with him. But I guess you couldn't wish a person back just because you needed them. Aunt Bessie moved to hug me tight, as if letting me know I could always come to her. At least we had each other and, between us, could help Mom navigate the next part of her life. The part where I was in it.

In a cloud of spicy-scented perfume, Amory entered the kitchen, her hair a tangle of wet curls. "Morning, again." She threw me a faux-dark look. "Aunt Bessie!" she exclaimed, kissing her on the cheek before her gaze darted to the pile of donuts on the table.

"Perhaps we can trudge up that mountain after all? Do a spot of midnight yoga?" she asked me sweetly.

Aunt Bessie and I caught each other's eye and laughed. "Just eat the damn donuts."

Amory let out a sigh of longing. "I'm so used to saying no. No sugar. No carbs. No…"

"No fun stuff." Aunt Bessie lifted the plate of donuts and held them in front of Amory's nose. "Don't let anyone tell you no. These are artisanal donuts and I don't like to see them go to waste."

Amory raised a brow. "Well, in that case, I'll have two. It's not like I'm a swimsuit model, is it?"

The Manhattanite in Amory was fast disappearing. Before she'd have only taken a great big sniff of the donuts, and eaten air instead. Away from that fast-paced lifestyle it seemed almost criminal the amount of restrictions we had placed on ourselves. Life at Cedarwood Lodge was changing us in ways we'd never dreamed of. For the better.

Once Amory had polished off two donuts, Aunt Bessie said, "So, why don't you two show me where you're going to set up for the expo so I can sort out what size table I'll need and how I want to display my donuts."

"Allow me," I said, excited by the prospect of working with my aunt and hoping that her table at the expo would generate lots of interest in Puft... Who could resist those delicious sugary treats? It brought out the sticky-icing-faced child in us, brought back a rash of memories of eating still-warm cinnamon-covered donuts, or getting covered in chocolate, as they melted too quickly in little hands. Even now, at thirty-three, I delighted in eating a donut the way I did back then, lips coated with sugar, hands tacky with frosting, colorful crumbs dusting my clothes.

"We're going to set the vendors up in here." Anticipation sizzled through me as I took in the ballroom. Christmas lights strung around curtain rails flashed intermittently, brightening up the gray morning. "We'll do our presentations here. What do you think?" Outside, the mountain ranges stood like watchmen, staring straight ahead, their snow-dusted peaks mesmerizing. The brides would be snug and warm inside, sipping gingerbread coffees or champagne and chatting about love and how to make their big day truly special...

I *loved* weddings!

"Perfect, my darling," she said, and I could see the pride in her eyes as she walked around the room mapping out where the tables would go, seeing it all as if through a crystal ball. "With the fire going it'll be so cozy, they'll be in awe of this room. With those chandeliers shining down, the grand old ballroom is a sight to behold. Once I've done my demonstration for them I'll help serve tea and coffee, candy-cane milkshakes and whatnot...?"

"That would be great, Aunt Bessie." An extra pair of hands, especially such skilled ones, would be a godsend. Aunt Bessie could charm the *zilla* from any Bridezilla.

"No problem. I'll head back to Puft now and make a start on things. I know you girls have everything under control here and this expo will be a roaring success."

I glowed at the thought and hoped she was right, "I'm going to visit Mom this afternoon and check in on her, before things get too hectic here."

She gave me a wide smile and enveloped me in a hug, rocking me from side to side like I was a small child. "She'll love that. And you tell her I'll come by after work."

Chapter Nineteen

Parking the car, I killed the engine and headed on foot up Mom's snow-covered driveway, slipping and sliding like I was on roller-skates. My screeches drew Mom's attention – she wrenched open the front door, frowning at the noise.

"Clio, golly, can't you walk without tripping?"

I grabbed hold of the bannister, and dusted my boots against it, clumps of snow falling to the ground. "It'd help if you salted the walkways at least."

"Come in before you hurt yourself," she tutted, the way moms do.

Inside was toasty warm, a fire crackling gently in the grate. "How are you, Mom?" Dark shadows played under her eyes, making them seem sunken, like she was ill. Her weight hadn't improved, she was scarily thin, and it hurt my heart to see it. In the time I'd been home, her health had clearly declined, and I blamed myself. Inadvertently I'd stirred up the past and she was paying for it. Would she just fade away to nothing if I kept going? My chest tightened at the thought. What was I doing to her?

"I'm good," she said. "I've been a bit rundown, before you go pestering me about why I haven't been out to see you."

"I'm not here to pester you. I just wanted to visit. Maybe we could have lunch? Make a pot of soup to warm us up?" Something, *anything*, to make her eat.

I stepped past and went to the kitchen, checking the contents of the fridge. Mom was the type who lived on bare necessities if she didn't feel like facing the world, and guilt gnawed away at me, making my gut roil. Why did I always presume she'd be OK, when I knew damn well how fragile she was? I played the *should have* game with myself while I searched for ingredients. Should have come over sooner, should have called more, should have…

The world was a lonely place sometimes, especially for people like Mom, and I grieved for the life she *should have* had. A happy one, full of friendships, and laughter, and love. But instead she'd lost her husband and that had changed everything. My mom, who had always been a little vague, had become reclusive. I was young, but I remembered it well, because it had been like someone had switched a light off and things had become very murky at home, save for Aunt Bessie's visits. As I'd got older and understood her grief better, I'd recognized the signs of someone fighting an internal battle every day, just barely holding on. Eating was a struggle for her, cleaning compulsive, her behavior erratic but excused as someone who was trying her hardest to stay here in the present.

Staring into the fridge I wasn't surprised to find it only held a range of condiments, half a liter of milk, and little else.

"Why don't I go to the store and buy some fresh fruit and vegetables? We can make a pot of hearty winter soup? We can freeze portions so you don't have to cook if you don't feel like it." Mom's cooking capabilities were on a level with mine so she never said much about the quality of our meals.

"If you want to, Clio. But aren't you busy with… things at the moment?"

"Not too busy for you, Mom."

Her bottom lip twitched ever so slightly. "Well, then, that would be nice."

I swallowed a lump in my throat, sensing we had taken the first step. Normally she'd have said no outright, craving her solitude. Slowly but surely it felt like the walls were coming down and maybe her health concerns weren't because I'd moved home. Baby steps were the way forward, and being careful not to upset the fine balance we were eking out together.

"Want to come with me?"

"No, no. I'll wait here. I'll... tidy the kitchen so we can cook."

I gazed around the pristine benches and said, "OK. I won't be long."

"Take your time. I've got some washing that needs hanging up too."

Mom couldn't relax if her chores weren't done. When the washing machine beeped its end-of-cycle warning, the laundry *had* to be hung up to dry – it couldn't wait an hour, it couldn't wait a minute. As soon as it was dry, it was ironed, with creases so sharp they could take an eye out. The garden was immaculate, the car polished to a shine. Mom's manic need to keep busy was almost a penance she did every day. Whenever we sat for five minutes you could see her gripping the arm of the chair, not ever able to fully relax. It must have been exhausting.

I kissed her cheek, trying not to notice how hollow it was, "OK, then. Back soon." Soup and maybe a glass of wine might help. I was determined to make her rest and recover and get used to the typical family routines that were so foreign to us.

In town, I grabbed a bunch of fresh of ingredients, and some extra pantry items to stock up Mom's shelves for the week. As the library was within walking distance from where I'd parked I decided to stash the groceries and head in. I'd only be a few minutes tops, and the library was still open – what harm could it do? I'd quickly check their archives, and if there was anything of interest on Cedarwood Lodge I'd come back later when I had more time.

The Evergreen library was silent bar a faint muffle, like a snore. Was someone sleeping here? The smell of old books, earthy and musty, was heavy in the air. I found the front desk and waited. A slim woman wearing a knitted pullover and jeans wandered over, smiling. I recognized her immediately, even though I hadn't seen her for a decade or so. My high-school friend Bennie's mom, Debra.

"Well, look who it is! Bennie told me he caught up with you recently. The old gang back together…"

I smiled at the memory. It had been great catching up with my friends when I first came back to town, and I made a mental note to reach out and arrange another get-together soon. "Yeah, after an hour and a few beers, it was like I'd never left. We just slotted back into the same place as before. How have you been, Mrs Talbot?"

"Good, thanks, Clio, and you? I heard you've made the old lodge into something pretty special once again."

"Yeah, it's going great, thanks! So much still to do, but I have high hopes we'll get more of the outbuildings renovated soon. What about you? Been busy?" It hit me what an inane question that was in a town this size.

She tucked a tendril of hair back. "I know it might not look like it now…" She gestured around the empty library. "…But we've been as busy as bees these last few weeks."

I couldn't see any other staff, just an old fluffy dog curled up by the fire, snoring merrily away. Ah, he was the culprit.

"Your assistant?" I motioned to the pooch.

She gave me a wide smile. "Bennie tells everyone I'm the head librarian. What he neglects to mention is I'm the only human one. Rufus here is my assistant and a fine one at that." She bent and gave the dog a chuck under the chin – he rolled on his back and waited patiently for another pat.

I laughed, forgetting how quiet the town could be. Dogs for assistants – not something you'd have seen in New York.

"As nice as it is to see you, I can't imagine you've come all this way just to have a chat with me. What can I do for you? Want some reading material for these long winter nights?"

"I'm not here for books for myself, Debra. I wanted to search the archives. I'm particularly interested in anything you might have about Cedarwood Lodge, any newspaper articles, or maybe historical references." Debra's smile vanished. She was gazing at me like the shutters had come down.

Double-blinking and bringing herself back she said, with a fluttery little laugh, "Oh, Clio... I don't think we have anything at all like that."

I smiled, trying not to take it personally. I knew Evergreen locals weren't keen on revisiting the past but I had hoped they wouldn't stop me outright from investigating it for myself. "Would you mind checking? You might have something tucked away that's been forgotten."

The air in the room thickened with tension as Debra stepped behind the desk, putting distance between us.

"We've just updated our archives and I'm certain there's nothing pertaining to Cedarwood. If I find anything, how about I give you a call?" She gave me a wide smile and picked up a duster, as if signaling the conversation was over.

"I'm happy to wait." I followed as dust motes danced in her wake.

With a barely suppressed sigh she spun to face me. "I'd love to help, Clio, but sometimes things in the library get lost. They go missing." She stared intently at me, and I knew she didn't mean misplaced books. "Sometimes the best thing to do, the *only thing*, is to understand that perhaps they're better off forgotten and just live in the now. If you get what I'm saying."

The warning was loud and clear, and part of me wanted to just walk away and leave the past buried, but I had an overwhelming feeling that if I found out what had happened I'd be able to understand my mom better. That maybe it was the missing piece of the puzzle, and with that last piece I'd finally understand why she hid away from the world. How could we repair our relationship if it was built on secrets?

"I hear you," I said, trying to keep my voice level. "But it's important. Really, it is."

"Like I said, I'll call you if I find anything." I had been dismissed, just like that. I nodded, knowing there was nothing much I could do if people were going to roadblock me. I'd just have to find another way around it.

"Well, thanks anyway, Debra. Say hi to Bennie for me and I hope to see you around." No point burning my bridges.

Outside, the icy wind took my breath away and I shrugged deeper into my jacket. I had a lot of thinking to do – did I take the risk and uncover something best left forgotten and potentially ruin what little relationship I had with my mom? Or just leave it be? I wasn't sure I could keep living the way we were now... but was it really my best idea, unearthing a secret from the past?

The wind picked up, sending an ominous *woo* across the field. Clouds above shivered from white to gray, as a spattering of rain sprinkled. A flash of lightning spiked the mountain range in front, and a rumble of thunder sounded. Was that some kind of sign?

Pulling up my hood, I inched along the slippery pavement, trying my best to stay upright. Shop fronts were gloomy as the gray sky cast a shadow over the day. Eskimo-like, in my various layers, I could barely see as I made my way to the car, bumping elbows with a passer-by.

"Sorry," I mumbled, searching for my keys deep in my jacket pocket.

"Clio!"

Oh, God. "Timothy! Hi!" I tried to make out his face through the fur of my hood.

He grabbed my arm and led me to a cove out of the inclement weather. "Freezing, huh?"

I flicked my hood back and stared into the deep brown of his eyes. He sure wasn't ugly. A girl could get lost in that gaze. Not me, though. We were past tense, weren't we? I darted a glance behind him for his children, and let out a small sigh of relief to find them missing. It wasn't that they intimidated me... OK, who was I kidding, they scared the

175

bejesus out of me. It was the way they sent laser beams into my soul, like they were trying to vanquish me.

"No kids today?" *State the obvious, Clio!*

A tiny line appeared between his eyes. "They're at school."

"Learning ABCs? Or, umm, one, two, threes…?" *Kill me.*

He cocked his head, probably mentally planning an escape route. "Ah… yeah. So, I got your text. You can't swing a dinner out before New Year? Surely I could tempt you for a feast at Shakin' Shack?"

When I was around Timothy it was much harder to remember why I was keeping him at arm's length. A fear of rewriting ancient history? The fact his life was vastly different to mine? His responsibilities? The flutter in my belly when I thought of Kai? It was just dinner, after all, not a marriage proposal. Dinner for two old friends. Dinner for two adults who had to eat. Why did I feel a little pang of guilt at the thought?

I realized my internal monologue had left us with an awkward silence so I grappled with something to say. "Gotta love a greasy burger, am I right?" *Just stop talking.*

"So that's a yes?"

Idiot. "Sure, sure. Maybe we can invite the gang?"

He grinned. "Maybe, maybe not."

I let out a creepy half-laugh, half-groan and said, "Well, I'd better be on my way. Got a lot of plans that need wedding, I mean weddings that need planning." Mentally I slapped my forehead hard – really, *really* hard. Why did I regress to a bumbling fool in front of him? I didn't truly feel anything, did I?

"You do that," he said and leaned in to kiss my cheek. I held my breath, waiting for my body to respond, but found it curiously quiet. No erratic heartbeat, no flushing cheeks, instead just a small fluttering in my belly, knowing him well, and knowing he was a great guy. But did that make it enough?

Inside the car, I turned up the radio as Michael Bublé crooned 'It's Beginning to Look a Lot Like Christmas'. I sang along as I wound through the snowy streets and remembered my time with Timothy, and how much I'd adored him when I was a teenager – that first flush of love when you were young, and how you felt the whole world would end if you lost it. Puppy love, I reminded myself. A million years ago.

Back at Mom's I unpacked the shopping, my mind reeling with the events of the morning.

"These herbs smell delicious," Mom said, giving me a ghost of a smile. She gave my arm a reassuring pat. I couldn't remember the last time *she'd* done something as simple as that, a brief touch, a measure of comfort, and I felt foolish as tears stung my eyes. I turned away so she wouldn't see.

Another day of no answers loomed, because there was no way I was saying anything that might halt this next step of our relationship. She was actually opening up to me, and it felt markedly different to when she just tolerated me.

"Want to chop the carrots?" Even I couldn't mess up vegetable soup, unless I burned it.

"Sure," she said. "I'll do the onions too. I know you hate chopping them. The trick to it is running the peeled onion under the tap first."

"I hate peeling onions." I managed a half-laugh, surprised she knew this about me. Afternoon light filtered through the curtains, and I settled in next to my mom, working in silence. But this silence was more companionable than ever before, and I indulged in the fantasy that we might one day be close.

Chapter Twenty

Questions buzzed around my mind on the drive home, but the answers were missing or murky and it was headache-inducing. Really, I didn't have time to get tangled up in the mystery of Cedarwood – what with a group of brides arriving in two days' time. For my own sanity, I needed to push the swirl of thoughts away and focus on what had to be done. With a rueful shake of my head, I tried one of Kai's crazy breathing techniques, feeling calmer by the minute. Damn him and his mumbo jumbo.

Back at the lodge, I went into autopilot, returning calls: the florist wanted to know if we had room in our fridges for the bouquets (yes); the liquor store had over-ordered and wanted to know if we'd take an extra crate of French champagne (always); and the linen company who provided our tablecloths and napkins wanted confirmation on color (white, the wedding centerpieces would be the stars of the show). That done, I ushered various delivery men through, showing them into the kitchen to drop off our new plate sets, or into the ballroom for boxes of special lighting, and waving them off again, but not before handing them a shiny, full-color pamphlet advertising Cedarwood in its best light. Any chance to promote!

Once they'd gone I double-checked the ballroom, making sure it was spick and span – despite boxes of supplies in one corner – and ready for us to finish up decorating. We were going for a winter wonderland wedding theme, to display what the ballroom would look like if they chose to celebrate their nuptials over the festive season.

From the ceiling to the top of the oak walls, Micah had draped white gossamer fabric embedded with Swarovski crystals, which twinkled even in the pale light of afternoon. Between the layers we'd hung glittery snowflakes and love hearts. In keeping with the color palette, everything was white, silver, and blingy, the stuff of every girl's dreams, and magical at any time of day, but more so on a wedding day.

Satisfied the ceiling had been finished, I reminded myself to check we had enough silverware and champagne flutes. It wouldn't hurt to order more, just in case. I made a mental note to do just that.

It was all coming together… when suddenly the clanging of pots and pans rattled in the kitchen reminded me that Georges was here, sorting the catering and waiting for me to taste and approve the canapés. I called out: "I'll be in soon to chat, Georges!"

"I'm OK. I'm pottering about. The menu tastings will be ready in an hour or so, OK?" he bellowed back through the kitchen doorway, and I couldn't help but smile.

We were damn lucky to have Georges as our chef. It would have been near on impossible to employ someone of his caliber in these parts on an ad-hoc basis.

"Sure, just holler and we'll come running." My stomach growled at the thought of the tiny canapés, veritable taste explosions.

But there was still so much to do and I'd left Amory alone for most of the day, what with going to Mom's and the admin I'd just finished off. Heading upstairs I wondered if Amory had made a start on making up the rooms. We wanted to show them off to the brides, especially the honeymoon suite. I followed the muffled grunts and groans to find Amory in one of the two-bedroom suites. On the door hung a green wreath made from holly, with little silver stars tucked in the loop. Being a Christmas aficionado, most of the decorations I'd hauled all the way from New York, but we'd also found some new ones in town. And just to be certain I had enough, I'd also had an online buy-a-thon one night to celebrate the fact it'd been weeks since I'd sobbed along to 'Total Eclipse of the Heart' by Bonnie Tyler, and that was really saying something... Perhaps this Christmas wasn't going to be as lonely as I'd imagined.

With the fire crackling and snow drifting down outside, the suite was charming and radiated warmth. Cedarwood was going to be the perfect destination for those looking to step away from corporate hotels with soulless rooms.

Amory hefted corners of mattresses up and tucked in the linen.

"Let me help," I said, pulling a soft white sheet up. "These feel so luxurious." I'd have to make up my own bed with the new linens. Sleep would be an absolute given wrapped in these and I knew our guests would agree.

"One thousand thread count, only the *very best* for Cedarwood guests." She winked. We'd bid on the linen online and got a great price buying in bulk. Our guests would have the very best money could buy when it came to linen, and fluffy bath towels. While the lodge itself was rustic, the accoutrements were luxurious and I hoped visitors would enjoy the effort we'd put in to make it so. "So, how was your mom?"

I sighed. "I just wish I could click my fingers and she'd be..."

"Be what?" Amory asked as we pushed fat feather-down pillows into cases.

"Happy."

I thought about telling her all about my trip to the library, but I wasn't ready to share it just yet, especially as there wasn't much to tell. So instead I shrugged, changing the subject to one I knew she'd latch on to and would lighten the conversation. "I ran into Timothy in town."

"The old flame?" Amory bounced on her toes as she turned to me. "I knew there was unfinished business there, you minx!"

I rolled my eyes. "You and your rom-com ideals for my love life!"

"Stop trying to buy time and spill the details. Did he ask you out?"

I pulled a pillow over my face.

"Oh, God, what did you say?" She flopped onto the bed next to me, and wrenched the pillow from my face.

"For some insane reason I get tongue-tied around him, I say the most incredibly stupid things! I practically sang to him. It's like my mouth has a mind of its own. Urgh."

"You sang to him?" Her eyes went wide.

"Not exactly. I asked where his kids were – obviously they're at school, but of course I didn't think of that. And then I sort of sang that they were learning about ABCs, and when he was cocking his head, probably wondering if I'd just come from a long lunch of drinking mojitos, I sang, 'or one, two, threes…'"

Laughter barreled out of her. "Oh, God, Clio! What were you thinking?"

"I wasn't!"

"And he still asked you out after that… little impromptu concert?"

"For a feast at Shakin' Shack."

She pulled the pillow onto her lap. "Shakin' Shack… well, it's not the most romantic of restaurants, but I suppose he could hide you in the corner booth in case you started singing again. Probably a smart move on his part."

I elbowed her. "I didn't say yes, or maybe I did, I can't remember. I told him we should invite the gang, and he fobbed me off."

She clucked her tongue. "Darling! Why would you invite the gang to a date? He's clearly trying to get to know you. Don't you feel anything for him? A rush of heat? A tiny leg quiver?"

181

I shook my head.

Exasperated she said, "Butterfly belly?"

I considered it. "Maybe. But I don't know if that's just the memory of him, or the way I feel in the present. It's so confusing." It struck me that, for someone who believed in love, who devoted a huge part of life to celebrating it, I was kind of lacking when it came to acting on it for myself. Being home made me more reluctant to make mistakes because a girl couldn't hide in a town the size of Evergreen, and I didn't want to be the subject of any more gossip.

I got off the bed and continued tucking the sheet in. Amory went to the other side of the bed and did the same. "Is it because of *you-know-who* that you're unsure?"

Heat rushed to my cheeks. "I highly doubt it," I said, my voice coming out more formal than intended. "Love is just so complicated. And when you live in a small town, you have to be a lot more careful in case things go awry."

"What a load of bollocks," she laughed. "But nice try, darling. In my humble opinion I think you should go out with Timothy. See if it sparks anything. Mr Ripped Abs isn't here, is he?"

"Mr Ripped Abs!" I laughed and propped pillows up against the antique ornate bedhead before doing an Amory-style subject change. "Do you think our future guests will be warm enough?" I asked as we fluffed the feather-down quilt and finished dressing the bed with a sumptuous gray faux-fur rug and some glitzy cushions.

"Sure they will. There's a fireplace in each suite. We can send Micah up to light them at dusk while they're having dinner, and stoke them before they go to bed. They'll be cozy and snug and will never want to leave."

I smiled. With the orange glow of the fire the suites would be like a winter oasis, the mountains with their colorful leaves in the distance, cheering the blustery view, the warmth, the wood, and the touches of indulgence in the rooms, from the Swiss chocolates by the bed to a shelf full of novels for their perusal. A bottle of complimentary wine cooled in each bar fridge, and there would be a bowl of fresh fruit on the table for those wanting a snack. Garlands of glittery golden tinsel twinkled in the filmy light, and a sprig of mistletoe was tacked above the door.

Hands on hips, we surveyed the room. Everything was neat, straight and in place, including soaps bearing the Cedarwood Lodge logo, and tiny little bottles of shampoo and conditioner lined up like soldiers in the bathroom.

For a moment I stood there, dizzy with awe. Seeing the suites dressed up, and ready for guests, made it feel so real, in a way nothing else had so far. Soon a guest would sleep in this luxurious bed, or read a book in the tub, with Cedarwood apple-blossom bubble bath scenting the air. They'd pull on boots while captivated with the view outside... Their biggest problem would be deciding what to eat for breakfast.

My lifelong dream of owning Cedarwood had come to fruition, and the sensation was a heady one. I knew it wouldn't be all snow and Christmas carols, that there'd be ups and downs, but that was life, right? And I basked in the fact I'd made it happen, that *we'd* made it happen. If we secured a wedding booking or two, I'd be able to breathe easier, but at least we were taking steps in the right direction. We had three families booked in for the summer season, a trio of neighbors who had swapped holidaying in Europe for outdoor pursuits at the lodge, and I was giddy with the thought of them swimming in the lake, and hiking up the mountains; indulging in an aperitif in the front salon as Georges made them dinner. But better still, we had a couple of singletons staying not long after New Year, who'd seen photos of Cedarwood Lodge on Instagram. It boded well. Our marketing was slowly but surely working.

If we kept up this momentum, the future would be rosy.

"Right, next suite?" I said, helping Amory lift the basket of freshly washed and pressed linen.

"Yep, and then we really need to double-check the chapel and make sure it's ready for the brides. We need to arrange the furniture and the fairy lights and make sure we haven't forgotten anything else."

My heart stopped. *The chapel!*

"Our brides will fall helplessly in love with the idea of marrying in such a beautiful little church. What is it?" Amory asked. "You look like you've swallowed a fly?"

"Oh, God!" I slapped a hand to my forehead. "The plans! Kai submitted the plans to the council for the chapel and I was supposed to follow up and make sure they were approved! We're not allowed to use it until then because the building was deemed unsafe and it hasn't been recertified yet."

I flew down the stairs two at a time, my heart racing. Micah had taken over managing the renovations after Kai left, so I could focus on building the business and touting for guests, but I still had to oversee the paperwork and the...

Amory half-tumbled down the stairs after me, trying hard not to fall in her heels. "Clio, wait. Don't panic, it will be fine. All we need to do is ring them and ask how it's going, right?"

"I can't believe I forgot! Kai told me to hassle them or else things get lost in the system and take longer than necessary. And I've left it until *now*!" I couldn't catch my breath; this one little slip-up could derail the whole expo.

This would never have happened when I worked at the agency. I'd taken my eye off the ball, and damn well dropped it. Kai had given me express instructions and I'd been all doe-eyed like a teenager, too busy worrying about him leaving the lodge for good to remember something crucial like the approval process. I skidded into my office and began searching the desk for the plans and Amory clattered in behind me.

"OK, don't panic, darling," she said, huffing and puffing from the dash downstairs. "You can fix anything you put your mind to! Why don't you call them and use that sweet and innocent voice of yours? Rave about your plans for

184

the local economy, how your guests will inject some much-needed funds. Invite them over and we can schmooze them if all else fails."

With a hand to my chest, I paused, contemplating what she was saying. "Yeah, it's not like they'll have a stack of pending approvals. There's only five hundred and three people in Evergreen!" Surely it was only a routine process, *read, stamp, sign*. My shoulders relaxed. I breathed in and out on the count of five. *Stress is an illusion*, a Kai mantra, popped into my mind.

"Yes," I said, feeling more confident. "OK, I'll phone up now." Amory nodded and slipped out of the room.

I turned back to the desk and flicked through the paperwork. I found a bunch of notes in Kai's handwriting and tried to make sense of them. From what I could tell he had everything in order and Micah had checked off the work orders one by one until the chapel was finished. I dialed the direct number of the planning officer Kai had been speaking to and sank back in the chair, focusing on the positives. I'd remembered now, and surely could fix this mess with a phone call. There was no need to panic.

"Ned speaking."

I took a deep breath and began. "Ned, how are you?" I didn't wait for a response. "It's Clio from Cedarwood Lodge. I'm calling about some planning paperwork that was sent in..." I pored over the notes again. "Back in October."

There was a sound, as though he was sucking his gums. "Yes?"

"You know the planning application in question? The one for the chapel on the Cedarwood property?"

"I do."

Golly, at this rate the conversation would take all day. "Great!" I smiled as Amory tiptoed into the room and put a glass of water on the desk before sneaking off again, presumably to finish the last suite. "I was hoping we could get it signed off and approved so we can go forward with our plans. We're hoping the influx of tourists arriving at Cedarwood will filter down to the other businesses in town, giving them a boost, especially over the winter. So... we're really quite excited."

"Right, right." There was a shuffling of paperwork. "The thing is, Claire..."

I coughed. "Clio."

"Clio, the thing is, I can't hurry these decisions. It would be remiss of me not to take into consideration variables about the property and what it could mean for Evergreen and its population."

I held in a groan. This did not sound like approval was pending any time soon.

This is your own fault, Clio! "I understand. But you see, you've approved the lodge itself, so guests are able to stay, right?" I didn't want the lodge closed down on a technicality. I rued the day Kai left. He was so much better at this side of things than me. The facts and figures of the planning and approval process were a nightmare.

"Right. *However*. What you're *not* allowed to do is use the chapel for guests. No weddings, no church services, no parties. The structure is a hundred years old, it's weathered, full of rising damp, and I have to know for certain it's safe before I can say yes."

"I totally understand. And you'll see if you do an inspection that it's had an overhaul and *is* safe for guests. I have a bridal expo planned. No one is actually hosting a wedding, but they'd obviously like to see inside the chapel..."

"No, they are not permitted."

Argh! I took a calming breath. Panic had never helped any situation before, so I really needed to get some perspective. "Why not? I can fax over reports about the work that's been done. The rising damp has been fixed, the beams have been raised, the electricals have been completely replaced including extra safety precautions..."

"*Clio...*" He said my name quickly, like a parent trying to get their child's attention. "Your builder promised me

186

the same things last time, and then a fire broke out... You can understand my worry, surely? I'm not being malicious, trust me, I'm being cautious."

The fire. Now his hesitation made sense. I closed my eyes. "The fire was extinguished promptly and we added a ton more safety procedures after that. And the fire was in the main lodge building, which is nowhere near the chapel. It wasn't actually our fault; the fire report outlines it in detail. And we were well equipped with extinguishers and other preventative measures, which stopped the entire lodge going up in flames." And when I said other preventative measures I meant Micah, ever the hero, racing toward the fire while the others raced away from it. Just thinking of that horrible day sent shivers down my spine.

He let out a weary sigh. "There's a process to these applications, Clio, and I have to follow them meticulously. If you check out our website you'll see the approvals process can take up to six months. Sometimes more."

Six months! "I don't have six months." Panic crept into my voice so I did my best to disguise it with calm. "Surely we can come to some agreement? I wouldn't push for this if it wasn't safe. I wouldn't put my guests at risk, ever."

Another phone rang in the background as Ned sighed for the third time in one very short conversation. "Look, send me the paperwork on your trades and I'll see what I can do. Better yet, send Kai over. You're still using your registered builder, aren't you?"

I gulped. *Where did it say that in the fine print?* This was exactly why I'd hired Kai for all the loopholes that cropped up.

"Yes, yes, Kai is still here, he's right beside me, actually. He can't hear me, what with all the safety gear he's wearing, ear muffs, and... and..." *Oh, God, Clio, stop talking!* "It might be a few days, or a week or so, because he's in the middle of something. Something big." *Stop, just stop, already!*

"Do that, Clio, and we'll see what can be done."

"Sure, and thanks."

"On the off-chance it's not approved before the expo, can the guests still peek in, surely that's allowed?"

"Just keep them safe, Clio. And get Kai over here."

I hung up, and slapped a hand to my forehead. Could I get myself into a bigger mess?

Amory wandered in and surveyed my pinched face. "It didn't go well?"

"He wants to chat with Kai, our *registered builder*..."

"Oh." She folded her arms, leaning against the doorjamb, and fanned herself with the postcard Kai had sent. "Guess you better call Kai and ask him to be Prince Charming just this once." Gone was the grimace, replaced by her Mona Lisa smile. The one she used when she was trying to act professional, but I could see straight through it.

"Don't give me that look." I narrowed my eyes.

"What look?" she said mock-innocently.

"Like you're the cat who got the cream. I'll call Kai and see if he can make a flying visit, but I'm not mentioning the kiss or any of that, so don't even think about trying to set us up. My focus is Cedarwood and getting this chapel mess sorted out."

She threw her hands in the air. "That's my focus too, darling! And *you're* the matchmaker, not me. I'm more of a casual encounter enthusiast when I'm advising my friends, aren't I? *Life is too short for bad men*, don't I always say that? On a serious note, Kai must stay at the lodge. You can't summon him all this way and expect him to pay for some sleazy motel out of town." The Mona Lisa smile was back.

I cocked my head. "I see what you're doing."

She feigned surprise. "Being a good host?"

Micah wandered in, face grimy with dust. He'd been clearing out the wine cellar since our eventual plan was to stock it with an eclectic mix of vintages for our guests. "What's up?" he asked.

Amory filled him in, taking great delight in the fact I had to call Kai back to Cedarwood.

Micah's eyebrows shot up. "Well, dang it, I didn't know we needed him on-site once the work was done. That can't be right? I think Ned is speaking out of his... What?" he said, surveying me. "What don't I know here?"

I squirmed, sinking into the chair hoping to disappear. Micah read my body language loud and clear.

Outside, gray clouds gathered, inching toward the lodge as if they'd crept forward to listen in.

"Well... we kissed, so it might be a little awkward at first," I admitted, grimacing.

He slapped a hand to his forehead, and let out a deep belly laugh. "And you let him *leave*? What about all that talk you gave *me* about following my heart and taking risks?"

Amory nodded in agreement with him. "Her heart is a vault, Micah. Matchmaker extraordinaire can't take her own advice."

I narrowed my eyes at her.

"She's always been like that," Micah said, nodding.

Amory's lips pulled down. "She just *cannot* recognize that in herself. There were plenty of keepers in New York but she always found fault..."

I jumped off the chair and spun to face them, snatching Kai's postcard out of Amory's hand as she laughed. "Umm, guys, I'm right here, you know! If you've finished your little psychoanalyzing session we can move on with, you know, important things – like business?"

They giggled.

"Admit it," Micah said. "You don't follow your own advice!"

I scoffed. "Because my advice is... bespoke, Micah! It doesn't apply to everyone and you're making it sound like I'm some kind of nagging Nelly, when all I did was tell you to open your frosty little heart to Isla, which, *I might add*, has made you extremely happy by the looks of it!" My voice rose with every inflection, as I tried to get my point across. "And you, Amory, I think you have to admit you care about Cruz more than you want him to know."

I was met with a weighty silence.

"What?" I asked, sensing their ploy. "All I need from Kai is his building knowledge, nothing more. So, if you need me, I'll be in my office!"

"We *are* in your office."

They had me frazzled! "Then... get out!"

Laughing behind their hands, they retreated. I took my cellphone and dialed. No point worrying over his reaction to my call; it was business, and I was a professional. Still, my stomach flipped as it rang.

"Clio! How's things?" His Australian accent was even more pronounced with the distance separating us.

I nervously shuffled papers, and tried to make my voice even. "Good, good. Well, not great actually. I have a problem."

"Yeah?"

"I need you here."

He laughed.

Oh, God. "I mean, I really need you for a very good *business* reason. Business at the lodge, you could say. Or *lodge business* is a more economical way to say it."

Say business one more time! With a manic little laugh I explained about the hold-up and what it meant for the lodge and how dire things would be if we didn't get approval in time for the expo.

He managed to ignore my woes and said, "Clio, you're not doing midnight yoga any more, are you?"

Surfer yogi strikes again. "Oh sure, sure, I am. Like clockwork. It's my favorite time of day. Well, night, but you know what I mean." Could midnight yoga solve this problem? I didn't think so.

"I can hear it in your voice. You're back to not sleeping too, I take it?"

Damn the man, how did he always know? All I needed to do was wrap myself in some of that fine Egyptian cotton and I'd sleep like a baby.

"Things have been a touch hectic, but I'm going to do some breathing... erm... exercises, as soon as I've hung up

190

from you. It's written right here on my to-do list. Breathe for the count of five. Make that ten, just to be sure." I smiled at the memory of him, hands on my shoulders, gaze fervent, as if he believed taking five deep breaths could cure anything. Crazy but sweet just the same.

"So, what do you need from me, Clio?" Kai's voice was calm and level, just like always, but I detected a twinge of sadness to it. As if big-city living stole the ying from his yang. Did he pine for home? For the Australian beaches and the surf culture he'd once been part of? Or just for the quiet? Fewer people, less noise, less bustle. Life pared right back to the elements.

"I need you to meet with Ned, and tell him you're still working for us, and that everything with the chapel is hunky-dory and *safe*, and we'd like you to be our guest at Cedarwood, so as not to put you out."

"Wow... OK. Let me see what I can do. I'm so busy right now in the lead-up to Christmas; everyone wants their jobs wrapped up. But I'll try to get there as soon as I can, yeah?"

Perhaps we'd get out of this situation by the skin of our teeth, just like we had so far with the other dilemmas at the lodge. I knew if Kai gave his word, he would try to make it happen, but it would obviously be up to his boss whether he could make it here or not. I crossed my fingers and tried very hard not to feel sick as worry washed over me.

"Thanks, Kai, I really appreciate it. I can't believe I forgot about the planning permission." Color rose in my cheeks, remembering his express instructions, now, when it was much too late. I wondered if my subconscious was setting me up on purpose... At least Ned was allowing the brides to peek in, so that was something at least. But there was no way we could take a booking if we didn't have approval, and the money we'd sunk into the expo would be wasted.

He clucked his tongue. "Don't sweat it. You can't do everything, and not slip up occasionally. I'm fairly sure

Ned has his facts wrong and you don't need a registered builder on-site, but let's not rock the boat. We'll follow his orders and see if that works."

"Small towns, hey?"

"Planning permissions." He laughed and it sounded like sunshine. "They love making it hard. Big towns, small towns, doesn't matter, something always crops up. Don't worry, we'll fix it."

I felt like Kai could fix anything. He was the sort of guy other men listened to and respected. Calmness radiated off him, and you couldn't help nodding your head and agreeing when he spoke. I missed him, hearing his voice. Missed him roaming around Cedarwood, double-checking the work, making sure it was right. Even missed contorting my body at strange angles under the cover of darkness with him.

"Are you getting a handle on the city?" I said, suddenly not sure I wanted the conversation to end there.

He sighed. "Sort of. It's just too cramped for me. There's people everywhere, all the time. No chance of hearing myself think, not in this chaos. What did I expect, though, really? It's San Francisco."

"Yeah, but it doesn't sound like it's your thing at all. Can't you ask for a different job?" Kai needed to be free, outside, being one with nature, away from the hustle and bustle, but I guess he didn't have a choice. He went where the work was.

"Gotta see it through."

Neither of us mentioned the kiss and it felt like it was too late now, like it would fall into the conversation chunkily, and jar.

"Cedarwood feels so different without you, and the team. But my friend Amory is here, and Isla and Micah, so I feel like I've got a ready-made family, but I brace myself for them leaving too one day. I wonder if I'll get used to goodbyes or if they'll always break my heart just a little."

He remained silent for the longest time, before saying, "Goodbyes that break your heart mean at least you feel something. And that's what counts, right? Otherwise all you feel is a certain numbness and that's even worse…"

Was there something upsetting Kai? Something other than city life? It struck me maybe his exit from Australia hadn't been as simple as he'd made out. Had he left some hurt behind? I'd never questioned it before, but he'd always been cool and calm, and now his voice had an edge to it, a touch of bitterness, though he tried to disguise it.

"Maybe a quick visit to Cedarwood will do you good," I said softly.

"I think it'll do me just fine. Say hi to everyone for me."

When we rang off I sat for a while, gazing outside, the view stunning as ever and a balm for the soul. My mind was still going a hundred miles an hour with all the things I had to remember to finish. I still had to check in with Georges and taste-test the canapés, but for a few minutes I just sat there alone and wondered if I should try to fit some midnight yoga in tonight. Would it be the same without Kai?

Chapter Twenty-One

The kitchen gleamed. Georges had tidied after we'd feasted on a range of mouthwatering canapés, and hugged us before heading off, promising everything was set for the bridal expo the next day. Amory made us cups of cocoa, and topped them with marshmallows that frothed and dissolved on the surface.

I said, "If the chapel doesn't get approved, we can't really take any wedding bookings in good faith, can we?" When the lodge was silent, bar its creaks and groans, reality had a tendency to come creeping in.

Soberly, Amory replied, "It's definitely a worry, darling. But we've faced greater obstacles than this. Let's focus on getting all the paperwork in order for Ned, so he can see you've paid for professionals to fix those structural elements, and you've met all the safety requirements they stipulate and then some."

"Yes," I said, sipping cocoa, trying to let her words sink in... but still, so much hung in the balance. I couldn't get Ned to sign off on the chapel if he was adamant it needed more work. And with the brides arriving the next morning, it made it almost impossible to forget.

Soft moonlight shone through the kitchen window. The lodge at night-time was a beautiful thing, with only the hoot of owls punctuating the quiet.

"Let's focus on what we need to do and hope Kai comes through for us. Yeah?"

For once Amory didn't joke, didn't try and lighten the mood. She always understood me so well, sometimes better than I did myself. And she knew the only way to stop stressing about it was to think of the brides, and making their time at Cedarwood magical.

"OK," I said. "Georges is well prepped for their arrival. Canapés first, followed by a festive lunch. The champagne is cooling, though we'll have to make room in one of the big fridges for the bouquets. The florist will be here by eight, and will decorate the table centerpieces, the chapel, and the suites."

Hope shone in her eyes. "Can you imagine how delicious this place will smell? Georges's amazing cooking and an abundance of bouquets?"

Splashes of color everywhere would brighten up the lodge, and make it so much more feminine. "It'll be beautiful. Micah's just setting up the stage for the orchestra now."

Amory took out her phone, and flicked open her notes section. We spent the next couple of hours making sure we hadn't forgotten any detail, no matter how small.

"I'm going to call it a night," I said, rubbing my belly, full after far too many cups of cocoa and a midnight snack of warm mince pies that we'd pulled out of the oven on Georges's instruction.

"I'll tidy this up, and I might head to bed too," she said. "Though I'm kind of wired… the usual pre-event insomnia, no doubt."

I gave her a big bear hug, grateful from my head to my toes she was here with me. "Thank you for everything, Amory. There's no way I could have done any of this without you."

She hugged me back hard and said, "As if, darling. You're a star and you know it. I could live here for ever and not miss New York, you know, so please don't kick me out any time soon. When you left, Manhattan lost its shine. I love working with you. We make a good team."

"The dream team. Stay for ever, Amory." She was a city girl through and through, and I'd thought, despite what she said, that her time here would be short-lived, while she worked through her feelings for Cruz. Hope bloomed that she might stay for good, but then guilt tapped me on the shoulder that it would come at the detriment to her relationship if so.

Trudging upstairs, I washed up, and did an Amory, throwing my clothes to the floor, and falling into bed in an exhausted heap. Just when I thought I'd nod off, Amory's voice rang out sharp in the silence. *What now?*

The front door banged shut, and her voice carried up the stairwell. Who was she arguing with? A man's voice drifted up, quieter, trying to calm her down.

Curiosity got the better of me, so I grabbed my robe and went to investigate.

I stopped at the top of the stairs and peeked down. *Cruz!*

"You don't get it," she said. "And you never will!"

He caught her by the elbow as she tried to stomp away. "Why is expressing my love for you so wrong?"

She huffed and crossed her arms. "Because you're rushing things. What we had was perfect as it was, so why change it?"

He shook his head, his eyes blazing at what she said. I was eager to hear his side of the story and crept down the first few steps.

"Because that's what you do when you're in love, Amory. Jesus. You *show* it, you *flaunt* it, you go to the next stage. If you're serious about calling it off, then I understand and I'll walk away, but I won't let you ruin what we have because you're scared of commitment. Why can't I tell everyone I love you?"

She huffed. "Why is it anyone's business but ours?"

He narrowed his eyes. "Why did you leave that night?"

"You know why! Because I had... an eyelash malfunction."

"And that made you plunge down fifteen flights of stairs?" His voice was incredulous.

"Well, I wasn't seeing straight, obviously, and I just needed to get home and apply eyedrops. And then…"

"And then…? That's the bit I don't understand," he said, in a voice that shattered my heart. It was full of such longing, such concern, but unmistakably full of love. Whatever had been about to transpire that night back in Manhattan, it was obvious it had come from a place of love. And Cruz had given Amory ample time to think things over in the relative calm of Cedarwood.

Even if it meant losing my best friend back to the big city, I hoped they'd work things out.

"And then I got spooked, Cruz. You've changed so much in the last few months and I'm trying to come to terms with the fact that you suddenly want different things than you wanted a year ago."

He pursed his lips, nodding like she was right. "I guess it struck me that my life was great to anyone looking from the outside in, but I needed more. I don't feel that same thrill about making big money – what am I, a glorified bean counter? It just doesn't make me feel alive any more. That whole corporate world depresses me, working all hours, sacrificing living so I can have a fat bank balance I don't have time to spend."

"So you want a different job?"

"I want a different life, but more than that, I want you."

"But you want the whole package, right? A house in the 'burbs with a big garden that needs constant attention, a traipse down the aisle, babies?"

He didn't answer for the longest time, and I held my breath, wondering what he'd say.

"I won't lie to you, Amory. I do want all of that. I want you to meet my family, for my mom to chatter away as I herd you into the kitchen and show you how to make llapingachos, which we'll eat together huddled around the bench. I want to show you where I grew up, and how much my life changed when I moved away."

"That's really sweet and all, but I'm not the type moms usually chatter away to, Cruz. I'm always too opinionated, too ambitious, too much for people, and I don't want to pretend I'm the perfect Stepford type... I don't want to pretend *at all*. I'm hopeless at being domesticated, and I think you're ready for the cute bungalow, the soccer mom SUV, and top-of-the-range dental plan for your yet-to-be-conceived dark-haired beauties."

Cruz shook his head.

"So, is your hesitation because you don't think you're enough, or because you don't want that same kind of life? Because I'm telling you right now, domesticated or not, you are enough, you are more than enough, and my family will recognize that in a heartbeat."

And *that*, I thought, is how you make a woman feel loved.

She mumbled something I couldn't hear so I crept closer, stepping on a groove in the wood which sighed like an old man. Two sets of eyes turned sharply toward me. *Damn it!* I squinted and put my hands out, groping for a wall that wasn't there.

"Don't try the old 'I'm sleepwalking' trick again. Get down here, you eavesdropper." Amory clucked her tongue but I kept up with the charade for Cruz's sake.

"How much did you hear?" she asked.

My hands fell to my sides and I slowly opened my eyes, making a show of squinting in the bright light, and adding a yawn or two for good measure.

"Ahhh... how did I get out *here*?" I gave Amory a go-with-it stare. "Oh... Cruz! Welcome to Cedarwood. What a nice surprise." I walked downstairs to greet him.

With his jet-black hair and exotic green eyes he was every woman's dream, and coupled with the spiel he'd just given he really was the whole package. I couldn't see Amory's issue – he said he wanted her, and would do whatever it was she needed to keep their relationship going. Maybe she thought him sacrificing his desires was unfair.

"Thank God you didn't tumble down the stairs! You might need to put another lock on your bedroom door to stop any accidents if you're given to wandering around in your sleep." He winked, my sleepwalking routine transparent as rice paper, and gave me a hug.

I gave him a toothy smile. "Yes, yes, an industrial-sized lock would be good. Can I make some tea?"

"If I'm not keeping you up?"

"Not at all! How about you go to the front parlor and we'll bring it in? Amory, give me a hand, will you?"

He sauntered off and once he was out of sight I grabbed her arm and dragged her into the kitchen.

"What?" she hissed.

I folded my arms. "He's driven all the way here to talk so you're going to talk to him!"

"We *were* talking until some creepy stalker interrupted!"

I gasped. "I am not creepy!"

She gave me a hard stare. "It was a little creepy. You may as well have donned a set of binoculars."

I whacked her arm playfully. "You would have done the same thing!"

She nodded. "But I would have been a lot more subtle!"

"OK, OK, you're getting off track on purpose. Go talk to him and find out what he was going to say that night when you almost plummeted to your death."

Leaning against the counter, she folded her arms, while I brewed chamomile tea and took the last of Georges's Christmas cookies from the tin.

"I must admit, seeing him drive up to the house earlier was a jolt to the system. I didn't expect him to follow me here. I could get lost staring into his eyes, and I need to keep my wits about me."

I sighed. "So, why keep him at arm's length?"

Her lip wobbled ever so slightly. "Self-preservation. I thought it might be better to make a clean break of it. There's no getting around the baby thing. I *can't* stop him wanting a family, it would be wrong to even try. Shouldn't

199

I let him go so he can find someone who does want the whole American dream?"

"Amory, the least you can do is let him talk without running away this time."

"Yeah, I guess." She took in a shaky breath and turned her glistening eyes to mine. "I just don't want him to see the moment when my heart literally breaks, that's all."

"Why would he?"

"Because if he says that's what he wants – a family – not now, not tomorrow, but in the future, I *will* have to say goodbye. And I love him, Clio. But I can't change who I am. And it just isn't right to stand in his way if he wants kids."

"Oh, Amory, who knew you were really such a softie on the inside? *Tell* him that, *show* him how you feel. True love always finds a way. It does!" I said to her skeptical face before reaching out to hug her.

"OK," she finally said. "Let me talk to him."

I handed her a tray with tea things and watched her walk forlornly down the hallway.

If he wanted to start a family and Amory was adamant she didn't want to be a mother, how on earth *could* they reach a compromise? Worry gnawed at me for my friend. I only hoped she'd be truthful with Cruz, and lay her soul bare. Only then could they move forward...

Chapter Twenty-Two

It was the day of the expo and I was jittery with nerves. Kai hadn't been able to get back here in time to clear the chapel; clearly at such late notice it was impossible for him, so that cast a pall of angst over the day. Ned had said the brides could peek in, but how long exactly was a peek? Surely they'd want to pretend to walk down the aisle, to get a feel for it, but I worried about something happening, someone tripping, any little accident that would plunge me into hot water, because I didn't have permission and that would veto any insurance. I *knew* the chapel was safe, that there were no tripping hazards, but it would be just my luck that a freak accident happened and I wasn't sure it was worth the risk.

I'd snuck in there earlier this morning after the florist had placed flowers everywhere and taken a range of pictures, the fairy lights creating that perfect air of magic and romance against the rustic wooden pews and pulpit. Maybe I could get away with showing the brides pictures on the big screen in the theater room instead. Safety first and all of that.

"Can you set that up in the lobby, please?" I asked a man wheeling a light machine that would send shooting stars up and down the ceiling. Just one of the options our brides might go for. Some liked super-glitzy elements to their weddings, others more low-key options. We'd tried to cater to them all.

Amory walked into the room and clipped on an earring shaped like a Christmas tree as carols echoed around the room. This was going to be one beautiful festive day, even the sun was shining – making the freshly fallen snow glisten outside. The sleds were parked near the slopes, and hot cocoa would be waiting for anyone who wanted to sip as they walked around the grounds in the snow. The ice-skating rink surface looked like glass. Most of the brides-to-be wouldn't want to participate in the winter activities outside, but we still wanted everything to look ready, as if they or their guests could head out for a fun-filled day at any time. Staging at its finest.

She said, "The florist has just finished the front salon and he's on to the centerpieces on the tables in the ballroom. The place smells divine."

I nodded as Micah came bouncing in, his full-wattage grin firmly in place. "What? What's that face about?"

He flashed a piece of paper. "Kai managed to get a *one-day* approval from Old Ned. You may waltz your brides down the aisle today, if need be."

Words froze on my tongue. "What?" I managed. "How? Ned wanted to inspect the chapel, didn't he? And Kai, our registered builder, was supposed to be on-site..."

"Ned came out early this morning and took a quick look around. It helped that Kai had used Ned's brother-in-law for the structural work. When Kai figured out they were related, he called Ned and explained about the quality of his tradespeople, and just so happened to mention his relative's name, and how we'd probably use him for the renovations of the chalets if all went well with the bridal expo..."

I shook my head in awe. "God, he's clever! So Ned won't want his brother-in-law to lose potential future work at Cedarwood?"

"Bingo," Micah said, grinning. "Ned still wants to meet Kai and go over it all with him properly, but you have one

202

day to wow your brides. And for the record, I told him Kai was running errands and wouldn't be in until later."

"Wow, Micah. You guys are amazing. Thank you!" My stomach somersaulted with glee.

I read the document and smiled when I saw the loop and swirls of Ned's signature. A one-day reprieve and just in time! Now I could get properly excited.

We went painstakingly through our list of suppliers, and where they'd set up their wares to show them in the best light. We hoped our brides would fall in love with the quality and detail and leave everything to us. A one-stop wedding shop.

"Canapés first up!" Amory said. "Then we'll introduce them to our vendors."

"Yes, and then we take them for a dance lesson in the great hall."

"The instructor's coming at eleven. Then they can wander the estate and check out the chapel before we regroup for lunch." Whew, there was a lot for them to do and see.

"I hope we get some bookings after all this work." I took another large gulp of coffee and marveled at both Amory and myself being out of bed and organized so early. Outside, Micah and Isla laughed as they finished festooning trees with fairy lights. They really were so in love, it was hard to look away. If only I could get Amory and Cruz to see past their differences too. I hadn't seen Cruz as yet this morning, but his car was still parked out front with a thick layer of snow atop it so he was rattling around the lodge somewhere.

"We will," Amory said, pulling me out of the thought. "The lodge looks stunning, and with the fires crackling and the ambient music drifting down the halls, what's not to love?"

She was right, it did look amazing, but seeing as I'd invested the rest of my funds into the expo, I couldn't shake the feeling this had been a bit risky. But if we could get even one booking it would all be worth it. Gambling was my new thing, it seemed.

A gaggle of suited men and women walked in. "It's the orchestra!" I motioned for help from Aunt Bessie. She gave me a nod, and ushered them into the ballroom. Wearing a long red dress and fitted blazer, she looked every inch the glamourpuss she was. "Follow me, friends," she said, "I'll show you where to set up. Now, are any of you hungry? I make artisan donuts, you see, and I've squirreled some away just in case…"

I hid a smile. That woman could make friends with the abominable snowman, and not blink. It was inbuilt in Bessie to care about people, and most importantly feed them up.

Next to me, Amory was immaculately dressed in a chic pant suit, her hair and makeup flawless, but I detected shadows under her eyes not even Max Factor could disguise.

With the chapel issue sorted for the moment, I could breathe easier, so I took Amory by the arm and led her to the corner for privacy. "Are you OK?"

She gave me a tight-lipped smile. "Sure, sure. Just a little tired."

"Don't lie, Amory. You don't always have to be the girl who is together all the time, you know." It was one thing pretending to be someone else at work, slipping on a different persona, but another to do it to your best friend.

She widened her eyes. "Well, you know me. Game face on. Big day and all."

"No one is here to see your game face except me, so don't worry about it for now. Just tell me what's going on."

She thrust her hands into her pockets, and slid her gaze away. "We stayed up late, too late, and went around in circles until words were just sounds, and had no meaning. Not my best idea when we've got such a busy day ahead of us."

"So where did you leave it?"

"At a crossroads. What would you do, Clio, if you were me? To ask him to stay with me and sacrifice actual living, breathing, blue-faced, screaming babies would be the epitome of selfish on my part. And he doesn't understand that my letting him go is being *selfless*. Sure, I could say, '*Great, you're giving in to me, perfect*,' but that's not fair. And what if ten years down the track he hates me for it?"

What a mess. I suppose I hadn't thought of the future, and whether he would feel robbed by not having the family he'd dreamed of. "There must be a compromise. There must be!"

She lifted a brow. "Can you tell me what that might be and then we'll both know."

I bit down on my lip. "I... umm... I'll have to think on it."

"Darling, don't worry. Let's get to work, yeah?" With a quick peck on my cheek, she turned on her heel, and met more musicians clutching instruments and standing wide-eyed by the entrance of the ballroom.

Click-clacking her way to them in her heels, she smiled – ever the professional. "Welcome, I'll show you where to set up."

I waved them off, clipboard pressed tight against my chest. Bridal expo day had well and truly arrived and with it a cast of people at the lodge, all vying to get their wares set up to display to our brides.

Through the window, snow drifted down as the orchestra started warming up, playing hauntingly beautiful Christmas carols. The wedding-dress designer caught my eye and pulled out a stunning white sheer satin gown and dressed a mannequin. The gown fell to the floor in delicate drapes, and I let out a gasp of delight as the small diamond beads twinkled under the lights. It was the kind of dress fairy tales were made of.

The florist was preparing the display of luscious bouquets and arranging them on tables. Some were seasonally themed, with white roses, pine cones and red cranberries, tied off with thick golden ribbon. My favorite was a posy of periwinkle, violet and lilac flowers, lilies, and something else I didn't recognize. The different hues of purple were spellbinding and drew the eye.

The florist, a robust, spectacle-wearing man walked to me. "Clio, these are for you." He handed me a bouquet of pale pink peonies.

"For me?"

He smiled and pointed to a card attached. "From a friend."

I thanked him and he went back to arranging the centerpieces. I took the card, wondering who had sent me flowers. I tried to remember the last time anyone had, and came up blank.

Clio,

I hope the bridal expo goes off without a hitch. Have I told you yet that I'm glad you came home? Life was never really the same after you left. Looking forward to that dinner whenever you're free.

Timothy x

Life was never really the same? But he got married and had a family about three minutes after I was out of sight! I'm sure I wasn't on his mind one little bit. I didn't hold any grudge or strong feeling about it – we'd been so young, really. But still, he had moved on fairly quickly and it wasn't something I was likely to forget. Would something bloom between us if I just let go and lived for the moment? The same niggle bothered me. Kai. Even if nothing happened with him, would it be fair to date Timothy when secretly my heart beat a double rhythm when I thought of my Australian surfer yogi?

Taking my cell, I hastily sent Timothy a thank-you text back, avoiding any talk about the dinner invitation.

This was why I loved work. Being busy gave me the ability to shelve any man dilemmas and focus on the task at hand. I found a crystal vase and took the bouquet to my office. That done, I went back to the ballroom and checked off my list.

Every vendor was accounted for, set up and ready to go. Isla and Micah had the activities organized. Aunt Bessie was getting her donuts out of the van and ready to serve… so what was I missing? I'd forgotten something, I could feel it.

I wandered around the tables we'd set up in different themes, lifting champagne flutes, checking for smudges. The cutlery was lined up perfectly, reflecting prisms of light from the chandeliers. Georges would serve canapés as soon as the guests…

Georges! Normally he'd be singing and bellowing in the kitchen, foodie scents wafting down the hallway making my mouth water, but I hadn't seen him arrive yet. I dashed down the hall to check. The kitchen was empty, not a pot on the stove and, more worryingly, not a sign of Georges. Snatching up the phone I called him, picturing the worst – a car crash, the roads were slippery this time of year. My heart was in my throat by the time he answered on the third ring.

"Hi, Clio, did you get my message? I'm sorry to let you down like this, but I couldn't say no. You understand, don't you?"

Blood drained from my face as I checked my watch. Three hours until our brides were due and my chef was telling me he wasn't coming. Trying to halt the erratic beat of my heart I said, "What message, Georges? Where are you?"

He groaned. "I left a message on your cell late last night."

"Saying what, Georges? You're supposed to be here!" I couldn't keep the desperation from my voice.

"I was offered head chef position aboard a private cruise ship. I had to say yes, Clio. I realize the timing isn't great…"

Just then Cruz walked into the kitchen, pointing to the coffee machine. I nodded, not sure whether he was asking permission or if I wanted a cup. My head was swimming with panic.

"Georges," I said, trying to keep anger from bubbling up. "Please tell me you're on your way here, and not en route to the bloody Mediterranean!"

I was met with silence. "Georges, I have a group of brides arriving in *three* hours, and you're MIA. Please tell me I'm imagining this. *Please.*"

"Sorry, Clio. Part of the deal was that I had to leave immediately. You know how much I need this."

It was all I could do not to scream, but I knew Georges's catering business was floundering in Evergreen. Still, did he have to leave the *day of* the expo! "Where am I supposed to find a chef, Georges, with *three hours'* notice?"

I could fix anything under pressure, but finding a chef in Evergreen with a three-hour deadline was a little too much, even for me.

The click-clack of Amory's heels rang out as I tried to steady my voice. "Clio," she hissed, "where the hell is Georges?" I pointed to the phone.

"Bessie can help," Georges said. "And most of the canapés are made, they just need to be plated."

I blew out a breath. There was nothing I could do. He was gone and yelling wasn't going to help. I tried my best to sound excited for him – I loved Georges and he really did deserve a break like this. I just wished it hadn't happened on the day of the expo. "OK, Georges, well good luck with the cruise. I'm sure you'll be great." My words may have sounded clipped but I'm sure he understood why.

"I really am sorry, Clio. I didn't want to leave you in the lurch."

"I know, don't worry about it." I rubbed my temples. "Look, I have to go!" I just wanted to end the call and solve the chef problem.

I hung up, and turned to Amory's pinched face. "What the hell? Where is he?"

"He's not coming!" I said, my voice rising.

"What!" she shrieked.

"He took a job on a cruise ship and he's already in transit. He left a message on my cell last night, he reckons, but shoot, Amory, what the hell are we going to do?"

Amory slapped her palm on the bench so hard the coffee cups rattled together. "How could he do such a thing?"

"I know... but where are we going to find someone this late?" I moaned. I pictured myself tackling the kitchen, and blanched. Why was I so hopeless in the culinary arts?

"Surely he could have left one day later!" Amory's eyes flashed, and her raised voice carried down the hall.

Cruz coughed, clearing his throat. "Ladies, I can help, if you're in a bind. I'm sure I can work out what Georges has done..."

Relief hit me. Hadn't he been a chef once upon a time?

"Really? Oh, Cruz, you're a total lifesaver!" I was ready to bow at his feet. "OK, Georges said most of the canapés are prepared. I'll go over the menu with you, and then leave you to it?"

"Sure." He smiled warmly, like he'd relish the challenge.

My heart beat staccato, disaster averted. But it had been another close call and my heart was feeling the damage. "Actually, Amory, could you help Cruz? There's some brand-new chef whites in the storeroom cupboard. Maybe some of them will fit?"

She squinted at me, but stayed silent.

Cruz rolled up his sleeves. "OK, my love, show me the way."

While I double-checked the menus, and wrote notes for Cruz, they walked away together, Amory speaking quickly about the various dishes we'd planned alongside Georges. I couldn't help but stop and watch them for a beat. They worked so well together in a crisis, their own worries shelved.

A few minutes later they returned and we chatted about the plan, and what time service would be. Cruz looked every inch a chef with his immaculate whites on, and I couldn't help but notice how at ease he seemed at being thrust into a last minute situation.

"OK, well, if you're confident with all of that, Cruz, I'll leave you to it?"

"Sure, sure." He smiled, tying his apron strings. "I'll be fine, Clio."

They huddled by the fridge, heads bent, surveying the contents. If all else failed, throw them together – didn't that always work in romantic comedies? Surely if they could solve the missing-chef dilemma, they could solve anything!

Following in the wake of Aunt Bessie's sugary-sweet perfume, I found her chatting to the florist while she set up her donut table. The donuts were cooling in the fridge, but she had elaborate stands for them, which she placed on the beautiful linen tablecloth. When she caught my eye she excused herself and sauntered over, her hips swinging in her Dolly-esque way. "I've been chatting to the other vendors from town and they're thrilled you invited them here today. And I said, well, of course you would! That you're planning to use them whenever you can. What?" she asked. "What's that line between your eyes for?" She rubbed the spot, as if she could erase it, making my frown deepen. I filled her in on the Georges debacle, her eyes wide with shock.

"He just upped and left?"

I nodded. "It was a requirement of the job that he start pronto."

She let out a breath. "Well, at least you've got a backup. How lucky are you?"

"Very."

"Take some deep breaths, baby girl. You've got this. It's going to be a huge success, I just know it. Mom sends her apologies, she had… other things to do today."

"Like?" Washing, cleaning, and gardening in the snow…

"Well," Aunt Bessie bumbled along. "You know, just things. Anyway, we'll have Christmas Day together, right? You'll come to me this year for lunch."

Neutral territory. We both knew Mom wouldn't step foot on Cedarwood soil, and Aunt Bessie knew I'd probably give all of us food poisoning if I attempted to cook. "I'd love that. Our first Christmas together in six years…"

Isla and Micah waved me over.

"You'd better go," Aunt Bessie said, pecking me on the cheek, and giving my butt a slap for good measure as I wandered away, her cackle following me. I shook my head, and laughed.

"Guys, you look great!" After working this morning, they'd dashed upstairs to change. They were helping serve today, and would then take the brides on a tour of the estate, pointing out the various activities on offer for guests. Micah was dashing in a suit and tie, and Isla was effortlessly chic in a full-length green dress with long sleeves.

Isla blushed, which brought out the freckles on her nose. "We wanted to look the part. I must say, it's nice to wear something other than my gardening gear and workboots."

I smiled at her and turned to Micah, who was rubbing his hands together. "Micah, I hate to ask because of your beautiful clothes, but can you light the fire in the honeymoon suite so Isla can take them for a tour before lunch?"

"Sure." He kissed Isla's cheek and I turned away discreetly while they did the lovey-dovey goggle-eyes. For some inexplicable reason, the wedding march played in my mind, followed closely by a vision of Isla getting ready in a suite upstairs, her mother arranging her veil, tears filling her eyes at the sight of her beautiful daughter about to marry the man of her dreams… *oh, she'd make a stunning bride…*

"Clio?"

"The tiara…"

"Clio?"

I blinked. Did I say that aloud? I made a mental note to research the kind of tiara that would suit Isla; something elegant, classic, not too blingy…

"Clio?"

211

I shook myself. "Sorry, was lost in thought about… weddings."

She frowned. "Right, well, it's the day for it. What should I do?"

I checked my watch. "Can you help me with the gift bags? We can set them up in the lobby to hand out before they leave."

We worked flat out for the next couple of hours until tires crunched on the gravel out front. *They were here!*

"Isla, can you tell Cruz we'll need the first lot of canapés in twenty minutes?"

She nodded and glided away.

Amory raced over, her face shining with happiness. Outside, car doors shut with a bang and high-pitched chatter filled the air. This was always the best part of an event, the moment all of our hard work came together, and our guests arrived, wide-eyed with awe.

Our brides entered the lobby, wearing big smiles. Amory and I stood next to each other and shook their hands one by one. We went into wedding and event-planner mode, and spent time greeting each bride, handing out name-tags to ensure everyone felt at home and important, before Isla ushered them into the ballroom where they let out gasps of delight at the wedding beauty displayed before them.

Suave Micah appeared carrying a tray of canapés. He winked and strode into the ballroom, but not before we snagged a Moroccan lamb cigar, a crispy deep-fried morsel of perfection. Discreetly wiping crumbs away, I said, "Wow, that guy can cook."

Amory raised a brow. "Wait until you try his South American dishes."

Would I get to try them? Maybe he'd stay around for a while. I did need help for Christmas Eve and the fancy dinner party I envisaged hosting for my friends. Not to mention the guests who'd booked in after New Year…

"What's my lipstick like? No crumbs stuck to me?"

"Fine, fine. And mine?" Usually we stayed well away from the food at our parties, but being the boss had its advantages. We were merely doing quality control, right?

"Let's mingle."

Moving with the group of brides, we took them from table to table, highlighting the ways in which their weddings could be spectacular and, more importantly, unique to them if only they held them here.

One of the more outspoken of the brides, a Texan named Barbie, grabbed my arm and ushered me to one side. "How quickly can you get a wedding organized?" With her bouffant blonde curls and twangy accent she was impossible to miss. Even lowering her voice, she drew the eye of the other brides.

"How quickly do you need it?" I wasn't going to shoot myself in the foot by saying a timeframe that didn't suit. I needed a booking, and just hoped the approval for the chapel came through in time.

Noticing she was being watched, she bundled me further away, and whispered. "Is January too soon? February at a push?"

It was December! When would we get a client who wasn't in a hurry? What if the chapel approval took six months? Amory must have overhead, as she gave me a desperate look and mouthed *say yes!* Wasn't that my own advice – say yes, always? Worry about the finer details later?

I managed a jittery smile. "Sure, we can do it for February, as long as you choose local suppliers as much as possible."

She patted her belly. "Time is of the essence, you see."

Ah! "There's something very special about the fact your baby will attend your wedding, whether anyone knows or not."

She gave me a genuine smile, one that reached her eyes. "I hadn't thought about it like that before. The jellybean will be our guest of honor, and you'll be one of the few who knows about him or her…"

"Did you have any themes in mind? Color combinations…"

"Vintage grandeur. Think Gatsby. The jazz age. That kind of thing."

I wanted to shriek! Vintage grandeur would suit the lodge and show it off in its best light. Did I risk taking the booking without approval? She hadn't confirmed yet, she'd only enquired about timeframes, so instead I focused on making her fall in love with the lodge. I waved Isla over. "Would you like to see the chapel? It has the most glorious stained-glass windows, and we can decorate it to suit the jazz era…"

"I'd love to," she said, and I made introductions and asked Isla to take Barbie on a tour. "Don't forget to visit the honeymoon suite," I said. "It's spectacular."

Another bride walked over exclaiming about the canapés. "Is this the same chef you'll use if we book Cedarwood as a venue? Please say yes!"

Amory answered: "Yes, Cruz can be requested, definitely."

I held my breath. She hadn't asked him, and surely this bride would insist on knowing it was in fact Cruz in the kitchen on her wedding day.

Just then, Cruz walked in carrying a plate of sweet canapés. "Let me introduce you?" Amory gave her a saccharine smile. "Cruz, this is Ebony, she's enquired whether you'll be the chef if she hires Cedarwood for her nuptials."

Without missing a beat, Cruz nodded. "That can easily be arranged."

They were totally on the same wavelength, and interpreted what the right answer would be. My heart just about exploded that they'd say yes, knowing it would help sway her decision. We'd worry about the practicalities of it later. *Worry later, Clio! Smile and schmooze and do your job!*

"Great," she said, beaming. "Let's talk dates."

Amory said, "Follow me, Ebony. Can I get you a glass of champagne while we chat?"

Two potential bookings! I wanted to jump for joy until I remembered the damn approval certification. I needed Kai and I needed him here fast.

At the florist's table, a trio of women stood chatting away, exclaiming over prices. I'd told the vendors to be vague about pricing, because we'd try to do the weddings as a package deal, but if they pushed for it, then to do their best to wow the brides with the quality of their products. The raven-haired beauty said, "I'm not sure it's worth all that! What are they, exotic blooms shipped from Amsterdam?" Her friends tittered behind their hands. I frowned and hoped the florist wasn't offended. His flowers were first-rate and worth every penny.

A twenty-something girl dithered alone, clutching her champagne glass so tight I thought she might break it. "Hello, Felicity," I said, reading her name badge. "Can I introduce you to my aunt who makes the most delicious donuts you'll ever taste?"

Felicity shot me a grateful smile and nodded. "Thank you, I'm a little out of my comfort zone here. Makes me wonder how I'll have the courage to walk down the aisle. Right now, eloping seems like a better idea." The apples of her cheeks were pink with nerves.

I took her by the elbow, and led her to Aunt Bessie. "Eloping is cute," I said. "But what about your family? Wouldn't they miss seeing you marry the love of your life?" I understood her nerves. Many brides felt the same way, until they'd done it. Then they wanted to do it over and over again. Once they started the slow walk down the aisle, time stopped, and all they could see was the person waiting at the other end for them, the one who loved them above all else, and was about to promise to love them for eternity.

"Yeah," Felicity admitted. "My mom would never forgive me. But she's one of those social types, and I'm more of an introvert."

"The good thing about location weddings," I said, "is that they can be intimate. You've always got that excuse to keep your party to a minimum. Keep it small, with only the people you feel totally comfortable around."

Her eyes brightened. "I guess you're right. Does that mean I can leave his mom off the invite list?"

I giggled. "Monster-in-law?"

"Times ten. She's a nightmare! I think that's half the problem, that I'll be worrying about what she's thinking about my dress, my hair, the way I'm walking. She intimidates me."

I clucked my tongue. It wasn't the first time I'd heard similar worries. Brides worried about so many variables, but it was my job to take that worry away, and make sure that in the lead-up – and, more importantly, on the day – they enjoyed themselves, and felt like princesses. Otherwise what was the point?

"If you have your wedding at Cedarwood Lodge, we'll do the worrying for you. We have expert hair and makeup teams, ones who usually do celebrities who can fly in from New York for the day. Your bridesmaids will walk ahead of you, and you'll have your father, right? He won't let you topple down the aisle. Trust me when I say, none of that will be in your mind when the music starts, and you see your fiancé waiting for you."

She squeezed my hand. "Thank you, Clio. I suppose I have to remember it's not a punishment. It's meant to be one of the best days of my life."

"It will be. You'll see."

"Hello there, pretty girl!" Aunt Bessie said. "Would you like to try some donuts?" Before waiting for an answer she pointed to a tray. "These are my Rudolf reindeers, filled with butterscotch custard and ganache. The antlers are made from dark chocolate, and the red noses are candy-cane flavored. Aren't they the cutest things?"

Felicity took the proffered donut, and said, "Almost too cute to eat!"

Just then a voice bellowed, "Not on your life would I pay five thousand dollars for a photography package! Are you trying to rob us blind?" The same trio again! I donned a serene expression and hotfooted it to the photography stand where the poor photographer stood aghast.

"What's the problem?" I asked, sweetly.

The girl turned to me, flipping her long mane of dark hair. "Your photographer is charging an exorbitant amount for a basic package, and it makes me wonder if the price is inflated for everything just because we're using the W word!"

This kind of person was party suicide, so I motioned for Micah to bring champagne. Better to kill her with kindness even though she was out of line. "Tory is one of the most sought-after photographers in New York, and we're very lucky he even agreed to visit us today."

"Yeah," she said. "I guess he's tacking his holiday bill on to our wedding packages."

Tory glared at her and said, "The package I quoted was including drone footage by the lake, and a variety of additions – definitely not the basic wedding package."

She blushed but rallied, "Still, it's a lot of money for a wedding in a hokey place."

"Right," I said, pretending to consider it. "Who just booked you for their wedding next year, Tory? Was it Hadley?"

"It was. But she obviously went for all the bells and whistles for her big day."

"Of course, you can't put a price on memories like those."

"They last a lifetime." He grinned.

"Hadley booked you?" Her voice was incredulous. "As in the singer?"

"I can't divulge the personal details of my clients." He pursed his lips.

She squirmed but tried to adopt a haughty expression. "Can I see those packages again? Like you said, you can't put a price on memories."

I left them to it, smothering a smile, fairly sure Hadley was the receptionist in the office next door to Tory's studio…

A few hours into the expo, the girls were pink-cheeked and grinning from excitement and perhaps a few extra glasses of champagne. Somehow the quiet, shy Felicity had convinced Amory to try on one of the couture wedding gowns so they could see it objectively. Always up for a challenge when it came to business, Amory had happily obliged, and I wondered what she secretly thought about wearing such a gown. For someone adamant they were never walking down the aisle, would it make her think twice, wearing something so fabulous, so utterly made just for one day... When she swanned out in it her expression was unreadable but her color high, and she made the most magnificent bride. Just then Cruz walked in, and his face said it all. For a split second, he brightened, his mouth parting in surprise, as if he'd never seen anyone so lovely. When Amory noticed him, she blushed, fumbling with the dress. Something had passed between them, a fleeting glimpse of what might be?

By nightfall most of our brides had left satiated after such a big day. Isla had impressed everyone with the range of outdoor activities, and our dance teacher, who was easy on the eye, had been a hit too.

We had one definite booking – Barbie in February – and a tentative yes from Ebony for the summer, but first she'd bring her family to the lodge for a second opinion. Micah and Isla had helped Aunt Bessie load up her car with supplies we'd borrowed and were meeting her in Evergreen to help unpack. Cruz was wiping down the kitchen benches, his chef whites no longer pristine, but a satisfied smile firmly in place.

I flopped down at the bench and said, "Do you want any help, Cruz?" I prayed he'd say no since my feet were on fire from wearing heels all day. I must have climbed the staircase twenty times, showing brides the honeymoon suite.

"I'd love a glass of wine," he said.

I lifted a finger. "No! Champagne for all!"

218

"Did I hear someone say champagne?" Amory took some flutes from the cupboard and went to the fridge, taking a bottle and expertly popping the cork with zero ceremony. I had to laugh. In times of crisis, or fatigue, she was a guzzler, and an expensive price tag meant little.

"You're a girl after my own heart," I said, clinking glasses with her and Cruz. "Thank you for today, both of you. I don't want you to ever leave! Can't we pretend there's no New York, and this is home?"

They exchanged a glance with each other. It was loaded with meaning, but of what, I didn't know. "Let's cheers to that," Amory said.

"Cruz, you were in your element! I thought chefs were usually grumpy under pressure, more sovereign-like, barking orders or some such."

He threw his head back and laughed. "I used to work under a chef like that and it was almost impossible not to laugh when he had one of his rages. I couldn't take him seriously when he was heart-attack red and frothing at the mouth. Instead of fixing the problem he'd have a conniption that lasted twenty minutes – which of course delayed us even more... It was insane."

"How depressing," Amory joked. "I was hoping to see you throw some pots and pans around – you know, christen the kitchen a bit?"

"There's still time," he said, his eyes twinkling. Was it a possibility he'd stay and take up the chef position at Cedarwood? It would be too good to be true, having my best friend and her partner here for good. But maybe out of the city they could sort through their differences... I sent up a fervent wish to the universe to make it so.

"And our beautiful brides! Weren't they amazing?" Amory said.

I took a big sip of champagne, bubbles bursting on my nose like little kisses. "They were, even what-was-her-name with the black hair?"

Amory rolled her eyes. "There's always one like that. Isadora. Doubt we'll hear back from her, though."

In a way, I was glad. You could only deal with so many dramas before it became old very quickly. I sensed Isadora would be a troublemaker just for the sake of it. Still, smile, nod, and solve the problem – we'd do it if we had to. "The vendors were really happy too. Might be the start of something big for them."

I knew how hard it was to make a living in Evergreen and I couldn't deny the thrill I felt knowing that Cedarwood Lodge was providing more customers for local small businesses too.

My face hurt from smiling but my heart was full.

***

The next morning we woke late, and the rest of the day spread out before us blissfully void of any work. We'd decided to relax and celebrate the success of the bridal expo and all the hours we'd put into it.

Cruz was humming away in the kitchen, searching the fridges, his zest for cooking back with a vengeance. He rejected my offers to help unload the dishwasher. "You girls have been run off your feet in the lead-up to the expo. Why don't you take a break? Go up to the library, and I'll bring tea?"

The thought of being still, lying supine, did sound appealing. "Are you sure?"

"I'm sure."

"Come on then, Amory," I said, dragging at her arm, desperate to lie down and chat lazily.

Slowly, like old women, we climbed the stairs. "You know, it hurts to wear heels these days. I suffer afterwards."

She gave me a bemused smile. "We sure did some miles in them. And going up and down these goddamn stairs every five minutes… We're going to have some serious calf muscles."

I thought of my wardrobe, packed with couture clothing, and various heels from kitten to stiletto… and all I wanted to wear these days were my yoga pants and ballet flats. To hell with keeping up with fashion. I didn't have to do that any more, and I didn't much care either.

We settled in the library, the scent of old tomes mixing with the perfume of rose posies scattered around the room. Our brides had loved the library – those with bookworm in their blood, anyhow. From my vantage point on an old, crinkled-leather Chesterfield I could see the snow-covered mountains and the frozen lake at their base.

Flashing fairy lights brightened the room, and I turned to Amory, who had her hands clasped over her belly, her lids heavy like she'd taken a sleep draught.

"It was great of Cruz to stay and help out. Without him I don't know what we'd have done." Neither Amory nor I could cook worth a damn, and Aunt Bessie had her donut table to attend to and brides to entertain. All of us had had jobs to do and, without Cruz's culinary expertise, we'd have been in real trouble.

Sleepily she said, "He told me last night that he quit his job. That's why there was a delay in him arriving at Cedarwood. He had to give them notice."

"He quit his job? Why?" As far as I knew he thrived on the fast pace of high finance.

"He seems to think it was our downfall, the reason we haven't taken the next step… Because we're always too caught up at work. He's sort of got a point."

I nodded. "Big-city burnout." It reminded me of Kai, and his feeling of being on a never-ending Ferris wheel. Was it worth it? I'd loved my job at the agency, and hated that my exit hadn't been my choice, but after buying Cedarwood and making a life back in Evergreen I was happier every day that the decision had been made for me. New York and that frenetic pace were a million miles from here and I didn't miss it any more. Instead, I felt a type of apathy about it.

We'd all been so caught up in racing to be the best that we'd lost our way – or at least that's how I felt now.

"What will he do?"

"He's got savings, so he'll live off that for the moment, until he decides – but I suppose he can be a chef, or at least use those skills somewhere, and you can tell by his pizzazz in the kitchen under pressure yesterday how much he loves doing it. He had fire in his belly again. It was lovely to witness that."

I sat bolt upright. "But what about for Cedarwood?"

She frowned. "You'd hire him? I thought that was just a ruse to get people to sign up – say 'yes' and all that?"

"Oh my God, no! I was totally serious. He is more than qualified. I mean, you saw him yesterday, he didn't even break a sweat, just got the job done as if he'd planned the menu himself."

"Don't you think that's too neat? We have problems, he shows up, boom he's hired. Do you think it'll make me change my mind?"

I leaned back into the chair and pulled a rug over me. "Do you want him to stay?"

She waited a beat. "Yes."

"Then why not?"

She sighed. "I worry I'm losing my identity, you know, and I get how uppity that sounds, but I thought I knew who I was. Thirty-something, career-driven, ambitious event planner to the stars. I had rules, so that vision stayed firmly in place. And now look at me…"

I smiled, and gave her arm a pat. "I know exactly what you mean, Amory. When I crept out of the city totally humiliated, I thought my dreams were done for. My confidence was wrecked. But it's been the best thing that's ever happened to me. And you're lucky you chose to leave. No one forced you. What do you want to be, Amory? That same girl, keeping the world at arm's length, or pulling those she loves closer?"

"Oh, you and your Hallmark clichés." She grinned. "I want to stay here, and never leave, Clio. Truly. I don't know if it's Cedarwood's spell, or if I've been living on autopilot in New York, but I love it here. I've never felt so at home. But how do I do that? Give up my job, my apartment..."

"Why couldn't you stay here, Amory? Sublet your apartment if you're not one hundred percent sure. And as for Cruz... Why not take it one day at a time? He'd be doing us a huge favor if he did stay on."

"It would be fun to help you here long term. The possibilities are endless."

"Then stay. I need your help, and I'm prepared to beg for it."

She laughed. "And Cruz?"

"Chef Cruz, it's got a nice ring to it." Her eyes twinkled and I knew she was thinking about it.

Chapter Twenty-Three

The next day I worked for a few hours, updating social media, emailing our brides to thank them for attending the expo, and catching up on the accounts. I thought about how to get some more bodies in beds, so I created some discounted package deals and uploaded them to various travel websites.

In the quiet of the office, I thought of Mom, and the sadness that consumed me at times that I could never share any of this with her. Why couldn't she be who I needed her to be and vice versa? When I'd first come home, I'd imagined us sitting side by side in the office, dreaming up marketing campaigns, new events for our guests, and window-shopping for sumptuous furniture we'd buy when our funds were in surplus. Instead, the lodge was like a cuss word, and we avoided any talk of it.

It was high time that changed. I grabbed my scarf from the coat hook, and wound it on, pulling on my coat, and donning a red knitted beanie. It took an age for the car to warm up in the freezing temperatures, but when it did, I took the drive very slowly indeed, slowing more as I drove past houses decorated to the hilt, inflatable reindeers blowing sideways in the bracing winds, and colored lights shining from windows. Wreaths decorated front doors, like a welcome home.

Twenty minutes later, I pulled into Mom's driveway, and shut off the engine. I rapped on the front door and got no answer. I called her cell, and she answered after the first ring. "Hello, Clio."

"Mom, I'm at your house, shivering on the porch. Where are you?"

"I'm at Puft with Bessie. She needed a hand with some orders. Grab the spare key, it's out back under the mat, and I'll be home in about half an hour, OK?"

"Thanks, Mom. See you soon." I felt a real pang of surprise, and happiness. Normally Mom would have said she was out and that was that. To have her come home on my account was definitely a step in the right direction.

After finding the key, I let myself in. The cottage was as pristine as ever, everything in its place and a place for everything, as my Aunt Bessie used to say, good-naturedly teasing Mom's tendency to clean everything within an inch of its life.

In the kitchen, I detected the faint smell of coffee. I rifled through the pantry to find some coffee beans. The one thing Mom always had in bulk was coffee. She might run out of food without much concern, but her coffee stash was always healthy. Finding the coffee, I pressed buttons on the machine, but it came up with an error code. I frowned, pressing more buttons, wondering what the little symbols meant. Being organized to a fault, I knew Mom kept all her kitchen-gadget instruction manuals in a file in the bottom drawer.

Sure enough, there was the file, just like I expected. But underneath it was a leatherbound book. It was thick, embossed, and looked out of place in the drawer. Mom didn't just leave things lying around. Kitchen things went in the kitchen and personal effects went in the office.

Interest piqued, I flicked it open. It was a photo album. The hair on my arms stood on end – part fear she'd catch me looking through her private things, and part curiosity that I might find something I shouldn't. The tiny book felt heavy in my hands, and my heart thudded in my chest. It was probably nothing, probably family photographs, and she'd mistakenly left them in this drawer.

Surely she wouldn't mind if I had a quick peek at my own family photographs? Didn't I have that right, the most basic of things?

I darted a glance over my shoulder, ears pricked for the sound of her car. I flicked the pages of black-and-white photos. The first picture was an old car with wide fenders, probably a classic by now. The second was a woman holding a baby. The young woman's hair was curled gently around her ears. The dimples in her cheeks, identical to ones in mine. *Mom.* She wore a sixties-style dress.

What I couldn't miss was the big, beaming smile on her face as she gazed with wonderment at the baby in her arms. Whose child was it? I'd seen a picture of myself in Mom's arms as a baby, and I knew this wasn't me. This picture had been taken a long time before I was born. Mom was shiny-skinned and smooth-featured like a teenager. Youthful.

I flicked to the next picture and my breath caught. It was Cedarwood. Beautiful Cedarwood like something out of an F. Scott Fitzgerald novel. The fountain out front was surging water into the air, the cherubs on its base unable to catch each other for eternity. The lodge in the background, the tree-crested mountains behind. It was unmistakably the lodge, but in black and white it looked so different, so young somehow... as though now the years of being abandoned had aged the old place.

The next photograph was Mom again, this time holding the hand of a toddler, her little bonneted head staring up at Mom. Who...? Just then I heard the crunch of gravel as Mom pulled into the driveway. Shoot! With my pulse thrumming, I closed the album and shoved it back in the drawer, and with it the file of instruction manuals.

Trying to calm the erratic rhumba of my heart, I pasted on a smile and smoothed down my hair before she came in, carrying a box of donuts.

"Clio, hi."

I was sure my skin was flushed with the secret, and averted my gaze so she couldn't read it in my eyes. I fought the urge to flee, my heartbeat still leaping in my chest, pumping so loud I was sure she could hear it.

"Hi, Mom."

To keep my hands from shaking, I hunted in the pantry for the biscuit tin, thoughts still spinning wildly, making assumptions about Mom and the mysterious child who stared up at her like she was her world. Did I have a sibling? Was she a teen mom? So many questions buzzed around my head, and I tried to think rationally about what to say to her that wouldn't make her clam up, and wouldn't make it obvious I'd been snooping, even though it had been mostly innocent.

For the life of me I couldn't think of anything to say. How did you bring up something like that? *Hey, Mom, did you have a child you forgot to tell me about?* Was that child now an adult living in Evergreen? Someone I'd walked past a hundred times in the street and didn't know?

When it came time to question her, words failed me. I froze. And for the first time I really understood people telling me to leave it be. Because once the words were said, you couldn't tuck them away again. I sat there for too long, silent. Wishing I had a crystal ball to guide me. Ask? Or not? Now I finally had some kind of evidence, although it was nebulous, courage failed me. I left with a lame excuse, giving her a loose hug, and rushed through the snow to my car. I just couldn't do it.

I drove sedately through the double gates of the lodge, seeing the place as it had once been, in the black-and-white pictures, and comparing it to now, in full color. And then, with the ghost of my mom as a teenager standing at the front, a small child searching her face, and now, bereft of anyone, rain soaking the spot.

Inside, I went to my office, and sat heavily, trying to push the worry away, and focus on work. Kai had emailed to say he would be here soon and hopefully our chapel-approval issues would be sorted before our very first wedding. I checked over the paperwork for the chapel once more, readying it to present to Ned. Invoices from each tradesperson who'd done the necessary safety improvements were all there, sorted into alphabetical order.

The phone rang, starling me. "Cedarwood Lodge, Clio speaking."

"How'd the bridal expo go?" Kai's Australian drawl provoked a smile.

Kai... just the person I needed to hear from. Even talking over the phone with him calmed me. "Well, despite Georges being a no-show the morning of, we got through it well, and secured a definite and one maybe. I just need that approval before I can put my wedding-planner cap back on."

"Georges didn't show?" I explained to Kai what happened. "Lucky you had a stand-in then."

"Very. Thank you for the magic you worked with Ned! I was iffy showing the brides the chapel without permission so that one-day pass was a godsend."

"No worries. Sorry I didn't get there – things have been hectic."

"Did you manage to see about getting any time off?" It was a week until Christmas, and if he didn't come soon, we'd have to wait until the New Year, because Ned's office was closed from Christmas Eve onwards.

"My boss wouldn't budge, no surprises there, but I managed to move some projects up, and got some extra help in, so I can get there in two days' time and stay for the week, because things shut down at Christmas. I know this leaves us tight for time with Ned, but I'm hoping I can convince him to visit Cedarwood while I'm there and explain the improvements and safety measures."

"Oh, Kai, that would be amazing. I hope you'll stay with us."

"If you're sure?"

"It's not like we don't have the room." I laughed.

"True. Get your walking shoes on, Clio. Rain, hail, or shine we're climbing that mountain."

I wrinkled my nose, and gazed out the window to the slushy, ice-covered ground. "It's *snowing*, Kai. And not just a little bit. Can't I convince you to take a leaf out of my book?"

"Yeah, sure, what will we do?"

"First we'll drink a bottle of wine, then we'll eat our body weight in candy canes, and then…"

He laughed, "And then we'll ice skate on the lake. Deal."

"Maybe we'd better do that before the wine then."

"See you soon."

We said our goodbyes and I couldn't ignore the little flutter in my belly that he'd be back soon. Back at Cedarwood…

Chapter Twenty-Four

The next day Cruz wandered into the kitchen, a sheepish expression on his face. "I've been ordered to take breakfast upstairs…"

I let out a laugh. "Yeah? Those princess instincts are really kicking in."

"They've never really been that well hidden to be honest," he said, and smiled. "Do you mind?" He pointed to the fridge.

"Go for it. I probably should go and do a big grocery shop before Christmas. I was going to host a little party, but now Georges has gone…" I let the words hang in the air.

"I can help, no problems," he said. "I forgot how much I love it. The sizzling of pans, getting the timing just right. While it seems more manic than number-crunching, it's actually a helluva lot more enjoyable."

"Why don't you cook again then, Cruz?"

"I had these dreams of owning a cute little café, somewhere where there are open spaces, no traffic, quiet…"

I raised a brow. "Sounds like Evergreen, doesn't it?"

He took bacon and eggs from the fridge, and turned to me grinning. "I guess it does." He ran a hand over his face. "It's funny. If you'd have asked me a year ago did I want kids, marriage, a different job, I would have laughed in your face. But something changed, like a switch was flicked, and I didn't recognize the person I'd become. It was so sudden, and I just felt like I'd been living a lie. The job, the

Amory continued to read: "*Like
touches turns to gold, and Cedarwood Loa

I hugged myself tight. "Well, the
changed their tune! That's a long wa
me of being a celebrity wedding wi
find out about the expo?" I asked.

"We must have had a rogue
screeched. "We'd usually have picked
Who do you think it was?"

"I don't know," I said, picturing th
"I bet you it was Felicity! That whole
was a farce!"

"Yes! And don't forget the try-the-d

"Or was it our troublemaker, Isador
Shrugging, Amory scanned the
"She mentions the food! She says:
*and seasonal, exceptional in every way,
luncheon was better than Mom's – but don*

"We have to thank Cruz a million ti
how he handled it with such aplomb."

"The rest of the article gives our deta
I have a feeling Cedarwood Lodge won't be a

"Let's celebrate! We have to plan
Christmas Eve dinner. We can deck o
adjoins the side deck, set up a table b
so we can watch the snowfall up close."

Her eyes shone, because there wa
a party planner than decorating ar
own party. "Yes! Let's go to town on t
another Christmas tree, something sm

"Shall we head into town and buy
and something for the center of the ta

"Yes! We still have a few more gi
rubbed her hands together. "We're goi
list. OK, well, get your granny shoes o
Evergreen."

I scoffed. "My granny shoes?"

work culture in NYC just seemed so meaningless. The only
thing that mattered to me still was Amory, and I realized
how much I loved her. When everything else fell away, all I
wanted was her, and a different life."

I took a frying pan from the hook and put it on the
stove, lighting the gas for him. "I did wonder why things
moved so quickly between you and Amory all of a sudden.
I thought it was because I was out of the way." Amory had
made it her mission to get me out and about in New York,
and often I felt guilty that I was encroaching on time they
could spend together, but at that stage Cruz worked long
hours, and Amory always reassured me it was fine.

He dropped a dollop of butter in the pan, which sizzled,
liquefying. "I probably scared her with my sudden intensity.
In fact, I know I did. But it was just so clear to me, you
know, like a complex math problem solved in the blink of
an eye. Now though, how do I make things right? How do
I show her I'm still the same guy, but with different goals?"

I flicked on the coffee machine and folded my arms,
contemplating it all. "I guess you just lay your cards out –
that's all anyone can do – and say, this is me, this is what I
am and... see?"

He placed bacon in the pan, which shriveled and shrank
back in the heat. "I know Amory thinks it's unfair to stay
together if I want children. She thinks it's like shopping
and I can walk down the supermarket aisle and pick one,
oh look she'll make a great mom, but you know, I love her
enough, too much actually, to let that one thing end us. So
she doesn't want kids now, and maybe she never will, but I'd
choose her over that any day. Sure, I'd love to have a family,
but not at the cost of losing her."

"Have you told her all of this, Cruz?" I knew they'd
gone back and forth over most of it a number of times,
but he was really ready to change his life, and all he
wanted was her. She wanted to stay here, and he wanted
open spaces and a quiet life. Couldn't they both stay

and at least explore a new s[...]
Amory told Cruz she, too, was ti[...]
demands of big-city living?

"Yeah, but I think she only hea[...]

"Cruz, I need a chef, and yo[...]
Think about staying, will you?" [...]
checked with Amory. These two n[...]
if they stepped away from their [...]
harmony here. Cedarwood had w[...]

Later that day I went online, and [...]
email full of queries about the loc[...]
about weddings, bridal showers, [...]
While I was thrilled, I wondere[...]
from. How had they heard about [...]

I went through them all, an[...]
attaching pictures, sample menus, [...]

"If you squint any harder, you'l[...]

"What's so fascinating?"

I laughed. "Well, for reasons un[...]
full of potential clients. Come see."

She leaned over my shoulder[...]
showing her the emails.

"I bet we've been written u[...]
that." She grabbed the laptop and[...]
mumbling to herself, as she[...]
combinations before saying, "Boo[...]
New York Observer!"

"No!"

"Yes!"

"NO!"

"YES-S-S!" She let out a squeal. [...]

"Let me see!" She turned th[...]
shrieked, clapping a hand to m[...]
headline: *Clio Winters rises again,[...]
hundred-year-old venue.*

"Rises again? Like I'm the undea[...]

"Those big clodhoppers of yours. Those boots, the ones that look like you're about to head into war after an apocalypse."

I hit her on the arm. "They're snow boots, I'll have you know. You're not the one who has to walk around the grounds every day, checking on things." I'd been escaping for long walks, telling whoever asked that I was clearing my head, when in actual fact I was searching for the maze. I knew it was somewhere on the east side of the property but that was thick forest, totally overgrown, and impossible to navigate in the slushy snow. Isla would have a better idea of where it was but I was loath to share my mom's secret because I'd promised her I wouldn't. There probably was no maze after all these years. By now it would be just one big overgrown hedge, but still I wanted to see it myself. So far, no luck.

"Well, get them on, darling, and let's go shopping!"

I grabbed her arm as she was about to leave. "Amory, you know Evergreen isn't actually a bustling little shopping capital, don't you?"

She threw her head back and laughed at my worried expression. "I think I'll survive. Now come on, we've got gifts to buy!"

In town, the street had come alive with shoppers wearing determined expressions. Storefronts were lit up with Christmas lights, and tinsel was draped behind windows. In the window of Puft were lush green-iced donuts, stacked atop each other in the shape of a Christmas tree. We waved to Aunt Bessie. I stuck my head in and told her we'd stop by after shopping. Wreaths blew sideways, their little bells jingling in the wind. The town Christmas tree was decorated with so many baubles they had their own music, clinking together in the wind, glittery dust blanketing the snow beneath.

We went to the little candle shop, and stocked up on candles for our friends and some for the lodge. Ruth, the owner, made the candles herself, and had a range especially for Christmas. From gingerbread scented to candy-cane striped, we had a hard time choosing.

"Let's get them all," Amory said. "They might sell out and then we'll be upset."

I held my laughter in check, doubting very much that anything would sell out in Evergreen except Aunt Bessie's donuts, but agreed to buy them all, knowing how lovingly made they were, and that if the same product was sold in New York, we'd be paying five times the price without blinking an eye.

"Why, thank you, girls!" Ruth said, wrapping our purchases as we kept finding other scents and adding them to the pile.

After that we went around the corner to a gift shop, tucked into the back of an alley. I often wondered how Henrietta ever made any money as tourists wouldn't know to look here, and the town wasn't big enough for her to survive on locals' purchases, but somehow she did.

"You know, we should make up a folder for each suite, with a map of the town and all these little hidden gems – like Henrietta's gift shop and Ruth's candle shop – so they don't pass through Evergreen completely. There's lots here, if you know where to look."

Amory nodded, and pushed open the door. Inside was toasty warm and decorated prettily for Christmas, in a pink and silver theme. "Hey there, Clio!" Henrietta said, grabbing me in a bear hug. "Bessie told me you're doing well at Cedarwood. I'm so happy to hear it."

"Thanks, Henrietta."

She stood back, surveying me, and smiled. "I'm glad the place isn't empty any more. Such a waste to have it lying there abandoned like that. S'pose there was good reason for it, though. The townsfolk are still very superstitious about the place, but they'll come around. I guess they think it's not fair to her memory... and I can understand that."

My chest tightened. "Whose memory?" I managed to sputter.

Henrietta's face paled. "Didn't your mom tell you before you bought the lodge? I thought…"

"I bought the lodge as a surprise and then told Mom. Who, Henrietta? Who did you mean?"

She waved me away. "I didn't mean a thing. I've had too much eggnog, is all. You know that old place, kinda spooky when it was vacant, that's all."

Just like the others, her mouth was closed on the matter. But it was closer than I'd come before. Had someone died there? And, if so, what did Mom have to do with it?

It was hard to continue shopping, as if nothing else mattered, but I did it for Amory's sake, pasting on a smile and chatting lightheartedly.

Chapter Twenty-Five

With only a few more days until Christmas, Micah had left early for the airport, to pick up Kai, who had finally wrapped up his jobs and was able to get away. Forget the kiss, forget the jelly-legged sensation, and focus on getting the chapel approved. *Yes, yes, yes.* Really, I had started to think I had imagined the whole take-my-breath-away moment of madness with Kai. Maybe I'd dreamed it up, maybe I was that desperate? Next I'd be journaling about our faux children, and their sporting prowess, their educational achievements… Where Kai and I would renew our vows (beachside, Mauritius) what I'd wear (backless, lemon-colored dress, flip-flops, hair loose), and what… I shook my head. Dang it, usually my away-with-the-fairy moments were about other brides, *real* brides, ones who were *actually* engaged or at least in a relationship. I put it all down to lack of sleep…

Isla, Amory and I had just finished inspecting the chalets, making copious notes just like always about how we wanted to furnish them, and what we needed to order, so that when renovations started in the New Year, we would be ready to go. The sooner they were done the better, and another income stream would open up. The chalets were completely self-contained, and also more private, being set away from the lodge itself.

Trudging back through the slushy snow, we chatted about Christmas Day and what our plans were. "I'm meeting Micah's parents," Isla said, grinning.

Amory gazed sharply at her. "Oh, God, really?"

Isla shrugged. "Well, it's Christmas! I'm looking forward to it actually. Micah said his mom is a sweetheart and his dad fancies himself as a prankster. Is that right, Clio? Are they as nice as he says?"

It was interesting to note Amory was hanging on every word. My usually confident, sassy friend was clearly still nervous about meeting Cruz's parents... Whereas Isla was happy to take the next step with Micah, because meeting the parents was always a good sign the relationship was moving in the right direction.

"They're even nicer than that," I said honestly. Micah's parents were caring, compassionate, and happy-go-lucky, just like him. They'd been there for me a lot growing up; I was sort of the daughter they never had. "His mom, Sue Betty, sewed my prom dress, and did my hair and makeup, and his dad gave Timothy the big talk about curfews and the appropriate way to treat a woman, i.e. don't even think about sex before marriage."

Isla laughed. "Oh, that is totally adorable! Imagine having" – she made air quotes – "'the talk' about someone else's daughter."

Silence fell between us. I remembered that night so clearly: the fact that my own father was missing another rite of passage, another event in my life he should have been there for; not to mention Mom, who should have been the one dusting on too much blue eyeshadow, and teasing my hair, choking us with hairspray fumes.

"It was hard to buy them Christmas presents," Isla said. "In the end I settled for Christmas-themed gift boxes, but I'm worried they'll think it's cheesy."

"What did you buy?" I asked, knowing it could have been a day-old newspaper and they'd still have exclaimed how perfect it was, and how thoughtful.

"Gaudy Christmas onesies, and a selection of Christmas movies, then I filled the box with candy canes, reindeer lollipops, and gingerbread men. I thought it could be a tradition, you know, start something new, celebrate my life here in Evergreen with them..."

I gave her arm a pat. "They'll totally love that, and no doubt wear them and make you all sit down and watch every last movie."

She grinned. "I hope so." I watched Amory consider it from Isla's point of view, and I wondered if it made her think of Cruz, and meeting his folks.

Back inside the lodge, we hung our coats, and unwound thick scarves, taking off our gloves, it was hot in the warm front salon with the fire roaring.

"Let's get the presents wrapped, yeah?" I said, taking various rolls of brightly colored foil from a shopping bag. The girls dashed upstairs to grab their gifts, so while they were gone, I wrapped theirs. For Isla, I'd found a chunky silver bracelet filled with floral charms – roses, peonies and lilies were recreated in thick silver and it reminded me of her and her love for flowers. Micah had been right when he'd said she could wax lyrical about flora for days... Amory's present was a Filofax. She adored them, and I'd had the leather cover embossed with her name. Inside, I'd stuffed two tickets to a ballet show she'd been itching to see. With red and golden ribbons tied around the shiny gold foil, I popped the presents under the tree just as they walked back into the room, arms full with shopping bags.

Amory produced her present for Cruz, which I rewarded with an eyebrow-raise. "An apron?" I asked faux-innocently.

"Not just any apron, a Santa apron! Won't he look adorable?"

"So... he's staying?"

She folded the ruddy face of Santa in half. "I mentioned that if he wanted to stay to help out, then that was really considerate of him. And that you were totally serious when you asked him."

"And?" I prompted.

"And what?"

"Did he say yes?"

"He did."

I let out a whoop.

"Have you talked about your relationship?"

She wrapped the apron in green foil. "We have."

It was like talking to a rock. "And…"

"And I've agreed to meet his parents, later."

I wanted to jump up and clap for her, but she was still so skittish about the whole thing. "And what about everything else?"

Her hands fell to her lap. "We've come to a deadlock. And, like you advised, we'll take it one day at a time. Cruz says he's happy to forgo his dreams of having kids. But I'm still not convinced he won't hate me for it later. So we've agreed to discuss the issue again in six months' time. If anything changes, if his desire to be a dad grows, then we'll have to address it all again. I don't want him to spend his life regretting the choice, but as long as we discuss it, and are totally open with our feelings, then I'm happy."

"I think that's a smart move." What else could they do? She was willing to break her own heart by letting him go so he could find the type of woman who wanted to have a family, but he only wanted her, and was willing to forgo his own desires. She couldn't have a baby just because it was expected in some circles, if she really didn't feel that was her path. I was glad they'd come to some sort of compromise in the meantime. And really, no one knew what the future held.

Micah's rust bucket of a car spluttered and belched its way nosily down the driveway, alerting me to their presence, and we all headed to the front door. Nerves fluttered at the thought of seeing Kai again, but I tamped them right back down.

Still, my breathing quickened when I caught sight of him unfolding his long, lean body out of the small hatchback. Micah said something I didn't catch, and Kai threw his head back and laughed, exposing his straight, shiny white teeth. As far as teeth went they were pretty spectacular, if you were into things like that. Which I wasn't. Just being observant.

Then there was his hair – too-long, surfer-style, wavy, a blond that made his tan more prominent. Where he got a tan in winter was beyond me, but while it had faded at Cedarwood it had never disappeared entirely. And maybe it was all the yoga, but he moved differently to most men; he sort of drifted forward.

"You absolute stalker," Amory whispered in my ear, making me jump in fright.

"I am *not*…"

She grinned and her face was transformed back into that of my beautiful, vivacious friend. "Listen," she said, lowering her voice, "why don't you stop pretending? You're the biggest advocate for love, yet you spend your life waiting for it to happen to you when really you should be a big girl and help it along…"

I opened and closed my mouth like a fish out of water. "I'll happily help it along if I find the right man."

She leaned so close I could see her pupils dilate. "Kai is pretty perfect. But you're never going to find out with your nose pressed against the window."

"Good advice." My voice was heavy with sarcasm. "Why would I hook up with someone who's working in another part of the country? That has disaster written all over it in big, fat, capital letters."

"Yet you offer to employ Cruz just like that. Kai could easily work here, and we *are* advertising for staff. You need a project manager for the chalets. Just saying…" She held up her hands when I went to protest.

"And…" she said, and I knew she had something up her sleeve. She flounced past me and sat on the desk. "Didn't you give Micah this exact kind of advice when Isla was going to leave Cedarwood? And now look… they've found a solution. I'm sure you can."

I sighed. "That's all well and good for them, Amory, but there is one little problem. They both liked each other. Kai and I are not like that. We're friends."

"Sure you are!" She rolled her eyes. "And what about that other guy? He was keen for a date and you've done absolutely zero about it. You accuse me of being scared, but I think *you're* the one who's scared..."

I frowned. "Timothy? You know, Amory, I was once so madly in love with Timothy, the sound of his name would provoke hazy-eyed rapture. But he's carrying more baggage than Louis Vuitton himself, though he tries to hide that behind that saucy smile of his. He's really on the rebound, if you ask me. The split from his wife is pretty recent, and I kind of can't forget he married her about two seconds after I left town."

"Ancient history, everyone changes. And you can cry busy your entire life and end up alone. When anyone mentions Kai, however, your eyes light up like that Rudolf figurine over there."

I really *was* busy! And while Timothy had made it clear he was interested, I still wasn't sure. In my heart of hearts, I was hoping things would change with Kai, but would I be brave enough to say anything? Probably not, because the moment we'd shared hadn't come up between us. It must have been that forgettable. At my age, when everyone was scrambling for love, commitment, their version of happy ever after, shouldn't I be acting more proactively about my future? It was easier to dither along, and hope the sun would shine one day soon and make it blindingly obvious.

I hesitated, Amory reading my facial expressions as well as if they were her own. "Start with hello." She grabbed my shoulders and marched me to the door.

When Kai caught sight of me, he gave me a slow smile that lit up the bright blue of his eyes. It was enough to make my heart pound. Really, I was a bundle of nerves. "Clio..." He held out a hand.

Behind me Amory hissed, "Ughay imhay!"

I turned and shushed her, whispering, "Pig Latin, Amory, really? Am I a child?"

She giggled. "Sometimes. Hug-the-damn-man!"

I blanked my face and trudged over, grabbing his outstretched hand, and pulling him in for a hug. *Happy now, Amory?* I was so focused on shutting her up that it took a moment to realize I was lost in the comfort of his arms – too long, I stood there, possibly murmuring to myself. He smelled so good, like hopes and dreams, and... *Get a hold of yourself!*

I extricated myself, apologizing profusely.

I glanced at Amory and she rolled her eyes again before reaching past me to shake Kai's hand.

"Hi, Kai, so great to meet you properly at last. I hope you got in OK." She smiled and then turned to Micah. "Sorry to bug you as soon as you're back, Micah, but can I get a hand for a minute? I need some help moving one of the tables into the salon..." She didn't make eye contact with me, the little minx. There was zero need to move any table, and she knew that full well.

"Sure," Micah said affably. "Chat later, Kai." They shook hands and Micah jogged up the porch, to move a table that didn't need moving.

We stood awkwardly, our eyes cast to the snow-covered ground. Words suddenly escaped me. How ridiculous, acting like a dumbstruck teenager at thirty-three years of age. It's not like we'd even seen each other naked, or had anything to be shy about. So, we'd locked lips. Big deal! I stared him full in the face, forcing myself not to look away, proving I could be the mature adult I was. I did my best *I'm totally together* impression and hoped he'd read my true feelings.

"Are you OK, Clio?" he frowned, concern clouding his eyes.

"Yes, why?"

"You haven't blinked once."

My lips twitched with laughter. Maybe my totally together impression needed a little work.

He gave me a bemused smile, or at least I think it was bemused – he might have been searching for an escape route. I certainly was.

"Shall we go inside?" He wiped a thick layer of snow from my shoulder. God, the poor Australian in him was probably freezing to death.

"Yes, let's get you warmed up by the fire. Get those wet clothes off you."

This time he really laughed, a full-bellied sort and said, "Have you been drinking?"

"No, why?" *Scatterbrained fool!*

"Nothing, let's go inside. I can dust off my coat on the edge of the porch."

Oh, he thought I'd meant get all of his clothes off! *Did he?* I wanted to die.

"Yes, of course."

I led him inside, and he hung his jacket on the coat rack in the mudroom, before joining me in the front parlor. "Wow, Clio, look at this place now." When he'd left, the lodge had been finished but not fully furnished, and most of our décor had still been in transit. He hadn't seen any of the completed rooms except the ballroom, which we'd done for Imelda and Edgar's party.

"Wait until you see the chapel. It's glorious. The pews are all set up and the pulpit – with the stained-glass windows funneling in light and the fire glowing in the grate – it's one of the prettiest spaces I've ever seen."

Whenever we discussed the lodge, Kai's face changed, like he'd found a pot of gold. He was always interested to know every little detail, when most people's eyes would have glazed over by then. I think it was a mixture of rapture about the expansive grounds, the beauty of nature, and the idea of providing accommodation in such a place, with old-school activities and lots of adventure. And let's not forget the mountain range he virtually ran up. For fun.

"You're amazing, Clio. To have so much happening. It's only been a month or so since the lodge got a makeover and already you've held an expo and locked in some guests and weddings."

Had Kai worried that no one would visit? Evergreen wasn't like other New Hampshire towns with big populations and tourist attractions galore. Unless you were a nature lover and happy to find your way around unmarked tracks, there wasn't much more to do in Evergreen. But that was kind of a joy in itself. It wasn't full to bursting with people, and when you went for a hike seeking solitude, you soon found it.

"It's not just me, Kai. I've had so much help from so many people. And now I have Amory here – the dream team, she calls us."

"A force to be reckoned with." He grinned.

"If you're getting married…" I stopped short. "Not you, but…" *Kill me.*

"Speaking of which, we'd better go over to see Ned. May as well see what can be done."

"Let me get the paperwork."

My head was suddenly clear. We needed this to go without a hitch so I could assure our brides the chapel was ready for their weddings. We needed their deposits too, to go forward with the renovations on the chalets, giving us another income stream for spring when the holiday season would truly begin.

After two hours of back and forth with Ned, me biting my tongue to prevent me speaking out of turn, and Kai keeping his cool and patiently explaining each improvement down to the type of nuts and bolts that were used, Ned agreed to approve the chapel at Cedarwood pending a visit to inspect the structure properly, before the year was out. We had a February wedding to organize, so it had to be done as soon as possible in case Ned found any problems and we needed to fix them. It was a weight off my mind, but I wouldn't fully relax until he put pen to paper and signed the document.

As we drove sedately back to Cedarwood, the silence weighed a little heavier. It was like we were tongue-tied and I missed our usual affable chats about every little thing.

Kai must have sensed my unease and finally said, "What are you thinking about? You're doing that squinty, hunchy thing of yours again, like you can't see."

"What squinty hunchy thing?"

He squinted and hunched over, letting the steering wheel go and hugging himself tight. "Like that. You always do that same thing when you're worried."

I peeked down at my body and found he was right. The Hunchback of Notre Dame had nothing on me. "Talk about bad posture, oh upright one."

His shiny white teeth shone under the soft sunlight, and he let the teasing go unchecked. "When we did yoga you stopped hugging yourself tight like that. Stopped folding yourself in knots."

"But you left." I attempted a smile. "My yogi."

He bit his lip, and turned away. "I wanted to stay."

The air thickened with unsaid words.

"Did you, though? You left so early after Imelda and Edgar's party…"

He stared straight ahead, gray clouds drifting toward us in an angry jumble. We were going to get stuck in the car, sheltering from the coming storm, if we didn't get home soon. I held my tongue, though. I wanted an answer.

"I was two weeks late for that job and my boss wasn't happy about it. I had to go." His voice had an air of anguish to it, and I thought something had changed with Kai. Something had stolen the light from his eyes. Was it his boss? There was a bitterness to Kai that was out of character when he spoke of his time away.

"What's going on, Kai? You don't seem like the same guy who left Cedarwood."

He smiled, but it was more like a grimace. "I'm not. I don't think I'll ever be the same."

By the set of his jaw, I knew to leave it alone, that whatever it was would come out soon enough. Kai harped on about how holding toxic emotions inside damaged a person, but I sensed he needed time to mull over whatever it was.

246

"I'm glad you're back, even if it's only for a little while."

With his hands on the wheel, he said, "Me too, I love it here."

***

At the lodge, Kai stood behind me, shrugging out of his coat. Voices carried down the stairwell. I stopped, straining to hear. It was Amory and Cruz, having a heart-to-heart by the sound of it.

"I'm sorry I've kept you at arm's length all this time. It was just easier if we were going to break up, to protect myself, my heart," Amory's voice carried down the stairs.

"Promise me you'll always say how you're feeling? Don't run away, don't hide it. The thought of losing you…"

It was such a happy thing to witness – two people so in love they were willing to forget their own dreams for each other. Not wanting to intrude, I tapped Kai's arm and pointed outside, and we crept away to let them chat in private.

We went to the chalets by the lake. I watched him for a beat, and it was as obvious as his shadow that something plagued him. He was quieter than normal and something inside me wanted to make it better, or at least show him I cared. When I'd been twisted and coiled tight like a snake, Kai had recognized it in me, and helped me, in myriad ways, by his cuckoo breathing techniques and enforced exercise, but mostly by listening, and not shrugging off my concerns. Sure, at the time he'd been my employee, but it went beyond that. And I wanted to reciprocate.

"Hey," I said, "do you want to head into town, and have a drink?" It tugged at my heart the way his whole demeanor had changed, like he carried the weight of the world on his shoulders.

"Sure," he said.

Twenty minutes later we arrived at the Shakin' Shack, and took a seat at a softly lit booth at the back. I ordered

247

us two beers, thinking alcohol just might loosen his tongue and get him to open up to me.

We made small talk for an hour before I figured out how to broach it with him.

"Remember when you said you were searching for something, a feeling, a place you belong...? Did something happen to prompt that?"

He nodded, a faint smile touching his lips. "That sounded a little too mystical, right?" He shook his head as if he was embarrassed he'd shared the idea with me. "Have you ever felt so lost you just don't know where you fit any more?"

I smiled and tried to find the right words, "Most of my life I felt that way, growing up with a mother who was there, only in body but not in spirit. The thing is, I know now that I can't change her. I can help, I can be there, but I can't change the way she thinks, the way she acts. I can only hope being around will help."

We hadn't talked about my mom, or her issues, but I'm sure he'd heard about it through the grapevine. It was a small town, after all, and word had got around that my mom had arrived at Cedarwood and stayed barely an hour, vowing never to return.

"What is it with parents?" Hurt crossed his face. "Before I left Australia, I found out I was adopted. Imagine, at the grand old age of thirty-one, your parents suddenly announce they're not your parents."

Shock rendered me mute. I couldn't imagine being told such a thing. Surreptitiously, I surveyed Kai, pain etched firmly on his face. Silence engulfed us. I was hesitant to say the wrong thing. In all the time he'd stayed at Cedarwood, he hadn't alluded to any problems back home, and I wondered if that had cost him, keeping it bottled up, and now it was finally spilling out. What had changed to bring it back to the fore now?

I'd pegged Kai for some kind of nomad, a drifter searching for adventure, but really he had been running from his past, from a secret. It reminded me of my mom and the baby in the black-and-white photographs. There was a momentary flash of anger toward these people, our parents, whether biological or not, keeping things from us – in Kai's case, something so major that it had caused him to flee.

"Why did they suddenly tell you now?"

Kai's face darkened. "My father had a close call in a car accident. He was fine but it scared him and I guess he wanted to right his wrongs. He called me over and they sat me down and blurted it out. It was tough, knowing my life was essentially built on a lie, but deep down I could sort of understand it. I mean, you hear these kinds of stories all the time."

I weighed up what to say that wouldn't sound like platitudes. "Do you know who your biological parents are?"

"That's the thing. I just packed up and left. Thought I'd worry about all of that later, come to terms with it first, see a bit of the world, and make sense of who I am now that I'm not Kai Davis, not really. Unbeknownst to me, my father did some investigating and phoned me last week to tell me my biological parents died, *years* ago. Substance-abuse issues… So now I don't even get to make the decision about whether I want to meet them. It's another choice taken out of my hands and I feel cheated. Like I'm adrift…"

For all his easy-going calm, Kai had been hiding his own pain. That's the thing about pain – it rises to the surface eventually and you have to deal with it. He'd obviously tried to forget, to keep busy, to run from it, but it caught up with him.

"I guess they did what they thought was best at the time, even though it doesn't make it right. I can't imagine any parent wanting to hurt their child, no matter how old he grew."

"Yeah, I would be able to see that if it was anyone else's story, but because it's mine and I'm living it… Sometimes their audacity takes my breath away. They should have told me. I should have got to meet my biological parents, or at least had the choice."

What if my mom had a secret like this? The child in the pictures... how would I feel? Probably the same way Kai did. I shuddered at the thought and once again weighed up whether some secrets should stay buried.

We sat in silence, pondering it all.

"I'm glad you told me, Kai."

He wouldn't meet my gaze. "Saying it out loud makes it real, you know? For some reason I feel like a failure, like I wasn't good enough to hold on to. I know it's stupid, but that's how I feel, and I can't shake it. Sorry, what a downer I am. But that's sort of where I'm at. I don't know what to do, whether to go home, or what..."

I gave his hand a squeeze.

He stared into my eyes, and my heart just about tore in two.

***

Back at the lodge, Kai headed out, so I told Amory I was going upstairs to do some paperwork, and took my laptop into my room. The phone rang just as I puffed my way up the stairs. I dashed to answer the extension next to my bed.

"Cedarwood Lodge, Clio speaking."

"You went through my things, Clio?"

I gulped. *How did she know?* "No, Mom, I would never do that. I was trying to fix the coffee machine."

"You saw the photographs." Her voice was heavy with sadness.

Did I put them back in the wrong drawer? Mom's fastidiousness was likely to blame.

"I honestly wasn't searching for them, truly Mom." This would set us back, I just knew it. My toes curled just thinking of the progress we'd made which would now be lost.

"Why won't you leave it alone? It's like you're obsessed with dredging up the past."

I sighed. "I was simply looking for the instruction booklet. The album was underneath."

"And your library visit?"

Damn it.

"Mom, how would you feel being me? I just know this mystery, this secret, is the key to us being a real mother and daughter. You can't pretend you've been there for me. I've never asked anything of you, but I'm asking you now: what happened at Cedarwood that stops you visiting?"

"Clio, Jesus. You just don't get it. I ruined their lives. Their family, their business. All of it. As surely as if I pulled the pin on a grenade, it exploded in an instant."

"I'm sure it wasn't your fault, whatever it was."

"It was, Clio. It was all my fault."

"Well…" Words vanished. What could I say without knowing what she meant?

"I tried this with your father, confiding in him, loving him, and then I lost him too. And now you're back at that place, and it feels like a punishment I deserve. Like God is reminding me of what I've done and what I have to live with."

"What did you do?"

There was a silence and then her voice came back distraught. "Something horrible that I'll live with until the day I die. And you just won't let it go. I'm asking you to forget it, please."

"Would you? If this was reversed?"

She sighed. "I don't know any more, Clio."

"Why don't you visit? Take me to the maze, explain what happened."

"I just don't understand why you don't listen, Clio." With that she hung up, but not before I heard a gut-wrenching sob.

Chapter Twenty-Six

I crept downstairs and made coffee and searched the fridge for the leftover donuts I knew were hidden somewhere in its depths. It wasn't long before Amory joined me, our early-morning coffee and chat being a routine as regular as sunrise, and a time we could confide in each other with no one to overhear. In her loved-up haze, it seemed depressing to bring up my mom and our phone call. I didn't want to say anything that would dim the light in Amory's eyes.

She sat down, grinning. "Coffee, stat."

I shoved her. "Here's your special new mug, Lady Amory." We'd found Santa mugs at the thrift store in town. Some poor fool had donated a box of them, and we couldn't believe our luck. Big, fat, red mugs with *Jingle Bells, Batman Smells* written on them. Kitschy but oh so cool.

She inhaled the coffee the way she did every morning. I gave her a few minutes to let the caffeine work its way around her body before probing. "What is that?" I said, making a show of sniffing. "Oh, I think love is in the air..."

"Oh my God."

I laughed. "So?"

"So... Well, I guess it is. I hope you really meant it, about us both staying on? It's a little like an orphanage here, all these lost souls gathering." I froze for a moment, thinking of Kai. And of my mom and the mysterious baby.

"I meant every word," I said, seriously. They didn't realize how much I needed them too.

"Cruz is keen to move to Evergreen to be with me and start a new life here as a chef."

"God, what a horrible guy."

She rolled her eyes. "Right? We thought we'd stay at the lodge over Christmas and then find a cottage in town in the New Year."

"But we have so many rooms here. You could move into one of the chalets?"

"Thank you, darling. But I think it would be asking too much of you. We'll hang out just like normal, but if we have our own cottage, at least I can be as messy as I like without facing the wrath of Mom – I mean, *you*."

We giggled, knowing it was true.

"But seriously, I don't want to get under your feet. The cottage will be a nice little sanctuary for us."

"So you're really moving in together?" For someone so adamant about not following the traditional path, she'd surely changed her tune. I was certain it was the magic of the lodge – the open spaces, the way time moved slowly here – that allowed people to think and ruminate about what their heart really wanted.

"Yep, I'm taking one giant leap, and seeing if the man still loves me when he trips over a mountain of clothes."

I switched on the radio and Christmas carols filled the room. "I got an enquiry about a New Year's Eve party. You'll never guess who."

"Who?"

"Timothy. The realtor he works for wants to throw a party."

"Your old flame?"

I laughed. "Glowing coals at best."

"We'll dance until midnight if we can keep you old fogies up long enough."

I laughed. With the early mornings and fresh air, I was usually in bed by ten. No longer having to hover at clients' parties until dawn, then head into work full of caffeine and promises... Life at the lodge suited the new me.

Pots and pans clanged in the kitchen and the delicious scent of roasting turkey wafted down the hallway. Cruz was a damn fine cook, and I was thrilled he'd agreed to work at Cedarwood. He and Amory were making goggle-eyes at each other, like they'd only just fallen in love, and I had to hide a smile each time I walked past the lovebirds embracing. Who knew what their future held, what any of ours held, but they were focusing on the fact they loved one another, and that was enough for now. Between them, and Isla and Micah, I felt conspicuously single.

The dining table was dressed in a gold tablecloth, adorned with glittery Christmas baubles. I polished the champagne flutes once more, admiring the perfect placement of cutlery and the poinsettia taking centerstage in the middle of the table. Flutes polished to a shine, I placed bonbons to the right of each place setting and silver napkins to the left.

Christmas carols played chirpily overhead and I tried hard not to let sentimentality take over. It had been a tumultuous year, and yet I'd come so far, surrounded by friends and family who'd also had their lives shaken up and were trying to come out the other side.

In the corner, the Christmas tree blinked merrily, and underneath was a veritable treasure trove of presents waiting to be opened. Even though it was Christmas Eve, we'd decided to exchange presents tonight. No doubt the couples would exchange their own presents the next day, but tonight it was all about what we'd bought for our friends...

Kai walked in, carrying bottles of chilled champagne, and a gift under one arm. He stowed the champagne in the ice buckets and hopped from foot to foot and wouldn't meet my gaze. "You can put the gift under the tree, Kai."

He cleared his throat. "Actually, I wanted to give it to you now." He handed it me, and I noted with a smile the delicate antique ribbon and superfine wrapping paper. It was almost criminal to open it.

"You didn't have to get me a present." Surprise colored my voice.

He shrugged, and gave me a loose hug. "Merry Christmas, Clio."

"Merry Christmas!" I slowly unwrapped the gift, letting out a gasp when I saw it. "How did you find this?"

"A lot of digging," he said. "Do you like it?"

It was a sketch of Cedarwood from its heyday. It was exquisite, the pencil strokes a touch blurred with age, the paper browned at the edges, but framed in a gorgeous antique frame that would protect it for the next fifty years.

"Kai, I can't believe this, it's the most beautiful thing I've ever seen. Look at the lodge!"

I peered closely to make out every minuscule detail. Nothing had changed, from the gable on the roof right down to the balustrades on the porch. It was all the same as now, except the windows were bracketed by heavy brocade curtains, and now we had sheer window treatments. And on the porch was a rocking horse, fit for a small child... Again I had that sense I was being watched, that someone stood just behind me. My skin prickled.

Before I could ponder it any more, Amory click-clacked her way into the room and said, "You're exchanging presents? Oh, Clio, that is utterly divine! Mine are under the tree in the salon – I'll be right back. But we're not opening them until after dinner, because yours might involve a drinking game..." She clapped a hand to her mouth. "Forget I said that."

Micah wandered in wearing a fuchsia-pink Christmas hat. "She made me," he said, laughing. Isla wore the same but in green. "And we've got our ugliest Christmas sweaters on, in honor of our first Christmas at Cedarwood."

They *were* ugly. Matching sweaters with a reindeer flashing uneven, eggshell-colored teeth – more like a bad-tempered donkey braying. Still, Christmas just wasn't

Christmas without an ugly sweater. "Delightfully ugly," I laughed.

Cruz put a plate of cheeses, green olives, and rosy-red cherry tomatoes on the table, all lined up in the shape of a Christmas tree. "Cute!" I said, loving that he was so festive with his food.

"Wait," he said. "I also made something else."

He came back a few minutes later carrying the most exquisite gingerbread house. It had candy-cane pillars, and a white-iced snowy roof; the windows were open and inside sat teddy bear biscuits, warming themselves near an open marshmallow fire. Trees were made from tempered chocolate and dusted white with icing sugar. Green candyfloss made up a Christmas tree decorated with star-shaped candy. "Wow, Cruz, did you make this from scratch?" The spicy scent of ginger permeated the air.

"Amory helped," he said.

We burst out laughing, knowing she would have hindered more than helped, just as I would have. Our skills were not culinary, that was for sure. But still, my mind spun with ideas for the future: cooking classes he could do with our guests, and perhaps even a little giftshop of our own where we sold handmade biscuits and treats like these.

Micah added a log to the fire, sending little bursts of fireworks up the flue.

While we munched on the nibbles Cruz had made, I drifted away, thinking of Mom and Aunt Bessie. My aunt had politely refused my invitation for Christmas Eve dinner – insisting us 'young people' spend it together, because we were having a gathering at hers tomorrow.

We went to take our places at the table, but not before I saw Kai standing innocently under the mistletoe. In the spirit of Christmas I pushed my chair back and dashed over to him, landing a big, loud kiss on his cheek. His eyes widened, and I pointed up. "Just following tradition," I said.

Amory winked at me. "Yeah, and she put mistletoe under every doorway just in case."

I laughed. "You're just jealous I didn't kiss you."

"Yes," she said. "I am. There's always next year."

"Shall we toast?" I asked, grabbing my champagne flute from the table, bubbles dancing like stars. My friends gathered around, each wearing a wide smile, relaxed and happy right here at Cedarwood Lodge. "Thank you for all of your help at Cedarwood. Without you I'd be a bumbling, incoherent mess. Here's to love, laughter, and good friends."

We clinked glasses, everyone letting out a cheer. Outside, night fell, and snow blanketed the ground.

Amory said, "Hear, hear. And on behalf of all of us, I'd like to say, you would never be a bumbling, incoherent mess, because that's just not your style, but we appreciate you taking us into your home and your heart this Christmas, and we look forward to making next year huge for Cedarwood. It's going to be amazing, and we're lucky to be part of it."

Over dinner, we laughed so much we cried, eating too much turkey and crispy roast potatoes. Cruz had gone all out on dinner, with all the trimmings... from honey-glazed ham to fragrant pecan and cranberry stuffing, and freshly baked bread rolls. We practically rolled out of the room, and groaned when he wandered in with a chocolate Yule log big enough to feed a small army.

"Maybe we should have a little break?" he said, taking in our satiated faces, and the way we rubbed our too-full bellies.

"Let's go sit in front of the TV," Amory said. "The Times Square Christmas carols are on, and I don't care what anyone says, I love watching them." Cruz raised a brow but took Amory's hand and led her down to the theater room.

Isla pulled Micah by the elbow. "Come with me? I want you to help me with something," she said mysteriously.

That left me and Kai, staring at each other over the table.

"Let's get some fresh air?" Kai said, pointing to the deck outside. I grabbed his gift from under the tree.

Stars glittered in the inky night, and the moonlight winked as if urging me on. It was déjà vu, but I wanted one minute alone with him before we were around other people for the duration of the night.

I handed him his gift, and held my breath.

He opened the gift box and took out the small album. Inside it were pictures of his time at Cedarwood, candid snaps when he wasn't aware I was there – iPhone at the ready. There were pictures of the team he'd led, arms wrapped around each other, big, goofy grins in place, and Kai in the foreground, eyes luminous, sparkling with the joy he'd found here. There were before and after photos of the lodge, and the improvements he'd suggested were right there in Technicolor. In the middle of the album I'd placed a handwritten note:

You said this place is magical, and I think you're right. There are so many adventures to be had here, and so much time in which to have them. You might feel adrift in the world right now, but we'll always be here for you, me and Cedarwood Lodge. If you need a place to get lost, a mountain to climb, a friend to talk to, a lake to swim in so all you hear is the tumble of water and not the heavy thoughts that are holding you down, then you know where to come. As you can see by the photographs, you belong here, like the trees, the mountains, and the rain. Always know that when you leave, we'll be counting down the days until we can welcome you back, home.

He worked his jaw as he read the message. Was it too much, too whimsical? I wanted Kai to have a tangible record of his time here, and photographic proof of the great work he'd done. It wasn't just your average renovation. It was restoring the past, and living for the present.

"Do you really mean that, Clio?"

"Every word."

He nodded and flicked through the album, smiling when he came to a picture of us toasting marshmallows, pulling silly faces. And then again when Micah was doing bunny ears behind his head as Kai surveyed building plans, resolute expression in place.

The last photo was my favorite. It had been taken by Micah when I was oblivious and was of me and Kai, sitting by the lake, bundled in blankets. Our faces were only inches apart…as if we might be about to kiss.

"Clio, I…" He stopped, his eyes ablaze, with what I wasn't sure. He lifted my chin with a finger and kissed me gently. I leaned into him, and kissed him back. It remained unsaid, but I knew Kai, and I knew what he was thinking. It wasn't the right time for us, was it? He was hurt, conflicted about his life, and starting a romance now was a bad idea. Until he'd made peace with his past… This was a kiss goodbye.

The Christmas tree blinked and shone, the lights radiating outwards, coloring the snow. Kai took me in his arms, and held me tight. I wished I could pause time and stay that way for ever.

In the distance, Micah and Isla ran back from the lake, their boots sinking into the snow, their faces red with cold.

"There's a maze!" shouted Micah as they ran to catch up with us. "It's hard to find, and it's overgrown, but it's definitely a hedge maze! How do you think we never found that before, Clio, on all our jaunts as children?"

I had the sensation that I was falling, dizzy and breathless all at once. Now Mom couldn't avoid it; the maze had been found. But I had the overwhelming sense I would lose her if I didn't handle it right. Micah noticed my stricken face, "Clio, are you OK?"

I'd have to be. I'd have to get this sorted out once and for all. "Fine, fine. Just a little cold." Again, I had the oddest sensation someone was standing behind me, but when I looked no one was there. Goose bumps prickled my skin, and Mom's face flashed in my mind, her teenage smile, and her bright eyes as she clutched the little girl's hand. What was the very worst thing that could have happened? Did she have a child out of wedlock? Did the child die? Or was she adopted out?

Tomorrow I'd be at Aunt Bessie's for Christmas Day, and my family and friends would celebrate Christmas lunch together. There'd be no time to quiz Mom alone, but maybe I could make her see how much we all loved Cedarwood, how we were making it great again, and whatever bad memories the place held for her, this was a new era, a new time, and I wanted her to be part of it. The only way forward was going back and saying goodbye to the past.

"Shall we fix the maze?' Isla's face was lit up.

"Strictly no work talk over Christmas!" I said, trying to sound upbeat. "Let's head inside before we freeze, and demolish that Yule log."

Kai and I exchanged a glance as we all trooped back inside, and my heart thumped in my chest, knowing I was saying goodbye to him soon too, maybe for good. If it was meant to be, it would be... Didn't I say true love would always find a way?

Chapter Twenty-Seven

The golden vocals of Frank Sinatra singing 'Have Yourself a Merry Little Christmas' drifted upstairs to greet me. Feeling decidedly festive, I wrenched the bedcovers back and raced to the bay window. Outside, the frosty ground was blanketed by snow and the mountains in the distance slumbered under dense white. If you squinted, you could make out tracks in the snow from Santa's reindeers. OK, maybe not, but a girl could dream...

From downstairs came the rattle of cups, the shrieking of the kettle – Cruz was up and about and, from the scents wafting my way, baking something Christmassy.

Not wanting to miss a thing, I pulled on my thick robe and went to investigate. Taking the stairs two at a time, I practically bounced into the warmth of the kitchen. Cruz had brewed a pot of gingerbread coffee and handed me a cup. The spicy ginger scent was synonymous with Christmas and gave me the desire to eat my bodyweight in baked goods – from gingerbread families to reindeer cookies, and as many of Aunt Bessie's donuts as I could carry in two hands. After all, New Year's resolutions were made for a reason, right?

"Thanks, and Merry Christmas, Cruz!"

"Merry Christmas, Clio. Nice PJs." He raised a sardonic brow.

Staring down at my ensemble I couldn't help but smirk. Isla and Micah had gifted us all kitschy Christmas-themed gifts. My pajamas were festooned with grinning red-nosed reindeers and merry mistletoe; the material was so vividly red they were blink-inducing. Let's just say you wouldn't have missed me even if you were in the next town over. My dressing gown covered most of the garishness but not quite enough apparently.

"Right?" I laughed.

A moment later, in walked Amory, wearing *her* gift from Isla and Micah. Flashing candy-cane earrings and a matching headband.

"Aww you look so... Christmassy." I grinned. I hadn't seen Amory embrace the holidays with quite so much flamboyance so early in the morning before.

"Coffee."

We laughed at Amory's usual one-word dawn greeting, her Grinch-like tone a total opposite to her flashing festive accessories. Even on Christmas morning she was unable to communicate until caffeine was pumping through her veins. I poured her a gingerbread coffee and she gulped it down, then held the cup out for another, which she sipped a little more *gingerly*.

I gave her the prerequisite three minutes to let it work its magic before saying: "Did you hear the sleigh bells last night?"

She rolled her eyes dramatically. "Is that some kind of euphemism? Because if you want to know about my sex life, all you need to do is ask."

A shocked giggle escaped me. "Amory!" Cruz turned away and did his best to appear busy, though I could see his shoulders shake with silent laughter.

"What? Isn't that what you meant?" She grinned, evil minx that she was.

"No, it isn't! I meant *actual* sleigh bells! I think someone in town must have been marching around as Santa last night. Maybe we missed a Christmas parade or something."

"Oh, my bad." Her face was the picture of innocence but it was hard to concentrate when she had all manner of kitschy Christmas jewelry flashing from her head. "Of course something like that would be happening in a town like Evergreen, darling! There seems to be a festival for everything here."

I smiled as I took a sip of coffee. Amory was right, Evergreen prided itself on having an event for every season. I'd missed the autumn food festival, but the switching on of the town lights and the ginormous Christmas tree had been truly spectacular. And before long, the spring flower festival would be here.

"And I see you're wearing *your* gift," Amory said, motioning to Cruz.

On top of Cruz's head was a novelty chef's hat announcing, *No soggy bottoms this Christmas!*

He grimaced. "Well, I figure I have three hundred and sixty-four days that I *don't* have to wear it. And I only whipped it on when I heard footsteps and thought it might be Isla checking up on me." With a grin, he pulled it off and threw it on the bench.

"Oh no, here comes Isla now!" Amory hissed. I darted a glance over my shoulder, sure Isla and Micah were elsewhere. They'd left in the early hours of this morning, after our Christmas Eve celebrations finally came to a close, in order to make it to Micah's family for Christmas.

Cruz's eyes widened and he fumbled and cursed as he stuffed it back on.

"Just joking! Isla and Micah aren't coming for breakfast today."

He narrowed his eyes and clutched at his heart. "You're evil. *Pure* evil."

Amory laughed. "But you make it so easy!"

Cruz was the epitome of politeness and it was almost impossible for us not to play practical jokes or tease him mercilessly. He took it in good humor, and it made the busy days a little more fun.

"And," I said, "Isla has spies. She'll know if you're not wearing your hat."

Shaking his head, he donned the offending item, and said with a smile, "It's a lovely hat. *The best.*"

"You're a lucky man." Amory stood to kiss him, and I felt a moment of pure joy for my friends.

"You should see what Isla got for Micah's parents. Bright-Kermit-green *Christmas onesies.* With matching slippers. They'll certainly be warm, if nothing else." Amory giggled.

I blamed Henrietta from the giftshop in town for encouraging Isla; still, when we'd given out presents the night before, our laughter had turned into a full-fledged cackle-fest as the gifts got sillier by the moment. When she produced a talking elf you could teach to speak, the night had disintegrated into chaos with everyone wanting to take a turn, teaching the innocent elf some not-so-innocent phrases.

It had been an endless evening of laughter until Micah had presented Isla with her very own real-life constellation that he'd named after her; we'd let out a collective *aww*, and the night had ended on a sweet note with everyone loved-up, and me dreaming of being loved-up...

Speaking of loved-up. "Where's Kai?" I knew full well that man did not sleep in, rain, hail, shine, or snow.

"Trudging up the mountain," Cruz said as he flipped pancakes. "He invited me but, tempting as it was, I couldn't let you girls wake up Christmas morning without a decent breakfast and gingerbread coffee now, could I?"

"Riiiiight," I said. "Sure, you couldn't."

He ducked his head and laughed. "I'm all for exercise, but not in a blizzard. Still, he should be back soon, he left ages ago."

I tutted, glancing out the window at the snowflakes seesawing down. The scene was Christmas-card perfect when you were warm beside a fire *inside*. Battling the elements outside was another thing entirely.

"I'll stoke the potbelly stove so he can defrost when he gets back, crazy fool that he is." I'd never known anyone like

Kai. There was something in nature that pulled at him, like he needed time each day to be alone, somewhere he could hear himself think. I couldn't believe he'd soon be heading back to San Fran. Cedarwood didn't feel quite right when he was gone.

Fairy lights blinked intermittently from window frames, brightening the somber skies. Cruz busied himself folding fresh berries into sheets of puff pastry, and Amory drank gingerbread coffee like her life depended on it.

In the silence I thought of my mom, and how she'd react when she found out Isla had discovered the maze last night. In my heart of hearts, I knew I couldn't bring it up today. She would shut down and it had the potential to ruin Christmas. Mom was a sensitive soul at the best of times and the idea of telling her made my stomach somersault. How would she react? I had no idea how to broach it with her.

"What are you making?" I asked as a pan sizzled, glad for the distraction. Cruz didn't just cook for the sake of cooking, he went all out, even though it was just the four of us eating Christmas breakfast. All good practice, he claimed, because he was rusty after having worked in finance for the last ten years, and wanted to get his skills sharpened before guests started arriving at the lodge in the New Year and ahead of the events we had booked.

"It's a *berry* nice Christmas tree. There'll be a star at this end," he said, indicating the top of an intricately folded pastry shaped like a tree, "and I'll serve it with lashings of Chantilly cream, and raspberry compote."

"I *might* have to walk up the mountain after eating that, to make room for lunch at Aunt Bessie's as well. I can see today is going to be mostly about gorging, and I am totally OK with that."

"Me too," Amory said, lifting her coffee mug in agreement. "After all, it's Christmas and it would be offensive not to. What time are we expected at Aunt Bessie's?"

"Any time before lunch. I was going to leave after breakfast and help her out..." I ignored Amory's snigger at the idea of me attempting to help cook. "...And you guys can make your way there whenever you're ready. Micah and Isla are spending the day with his family, but they might pop over late afternoon if they get time."

"And Kai?" She waggled her eyebrows.

"Are you having another eyelash malfunction?" I asked innocently.

She laughed. "Touché."

"Kai can come with me, or hitch a ride with you guys. It's up to him."

With a flick of her hair, like she was considering it, she said, "Oh, we're full up, sorry. He'll have to go with you."

"Is that so?" I folded my arms and stared her down, knowing she was trying to push us together, and secretly glad about it – not that I'd let her know that! "Full up with what exactly? There's only two of you!"

"Presents." She waved her hand. "You know how it is."

Cruz deftly ignored our conversation and put the tray of berry pastry in the oven, the jammy smell of warmed fruit scenting the air.

"Well, I'm sure you can squeeze him in if he doesn't want to go so early. He might have other things to do first."

Like call his parents. In Australia it would be dinnertime on Christmas Day, and I wondered if Kai had called them yet.

Were they sitting around their Christmas dinner table with long faces, trying to be jovial for guests but failing miserably, worried their son was elsewhere in the world and hadn't made contact? I knew the whole situation was complex but Kai was too caring to let anyone suffer. Especially on such a family-oriented day. Or so I hoped.

"Darling, here he is now. Let's ask him, shall we?" Amory gestured to the window and I caught a glimpse of Kai as he jogged past, shoulders dusted white with snow.

A few minutes later, he walked into the kitchen. "Morning all," he said, rubbing his hands together for warmth. His wavy blond hair was mussed from the sheeting wind and snow, his cheeks stained pink from the crisp air. If you were into rugged, super-hot guys with a toned physique, he'd have been right up your alley.

Phwoar, he was certainly breathtaking to look at. *Smile, act normal!* The kiss from the night before replayed in my mind, and it was all I could do not to get starry-eyed and fall into a Kai daydream.

I nodded hello, not trusting myself to speak, lest I say something inane.

"Morning," Amory said, flashing him a smile. "We were just discussing the logistics of Christmas lunch. Is it OK if you head to Aunt Bessie's with Clio a little earlier than us? We've got some errands to run and don't want to hold you up."

Errands to run on Christmas Day? She was incorrigible.

Still, Kai swallowed the lie. "Sure, that'd be great." When he smiled at me I pretended to be interested in a spot out the window, so I could let the blush creeping up my cheeks settle. But boy, it was hard to know how to act, or what to say, when we kept stealing kisses and then acting like nothing had happened. With Kai's current family issues lurking in his heart, I didn't want to be another complication, and he would be leaving soon anyway. Maybe back to Australia, if they mended bridges, and did I really want to pine for someone who was that far away? It was better to protect my heart, and wait and see what happened before I plunged headfirst into anything.

When Kai grabbed a coffee and sat next to me I tried hard to look composed. The kitchen was a cozy nook, warm from the old belching potbelly stove, and full of delicious foodie scents as Cruz cooked a feast while we chatted about every little thing. The only problem was, Amory kept throwing me secret looks that any fool could see. Each time, I frowned at her and gave an almost imperceptible shake of my head. She knew Kai was leaving soon, so I don't know what she expected me to do about it. Instead, I waited patiently for the breakfast Cruz was preparing. He seemed to be whipping and baking what appeared to be enough food to feed a small country. Oh, how I loved Christmas!

"Cruz, you know there's only four of us, right?" Amory called over as he placed another tray in the oven.

"You can't call it Christmas morning if there's no monkey bread," he said, as if we were crazy for even thinking such a thing.

"Monkey bread?" Amory asked.

"You haven't had monkey bread? Please tell me you've at least tried Christmas tamales?"

She gave a quick shake of her head, her candy-cane earrings swinging and blinking merrily.

"You, my lucky lady, are about to be educated on what makes a perfect Christmas breakfast."

I wasn't sure what monkey bread was either but it certainly looked pretty damn good. A man who could cook, and better yet was actually professionally trained in the culinary arts, was a keeper. Even *un*domestic goddess Amory could see it and was coming around to our small-town ways. In Evergreen, if someone cooked you food, you damn well ate it. There was no *I'm on a diet* here. People would frown like you were insane if you so much as uttered the words *put the dressing on the side…* or *hold the butter*.

Once upon a time there'd been zero chance Amory would have sat down and consumed so many varieties of carbs – neither would I, for that matter! In New York we'd been so accustomed to following fads. So much had changed in just a few months being back home and now she was much more lax about restrictions and would end up fighting me over the last gingerbread cookie. Another positive to living out here meant we got plenty of exercise – zooming around the grounds and inside the lodge all day every day, including trudging up the stairs a million times, sure worked up an appetite; that and the abundance of fresh air, or that was my excuse anyway. Sure, it wasn't a gym on the Upper East Side, but it was a hell of a lot prettier and a lot more fun.

An hour later the table was laden with the biggest Christmas breakfast I'd ever seen. I touched my belly in apology, because there was no way I was going to be able to hold back from demolishing it all: from the monkey bread and caramel sauce to the crisp *berry nice* Christmas tree; the steaming cheese and chili tamales; and a helping of eggnog pancakes with lashings of butterscotch cream. And that's what I could see in front of me. Cruz was still stirring pots and flicking frying pans. We'd be living on leftovers for a week at this rate.

Beside me, Kai sent a look to the heavens as if he was also apologizing, then helped himself to a huge serving of the pastry tree, the bright berries as fragrant as they were pretty. With a grin, he took up a slice of monkey bread and drowned it in caramel sauce.

"Your body is your temple, hey?" Amory teased him.

I grinned. I could hardly believe it. Kai – who ran up mountains for fun, practiced yoga at midnight and waxed lyrical on the pros of fermented vegetables – had a sweet tooth? It was good to see he was a mere mortal...

He blushed. "Well, I'll be extra nice to my body tomorrow."

"And what a body it is," I said, and instantly wanted to slap my forehead. I coughed. "What I meant was..." *Yeah, Clio, what did you mean?* "...You can obviously see that you work out, and um... eat well, and that reflects in your... erm, physique." *Kill me.*

He winked, which of course provoked what I'd come to call *tremble-leggedness*, and I wondered if there was actually something wrong with me. Honestly, my brain was betraying me in the worst way. I didn't dare look at Amory, even though I could feel her gaze on me like a laser beam.

Heat crept from my toes to my nose, and I concentrated really hard on staring into the coffee in my mug. I'd have buried my head in it if I could have. It was like being a teenager all over again... Was it glaringly obvious to those around me?

It was kissing him again that had done it. My lips twitched every time I remembered, and he'd even stolen into my dreams. It was almost impossible to eat because my nerves were fluttering in my belly like the tips of butterfly wings, but I made an effort, since it was Christmas and Cruz had cooked such a feast. I couldn't possibly let any of it go to waste...

Chapter Twenty-Eight

After the gargantuan breakfast we'd put away, we were about to head off and somehow eat more. I already felt like napping, a surefire sign it was Christmas, because I was floppy with relaxation and a very full belly.

Kai and I piled the backseat of my car with gifts and bottles of wine for Mom and Aunt Bessie. The sudden need to be organized and make sure we didn't forget anything calmed my nerves. It was only a fifteen-minute drive to Aunt Bessie's, but with icy roads it would probably take twice as long to get there.

All set, we jumped in and turned the heat to high. We wove through the slushy streets, passing children bundled up in scarves, puffer jackets and mittens making snowmen in their front yards. Others tried out their new sleds, careering down long driveways and landing in a giggling heap amidst piles of snow. I smiled, remembering the excitement of Christmas as a child, waking up to find Santa had visited, discovering reindeer footprints in the snow, left by Aunt Bessie, who always made the magic real, despite whatever was going on at home.

"What are Australian Christmases like?" I asked, breaking the silence. Did his parents fuss over him, wearing beaming smiles, proud that they'd raised him right? The thought of them missing him today of all days hurt my heart.

"Hot." He grinned and his eyes lit up as if with memories of merry Christmases. "We have a traditional

271

lunch with turkey and all the trimmings, but we also do seafood on the barbecue, and eat outside to escape the heat in the kitchen. My parents live by the beach so we usually go for a swim at some point, and share a bottle of wine as the sun sets. It's always a scorcher of a day. Summertime in Australia."

"It must be so strange being here – all the snow and cold?"

He laughed. "It is, yes, but I like the change. It's good to experience that American Christmas you see in the movies."

We lapsed into another silence as we drove the snowy route. "I wanted to thank you, though, for inviting me to spend Christmas with your family. It means a lot, Clio."

His gaze was intense, as if he wasn't only thinking of *my* family. "They must be missing you this year," I said, sensing he was thinking of his parents. His body stiffened slightly. Bingo. Part of me was relieved he cared; of course he cared, he was Kai after all. Maybe he just needed a push to reach out to his parents again. Someone to be the voice of reason? "Did you speak to your parents today?"

He took a full minute to answer. "No, I haven't called yet." He let out a sigh. "I don't feel great about it either. I dialed so many times, and then hung up before it connected. Like, what do I say? *'Hey, Merry Christmas! It's your son who's not actually your son.'*" There was a bitterness to his voice, and real pain shone in his eyes. I knew he didn't want to hurt them; he just didn't know how to be this new Kai who'd found out he was adopted.

I gripped the steering wheel tighter as I turned a corner. What would I do in the same situation? Probably retreat too. Isn't that what I had done when things had got too hard with my mom? Packed a suitcase and headed to New York, and I hadn't looked back until I'd been forced to.

But I couldn't help think that, whether Kai was related to them by blood or by love, did it really matter in the long run? Love was love, right?

272

"You should call them, Kai. They're probably heartsick over it all too, you know. I don't think it matters much what you say. Just call them, for their sake, if not your own."

What I was picturing was my own mom, sitting at the table on Christmas Day for the last few years, missing her absent daughter. Guilt roiled inside me that I'd left her alone so long. I had left for good reason and stayed away for self-preservation, but that didn't change the fact that I should've reached out sooner. While our relationship hadn't been normal in any sense of the word, I knew she wouldn't ever ask for help, even if she desperately needed it – and I'd simply packed up and left without so much as a backward glance. Maybe I could stop Kai doing the same thing; he shouldn't have to live with the regret, or wishing things had turned out differently.

As it stood, I wasn't even sure if my mom would hug *me* and wish me a Merry Christmas today. Her moods went up and down like a yo-yo, and I was never certain how she would be. Sure, things had been getting better, but would she even look me in the eye and *really* see me?

Kai had dream parents, ones who'd cheered him on at his surf comps and football games, then later supported him through university, all with one goal in mind – a successful future for him. He'd told me all about them and it was hard to think they'd want anything for him but the best. Yeah, they should have probably told him he was adopted earlier – but they'd kept silent out of fear they'd lose him, and now they had.

He rubbed at his face. "I know. And I don't want to hurt them. *Really*, I don't. My silence isn't some kind of revenge. It's more that I'm lost about how to be, what to say. They'll hear it in my voice. I just can't believe I had birth parents I won't ever get to meet. I won't be able to see if I have the same color eyes as my dad, the same smile as my mom… you know? I *am* angry, and I can't help it. I keep hoping that it'll subside and then we can move on. But it hasn't.

273

What if it never does?" His voice was low and anguished and I wished I knew the right thing to say.

Houses crowded closer together the nearer we got to the town; twinkling Christmas lights flashed behind lace curtains, tinsel was strung across neat hedges, and wreaths blew sideways on front doors. Every house looked like a fully decorated gingerbread house, only on a real-life scale.

"I understand all of that, Kai. I think I'd feel the same. But I think the only way forward is to deal with it now, otherwise you're just sweeping it under the carpet, and you of all people know how toxic that is."

Using Kai's philosophy against him seemed fitting. He was a big believer in letting out negative emotions, and concentrating on the positive, through breathing exercises, yoga, and meditation. While I teased him relentlessly about his surfer yogi guru prowess, it really had made a difference to me, no matter how crazy doing the lotus position at midnight might have looked to an outsider. And I think he probably needed to practice what he preached, for his own sanity.

"You make it sound so easy, Clio. But how do I articulate to them how I really feel without letting my anger creep in? I know they're hurt too. What if I make it worse? Wouldn't it be easier to just keep silent until I work it all out?"

I considered it. Who was I to advise him anyway? I still hadn't mended things with Mom and I was walking into Christmas keeping a secret from her. But not as big a secret as she was keeping from me. For some inexplicable reason, I felt calling his parents was the right thing for Kai to do. "I don't know them, Kai, but I'd hazard a guess they'd prefer you yelling down the phone line than silence. At least that would be progress." I shrugged, hoping I wasn't wrong. "The longer you leave it, the harder it will be to bridge that gap. It doesn't have to be all sunshine and butterflies. Just be honest, say how you feel, and go from there."

He nodded, his jaw tight. Kai wouldn't yell at them – he wasn't the yelling type – but his hesitation said a lot about the black cloud hovering over him. "Maybe," he finally said.

I gave his arm a reassuring pat, feeling like a fraud – I could dole out advice easily, but when it came to my own life I kept it bottled up tight too, not sure which way to go with my own mom.

Sensing a subject change was in order, I said, "I hope you're hungry. Aunt Bessie has been talking up her festive donut tower, and says we're not allowed to leave until it's all been eaten, because…"

"They're artisan donuts," he finished, and we burst out laughing. Aunt Bessie took her donuts seriously and Christmas Day was no different. I expected it wouldn't be long before we fell into some sort of sugar coma with the amount of eating that was expected at any soirée at Aunt Bessie's. For a moment I almost regretted the second helping I'd had at breakfast, but who would ever wish away a single forkful of Cruz's sinfully delicious berry nice Christmas pastry tree?

"If I eat any more, I'll explode," Kai said with a grimace.

"Me too," I laughed. "Damn Cruz for making such a huge, delicious breakfast. Let's just hope Aunt Bessie is running behind schedule." I turned on the radio and as we drove down the last few streets Kai and I sang tunelessly along to 'Rockin' Around the Christmas Tree'. When I surreptitiously glanced sideways at him I noticed he was grinning – our conversation hadn't been forgotten, but at least he didn't seem to be burdened by it.

In Aunt Bessie's driveway, I shut off the engine. A gasp escaped when I caught sight of her house. "Golly," I said. "It's got to be the most decorated on the block!" Aunt Bessie never did do anything by halves! It was the most fabulously festive cottage – which said a lot as competition in Evergreen was fierce. There was a sleigh complete with reindeer on her roof, and even Santa's legs visible – as if he was heading down the chimney head first to deliver presents. The look was completed with thousands of twinkling fairy lights, and I'd bet money that the enormous wreath on her door was a musical one. I peeked at Kai, who wore an expression of surprise – maybe they didn't decorate quite as fantastically where he came from?

"Aunt Bessie *really* likes Christmas..." I said as I climbed out the car.

He winked at me across the back seat as he started to gather presents. "Ah, I had been wondering where you got your love of excess from."

"So, I like buying gifts!" I said with a flick of my hair, and laughed as he pretended to teeter under the weight of his pile.

I loved Christmas, and gift buying even more so ... I couldn't help but put things away all year round when I found perfect presents for those I loved. Which would have been fine, except I kept forgetting what I'd bought, and ended up with more than I had intended – though it was fun to exclaim over them, and remember what store I'd found them in, and what I'd been doing at the time.

When we reached the porch I leaned over to press the doorbell and tamped down giggles as 'Jingle Bells' rang out.

"Come in, come in," Aunt Bessie trilled from inside the house, before throwing the door open. She wore a bright green Christmas sweater, her hair curled and makeup immaculately applied... if not a touch heavily, as was her way.

"Don't you look fabulously festive?" I said, hugging her with one arm as I grasped the wine.

She waved me away. "This old thing? Shucks."

I grinned and moved aside so she could hug Kai, managing to maneuver her arms around the presents he clutched. She held on for a moment or two longer than strictly necessary and then stage-whispered over his shoulder: "At your age, I wouldn't waste any more time getting to know the man, *if you know what I mean.*" She then gave me a salacious wink and I almost died right there.

Scandalized, I hissed, "Aunt Bessie!" as any other words failed me. What was she playing at? Kai did his best not to laugh as he squeezed past her into the house. Had Amory sent out a memo or something: *Let's not rest until Clio admits she has feelings for Kai!*

What did she mean *at my age*!

Was I left-on-the-shelf age already?

"What?" she said, wide-eyed, playing the innocent. "Just saying it like it is."

"Well, you may as well have told him I'm old and desperate! *At my age*, jeez, Aunt Bessie!" I hissed at her.

Aunt Bessie just smirked at me and turned to follow Kai in. "Oh, let me help you, Kai."

I shook my head and laughed. Seriously, she was the limit.

Aunt Bessie's cottage was just as I remembered it from Christmases as a child. There was a fire crackling in the grate, and Christmas carols playing chirpily. The living room was decorated from the ceiling, where shiny silver lanterns hung, right down to the floorboards, where a Nativity scene played out, including hay in the manger for baby Jesus.

"Now come through, I've made some candy-cane milkshakes, but you can't have a milkshake without a donut and you can't have a donut without candyfloss, so I hope it won't spoil your lunch."

I groaned. "We've only just had breakfast, Aunt Bessie."

She tutted. "It's only a drink, Clio!"

There was no denying her. We'd be marshmallow-shaped when we left.

"See what's for dessert?" Kai said in awe as he unloaded presents under the tree, a tree that seemed to be more lights than branches.

On the kitchen bench sat Aunt Bessie's donut tower, and I gasped. I'd been expecting something extravagant, but not this. It was truly a marvel, iced donuts in festive red and green stacked atop each other in the shape of a Christmas tree. Edible diamonds twinkled on each layer. A golden star gleamed from the top. "What on earth…" In the window of Puft she'd had something similar but on a much simpler scale. This was another level!

"Your mom helped," she said, her eyes shining with pride. "She sure has a steady hand for it. It took us just over four hours to assemble, and that doesn't include making the donuts."

"Mom helped?"

Aunt Bessie grinned. "She sure did. She's becoming quite the baker, you know. Her visits to Puft are more frequent. Sure, to start with she just helped out the kitchen hand, cleaning and sorting the fridges, but now she's learning to bake too. And decorate. She's got the patience for the finicky work."

My eyebrows shot up. I knew Mom went to Puft and 'helped' but I'd thought it was just a reason to catch up with Aunt Bessie, and have some time outside the house with someone she felt safe and comfortable around. I'd never for one second thought she would be learning to bake. Also, I'd inherited my terrible cooking skills from my mother… or so I'd thought! I stared at the tower again, fresh pride coursing through me.

She gazed in the direction I looked. "Oh, the star? It's made from tempered dark chocolate and covered in gold leaf. It cost a pretty penny, but it's worth it, don't you think?"

"Aunt Bessie, it's totally amazing. It's so grand!" The stack of donuts had been truly transformed. It was a piece of art. "You've got such an incredible talent, sometimes I think you're wasted here in Evergreen," I said.

"Well, funny you should say. About that…" Aunt Bessie said, dipping her head as if shy, which was out of character for her. "I'm not technically minded, I'm more a 'get your hands dirty in the kitchen' type, as you can clearly see, but I've had a lot of *the emails* recently…"

"*The* emails? Go on." I bit down on a smile.

"Yeah, so the emails are all basically asking the same thing. Where can they see pictures of what I make, what's my handle on Instagram." Her face went blank. "I replied I don't have a handle on it, I don't have a handle on technology at all."

Laughter sputtered out of me. "Oh, Aunt Bessie! They mean what's your *name* on Instagram, so they can follow you! Not whether you have a handle on using it! Handle means name – for example, it could be something like: @PuftArtisanDonuts."

"OK, OK, I understand, but what exactly is Instagram?" Her eyebrows pulled together as she poured out enormous candy-cane milkshakes, decorating both with white-and-red sprinkled donuts and a spiral of whipped cream.

I laughed in spite of her bewildered expression and took my milkshake before I pulled out my phone to teach her the intricacies of Instagram. "So, social media looks scary, but really it could take Puft to the next level. Introducing it to more customers, from, well, pretty much anywhere in the world."

"So..." Her nose wrinkled. "You're telling me I'll post pictures of my artisan donuts and strangers are going to *like* them? With a click of the button? And this will sell more donuts?" Her expression remained bewildered.

I nodded and took a gulp of my milkshake, relishing the minty freshness. Puft definitely deserved more fans, even if demand in Evergreen was already pretty high. I just knew New Yorkers would love to 'discover' those artisan creations.

Still confused she asked, "But how will they find me?"

"Hashtags." I tried to hold back the laughter as I caught Kai's gaze. Explaining social media seemed completely mad – hashtags, handles, likes? "Okay, so let's not worry about all the terms or anything, let's just get you an account set up. It's easier to show you that way."

With a big smile, and a lot of dramatic sighing and exclaiming over remembering passwords and how her nails were too long to click-clack at a phone, we set up an Instagram account and I promised to help her with Facebook and Twitter once she got a handle (!) on using Instagram first.

"So these strangers will *like* my posts and send orders through my website? Seems pretty crazy to me…"

"It's the way of the world, Aunt Bessie," I said, smiling. "Amory will design you a stunning webpage that will suit Puft and she can link your social media accounts to that. Then when you get an order you simply ship it. Easy peasy. We'd better sort out some nice packaging for shipping too, because I bet it won't take long for the word to spread."

"You're a sweet girl, Clio, believing in me like that. This all came about after Cedarwood was written up in the newspaper, you know. It's more to do with you than me."

I kissed the top of her head. "It came about because you're exceptional at what you do. It has nothing to do with me."

Looking up at the clock Aunt Bessie suddenly exclaimed, "Look at the time! We'd best get a wriggle on now or this Christmas lunch is going to be a real *turkey*!" she cackled at her bad joke and I followed her back to the kitchen.

I sat at the counter and watched Aunt Bessie work as she pulled out vegetables and instructed me to stay well away from any pot or pan. But she called Kai over to be her helper and I watched as he confidently chopped and prepared the carrots. I was almost jealous – seeing as Aunt Bessie had been able to teach Mom how to bake, I wondered if she could teach me how to boil water without burning the pot…

"Where's Mom?" I asked.

Aunt Bessie stopped stirring and checked her watch. "Should be on her way." She paused, turning toward me and catching my eye. "Clio, you know it's a big thing for her, coming here today when there's going to be people she doesn't know." She motioned to Kai, who seemed to be in his own world meticulously julienning carrots to the same length.

I nodded. My mom could hide out in the kitchen at Puft, stick her head into the bakery and say hello to a friendly face, but real socializing – sitting down, eating, drinking, and making conversation for hours on end – was another thing entirely. I couldn't remember ever seeing my mom handle a social situation well – I guess she just used the avoidance tactic, or made excuses and we left it at that.

"I know, Aunt Bessie, but they're all really sweet people. No one is going to make her uncomfortable." She nodded and turned back to her stirring.

It was nice to be spending Christmas with family this year. Of course, last year – spending it with Amory in a Chinese restaurant in Brooklyn – had been amazing in its own right, but I sensed things were changing for all of us. Family should have come first, and I vowed it would from now on.

Chapter Twenty-Nine

A car crunched on the icy driveway, interrupting our rendition of 'Last Christmas', with Kai pretending to be awed by our singing but probably wanting to cover his poor ears from the abuse he was suffering. None of us could sing, not a note, but still, we enjoyed caroling, so what did it matter if it sounded like nails on a chalkboard? I leaped up to see who had arrived. Mom. She'd made it.

I knew today would be difficult for her, but I remembered the advice I'd given to Kai. I needed to start dealing with things head-on too. So I went outside to greet her. As I got closer she started, and then gave me a tight-lipped smile.

I opened the driver's door. "Hi, Mom! Merry Christmas," I said brightly.

Her eyes widened at my exuberance. "I was… just organizing my thoughts," she said as she pulled her handbag into her lap.

"OK, well, great! Let's go in and get out of this cold." She didn't move, so I said as soothingly as possible, "There's only Kai and Aunt Bessie here so far."

She flashed me a small smile and undid her seatbelt.

I reached out and took her hand and led her inside, chatting away about this and that to put her at ease. I sensed she was trying hard to appear relaxed, but although her smile was stiff it was still a smile, and she wasn't so folded in on herself. She'd made an effort to dress up, and wore a slick of lip gloss and some blusher. I debated whether to mention how pretty she looked, or if noting it would make her feel self-conscious. In the end, I just gave her hand a squeeze, and hoped she could read it in my face how happy I was she was here.

"Merry Christmas!" Aunt Bessie said, kissing Mom's cheek, and giving her the once-over. "Don't you look nice, Annabelle! That color suits you." She motioned to Mom's teal-colored shirt.

Mom tucked a tendril of hair back and smiled her thanks.

"Help me get these vegetables chopped, would you? I didn't dare ask Clio in case she lopped a finger off or some other disaster. She's quite hopeless in the culinary arts."

"Hey!" I protested half-heartedly, knowing Aunt Bessie knew how to put Mom at ease without it being obvious. Mom took an apron from the hook and put it over her head, her demeanor changing now she had a job to do.

"Mom, this is Kai, Kai my mom, Annabelle."

Kai gave her a wide smile, and shook her hand. "Pleased to meet you, Mrs Winters."

With a tentative smile, she said, "Likewise, Kai. I've heard a lot about you, and it's all good."

He laughed. "That's a relief." Mom's charming side surprised me; it boded well for the day. Maybe she'd always wanted to be around people but just didn't know how to after hiding away for so long.

Mom and Aunt Bessie pottered around the kitchen, continuing to prep for lunch. They refused our offers of further help, and ushered us into the living room. "Go watch a Christmas movie, relax, unwind, you're my guests," admonished Aunt Bessie as she handed us two fruit mince donuts – to keep us going!

In Aunt Bessie's living room we went through her alphabetized Christmas movie selection and decided on *Love Actually* and I pressed play, before sitting next to Kai on the lumpy red sofa. We sort of fell into each other as the cushion sagged beneath us, and we brushed hands as we tried to scramble back into a sitting position. I sent a thank you to the universe that Aunt Bessie hoarded her old things and refused to update her furniture.

When Hugh Grant's character danced around in 10 Downing Street, we laughed when he was busted by a steely-faced aide. It had to be a sign – a man who liked a rom-com had to be of the finest order, right? Emma Thompson's Joni Mitchell scene played, and I felt her sadness as surely as if it was my own. Surreptitiously I wiped a stray tear, but Kai caught me.

"He's a bit of a bastard for doing that."

I bit down on my lip, and let out a half-sob, half-laugh. "I love her, and even though it's fictional I still can't quite help thinking it's real and he's such a fool for hurting her. And for what? A passing flirtation with scarlet lips. It's just the worst!"

"I totally agree." He leaned over and I caught my breath as he wiped a lone tear from my cheek. "It's like he can't see what's right in front of him, and he is utterly stupid for that." He gazed at me so fervently, I thought for a second he meant me.

The air in the room hummed around us as my mind raced. Was there hidden meaning, or was I just hoping so? I'd never wanted to kiss anyone as much as I did at that moment. The man enjoyed *Love Actually*, for God's sake! Didn't that make him great? Forget heartbreak, forget about the future, all I cared about was this minute right here, so I closed my eyes and kissed him, all at once dizzy with the touch of his lips against mine. He brushed his fingertips against my cheek, and kissed me back softly. And I thought if I never felt like that again, life would be so dull. So empty.

With my heart racing, I pulled away slightly, hoping he wouldn't see the quake in my hands. If I ever got naked with him, I was sure I'd pass out with the wooziness of it all. Wouldn't that be the most embarrassing thing? *Stop picturing him naked, Clio!* It wasn't like I was a prude, or hadn't had relationships before, but with Kai, even the simplest of touches felt charged, like Cupid was making sure I knew this guy was the one. And suddenly I decided to throw caution to the wind. One week with Kai was better than none, and maybe the memory of his kisses would last a lifetime...

"Clio..." he said softly and pulled me in for another kiss.

The crunch of tires had us leaping apart. Cruz and Amory had arrived, and that put paid to any more private time.

"I... ah... I really love that movie, thanks for watching it with me." *Lame, can anyone say lame!*

He laughed as I scrambled out of the sofa. "Any time, Clio."

For someone who spent their whole life around love I was completely useless at it myself. Kai probably thought I was unhinged, or something.

I raced over to open the door for Cruz and Amory, who were stomping snow from their boots.

"Come in," I said, a little breathless still but trying to disguise it with festive cheer. Amory narrowed her eyes as if she knew something was up. I let out a slightly manic laugh and smoothed my hair down.

Suddenly Cruz clicked his fingers and tutted. "Dang it, I left the wine at the lodge. I'll be right back," he said as he turned to go straight back out into the snow.

"We have a ton of wine, don't worry," I called, but he was already at the car holding the keys up.

"I won't be long, promise."

"Drive safe on those roads," Amory called, but he'd already closed the door and was starting to reverse out of the drive.

Amory turned her laser beam on me and smiled. "Why are you so flushed?"

I pulled her inside and out of the cold. "Oh, you know, sitting by the fire and all that!" She didn't believe me, I could tell by the textbook squint of hers.

To distract her, I steered her toward the kitchen and asked, "Why does Cruz want more wine? We seriously have loads here." It was a good thirty-minute round trip back to the lodge, and seemed like a lot of effort, especially when the roads were on the hazardous side.

She shrugged and unwound her scarf. "It's probably some fancy wine that pairs with a certain type of dish. Don't know why he keeps bothering with all that. I'll just guzzle it anyway."

I laughed, knowing it was true. Amory gave not one jot about the quality – even after taking wine-appreciation courses as part of our job. Whether she was hosting glamorous parties with fridges full of expensive champagne, or intimate gatherings with full-bodied reds that had been cellared for decades, she'd drink them down just the same as a bottle from the bargain bin and exclaim 'not bad'.

Amory swept into the kitchen, greeting Mom as if she'd known her for ever, giving her a tight squeeze, which had Mom's eyes widening, and said a cheery hello to Aunt Bessie, who squished her in return.

"That is a work of *art*, Aunt Bessie," Amory exclaimed over the donut-tower Christmas tree. "Seriously, you have to start sharing these with the city crowd, they would love it!"

I laughed as Aunt Bessie donned her specs and snapped pictures of the edible diamond decorations, all the while filling Amory in on her newfound love for Instagram. "And you see, my friend…" She made the @sign with her fingertip. "… @Donuts4Life asked me for a close-up of the edible decorations on the tree. She's thinking of placing an order for her daughter's birthday. A candyfloss donut tower. Pink frosted donuts, pink candyfloss, and pink edible diamonds. Wouldn't that be every ten-year-old's dream?"

I sat there with my jaw hanging open. She'd embraced Instagram that quickly? I'd only just taught her what a hashtag was and here she was with followers and everything already! Calling them her friends? She seriously could charm anyone, this woman, and I loved her for it.

"This all happened in the two hours you've been on Instagram?" I asked.

Aunt Bessie looked at me like I was dense. "Yes, Clio. @Donuts4Life lives in Oakville, so she's going to visit after Christmas. I used the hashtags like you told me to, and she clicked on #Evergreen and found me. And so did thirty others, but so far we haven't spoken. I will, though. I'll introduce myself to them tomorrow, tell them a little bit about my artisan donuts and how much I love baking."

"That sounds… great, Aunt Bessie." I tried to keep my laughter in check. "It is called *social* media, so introducing yourself is part of it, I guess." They wouldn't know what hit them. Aunt Bessie could win anyone over with her affable personality and I bet they'd order donuts just because she wooed them with her zest for life.

We were still laughing about my techno-phobic aunt embracing Instagram when Amory clapped her hands and said, "Now, what's the protocol here, is it too early for wine?"

"It's actually a little late." Aunt Bessie winked, reaching for some glasses. "We've got mulled wine steeping away on the stove, or take your pick with something else. Just make yourselves right at home, we're all friends here."

Amory poured everyone a glass of mulled wine, the scent of cloves, cinnamon, and orange rind spicing the air, and I made a mental note to get the recipe. Surely I could throw a few ingredients into a vat of wine without ruining it?

Just when everyone had settled down again, a car pulled into the driveway and we all turned to look. Cruz couldn't have got to the lodge and back in that amount of time. Amory's eyes narrowed, and I sensed a ploy afoot too. Cruz had always been good at big romantic gestures. A Christmas gift, perhaps? He'd been so keen to get back into the kitchen at Cedarwood, I don't think he'd even ventured into town since he arrived, so he wouldn't have had time to buy a gift, unless he'd organized it by phone…

We peeked out of the window, Amory watching him intently as he opened the back door of the car and shuffled backwards with something in his arms.

Realizing it was something important, and definitely not wine by the looks of it, I ushered Amory away. "Let him surprise you," I said.

While I was pushing Amory back into the dining room, Kai opened the door for Cruz.

"All right, all right," Amory said when I shoved her a little harder. "There's no need to manhandle me."

"Oh, please," I said, smiling. Mom and Aunt Bessie stopped what they were doing and waited for Cruz's big entrance too. What was taking him so long? I was dying to see what Amory's gift was.

"Close your eyes," Cruz called out from the doorway as we all hovered in the living room expectantly.

Amory duly closed her eyes.

He tiptoed in, and we collectively put a hand to our mouths to stop *awws* spilling out. In his hands Cruz held a little fluffball of a pup, with black and tan fur and the most beautiful big blue eyes.

Putting a finger to his lips, Cruz sneaked in and placed the puppy onto Amory's lap. She gasped, and opened her eyes. "Merry Christmas, Amory."

We froze, not sure if this was meant to be a private moment or not, so we just stopped moving and pretended to be invisible. Dropping to his knees (*both* knees, thank God; no chance of a proposal fiasco again) in front of Amory, he said, "This little rescue pup needed a home for Christmas, a for ever home, where he's safe, and loved, and well fed. I told the shelter we'd show him what real love was and he'd have a happy life with us."

"This little guy was going to spend Christmas alone?" Amory asked, her eyes glistening as she stroked his fur.

Cruz nodded solemnly. "But now we can give him the Christmas of every puppy's dream."

"He's so beautiful!" she said, and for a split second or two her mask fell away and she looked really quite vulnerable. Her face softened and her eyes shone.

"Amory, I know we both had different visions about starting a family, and about marriage, but we got through that hurdle by being open and honest, and if we can get through that we can get through anything, together. So when I spotted this little guy, I just felt like he was right for us. The same way I knew, as soon as I saw you, that day in Manhattan when we first met, that you were the one for me. It was like my soul recognized you, and I had that same feeling with this fluffball. And I hope you do too."

I cast my eyes to the floor, feeling like I was intruding, but my heart was beating fast for my friends. Their love was so strong, so evident in everything they did, that even huge dilemmas couldn't force them apart. Cruz's gift of a rescue pup was perfect.

"I love him already," she said, holding back tears. "And I felt the very same way about you, but of course, I couldn't tell you that. I'm a born and bred New Yorker, we don't share our feelings so easily." She tried to joke about it, but it was clear Amory was letting down the defenses she'd built in the past. "I love you, Cruz, I really, really do, and I don't care who knows it," she said as she reached for his hand and then looked down at the new addition to their family.

I exchanged a quick glance with Kai, who was trying to contain a smile too; Mom and Aunt Bessie were grinning behind their hands. It was a beautiful thing to witness, two people so in love.

Then the puppy glanced up and licked Amory's nose, provoking a giggle which he took as a sign to pee in her lap, lightening the mood instantly. "Oh," she laughed. "We need to housetrain him."

The puppy jumped, his front paws landing on her chest, and licked her chin as if he was saying hello. She threw her head back and laughed. "OK, you're forgiven."

Mom came back in with a wet hand towel so Amory could clean herself up, which she took gratefully and uselessly wiped at her jeans.

"Do you want to borrow something of mine?" Aunt Bessie asked.

I stemmed my own giggles, picturing Amory in one of Aunt Bessie's sparkly ensembles. Amory laughed too. "That would be great, Bessie, if you don't mind."

"Be right back," she said, leaving the rest of us to coo over the puppy.

He was a ball of energy, and jumped and rolled on Amory's lap. She lifted him to her face and kissed him on the nose. "Oh, he's adorable. Thank you, Cruz. He's a little ray of sunshine."

"What are you going to call him?" Cruz asked, bending down to pat him.

She gave Cruz a peck on the cheek. "I don't know, I'll have to think about it. Get to know him first."

As Amory went off to change, Aunt Bessie bustled to the kitchen. The scent of roasted meat and crispy potatoes had my mouth watering, despite the amount of food I'd already eaten.

"Stir the gravy, will you, Clio?"

"Sure." She trusted me with the gravy? Yikes.

The turkey came out, roasted golden, then the root vegetables, which were crisp and glistened with butter. Aunt Bessie parboiled some green beans, drizzled them with olive oil and mixed through some pomegranate seeds that resembled shiny rubies. My old childhood nemesis, Brussels sprouts, were crumbed and deep-fried, and served with a melted cheese dipping sauce. They were disguised so well I was eager to try one and see if I really was a grown-up now – didn't you achieve the highest level of adulting when you could eat Brussels sprouts?

Cruz wandered in. "Do you need a hand?"

Aunt Bessie threw him a grateful look. "Can you carve the turkey?"

He nodded and set to work.

She dusted her hands on her apron, and wrinkled her brow. "What am I forgetting?"

"The carrots?" I ventured, noticing that the neat julienned stems Kai had chopped were now swimming in a pan of garlic butter.

"Yes!" she laughed. "Also I made bread and butter sauce this year. Now don't turn your nose up at it, it goes very well with the richness of the turkey."

I held my hands up in surrender. "I'm not saying a word. I'm more than happy to eat a feast someone else cooked. And I'll try all of it."

"Good girl." She kissed my cheek. "Start taking these to the table and I'll bring the serving spoons."

Once Amory had changed we all sat at the dining table, now laden with food and decorations, ready for our second feast of the day. With the puppy asleep in Amory's lap I couldn't help but smile as I saw how sweet they were together. I'd never thought Amory was a pet person, but here she was falling head over heels for a puppy.

I poured everyone a glass of wine, and Mom and Aunt Bessie went to fetch more platters before joining us at the table.

Jostling around in our seats, we turned when Aunt Bessie clinked her glass with a fork. "Now, I wanted to raise a toast before we start eating. Here's to our first Christmas together in a long time." She held her wineglass aloft, and blinked back sudden tears. "A big welcome to our guests," she said, turning to look at each of my friends in turn, "and thank you for spending the day with us. Let's hope it becomes a new tradition." She beamed so hard it almost broke my heart. I hadn't really thought in all the years I'd been away that it would have just been Mom and Aunt Bessie sharing a turkey lunch with all the trimmings. Why hadn't I come home more? Since being back I'd realized I was as much to blame as Mom for the radio silence. Still, I was here now, and things were changing – albeit at a snail's pace.

When Aunt Bessie sat down I was astonished when Mom lifted her glass, and cleared her throat to speak. I leaned forward so I wouldn't miss a thing.

With downcast eyes, she said, "Thank you all for looking after my daughter. I know you've been there for her in one way or another in the past few months. It helps..." Her voice petered off, and tears sprung in my eyes. "...It helps knowing she has support and friendships that will carry her through the good and bad."

Silence fell.

I was so shocked I couldn't think of a thing to say, but the smile on my face must have spoken volumes because Mom gave me a small nod and a wobbly smile of her own.

Aunt Bessie broke the hush by saying, "Well, now we've got the toasting out of the way, let's drink and be merry!" We all leaned forward and clinked glasses. I darted a quick glance at Kai, who was lost in thought, and I figured Mom's words might have touched a chord with him too.

The chatter rose as we feasted on every delicious morsel. Even the bread and butter sauce was a hit, mixing with the steaming-hot gravy, and perfect for dipping each mouthful into. Combined with the nutty, herbaceous stuffing, it was a meal made in heaven, and one I wished I had the skills to recreate. I was awed by people who could cook so many things at once and not burn it all. Sadly, I didn't reach peak adult status because the sprouts, no matter how dressed up, still tasted like bitter greens to me, and in a way I was thankful – who wanted to be an adult anyway?

The puppy chose that moment to steal a piece of gravy-covered turkey off Amory's plate. It was too big for his little choppers, and somehow missed the napkin on her lap, but found her clothes. She slapped her head. "Outfit number three coming up! He's a wardrobe menace!"

"Your jeans should be dry by now," Aunt Bessie said. "You can change again after lunch."

"Thank you." Amory grinned. "I'll throw these in the wash at the same time."

Mom didn't say much, but actually ate rather than picking at her food like she would usually do. She was so thin, it scared me, but just *maybe* this was a tipping point.

Empty plates sat in front of us all and no one moved. We were too full to do anything except sit with blank faces. Aunt Bessie was the only one still sprightly, and she ambled to the kitchen and returned with more mulled wine and a tray of peppermint chocolates.

"Thank you, gang, for making this one of the best Christmases we've had in a long time. I'm hoping your youth rubs off on me."

We laughed, and sipped our wine, and my eyelids grew heavy from contentment.

"Have you all called your families?" Aunt Bessie asked into the satiated quiet. "They must miss you, being so far from home."

Amory spoke up first. "I rang them this morning. My parents are enjoying their very first child-free Christmas! They're traveling in India, and quite content to swap turkey for goat curry and not bother with the cleanup, or waiting on their grown-up children. Can't say I blame them. I'd choose India too. We are a bit of a handful when we're all together."

"I'm sure they're missing you too, though," Aunt Bessie said. "But I'm glad they're enjoying India. I've always wanted to go there. What about you, Cruz?"

Cruz filled them in on his phone call home – and the fact he'd had to speak to every extended family member, *and* some of the neighbors. And that they were excited about him and Amory visiting as soon as they could.

"And Kai? I suppose Christmas is over for another year in Australia?"

A blush crept up his cheeks, and I was about to save him by making some excuse when he said, "I'm all set to Skype them when I go back to the lodge this evening."

Sitting beside each other, we locked gazes for a moment, and I was lost to him, and everything around me.

293

"Is it hot in here, or is it just me?" Amory made a show of fanning herself. I kicked her under the table but must have hit Cruz instead, who let out a yelp of surprise.

"Sorry," I said. "Pass it on," I motioned to Amory, and he grinned.

Under the table, Kai clasped my hand and held it firm against his jean-clad thigh. I couldn't remember a better Christmas, being surrounded by friends and family, and even my mom, who was smiling at Amory's joke. Things were looking up for the New Year, especially with all of these people here to stay... or at least most of them.

Chapter Thirty

Back at the lodge, Amory and Cruz made excuses and headed up to their suite with the puppy, who was once again asleep in her arms. My big-city, party-the-night-away friends were no match for a long festive lunch and a country walk in the fresh air. They were wiped out and bleary-eyed, all set to nap.

I flopped on the chaise in the front parlor, and Kai did the same. It had just gone six, and outside the sky shifted from blue to inky black.

"What's the story with your mom, Clio? You've told me bits and pieces but I didn't realize she'd be so... reserved. She's very different from you."

As usual with Kai, the words held no malice, just a greater need to understand. Today had felt like a dream, like life was on the right track. Mom had overcome her anxiety to join us, and even spoken up a fair bit. But I didn't really want to burden Kai with the whole story when he had so much going on, so I kept it light, told him an edited version. Some secrets should stay secret, so while I told him about my upbringing, my father's death, Mom's pulling away, and finally, her mysterious connection to Cedarwood, and the fact no one would fess up to what exactly had happened here all those years ago, I kept some things back too, and sped through it like I was recounting someone else's story.

"Wow," he said.

I sighed. "I know." Things were complicated, and there was no pretending that one Christmas lunch had solved everything. I hadn't told him about the photographs I'd found or the significance of the maze Isla had discovered. "Mom's always been that way. I used to think she was cold, sort of bitter about life, but now I can see it's more than that. She's fighting an internal battle every day just to be here. I wish I knew what to say or do that would pull her up."

His brow knitted. "Watching her today made me think of my own mom, and how my silence is probably hurting her. I think you're right. The longer I wait before talking to them, the worse it's going to be. So I'm glad I messaged them after our chat."

I sat up straighter. "I don't think there's ever a 'right time' with these things," I said, thinking of my own predicament, and knowing it applied to Kai too.

"You're doing the right thing with your mom," Kai said, reaching over and smoothing a hand over mine.

"We're getting there, slowly but surely." I smiled up at him, appreciating the gesture. "Go call them, Kai. I'll be here if you need me."

He consulted his watch. "OK. Mind if I use your office?"

"Go for it."

When he left, I went to the kitchen and brewed some herbal tea. My phone beeped with a text.

Merry Christmas, Clio! Hope Santa spoiled you… If it's OK I'll pop around tomorrow to discuss the New Year's Eve party? My boss is thinking masquerade ball now, think there's time? I'll bring a bottle of wine. Love Timothy x

In all the craziness of Christmas I'd nearly forgotten about the New Year's event we were planning. Like always, the thought of organizing an event sent a thrill through me, but so far we had been time poor with every party we'd held at the lodge and this would be no different. A masquerade ball would require a lot of prep, and we'd have to order decorations and pay for quick delivery. Still, then we'd have those props for future parties…

I fired off a reply:

Merry Christmas, Tim! Hope the kids had a ball! Tomorrow is perfect, we'll have to move fast if the theme is masquerade but we can definitely do it… I have wine, so don't bring a thing. See you soon,

Clio x

With the scent of lemongrass and ginger in the air, I sat cradling the steaming-hot cup of tea, and thought about what we'd need for the party, and what kind of menu would suit, what drinks, music? Cocktails, pink champagne, and hors d'oeuvres, feathery masks, jazz music? Or classical guitarists? A black-and-white masquerade ball! Everything in monochrome…? The lodge was the perfect venue for such an elaborate party. I just hoped we'd be able to pull it off.

Instead of worrying, I grabbed a notebook, its pages swollen already with to-do lists, and started scribbling my thoughts down. I thought a photo booth would be fun, the old-school type that shot a length of film out which guests could take home. Aunt Bessie could do donut towers… As the ideas came thick and fast I was tempted to fetch Amory and brainstorm, but reminded myself Christmas night probably wasn't the ideal time to talk about work.

Without meaning to, I pricked my ears for the sound of Kai; he'd been gone twenty minutes, a good sign that they were really talking and not just making pleasantries. I smiled and got back to my planning, falling into deep concentration. Before long his footsteps echoed down the wooden floors, and I hastily jotted down an idea before I forgot it as he walked into the room.

He sat opposite me, and I pushed a cup of now lukewarm herbal tea across to him.

I waited for him to say something, but he didn't move. "How did it go?" I asked softly.

The grandfather clock in the hall tick-tocked while he formulated a response. "As well as it could have in the circumstances, I guess." Raking a hand through his hair, he pursed his lips and gazed past me. "They wanted to know if I was planning to head back to Australia soon."

My belly clenched at the thought of him leaving the US for good. It was hard enough seeing him leave for other parts of the country. And it wouldn't be long before he left for San Francisco again – even that was too much to bear. He seemed to think of Cedarwood as a place of calm, somewhere he could get lost if he wanted to, find that solitude he craved. All he had to do was head up the mountain and he could clear his thoughts, and think without the daily grind of the big city. There was a part of me that just knew he belonged at Cedarwood, but it had to be his choice.

"Of course, they want to see you in person and make sure you're really OK. If it was me, that's what I'd want to do too…"

He gave me the ghost of a smile. "I'm not leaving America, Clio. Not yet."

Selfishly, I was over the moon he wasn't leaving the country – Australia was so far away. "Well, you've taken the first step, and I know it wasn't easy." I reached out and squeezed his hand. "Now you've spoken the first time, it will get easier going forward, trust me."

Kai had to follow his own path. Our timing may not have been right – we were both dealing with messy fallouts from real life – but my world made more sense with Kai in it. Even if I only saw him once a year, it would be better than nothing. Maybe our paths would cross again in the future when he had worked things out, and was where he wanted to be…

"Thanks, Clio. For everything. Having someone to talk to, someone I could trust with all of this has made it so much easier."

We clasped hands a little tighter. "I'm glad you trusted me."

We stared into each other's eyes as moonlight shone through the gauzy curtain, and for a moment everything was right with the world.

Chapter Thirty-One

In my office, I added a log to the fire and watched it until it caught alight. Boxing Day was always a mixed bag for me. While the fairy lights still flashed on the tree, the fun itself was over for another year. Still, this Christmas had been a good one.

While the lodge inhabitants slumbered, I worked. I checked various tourism websites we used that helped connect guests to accommodation, and was happy to see a few enquiries about the special offers we'd introduced, and one booking for March. I replied to the queries: did we offer guided walks? (Yes! Micah had climbed those mountains since we were kids, he knew them backwards.) Were there enough things to do to keep a tech-obsessed ten-year-old busy and away from his phone? (Yes! Plenty of indoor and outdoor activities, enough that screen time would be forgotten.) Did we cater for gluten intolerance? (Yes!) And lastly, could dance lessons be booked ahead of arrival so they didn't miss out? (Sure!)

I felt a real thrill replying because obviously our marketing campaigns were working, judging by the sorts of questions we were being asked. With that done, I went about the lodge taking photos, ready to share them across our social media accounts, knowing that, for most Americans, today would be a quiet day, and a lot of people would be lazing at home scrolling through their phones.

Outside, I took photos of the sleds by the bank of the ice rink, catching snowflakes drifting down, and uploaded the best one to Instagram with the hashtags

#WinterWonderland at #CedarwoodLodge. I enjoyed the chatty aspect of social media, and liked to see our pages growing, knowing it was all about the numbers – the more followers we had, the more people were aware of the lodge, which always gave me a little buzz.

I tucked my phone into my back pocket, and headed to the eastern side of the property. I debated with myself whether to hunt for the maze again. I could have asked Isla to show me, but it didn't feel right. So instead I turned back to the lodge, leaving it hidden for one more day.

Micah and Isla were standing together in the front garden, Isla gesticulating wildly as she directed Micah toward a hedge. "What are you two up to? I would have expected you to still be asleep or even spending the day lolling around on the sofa?" I said as I came up next to Isla and watched Micah trimming the top of the hedge.

"Clio," Isla said, snaking an arm around me and giving me a squeeze. "We're so sorry we missed seeing your mom and Aunt Bessie yesterday. We just got so caught up with Micah's family, and then we watched Christmas movies, and before we knew it, pretty much everyone was snoring on a couch somewhere."

Seeing them work together in the snowy landscape, their laughing and teasing, turned my wedding-planner mode back on. For some reason I couldn't help picturing their nuptials, and they weren't even engaged. A spring wedding… Flowers blooming, a bright bouquet of yellow tulips, a simple white sheath dress for Isla, Micah wearing a casual, cream-colored linen suit. A violinist in the corner playing a sweet song as Isla walked down the aisle…

"Hey," Micah said, pulling me into a tight hug and out of my reverie. "How was Christmas? Get everything you asked for…?" He raised an eyebrow suggestively and I gave him a sisterly shove.

"Yes, I did actually!" I said, faux-haughtily. "Yesterday was great, even Mom was there and, well, it went pretty well. She stayed the whole time, and get this – she's even started baking with Aunt Bessie."

Micah's mouth fell open. "Annabelle is baking? And had Christmas lunch with all of you?"

"Right? Wonders will never cease."

"Maybe she just needed time, Clio. Or needed you back," he said more softly.

I nodded.

We chatted more about their Christmas, laughing about the bawdy songs they'd taught the talking elf and exclaiming over Micah's family traditions, which basically involved watching every Christmas movie ever made.

As we were walking back toward the house, Kai walked out from the woods, his presence making me jelly-legged. Damn it.

"Hey, guys," he called out, "need some help?"

They waved him over, and wished each other well.

It reminded me… "What *are* you guys doing here? The garden could wait another day…"

Isla shook her head. "Not really. We wanted the front to look perfect for guests for the New Year's Eve party, so we figured we'd make a start. Besides, I had to do something, I spent all day yesterday on my butt, eating."

We laughed. It felt good to be outside, moving around, the lethargy of the day before vanishing.

"Can I tempt you in for coffee?"

"We'll get this hedge sorted and join you," Isla said.

"Great." I wandered back into the lodge, Kai beside me. We kept sneaking looks at each other, and eventually giggled as it got the best of us.

"Nice to see you're treating your body well again," I joked.

He waggled his brows. "Didn't want to let you down, after what you said."

I blushed, remembering. "My mouth doesn't always link with my brain."

"That's what I love about you," he said.

Love? Just a figure of speech, Clio.

Chapter Thirty-Two

After coffee Kai went for a shower and I went to the office to finalize my plans; Timothy was due and I didn't want to be caught unprepared. Masquerade balls were such fun to organize, but they were lots of work and we were already on the back foot time-wise.

I sat heavily, and tried to focus on the paperwork in front of me. There was a knock at the door and Timothy stuck his head in, surprising me, as I hadn't heard his car in the driveway and wasn't expecting him until later that afternoon.

"You're early!" I said, getting up to greet him. He cut a fine figure with his tight jeans and fitted black-knit sweater, smooth skin, and deep, intoxicating gaze, like he'd just stepped off the cover of a men's fashion magazine.

Those deep-hazel eyes of his bored straight into me, and for a moment I was a teenager again, belly flip-flopping, before I reined myself in. Being back in Evergreen sometimes brought out that gangly, bright-eyed girl, especially when Tim gave me the special smile he'd reserved only for me, once upon a time.

When he smiled a dimple appeared in his cheek. A memory rushed at me – I used to kiss that spot on his skin. "Yeah, sorry, I should have called. My boss has given me a checklist so long I don't know if the party will even be possible in such a short amount of time, so I figured we'd better meet earlier." By the pitch in his voice, it was clear Timothy was nervous. I couldn't remember ever seeing him anything other than assured. This party was important to him.

I gestured for him to sit down and said, "Well, early is better than late. Would you like some coffee? Or hot chocolate?"

"No, I'm OK. Before we get started, I wanted to give you this." He reached into his bag and produced an exquisitely wrapped box.

"You shouldn't have, Tim!" I blushed, feeling like a teenager all over again in his presence. I didn't know why he had that hold over me. It was like I regressed to the old me – and I wasn't sure it was a good thing.

"It'll make you smile, that's all."

Unwrapping the present, I pulled out a cassette from the box and laughed. "Oh, God, is this our ultimate mix tape? From way back when?" I flicked it over to read the artists and song names, scrawled in Tim's block writing.

It read:
Clio's hits of 97
Tubthumping
Barbie Girl
Truly Madly Deeply
Foolish Games

When I came to the fifth song, I burst out laughing, "'Spice Up Your Life'! Oh my God, do you remember dancing around to the Spice Girls, and thinking they were just the bee's knees?"

His eyes twinkled with memory. "I remember watching you dance and thinking you were the bee's knees, if not a little out of tune…"

And just like that I was back in the past – Tim just like he was now, but lankier in his teenage years; I'd taken to wearing sneakers and shiny velour tracksuits, just like Sporty Spice. Reminiscence was a wonderful thing because the fifteen-year-old Clio had had her life all mapped out: she was going marry Tim, have a million babies and work in fashion… It hit me suddenly that none of that had happened. I'd grown up and that girl was a distant memory, just someone I used to know. Still, it was sweet remembering a time I'd felt truly loved by Tim, no matter how young we'd been. You never forgot your first love, and seeing the man Tim had become, I thought I'd chosen well when I was younger.

"We must have been the only teenagers without a CD player back then. Remember?"

He smiled, bringing out the dimples in his cheeks again. "Things have never moved fast in Evergreen, and probably never will."

"I bet you Aunt Bessie still has her old tape deck that I could play this on. Thanks, Tim. It's one of the sweetest things I've ever been given." It was full of sentimentality and the perfect gift. Each song would conjure a different memory, a different time and place.

"You're welcome."

"Right," I said briskly, setting the cassette on my desk. "We'd better get started. We have a lot to discuss and not much time to organize everything."

Usually, I could fix any party problem, especially under pressure, but so far all of our events at Cedarwood had been on a tight schedule. I couldn't wait until we hosted one with some breathing room.

"So, you mentioned a masquerade ball, which is great, they're so much fun. Today, though, let's make some of the bigger decisions so we can order what we need and get moving quickly." We sat across from each other at my desk.

Tim pulled a file from his briefcase. "OK, great." He ran a hand through his hair. "My boss, Vinnie, wants a masquerade ball with all the bells and whistles. Money is no object. He's inviting the owner of a construction company, Mr Whittaker, because he's trying to win the right to sell his group of luxury condominiums, so in essence this party is to win him over."

I leaned back in my chair, pen in hand. "OK, so we'll give Mr Whittaker the VIP treatment."

Timothy's eyes twinkled. "Yes. We want to woo him, and the New Year's Eve masquerade party is the perfect place for that. He'll see we can get things done quickly and efficiently."

I clapped my hands together, excited. Planning parties was always fun but New Year's Eve was even more so – glitz and glamour was a given and we could go all out, making sure the lodge looked the part and that our guests had the time of their lives... all behind the mystery of a beautiful mask!

There was a tap on the door, and Amory poked her head around. "Sorry, I didn't realize you were here already, Timothy."

"It's OK, Amory, we've only just started," I said, and introduced them. I got Amory up to speed with the party and what Tim wanted; she flipped her laptop open and went to work, designing interactive invitations that would be emailed to guests. I grinned as we went through the main points of planning any party: the invite list, the budget (unlimited!) and the music, food, and drinks menu. As we chatted away, the puppy wandered in through the open door, and jumped straight on to Tim's lap.

"Who's this little guy?" he asked, clearly smitten with the little fella who'd so far managed to steal everyone's hearts.

Amory grinned. "That's little Scotty. Give him two minutes and he'll be snoring on your lap. He's like a wind-up toy, a bundle of energy one second, and asleep the next."

Timothy chucked him under the chin. "He's cute."

Pride practically shone from Amory's eyes. "Thanks."

We fell into a serious discussion about the party, and managed to lock in almost every detail from the music (a string quartet) and table centerpieces (ornate gold candelabra), right down to the color of the napkins (rose-gold linen). Tim was certainly organized, which made our job so much easier.

"Right," Amory continued, closing her laptop. "I'll finish these invites in my office, and I'll email them to you for your approval. Once that's done. I'll meet with our chef, Cruz, go over the menu, then email you a range to choose from. Cruz can then organize a tasting plate for you to approve. Clio will orchestrate everything else."

I nodded, and Amory shook Tim's hand, before he reluctantly handed back a snoring Scotty and she retreated to her own office in the parlor next door. "We have to move exceptionally fast to have everything delivered," I reminded Tim, jotting more notes down, and hoping our suppliers would agree to help on such a short timeframe.

He smiled. "I'll run everything by Vinnie as soon as I get back to the office. It'll be the party of the year, Clio, I just know it."

"It will," I said, imagining the ballroom full of women in spectacular glittery evening gowns, holding Venetian masks to their faces as they flirted with strangers, the secrecy and mystery of a masquerade ball giving even the shyest person the chance to slip on another persona.

Tim tidied his paperwork away and sat back, clasping his hands together. "Who'd have thought we'd be sitting here like this, together again, after all these years. You're amazing, Clio, not only buying the lodge and restoring it, but building a business people are already flocking to. No wonder you were always written up in the papers in New York. You were their events darling, and rightly so."

I gulped, hoping he hadn't read *every* article that featured me. The scandal that had left me jobless and fleeing to Evergreen was thankfully behind me, but no girl could ever get over being called a groom-stealer in black-and-white print. And even though the gossip had eventually faded as juicier stories came along, it still smarted – I didn't want my friends to think I was that kind of person.

"Oh, they weren't so much talking about me, rather my clientele when I worked in New York." In my former life in the Big Apple, my celebrity clients always tipped off the press about their soirées. Everyone wanted to be known for having the most extravagant, exclusive parties. It helped me no end being written up as the party planner to the stars, but that life was over and I preferred anonymity at Cedarwood Lodge. Though we'd had a rogue reporter cover the bridal expo, it had been about the lodge as a venue, rather than the guest list, and I thought that was a step in the right direction.

Outside, snow drifted down, settling on windowpanes. The fire crackled for attention, so I stood to stretch and throw another log of wood on it. Timothy joined me by the fire, stepping a little closer than seemed necessary.

"It's their loss," he said quietly. "We have you now, and we're not losing you to the big city again." Tucking a tendril of my hair back, he stared into my eyes and I stood there stock-still, wishing I felt more for him than I did. Because I knew right then, that my heart belonged to another.

How the man in front of me was single still was beyond me, but I figured he was still getting over his divorce. Except, right now, he was flashing me enough signals that even a daydreamer like me could pick up on them. If only things had been different between us. But timing was everything and it was too late. Wasn't it? As usual, when I even considered what could be with Timothy, Kai's sun-kissed face popped into my mind.

I smiled, unsure of what to say. "Thanks for thinking of Cedarwood."

"I was thinking of you, I must admit."

The look he gave me was one I recognized so well from all those years ago – the type where he'd say something and follow it up with a slow, sultry kiss. In the quiet of the moment, we could still be those two teenagers who only needed each other... But we weren't those people any more.

Trying not to look too obvious, I retreated to the safety of my desk, his presence overwhelming in close proximity.

"Well, I appreciate it," I said, pretending I didn't understand his meaning. "And I promise it'll be the party of the year!"

"Did you ever think of me after you left, Clio?"

Oh boy. "Sure. I thought of you all."

He rubbed his chin, like he was weighing up what to say. "I thought about you constantly. Picturing you in the big city, going from party to party, dressed to impress, meeting interesting people. Living this exotic life. I kicked myself a million times for letting you go."

I waved him away. This was all getting way too sentimental for a business meeting. "That's all in the past. We didn't know any better back then..." And when I said we, I meant *him*, clearly. He was the one who'd got married and moved on quickly, and made babies with someone else: real, living, breathing children and whatnot. Still, I didn't begrudge him anything. It really was a distant memory for me. And in hindsight had probably made staying and living in New York easier, because I hadn't been pining for a long-distance love, just nursing a broken heart that had been surprisingly easy to heal in the bright lights of the big city.

"You say that, but I always wonder, you know? Would we have made it if you'd stayed? Would we have had a family, a house, a business together?"

He was speaking so fervently I had the urge to flee. What was the point of looking back? None of those things had happened, and they wouldn't either. He'd *had* a wife, a family, the dog called Buster, the cookies baked from scratch, and some of it had worked out for him and some of it hadn't.

It was too late for us. And yes, the thought made me a little sad – Timothy was one of the sweetest guys around – but he just wasn't right for *me*. No matter how many times he asked for a date or turned up unannounced, all my fleeting feelings had been those of a long-forgotten teenage crush.

Here was the universe placing a good man in my path and I wasn't interested. Instead I was pining after a man who would most likely head back to Australia once his family rift was fixed. Was I destined to be alone? I shook the thought from my mind – I didn't want to be anyone's second choice and, while Timothy wasn't that kind of guy deep down, that was sort of how it felt. Like, *you're back, and you're good enough, let's pick up where we left off.* But I wanted the fairy tale. The fluttery belly, the air sucked from the room when he walked in, the thought that I was number one in someone's eyes. Not a consolation prize.

I coughed, and let out a nervous little laugh, trying to lighten the mood. "Ah, but you had all of that with someone else, and now you have two love, love..." I skidded on the word. "...Two *lovely* children, and you should be very proud. We'd have broken up after our first fight about where the couch went, and whose turn it was to put the trash out. We were never much good at agreeing on things." I smiled at the memory of our epic fights – the slammed doors, the threats that we were finished, the fervent apologies and making up. We were such utterly different people. Tim had been an athlete through and through, and I'd been the dreamer with firm ideas about décor who'd yearned for another life somewhere more exotic than Evergreen.

With a deep breath, Tim smiled and said, "Feng Shui, I never really understood it."

I laughed. "Feng Shui was forgotten by the time I got to New York. Out there it was something else every other week. A new hobby, a new passion. Following the latest craze, as you do."

The sultry smile was back in place but dialed down a notch. Had I got my point across? "Well, no matter what, New York was good for you. But I'm glad you returned home safe." His cellphone buzzed, and he tapped his vibrating pocket, his mouth tightening. "That'll be Vinnie. I'll call you later." With a quick peck on my cheek, he walked out, answering the phone as he went.

I watched him drive off and counted the seconds, wondering how many it would take before Amory rushed in ready to grill me about Timothy. And sure enough: *One, two, three, boom!*

"So, what's the deal with Timothy?" she asked, her forehead furrowing. "He practically had love hearts for eyes!"

I scrunched up my nose. "We're strictly in the friend zone. My choice."

She sighed, drawing out the sound.

"I know, I know," I said. "I'm too fussy. But the thing is, I just don't feel anything for him, not now." I shrugged. "There's no point pretending."

She held up her hands. "I want to shake you until you see sense sometimes! Why can't you go on a date and see what happens?"

There was real confusion in her voice. Poor Amory could never understand my hesitation with men. I just had to be sure, and I found taking that step so difficult. "Well, you know why, Amory! Yes, he's sweet, buff, financially secure... but my heart doesn't beat a rhumba when he's around. It just beats the same old boompety boom, as usual. And I don't want to give him false hope if there's nothing there for me."

"Oh, darling, you and your obsession with visceral reactions. Won't he do? For some fun, someone to have dinner with, dare I say someone to tangle in the sheets with after a bottle of wine on a Saturday night? Don't you miss men?"

I debated whether to lie. "Not really. I don't think about tangling in the sheets at all, because I know how much those sheets cost."

Her mouth fell open and she laughed uproariously. "Clio, darling, you're hopeless. You go around kissing Kai and then pretend you haven't." I opened my mouth to protest, but she held up her hand. "Don't think I don't know about that! But what does it mean? Look, if you won't tell Kai you like him, and you won't consider a measly date with Timothy, what are you going to do? Snuggle up to your Egyptian cotton sheets for the rest of your life?"

"You have to admit they are nice sheets."

"Seriously, Clio!" Pink spots appeared on her cheeks. Scotty chose that moment to run over and try and climb up my leg like a tree. I scooped him up and buried my face in his fur; he really was the sweetest thing.

"OK," I said, trying to take her more seriously. "I don't know who I'm going to snuggle up to. I might have to borrow your puppy."

"Nice try, but you cannot get away with a subject change like that with me and expect I won't notice. You need to be honest with yourself, Clio. Don't let two good men walk out of your life because you're scared to admit how you feel."

"Who said I'm scared?"

"It's written all over you, in big, fat, capital letters."

I sighed. "I think *you're* loved-up and you want me to be loved-up too, so everyone at the Loved-Up Lodge can be joyous and loved-up. Not all of us are so lucky, you know."

"I can see you won't listen to reason." She tried to appear huffy and I stifled laughter, but it spilled out regardless.

"Darling," she moaned. "Why won't you just give love a chance?"

I fell back on my chair, and she followed suit. "I would, I really would this time. But he's not ready."

"Who?"

"Kai."

She raised her eyebrows, "How do you know? Have you asked him?"

"Trust me, I just do. He's going through something major in his life right now and love is not on the cards. The timing just isn't right, which is the story of my life."

"And yet he's *here*." The sparkle was back in her eye and I realized I'd said too much... she wasn't going to give up that easily. "Kai's sorting out Cedarwood again, just like he never left."

Chapter Thirty-Three

The next day, I called a team meeting. We had to move at lightning speed if we wanted the party to go smoothly, and luckily we were well adjusted to working under immense pressure. A lot of companies were closed over the Christmas/New Year period but we'd managed to get a number of things sourced and wheedled the suppliers into delivering on time.

We crammed into the kitchen; even though we had newly renovated and painted offices, we hung out like college kids around the table, close to the coffee pot and cookies. It was good brain food, right?

Thankfully, after Timothy's visit yesterday, we'd already got the ball rolling on a lot of the finer points. As Amory lifted her iPad and showed us the invitation she'd made we all sighed. "Stunning, Amory. Did it get approved?" I asked. She had such a talent for design, I often thought she should use it for something other than just party invites.

"Still waiting to hear back. I've emailed…"

We had zero time to play phone tag, let alone email tag. I held up a finger and dialed Tim's number, putting it on speaker so I didn't have to relay the conversation. "Tim, it's Clio. What did Vinnie say about the invites and overall plan for the party?"

There was a groan and I held my breath.

"Sorry for the hold-up, Clio. I've literally just hung up from him. He's decided to go for a Gatsby theme. You know, black and gold and all that jazz. So I'm really sorry but the invitation will need to be changed."

Gah! The team twitched nervously. A last-minute change in theme could really set us back. There seriously weren't enough hours in the day to be making huge changes like that. But I bit my tongue and pressed on, remembering that the customer was always right: "Roaring Twenties, got it. Is he *sure*, though? Because if I order everything, we won't have time to send it back if he changes his mind again." It was almost impossible to keep the frustration from my voice because Amory and I had spent the morning sourcing table centerpieces and décor for the masquerade ball, not to mention that we had ordered most of it and convinced the suppliers to deliver the next day. Maybe we could swap it all for Gatsby-style products if we called them and explained our predicament as soon as I'd hung up from Tim... I nodded at Amory, who opened up our spreadsheet of suppliers and highlighted the ones we would have to call and plead with to let us change our order and still get it delivered on time.

"I know," Timothy said with a sigh. "I tried to convince him we just don't have time to change everything now, but Vinnie is convinced a Gatsby party reeks of glamour, and apparently that's what we were missing."

I laughed, but it came out more like a nervous, jittery squeak. "And the menu?" Cruz had sent in an order for a long list of ingredients already, and I knew for a fact they wouldn't allow for any changes – we'd had problems with our supplier already, but we didn't have much choice as there weren't any other grocers in town.

"He wants a different menu."

Cruz clutched his head, while Amory reached over to pat his back.

"What kind?" I asked, hoping he would say something simple.

"How about I email it over?" That didn't sound good. I'd hoped Tim's boss wasn't an indecisive type. Maybe it was just nerves on his part? Either way, we couldn't mess around our suppliers by chopping and changing orders. They'd soon tire of us, no matter how much future business we promised them.

"Email it now, Tim. And if we can't return what we've already ordered, Vinnie will have to cover it. We'll try and swap what we've sourced but I can't promise anything."

"I know, and that's fine. I'll email the new menu and call you this afternoon."

"OK, thanks, Tim."

I hung up feeling wired and frazzled. I hadn't met Vinnie in person, and going through a middleman always created conflict. As Vinnie was out of town it made sense for Tim to be the go-between, but not if Vinnie was going to change his mind all the time. My phone pinged with an email.

"Go on, read it," Amory said. "I bet he's got something ridiculous written there and that's why he wouldn't say it on the phone."

I shook my head. "If it says Beluga caviar from the Caspian Sea, I'm quadrupling the price. We don't have time for this."

"Do you think Vinnie's a flake?" Amory asked, wrinkling her brow. What she meant was, someone who'd pull out of the party last-minute, with nothing paid, nothing promised, a time waster of the worst kind.

"Maybe we should send a pre-party invoice?"

"Let's," Amory agreed. "Just in case." We'd been stung before at the agency in New York. I'd learned pretty quickly that, just because people had recognizable names, it didn't mean they were on the level. After a few mishaps where we'd been left *sans* client, we'd changed our practices and got a deposit upfront if they were a little skittish. No one liked paying ahead, celebs hated parting with their money (go figure), but it was insurance, not only for the agency but also for us keeping our jobs. Here at Cedarwood we definitely couldn't afford to be left in the lurch.

"Perhaps we make that a stipulation going forward, Amory?" I said. "While our clients so far haven't been celebs, we also don't want to foot the total bill if they're a no-show."

I wasn't used to worrying about the money side of things – in New York someone else had always done the tallying – but here I had to be in charge of it all, and we were learning on the run. Thank God Amory was here.

"I'll email Tim an invoice and all our terms now," she said as her fingers flew over her iPad. A few minutes later she said, "Done. Right, so come on, read his email…"

Cruz waggled his eyebrows, "Yeah, the suspense is killing me. Let me guess, black and gold finger food?"

I read the email and laughed. "Oh my God, yes. He wants everything black and gold, including gold-covered strawberries. 'Think edible glitter, think edible gold… the more glam the better!'" I quoted, rolling my eyes. "Golly, how on earth are we going to get this done?"

"Allow me one second to face palm," Amory said. "Right, that's done. Now, this sounds like an Aunt Bessie job to me. A gold-plated dessert table sounds right up her alley."

I nodded at Amory. She was right. Aunt Bessie would love this challenge… and considering how involved Mom was with Puft, perhaps she could help out too?

"Micah and I have to meet Ned from the council this morning. He's inspected the chapel and hopefully he's going to sign off on it today. So we can drive you into town to see Aunt Bessie," Kai said.

"I have to get these suppliers sorted out first," I said, hoping they'd swap the elaborate candelabra we'd ordered for something Gatsby-ish instead… If they couldn't, at least they were gold. Perhaps they'd do at a pinch.

"I'll go," Isla offered, and I smiled at her, so grateful to have such a brilliant team around me. "I'll explain to Aunt Bessie, and help her hunt online if she needs to find edible glitters… While I'm there I can look in the giftshop in town. I'm sure I saw some Gatsby-esque photo booth props, and some vintage posters that might work."

"What's our motto, team? *Always say yes!*" I joked, the pressure fading a little as we divvied up the rest of the jobs.

Cruz read the rest of the email about the menu updates and said, "So, do I cancel the seafood? It's not exactly black or gold is it?" He wrinkled his brow like the new menu was insane. He'd learn. This was nothing compared to some things we'd catered for. We'd had lots of odd requests over the years, including a yellow-themed party – you haven't catered for odd until every single morsel is yellow. Thank God for saffron! We'd managed to dye a lot of the food to suit.

"You could do nori rolls? Seaweed is black, or you could encrust them in black sesame seeds…" The more I thought about it the more ideas sprang to mind. "We'll wow them with the gold, glittery stuff. Trust me, they'll love your menu."

He smirked. "I'll go see what I can dig up, and get back to you with some ideas before I order any more stock in."

"Thanks, Cruz." I liked how amenable he was to any spanner in the works. A lot of chefs I'd dealt with would have clutched their spatulas and spit out a torrent of abuse about indecisive clients, which only hindered the process. But not Cruz. After a quick moan he rolled with the punches and found their curiosities just that: curious. I hoped he'd never change.

As everyone rushed off to do their jobs, Amory and I faced our laptops, ready to do battle with suppliers. I turned the coffee machine on again, thinking that if nothing else we could get through this with coffee – we always had in the past! And of course champagne to celebrate our successes…

"Right, waiters, bar staff, and kitchen hands – we can hire a crew from a skill-hire place which guarantees a certain number on the night, but we won't get to meet them ahead of time, and we won't know their level of expertise. At this late stage, though, we might have to go with it, and then see about getting some local staff to agree to ad-hoc work?" Amory said as we rifled through our to-do lists.

I bit down on my lip, contemplating. Staff were always hard to find, especially in such a small town. "Yes, we don't have time to ask around town for this party. But let's advertise afterwards and find some reliable locals."

Amory made a note on her calendar. "Done. I'll call Sylvia from the skill-hire place and let her know. Next on the list – party prep."

"OK, we've done a few Gatsby parties in the past so let's roll with the same ideas… everything glittery, sparkly, we have to hire musicians, drape the chairs with clusters of pearls, we need feathers for vases, and signs that say, *Prohibition stops here, dollface*, that sort of thing."

"You're actually getting excited, aren't you?" Amory asked, and I recognized the same look in her eyes.

"Gatsby parties are the best! Obviously we'll have to order flapper dresses."

"And flapper headpieces."

"Clearly! It's part of the job to look the part." We grinned at each other. "OK, let's get everything ticked off our list. First things first… I'll see if we can exchange the things we've already ordered. Once that's done our reward will be dress hunting online over lunch?"

She threw her head back and laughed. "Deal. Gone are the days when we wandered arm in arm down Fifth Avenue…"

The change in our lives was so great it had the ability to take my breath away at times. "Are you happy here, Amory?" I asked, suddenly nervous that my crazy dream to run back to Cedarwood and start a new life had also pulled Amory from her high-flying corporate existence.

Her eyes twinkled. "You know, never in a million years would I have thought I'd end up in a small town in New Hampshire by choice. But it's the best thing I've done, I can feel it in my bones." She stretched out and I noticed her slippers, jeans, and big warm jumper and almost laughed – this was a far cry from the Amory who'd only ever worn six-inch heels. "I'll always love New York, but being away from the hustle and bustle is so damn nice, I wonder why I didn't do it sooner. Working here is a whole different ballgame, and I just know we're going to make it great."

I smiled, and felt happiness all the way down into my soul. "I'm pretty sure at the ripe old age of eighty our feet will thank us for the change. I see you've moved from stilettos to ballet flats."

"Why fight it?" she said. "I've swapped Fifth Avenue for Amazon, why not go all the way?"

"Right? And look how far our dollars will go!"

Chapter Thirty-Four

Later that afternoon, we'd finished all the reordering; charming suppliers was one of Amory's specialties so I had left that to her while I made progress with the rest of the list.

"Just quickly," I said, refilling my coffee. "Amidst the NYE party, we've also got to make a start on our February wedding. Can you touch base with our bride and get her RSVP list? Once that's done, we'll knuckle down to what else we need to do."

"Already done, darling," Amory said, holding out her empty mug.

"You're a superstar." That's what I loved about Amory – in business she was always a step ahead. She truly loved her job and thrived on being busy.

"Thank you, darling. It's sweet of you to state the obvious."

"Humble too, so utterly humble."

"I try."

"Shall we set up a time to Skype our bride?"

"Yes, I'll email her and lock in time for this week, yeah?"

"Perfect." We may have been midway through planning a NYE party, but weddings normally needed more than a month's notice and we needed to ensure our first Cedarwood nuptials went off without a hitch.

After giving me an air kiss, Amory went to her office and I called the grocer. Difficult suppliers that they were, he wouldn't budge and gave me a stern talking-to about food waste and being flighty. Holding in a scream, I reassured him we'd take what we'd ordered and sort out the new menu soon. Really, we'd have to find someone more accommodating in the future, but for now, he would have to do.

Cruz rapped on the door and came in with a plate of sandwiches. He popped them on my desk and left as quickly as he'd come – I yelled out thanks. While I nibbled, I switched gears and scoured the internet for props for the party, like feather boas and moustaches on sticks that guests could use in the photo booth. Scotty smelled something delicious on offer and scampered in, paws up on my shins, little nose twitching. I snuck him some of the ham from my sandwich, and wondered briefly if we were all sneaking him food. He was irresistible and I now knew the meaning of the term 'puppy-dog eyes'. Once he'd taken his fill and knew I was fresh out of scraps for him he toddled off, probably next door to Amory to repeat the process.

My cellphone buzzed, and I checked the screen before answering. Mom. I smiled, hoping she was calling about all the gold and glitter desserts we'd ordered.

"Mom, how are you?"

"Clio, what have you done?" Her frosty tone froze me down to my bones. "You promised me you'd leave it alone, and now Isla comes into Puft and tells us all how she's found a maze, and is going to restore it back to its former glory. You *promised* me, Clio."

Damn it. I hadn't thought to tell Isla to keep it hushed up for now. To be honest, I hadn't expected her to mention it to anyone, least of all my own mother.

I took a steadying breath. "They don't know anything about it, Mom. Isla stumbled on it and showed Micah, and they announced it to all of us on Christmas Eve. There was nothing I could do since they found it by pure accident. And I didn't mention a word about it, I just changed the subject and hoped they'd forget."

Mom sighed, a world-weary, I-can't-handle-this-any-more kind of sound. I was at a loss for words and was bone-weary about it all myself. Hiding someone else's secret was exhausting, especially when I didn't know what it was exactly.

Mom's delicate health concerned me, and I worried about what she'd do if she felt cornered, but surely it had to come out. It's not as though the townsfolk didn't know... They *did*, and they were keeping their lips pressed tight when questioned over it. And me, her own daughter, wasn't trusted enough to confide in. It was mind-bending.

"Mom, look. I know it's difficult for you and I'm not trying to push you or anything, but don't you think it's time you told me? Cedarwood is getting busier by the day. We've got guests booked to stay in the lodge soon. We've got parties and weddings planned. I can't keep it a secret for ever. People will stumble over it if they hike, and especially as Isla clears the grounds come spring. Don't you think it's better if I know what happened?" She didn't say anything but her breathing was audibly shallow. With a soothing voice I tried a different tack. "Why don't you come visit, and we'll find the maze together?"

"I never want to see it again as long as I live." Her voice broke but I pushed on. At least she hadn't hung up on me... not yet anyway. That had to be progress.

"I know you don't. But avoiding the situation isn't working, is it? Lots of people have kept your secret, Mom, which says a lot about how people feel about you. It's time to trust me. I am your daughter, and I do love you unconditionally."

The line went silent, and eventually she said so softly I could barely hear her, "I haven't exactly been a mother to you."

I closed my eyes, wishing so hard that she'd just forgive herself for whatever it was. "I love you, Mom. You've done the best job you could. I'm home now and I want to work on our relationship, and that means we have to be honest with each other."

Once upon a time I couldn't get out of town quick enough, bereft that my mom didn't care one iota about me. I'd been ready for a new life and new friends who would eventually become my family. But I'd been young and naive and hadn't known that whatever had happened to Mom had shaped her future and made her turn in on herself. Now, I was ready to help her navigate whatever it was, and be there for her, without any recriminations on my part. It was the only way forward. Any grudges I'd held had evaporated a long time ago and all I cared about was that she got better.

The faint sound of crying traveled the length of the line, and my heart just about tore in two. "Think about it, yeah, Mom? We can get through anything, me, you, and Aunt Bessie."

She cleared her throat, and managed to compose herself enough to say, "I'll think about it, Clio. Will I see you for Friday night dinner?"

"You sure will, I'm looking forward to it." The hope in her voice told me to leave it for the time being. That she was happy to have dinner with me was enough. It was a step forward and not something I would ever take for granted.

We hung up, and while it had been an emotional phone call, I felt like we'd finally gotten somewhere. Now I just had to tell Isla to leave the maze be for the time being; as thrilling as it would be to see it restored, we had to bide our time.

While the sun sank behind the mountains, pitching the sky into shades of dense gray, I thought about love and loss, and what shaped our lives. Could my mom find peace? I hoped so. If I didn't truly believe she could find peace, I wouldn't have pushed her so. She'd been living as if she was paying a penance, obsessively cleaning, hyper alert, not interacting with people if she could avoid it. I couldn't predict the future, but I hoped my good intentions wouldn't backfire.

Before I could get lost worrying, the phone rang again.

"Cedarwood Lodge, Clio speaking." A mumble of static greeted me.

"Clio! It's Georges. Sorry, the phone reception onboard is appalling."

From the choppy wind in the background, it sounded as though he was calling from above deck, not below. "Georges, how's it going? I bet you're staring into the beautiful blue of the Mediterranean!"

He let out a deep belly chuckle. "Sort of. I'm bracing myself for another storm actually. With the pitching of the vessel, I'm quite nauseous all the time…"

Poor Georges. Even though he'd left us in the lurch when he'd run off to be an onboard chef for a celebrity's cruise ship, I'd never be able to be angry at him – and look how well it had turned out! I was surprised, though, at the tone of his voice. He was quite plaintive, which was unusual for him. "You just have to develop your sea legs, Georges. All great adventures have their downsides, so I'm sure it's only temporary," I reassured him. "Soon, you'll be screeching you're the king of the world at the bow, or whatever that pointy front bit is called."

He laughed, but it was hollow. "Yes, yes, you're probably right. I just have to get *acclimatized*. It's just a matter of becoming *one* with the sea, the beast that it is."

"That's the spirit, Georges!"

"Did you find a new chef? I'm so sorry to have left you in such a bind, Clio. You know I could always come back… if you insisted."

Oh, Georges! I suddenly understood his phone call. "Well, we were lucky actually, Georges, and we managed to hire Cruz as a part-time chef until he figures out his new direction. I'm hoping, though, that we'll be busy enough and give him enough creative freedom that he'll stay on for good. I am sorry, Georges. But really, I just think you're a little homesick. If you give it a chance, this will be the best thing you ever did."

I could empathize with Georges. I'd felt the same when I'd first arrived in New York. A country girl suddenly thrust into the big city, blinded by bright lights, fast talkers, and so much traffic. But each day had got a little better until I'd become one of those subway-catching, cosmopolitan-drinking locals, snatching every minute of the day to do things I'd never tried before. And it had been so worth it. Worth the nights I'd cried into my pillow, the mornings I'd been fuzzy with confusion, lonely among so many people. It was a learning curve, and when you'd done it once you could do it again, quicker, braver.

"Thanks, Clio. I know you're right. I do. It's just so different, but that's what I wanted, right? To be busy, to not spend every waking minute worrying about making enough money."

"Now you'll have money to burn, Georges! And when you have your days off, think of the places you'll see! Sailing around the world on someone else's dime is nothing to sneeze at."

It was like I could hear the cogs in his brain whirr as he warmed to the idea. "Yeah, not many people get to travel the world and get paid to do it. It was nice talking to you, Clio. Keep in touch, yeah?"

I smiled. "Send us postcards at every exotic port of call."

"Will do," he said jovially. "Give my love to everyone."

Just then I heard the pitter patter of tiny feet and that could only mean one thing. Trouble. "Where are you, you little varmint!" I said jokingly, watching as the fluffy ball of fur heavy-breathed his way under my desk. I bent on hands and knees to grab him before he used my antique handwoven rug as his personal toilet or nibbled on one of my spare pairs of high heels, tossed under there in case of surprise customer arrivals.

I scrabbled for him, darting a hand and grabbing air. I huffed.

"What on earth are you doing, darling? Is that one of your yoga moves?"

I started and smashed my head into the top of the desk as I tried to retreat, realizing it probably wasn't my best angle, rump in the air, jiggling around for the world to witness. The little fur ball barreled backwards out of sight, and my hand came to rest in a still-warm puddle. "Amory! He's peeing all over the place!"

She laughed from behind me. "There's absolutely no point harping on about it now, darling. What's done is done. All the puppy-training manuals say you have to catch them *before* they commit the act; yelling like a banshee after does absolutely *nothing* except confuse the poor mite." Scotty dashed out of the office and down the hall to the front door, his little paws clip-clopping on the wooden floorboards.

Ungraciously, I managed to shimmy my way out from beneath the desk and Amory handed me a wet-wipe to clean up as she laughed. "Jesus, did you have a nap down there? Darling, you're quite *bedraggled*…"

"What?"

Before she could answer, Isla, Micah and Kai trooped in. The trio gave me a slow once-over, alarmed at my heavy breathing and red face, hair sticking up at odd angles. Running my hands through my riotous hair I pasted on a serene 'I'm in control' smile and said, "How'd it go with Ned?"

"Great," Kai said, hiding a smirk. "He's signed off on the chapel, and has agreed to the plan for the chalets. Only kicker is, you need a registered builder on-site at all times…" He trailed off.

"Oh, but—" I stopped short as a car slipped into the driveway, pulled to an abrupt halt, and Timothy climbed out. I frowned, hoping it wasn't another issue with the New Year's Eve party. Looking back to Kai I smiled distractedly. My mind was whirling as I tried to troubleshoot any potential problems while thinking I should really respond to what Kai had just said. "Sorry, Kai, could you repeat that?"

Amory nodded at Tim through the window, then headed toward the front door to let him in. Turning back to Kai I tried once more to concentrate on what he was saying.

Just then, out of the corner of my eye, I spotted Scotty careening through the snow and running straight for Timothy. Before I could even so much as shout out, he skittered under Timothy's feet sending him flying. *Holy moly!* Timothy fell in a heap, letting out an *oomph* as he landed hard on the ice.

"Oh, no!" I raced outside, pushing past Amory, who'd frozen on the spot, her face pinched with worry. "Are you OK?" I asked breathlessly.

Tim stood and brushed snow from his jeans, a rueful grin on his face. "Sure, sure, he caught me by surprise, is all."

Amory scooped up Scotty and held him to her chest. "I am so sorry, Tim, he just ran out! I thought for a minute you'd landed on him, and my heart just about stopped."

"Hey, he's a puppy, he didn't do it on purpose," Tim said. "And he was well clear of me, don't worry."

"Are you OK, little man?" Cruz said as he wandered out, standing next to Amory while she searched Scotty for any cuts or bruises as he wriggled in her hands. The care she was taking over him showed a completely different side to Amory. All of her untapped maternal instincts were coming to the surface and although, sure, she might never have wanted to be a mother in the real sense, her protective instinct was still strong.

"He's fine," I said to Cruz. "Tim took the brunt of the fall, Scotty scampered out of the way."

"Sorry, Tim," Amory said again, pulling her attention away from the squirming puppy. "It's just he's so little and fragile, you know. He's just a baby really."

"Is everything OK with the party?" I asked Tim, worried another unofficial visit spelled trouble.

He slung his hands into his pockets as we walked to the door. "Yes, Vinnie's happy, invites are sent, and Cruz has the new menu sorted. I'm here to steal Cruz and Amory away actually. I've lined up a range of cottages to show them in the area."

"Oh, of course." They really were serious about moving to Evergreen and starting a life here. Part of me understood their need for a space of their own, but still, I'd miss them at the lodge. My mornings with Amory, slowly awakening as the sun split the sky, our chats over coffee and cake.

"We'll just grab our coats," Amory said, pulling Cruz inside with her.

As we followed slowly behind, Tim motioned toward my office and said, "Can I talk to you for a sec, Clio?"

"Sure."

In my office we sat at the desk. "What's up?"

He fumbled with the sleeve of his sweater. "I was… It's just that… How did you get on with the cocktail menu?"

The cocktail menu? I sensed that wasn't what Tim really wanted to ask. No one normally got nervous asking about gin and tonics. "I thought I emailed you? Anyway" – I smiled – "we've hired a mixologist for the evening, so he can fling those cocktail shakers and wow the guests, without spilling a drop." Mixologists were worth their weight in gold. They had an innate sense of how to entertain people, not only with their cocktail knowledge but also their upbeat personalities and general sense of fun. They were worth every penny, and we never scrimped on hiring the best we could find for the job. Amory had convinced one of our favorites from New York to fly in for the evening, and we were lucky to secure him so late, and that was only because he'd had a cancellation.

"Great, that should be lots of fun…" he tailed off.

I nodded, hoping he would get to the point soon. "Anything else?"

He clasped his hands and looked beyond me. "Erm… That's about it, I guess. You'll save me a dance on the night, won't you?"

I laughed. "Of course."

"I'd better go, they're waiting for me." His face was etched with concern. What had he really wanted to ask? Part of me didn't want to know. Maybe I had to be more upfront with him, but what if I was presuming too much? Then I'd look a fool.

"I'll walk you out."

We joined Cruz and Amory outside once more. Both were bundled up and ready to find their very own dream house. Kai stood peering under the bonnet of Micah's rust bucket of a car, while Micah tried to explain that he was sure it would work again if they just did this or that. Again, it was having some kind of mechanical issue, and I wished he'd scrap it and drive something more reliable.

The car diagnosis over, Isla started a tense discussion with Micah about what movie to watch on the upcoming movie night we'd been planning. Micah was deeming all of Isla's suggestions 'too girly' – when in fact I knew he'd watched many a chick flick back in the day.

"Why don't you guys go to Shakin' Shack that night and leave us to it?" I said, diplomatically. There was no way I wanted our movie night ruined by men pretending to hate chick flicks!

"I've got *Grease*," Isla said. "And a selection of other musicals. But the boys here seem to think that's LAME, in big, fat, capital letters."

We'd need donuts, and lots of them.

"Deal," Micah said, laughing. "I'll take the boys for burgers and you girls can snuggle up and dream of John Travolta sweeping you off your feet."

Isla bumped him with her hip. "Oh, so you just so happen to know the star of the movie, huh!"

A blush crept up his cheeks. "No, it was… a lucky guess."

"We'll still think you're manly if you admit you're a fan of musicals, Micah," Amory said, grinning.

Micah reddened. "Help me out here, guys."

"We won't judge you, Micah," Cruz said, deadpan.

Micah swatted his arm and said, "Get outta here before I change my mind and we all watch it together."

The gang burst out laughing and Micah's color deepened. We used to watch musicals together a million years ago, and I couldn't remember him complaining about our famous singalongs back then. The joys of your best friend being a girl, I suppose.

Timothy gave me a loose hug and took Amory, Cruz, and little Scotty in his car to view cottages in Evergreen.

Isla and Micah waved them off and then walked back in the direction of the chalets. They were preparing them for the painters who'd arrive in the New Year.

"Make sure you light a fire, Micah," I yelled after him. The chalets were ice-cold with the frosty breeze blowing off the frozen lake beside them. Kai and I left them to it, instead opting for the warmth of the lodge and a little hot chocolate to take the chill away.

Once I'd made a pot of cocoa we stood nursing steaming mugs in front of the potbelly stove, which belched its usual greeting. We sat for an hour, chatting, and then lapsed into silence.

"It's so quiet," he said suddenly. "No puppy, no banging of pots. It's weird how you get used to a choir of sounds, until they're gone."

"I know," I said. "The lodge is going to be so lonely when you all leave again. Isla has moved in with Micah, and Amory, Cruz, and Scotty will no doubt find a nice cozy cottage, and you... you'll be heading back to San Francisco. Soon it'll just be me, rattling around the big old lodge again."

And you and Bonnie Tyler will be back to sobbing into your wineglass. Shut up, brain.

Kai gave me an understanding smile. "It's like we're big kids at camp, having the most magical time, and then it's going to be over, and become a distant memory that makes us smile. Cedarwood certainly gets under your skin."

"It does..." It was bittersweet, hearing him talk in such a way. "I wonder what it'll be like having real guests stay here? It's not like I can force them out of bed to have coffee with me, or yell at them for leaving their clothes everywhere. I'm really going to miss having Amory here." *And you.*

"You'll get used to it. Soon you'll be so busy you'll fall into bed and forget you ever lived any other way."

"I don't think so. These times where we've shaped the lodge, and have all come together to make things happen... it feels so special, and so different. I don't know how long I'll have Amory and Cruz for, not really, and the same with Isla and Micah. And then there's you. I just hope you'll all come back some day. That we'll make it a tradition to celebrate Christmas or New Year together." I swallowed a lump in my throat. I wanted everything to stay like it was, right then, at that moment.

"Count me in," Kai said.

"You'd come all the way back here every Christmas?"

"Why do you act so surprised?"

I shrugged. Kai could be so hard to read at times and I often couldn't distinguish between what I wanted him to say and what he really said. "I just am."

Quietly he turned to me and put a finger under my chin, tilting it up so we were gazing into each other's eyes. "Clio, you have no idea how people see you, do you?"

"What do you mean?"

"People *want* to be around you. That's why they come here and don't want to leave. It's not just the scenery, the picture-perfect setting, it's you as well. You paint this picture of a different kind of life, and you sprinkle your magic dust over it, and they're spellbound. People want to be where you are. Cedarwood has its own pull, but then there's you..."

I let out a nervous laugh. "I..."

"You're intoxicating, and you have no idea how special you are. When we were here renovating with the team, did you not see everyone coming to you every five seconds with inane questions they knew the answers to? Six phone calls from

330

one painter, to query the color you told him a hundred times already? The way they tell you joke after joke just to hear you laugh?"

I double-blinked, sure he was making it up. The team was tight-knit, and we'd had a barrel of laughs. "They were just good guys."

"They were. But you have this extraordinary power over people, Clio. You make them want to be in your spotlight. They want to be your friend, your confidante. Anything to be near you."

I couldn't reconcile the person Kai was speaking about with myself.

His finger smoothed a trace down my cheek and I felt myself lean in to his warmth. "Believe it, Clio."

Any rational thought escaped, and I was lost in his deep, ocean-blue eyes. *Kiss him, Clio.* Before I could debate with myself, I reached up to cup his face and pressed my lips against his. A frisson of desire raced through me, provoking jelly-legs. Kai stepped closer, pushing his body hard against mine, and kissed me back, deeper and more slowly. Heat flooded me, and it was all I could do not to gasp when he broke away, with heavy-lidded eyes. How did he learn to kiss like that? It took my breath away.

A second later Amory appeared in the doorway. "We found the cutest cottage... Oh, um, never mind," she said, ducking back behind the door.

Kai dropped his hands and laughed, calling out to her. "It's OK, Amory. I'm going to help Micah and Isla with the chalets. I'll talk to you later, Clio." He headed out, giving me a look that said *this isn't over* as he walked away.

Knowing what was about to come, I went to follow, but Amory hooked my elbow as I walked past. "You're not getting away that easily," she said, eyes bright. "What happened? Your cheeks are rosy pink and you've got those dazed-up manga eyes happening. He kissed you, didn't he?"

"I kissed him!"

"And?" she said, hopping from foot to foot with excitement.

"And then again you walked in! Do you have some kind of radar?"

She cupped her face. "God, I want to slap my *own* face! We need a signal, like a napkin on the door handle, or a…"

I laughed. "Amory, it wasn't planned! It was a spontaneous thing! It's not like I plan to swoon my way around the lodge, flinging myself against every surface so he can ravish me!"

"Why not?" she asked, her face a mask of seriousness. "It's your lodge!"

I sat at the kitchen table and cradled my head. "Urgh. I'm thirty-three, almost thirty-four in fact, and I'm acting like a lovestruck fool. He completely befuddles me, and the brain in my head goes on vacation."

"Lust, pure and simple," she said with a firm nod. "I've seen it before; you'll survive."

"It's more than lust." I wanted to snatch the words back as soon as they escaped. "Well, what I mean to say is, it's just, it's not…"

She rolled her eyes and sighed dramatically. "Clio, you like the damn man, and he clearly likes you. It's really a very simple equation. Girl tells boy, or boy tells girl, *hey, I really like you, and I want to take this kissing thing a few steps further…*"

I held up a hand. "Oh, my God, please don't school me on how to date a guy."

She huffed. "Someone needs to!"

"They do not!"

She stared me down, and I knew by the set of her lips that she had a trump card. Damn it, she always had one up her sleeve. "OK, tell me the last guy you admitted your feelings to?"

"You want me to go back through my past boyfriends?"

She wrinkled her brow. "Clio, you dated them for about five seconds. I don't think you committed to anyone in the whole time you were in New York!"

Damn it, she had a memory like an elephant. "There's no point dating someone when they're not *The One*. Why waste my time?"

"Stop trying to avoid the question. Who have you ever told you're keen on them? Given them the green light? Fluttered those silky long lashes and said with real words, 'I, Clio Winters, think you're a bit of all right, and I'd like to invite you to share my thousand-thread-count cotton sheets for the evening'. Give me a name. One name."

I let out a peal of laughter. So, I really liked expensive sheets? They made good bedfellows! "I can rely on my sheets, you know? They're always there, just how I left them. I get into bed and they wrap their silky threads around..."

"Stop! You're doing it again! When have you ever admitted to any man how you felt? Have you ever?"

I considered it. Had I ever told anyone how I felt without knowing for sure how they felt about me first? There'd really been no one serious except for Timothy... Puppy love, I reminded myself. Too many years ago to count.

"You know, I don't think I have." This time I stopped her from interrupting by placing a hand over her mouth. "And that's only because they didn't set my world on fire. My heart didn't race, I didn't think poetically. If I was away from them, they didn't cross my mind. Shouldn't real love be arresting, and stop you in your tracks, make your heart sing, your body tingle, make everything else seem unimportant? And anyway..." I took my hand from her mouth. "Why does it matter? You've distracted me on purpose to hear me blather on like a fool."

"Why does it matter? Because Kai is *exactly* like you! He's not going to admit to it, and you're pussyfooting around him, and I want to grab you two and bash your heads together."

I just stared at her, so she sighed and continued: "You're both happy sneaking kisses here and there, but neither

333

of you is brave enough to admit how you feel! He'll leave, and you'll pine for him. Admit, even just to *me*, that he does make your heart sing, your body tingle – that's how you know what real love feels like." She folded her arms triumphantly.

I still wasn't convinced. "He did say the most beautiful things just now, but it was like he was talking about another girl," I said, slowly.

She laughed. "Oh my God! He's trying to let you know, it's OK to love him! GOD, WOMAN!"

Was I that bad at reading his signals? Sure, I'd made the leap and kissed him a few times; it was impossible not to. But love was so complicated! Could I even call it love? This whole love scenario was so much easier when it was about someone else.

"You see, he's having some really huge issues with his family, and I don't want him sort of using me as a pick-me-up and then realizing it was a mistake."

Just when I was hoping to change the subject Micah walked in wearing his perpetual half-smirk, carrying in a parcel that had been delivered. He glanced from me to Amory and tutted, plonking himself on the seat next to me.

"Boy talk?" he said, earnestly.

"She's at it again," Amory said.

"Oh no you don't. Don't think you're talking over me again, you two."

They just ignored me, and continued: "So she's kissed him again, but he's got some family problem – I mean who *doesn't* these days, but for the sake of argument, let's roll with it – and she seems to think *he* thinks she's a nice soft landing pad on which to lick his wounds, but then once healed he'll flit off to the never-never."

Micah nodded, and linked his fingers, taking his time to consider it all. "But she knows him, right? She knows he's not exactly the love 'em and leave 'em type? I mean, we haven't seen him act remotely like that, have we? He's

334

been almost gentlemanly with his favors, like something out of a period drama."

"Right? It's amazing people like her manage to procreate. At this rate they *might* hold hands by 2020."

I held up a finger. "Aha. We've held hands, thank you very much."

They continued to ignore me and instead diagnosed my love life. "So what *is* her problem? Commitment-phobe?" Micah asked, wrinkling his brow.

Amory shook her head. "Even though that's the kind of vibe she gives out. Like, *stay away, I am too busy for the likes of you. Here's me, running my business, crooning to Bonnie Tyler when I've had too many glasses of red wine. Here's me buying one-thousand-thread-count sheets online again.* And so they stay away. Really, she's scared of rejection. Would rather keep her steely heart in one piece even if it means the only love in her life is an eighties ballad and some freshly washed Egyptian cotton."

"Guys, seriously, you're not Oprah, OK? Not even Dr Phil. You're so far off base it's not even funny."

Micah gave me the sweetest smile, but it was sad too, like he could see something I couldn't.

"What is it, Micah?"

The day stilled. He and Amory exchanged a glance and she nodded. "I have to go help Cruz." She air-kissed me. "Micah, you talk some sense into her."

Softly, he said, "It's your mom, Clio. You act this way because of your mom. You don't let any man close in case they push you away, because you grew up lonely, with a mother who was absent almost all of the time, even when she was sitting right beside you."

It felt like I'd been punched. It was one thing for me to recognize that, but another for my best friends to notice. "It's not because of that," I said, thinking I'd come to terms with all of it a long time ago. With Mom and everything that had happened. Or… maybe I'd been trying to heal everything too quickly? Sure, she'd admitted she hadn't been there for me and that had helped, but had I really dealt with everything that had happened? All the years of feeling hurt and lonely. Was it time for me to finally open my heart up to someone again? Someone who could smash it into little tiny pieces?

Chapter Thirty-Five

At a quarter to midnight, headphones in, Bonnie Tyler crooned to me as only she could. Tears stung my eyes, and I swatted at them angrily. What Micah and Amory said had shaken me up, but I knew they were speaking from a place of love. Still, it hurt. Sure, I could forgive my mom as an adult, but the memory of my childhood would always be there.

There was a light tap on the door, and I took an ear jack out. "Yes?" I called, wondering if Amory had a sixth sense when it came to me weeping away to Bonnie Tyler.

"Up for a little midnight yoga?" Kai whispered through the crack in the door.

I froze. Firstly, I wasn't climbing up a snow-covered mountain, I'd be swept away in a mini avalanche, I was sure of it. Second, I was a puffy-faced mess. No, I had to avoid him at all co…

He opened the door and walked in. *Damn it!*

Surveying me and the multitude of screwed-up tissues surrounding me, he frowned. "What's wrong?"

I took a shuddery breath, trying to formulate a lie. An eyelash malfunction had been used already so that was out. Work issues – no, he knew too much. In the end I settled for the truth.

"Sometimes I feel like I'm the only person on the planet who doesn't know her own mother." I wanted to slap myself when I realized what I'd said, and to Kai of all people, whose birth mother had died before he'd even known about her. Wasn't he suffering the very same fate, albeit in different circumstances? "Sorry, I mean…" I tailed off.

"Don't apologize." With a smile, he walked over and settled on the bed beside me. "And why has that suddenly upset you tonight?"

I tried not to sniffle and snort because, how unattractive was that? But it was impossible. Once I started the 'woe is me' game, it was hard to stop. "Micah and Amory were giving me a kind of pep talk, and then they mentioned that the reason I don't really ever put myself forward..." Urgh, how to say it without mentioning Kai's name? "Put myself out there, you know, *in life*, is because I'm scared of getting rejected. Which stems from the way I grew up *beside* my mom, but not *with* my mom."

He put an arm around me and pulled me close; leaning into his warmth, I felt calmer. "And what do you think? Is that how you feel?"

"I guess I stopped thinking about it, because why keep reliving it? Mom was Mom, and I knew from early on things would probably never change. The thing is, I didn't think I'd internalized it, and put up barriers. But I guess I did and just pretended I hadn't. And for Micah to recognize that in me, well..."

"For what it's worth, I don't think your mom's able to see much out of her peripheral. It's like tunnel vision; she gets through each day the only way she knows how. But to me you come across like the girl who knows what she wants, but is careful and considered about it. Except maybe when you bought Cedarwood on a whim... but everything else you've told me about has been well thought out. I don't think it's necessarily a barrier, more a process of yours, and that's OK. We all deal with things differently."

I closed my eyes and listened to the thrum of his heart. "I know you're right, about Mom I mean. Being back, it's made such a difference. I can see it now and I hope together we can move past it."

He stroked my arm softly as we both stared off into the darkness, contemplating it all. "What about you, Kai? Have things got any clearer for you?"

Turning to face him I realized how close we were, almost coiled together like lovers, but somehow it felt like more than that. It felt deeper, as if Kai was someone I could trust and lean on, someone who'd listen and understand when I talked.

"Things are better for me," he said, sighing softly. "There's a lot to be said for having space to think. Up the mountain, where it's just me and the birds, I realize I'm just a tiny speck in this huge, wide world. You know? So yeah, my parents could have been honest with me from the get-go, but I can't hate them for hiding it. I get it. They would have said something like, 'We'll tell him when he's old enough to understand, when he's ten,' and then I'm suddenly ten and it's not the right time, and then twelve and that's not either, and before long it's too late, and they sleep with that knowledge every night and it eats away at them, but they don't know how to say it, how I'll react. And so they try to forget."

"But then they did tell you."

"And look how I reacted. Which is exactly why they didn't tell me before." He scrubbed his face with his hand. "I've come to terms with it, more than I thought I would a few days ago anyway. Like when I hike, and I'm surrounded by the fog, the low-slung clouds, I think if the worst thing that ever happens to me is knowing this secret, then I'm doing OK."

"We humans do like to complicate things." In Kai's arms the world started to make sense. Big things, past hurts, loss and loneliness dimmed, and all I could feel was his particular kind of calm washing over me. I didn't want to say anything to ruin the moment. I was happy just *being*, euphoric even, and grateful to the universe for showing me the kind of person I wanted to love. And that was Kai. I'd tell him, before he left, but not right now. Right now I wanted to enjoy the moment, this realization that I was ready to take a risk on love. Just the knowledge of that made me smile.

Stars twinkled through the snow-dusted window as we lay there and I fell asleep in his arms.

Chapter Thirty-Six

Friday rolled around bright and clear with the snow glistening across the ground. After a long day at the lodge, I'd showered and changed and hotfooted it to Mom's house. We worked quietly together assembling dinner and Aunt Bessie was joining us as a last-minute surprise. It was the perfect way to finish off a long week of planning, ordering, decorating, and overall panicking that we could pull off the Gatsby party. As I chopped potatoes into rough cubes, certain even I couldn't mess up mashing them, Mom was baking some chicken concoction of hers. I wasn't sure chicken needed so long in the oven, but I kept my lips zipped. She was the one who had been taking lessons from Aunt Bessie, so what did I know?

Aunt Bessie sashayed in, kissing our cheeks and unwinding her scarf as she went. "How are my two favorite people?" she said, her voice high with happiness.

"Good, good," we said. Mom and I had been working beside each other in perfect synchronization. There'd been no tension over Isla's discovery of the maze, and no real mention of her phone call to me about it, and I was hoping this was a good omen for the evening. Maybe she would show me the maze herself, of her own free will.

Aunt Bessie put some groceries in Mom's fridge, including the obligatory box of donuts. She gave me an encouraging smile and double-checked the cubes I'd cut. Then she opened the oven and lifted the foil off Mom's chicken dish. "Annabelle, what's this?" she asked. "I thought you were doing the basil lemon chicken recipe I sent over?"

Mom stared at her. "I am."

Aunt Bessie's mouth opened and closed like a guppy. "Did you read the recipe?"

Mom folded her arms across her chest. "I'm not completely hopeless, you know. Of course I read the recipe. What are you like?"

With a dramatic sigh Aunt Bessie took the tray from the oven and ripped off the foil. "That recipe called for a *whole* chicken. Not teeny tiny pieces like this. You've gone and made cardboard out of it."

It was Mom's turn to do the guppy impression. "Chicken is chicken."

Aunt Bessie hooted. "No, chicken *isn't* chicken, Annabelle. Right, well, there's nothing we can do with this, so let's see what we can salvage out of the fridge." She rummaged around, mumbling to herself before closing the fridge door.

"OK, we're going out. Get your coats. We'll have burgers and beers at Shakin' Shack and I don't want to hear any excuses."

I waited a beat. Waited for Mom to refuse point-blank. We'd made it through Christmas, but even that had been a huge step for Mom. Going out to a restaurant... Instead, Mom took the tray from the bench and tipped the cardboard chicken into the bin. "Well, sure, but I can't leave the kitchen like this," Mom said.

I suppressed a victorious smile. "We'll clean up now, Mom, all of us, and then we'll go."

There was no way Mom could leave the cottage if her kitchen was untidy – she'd never be able to relax, and this was a big step for her – so we all bustled around, tidying as quickly as we could in case she changed her mind. When Mom put the trash bag in the outdoor bin, Aunt Bessie whispered, "I didn't think she'd say yes!"

"When was the last time she went out to town for dinner?" I whispered, still surprised.

"Ages ago."

I nodded, "OK, let's make it a really fun night."

This was one gigantic Neil Armstrong kind of leap forward. We were getting closer to that sitcom mother and daughter vision I'd always had. I knew it could all crumble when she visited Cedarwood and set eyes on the maze again, but for tonight so far so good.

Turning back to Aunt Bessie I wound my scarf around my neck. "How's your Instagram account going?"

Aunt Bessie's eyes shone, and she grabbed her cell from her bag. "Oh, Clio, it's one of the best things I've ever done. I borrowed one of those *Social Media for Dummies* books and worked out how to ramp up my followers. I've been getting orders from all over the country, but are you ready for the kicker?"

"Yes."

"Helena from *America Today* re-Insta'd my death-by-chocolate donut tower. You know the one – thirty-six chocolate ganache-filled donuts stuck together with dark chocolate icing, and topped with shards of toffee and spun sugar."

"Yes, I know the one!" I exclaimed, amazed at how far Aunt Bessie had come in a matter of days.

"Well, anyway, she got thousands of comments from her followers and I mean *thousands*, Clio." Aunt Bessie's cheeks pinked with happiness. "So she asked me to come on the show and do a baking demonstration. I was waiting until dinner to tell you and Annabelle all about it."

With a shaky hand Aunt Bessie held up her phone and showed me Helena's re-Insta of the spectacular donut tower, and, sure enough, there were thousands of comments underneath the picture. "Oh my God, Aunt Bessie, that is incredible!"

"I know, I know! I couldn't believe it. Now, what do you think I should wear on the show? My tastes might be a little outlandish for primetime morning TV." Her eyebrows pulled together.

"I think you're perfect the way you are, Aunt Bessie, especially for primetime TV. Why don't you wear the cobalt-blue pant suit? Your scarlet lipstick goes perfectly with that color."

"OK," she said, grinning. "I do love that suit."

"My aunt the celebrity."

Mom wandered back in so we turned away from each other and finished cleaning the rest of the kitchen in companionable silence.

***

Later that night, I was back in the office, smiling like a loon. Not only had Mom had dinner out for the first time in years, but she'd agreed to visit Cedarwood and show me the maze. Then I'd returned home to a flurry of emails about potential spring accommodation bookings at the lodge. At the rate we were going I'd have to employ Cruz to cook full-time. And really, we needed someone to handle the guest activities too.

Isla had been flitting from job to job as we needed her, but once spring had sprung she'd have her work cut out for her managing the expansive gardens alone.

While I was adding another role to our list of job vacancies that needed filling, Amory came in carrying two cups of cocoa. "Can't sleep?" I asked, noting it was almost midnight.

She shook her head, handing me a mug. "We haven't had two seconds to talk lately and I'm bursting with news. We rented the cottage! Oh, it's the loveliest place just outside of Evergreen. It's tiny but cozy, and I'm so looking forward to decorating it."

"That's great news, Amory! I'll miss you, even though I spend my life taking your empty coffee cups back into the kitchen," I said, just as Scotty came barreling in looking for hugs. I'd miss him too, with his boundless energy and soft cuddles.

"Oh, darling, that won't change. I'll still leave them scattered about during the day, so it will give you something to do at night."

"You're a true friend." I laughed and filled Amory in on dinner with Mom, and the latest bunch of emails and what was left to do for the party.

"Amazing, Clio! I've got a feeling things are going to be hectic over the summer." She gave me a smile. "Oh, that reminds me. Tim called while you were out, and wants you to call him back."

I blew out a breath. "What now?"

She shook her head. "I don't know, he didn't say why, but the whole time we were looking at cottages, all he did was talk about you."

"What did he say?"

She sipped her cocoa. "Well, it was like a celebrity tour of town. *This is where Clio and I used to buy tapes. This is where we kissed in the rain. This is where I asked her to the prom.* It was sweet and all, but methinks the boy has *not* moved on."

I grimaced. "That's a little awkward. He is *so* lovely, seriously, but I just don't feel that connection. And I wonder whether he really does either, or whether he's just remembering a time in our lives when things were simpler, you know? Like slipping into your oldest, most comfortable jeans…"

The old lodge creaked and groaned like it was agreeing with me. "Yeah, and first love does leave a sort of fingerprint on your heart."

I raised a brow. "Wow, Amory, how poetic of you… she of the steely-heart, non-soppy love club."

"The what club?" she laughed, and shook her head. "Anyway, did I see Kai wander downstairs from your suite?"

I scoffed. "As if *you'd* have seen anything; you would have been in the land of Zeds. Got spies have you?"

"Of course! Cruz told me. So you admit it? What the hell is going on, darling? Some best friend you are, who keeps all the good stuff under lock and key!"

I shrugged. "We just had one of those long, deep and meaningful conversations, putting the world to rights, that kind of thing, and then we fell asleep. It was nice."

She stared me down. "Nice? Just nice, darling?"

"Nice."

"Nice is a lie-in after too much champagne, nice is breakfast in bed, nice is…"

I clucked my tongue. "I get it! OK, OK, it was amazing. *Totally* amazing. Something has changed and I'm ready, I think… you know, to admit it first. But he leaves in a few days…"

"He's due to depart in a few days. Whether he leaves or not is surely up to you and him?"

"But he has to go back to work. And I'd hazard a guess it won't be long before he heads back to Australia for good, once things are sorted with his family. Why start something and get my heart ripped out when he moves back to his beachside lifestyle…? I'll be a distant memory, the pale-faced girl wearing fur, when he'll be around all the sun-kissed girls in bikinis…"

With an exasperated sigh Amory said, "Stop imagining the worst, darling! As far as I can tell he's got no inclination to go home, but you're not exactly giving him a reason to stay by not admitting how you feel, are you? He probably thinks you're only kissing him when you're bored or something, because afterwards you act like it hasn't happened! You need him for the chalets. Ned practically insisted." At the confused look in my eyes she sighed. "Ned's report said you need a registered builder here during the chalet refurbishments, no 'maybe' about it. And Timothy mentioned there's a ton of building work going on in the next town over. So… what this means is, if you really wanted it to happen, it could happen. Stop making excuses, Clio. Stop hiding. *Really*."

I tapped my pen against the desk, glad she didn't push any more. "Imagine if he stayed."

She waggled her eyebrows and hummed the wedding march, just as Kai walked in. I blushed furiously. How many people were up at midnight around here! Quickly I said, "So, yeah, we need to order those martini glasses, and…"

"On it," she said with a smirk. "I'd better go to my office and get that done straight away. It's totally soundproof when I shut the door. Which is good. Means I can concentrate. Gotta love a big oak door, don't make 'em like that any more. *Can't hear a peep.*" She leaped up and made for the door. "Come on, Scotty, we'd better leave these two alone…"

I made faces behind Kai's back for her to shut the hell up as the puppy raced to her side. He turned and caught me waving frantically at her to leave. I snatched my arms back and pasted on a smile. "Numb fingers," I motioned to my hand. "*So* much writing. *So* many to-do lists. Really, I should probably type them." I was rambling, Amory was ridiculous, the whole situation was too slapstick to be believed.

Kai gave us both polite smiles and we paused.

"Toodles!" Amory said and waltzed out of the room with the puppy under her arm.

Toodles? "Sit down," I said. "If you want." *Gah.*

"Sorry about the late-night disturbance, but my boss called. He wants me to head back as soon as possible. I tried to put him off, but he really needs me since more contracts have arrived. No rest for the wicked, hey?"

My heart fell. Plummeted, even. What horrible timing. Just as I'd built up the courage to say something. Was it even worth the risk…? How long would it be before his parents called him back, or he craved the Australian sunshine, the beach culture? "I don't want you to go," I said suddenly, the words escaping before I could stop them.

He stared at me and I hoped he'd read between the lines. Did I have to spell it out? "Really, Kai. I *don't* want you to go."

"I'll fly back to Cedarwood when I can," he said hurriedly, "and help with Ned when the chalet renovations start in earnest. Micah knows the plan and I can keep Ned sweet with phone calls, and lots of talk about meeting code, and…"

I swallowed panic. It was now or never, and I sent up a silent prayer to the universe that he wouldn't laugh in my face. "Kai, stop. I don't care about the chalets, the code, or Ned. I care about you. The reason I want you to stay is…" *Why was it so hard to say how I felt?* "…The thought of you leaving depresses me. When you're gone, I feel like a piece of my heart is missing. Even though we lead two very different lives, and you may leave the US for good, I want you to know I have feelings for you…" Heat rushed to my face and my hands shook. There, I'd said it. It was almost a relief, until I realized he hadn't said a word.

"Clio…" he breathed, and without giving him a chance to say anything more I pulled him forward into a kiss and put everything I had into it. I didn't want him to leave without knowing how I felt. It was damn good to be honest with him – and honest with myself too. I'd spent the better part of my life hiding from my feelings, so panicked about possible rejection that I hadn't really been living, or maybe only living vicariously through the brides-to-be I planned weddings for. Well, that had to stop. It was time for me to be just as ambitious with my love life as I was with my career…

Chapter Thirty-Seven

The next morning I was lolling in bed replaying my confession to Kai and coming to the horrible realization that he hadn't exactly reciprocated with the whole sharing-your-feelings thing. Sure, I hadn't really given him a chance, instead choosing to lock lips with him, but how did he feel in return? Would he leave in the early hours of the morning, avoiding a goodbye again? Surely not this time, after I'd opened up to him. This was why I tended to avoid romance; it was so damn messy and complicated. But oh so rewarding when a man could kiss the way Kai could and make you forget about the world around you. The problem was, I had forgotten everything and, after we'd chatted for a while about this and that, he'd headed up to bed. Alone. Was that a sign? A nice way of telling me no?

Rolling out of bed to start the day, I jumped as the phone rang. "Cedarwood Lodge." I made my voice bright, even though it was a little early for phone calls and I hadn't even had any caffeine yet. I went to the bay window, catching sight of Kai as he headed to the chalets, wearing his tool belt. He was still here, then, hadn't done another midnight flit. My heart fluttered at the sight of him.

"Clio! It's Tim. Have I caught you at a bad time?" I wrenched my gaze away from the window and traipsed downstairs, wondering why Tim needed me so damn early in the morning. "It's OK, Tim. I'm just about to make coffee," I said, pulling on my robe as I went.

"Still have it black with no sugar?"

I smiled, amused he remembered. My head was still so full of last night with Kai I needed a double shot of caffeine to get my brain into full-on party-planner mode. I shook the Kai daydream away, and focused on the call. "Still the very same. What about you? Milky white with two sugars?"

He laughed. "No sugar these days. Life is so boring when you're an adult!"

When we were younger we'd had plenty of study sessions, cramming for exams, wired on so much coffee. The good old days when life was simple.

"What can I do for you, Tim?" I asked, pulling down a mug and reaching over for the coffee pot. Cruz must've been up already and brewed an extra-large jug for us, knowing that between me and Amory we'd guzzle it down like water.

"Just confirming you received my email about the jazz band?" The string quartet had been canned and we'd chosen a jazz band to fit the Gatsby theme instead.

"Yes, I did. All booked and confirmed." Was he not getting my replies? I'd definitely emailed him straight back.

"That's good to hear," he said, his voice suddenly wistful. "What about the fireworks? Did the company return your call?"

Had they? I struggled to remember in my un-caffeinated state. Between us, Amory handled some of the suppliers, and I handled the rest. "I'll have to double-check with Amory. I think she was pushing for silent fireworks so we don't upset the animal life around Cedarwood, but still have the wow factor from the colors and patterns." Proud puppy owner Amory had definitely changed her attitude since becoming a canine mom.

"OK, that makes sense. Let me know?"

"Sure, I'll send you an email as soon as I find out."

"Just call me, Clio. It's easier when I'm out and about with clients."

I frowned. Maybe he was simply nervous because there was so much hanging in the balance, and kept detail-checking out of angst? "OK. I'll call you as soon as I talk to Amory."

We hung up and I took a sip of my coffee, feeling it work its magic through my bloodstream. I checked my sent emails, and found I had sent all of the confirmation emails to Tim, and there was also one from Amory CC-ing me about the fireworks, which had been booked and were silent for the sake of the animals. Was it a technical glitch? Or was he making excuses to call me?

***

I stepped out of the front door and headed in the direction of the chalets, but froze in shock as Mom's red hatchback turned into the driveway. We'd agreed she'd visit and we'd go to the maze, but I hadn't thought she'd actually turn up. I thought she'd renege, or make up some flimsy excuse.

Watching her exit the car, she looked every bit her age today, and I knew this visit was costing her. She held the driver's door for a moment, and looked in the direction of the woods. Hanging her head low, she shut it with a bang, and made her way to me.

"Mom, you came," I said, going toward her and enveloping her in a hug.

She gave me a wobbly smile and nodded.

"Are you sure about this?" Now it was time to confront the past, I wasn't sure it was such a good idea. She was so thin, so fragile. I didn't want to lose her again after the progress we'd made.

With a shuddery breath she said, "I'm sure, Clio. Let me show you my maze, my downfall."

I grabbed my coat and gloves, and gave Mom another wooly scarf.

We headed toward the woods, heads bent against the sheeting winds. It was a long trek, and probably one of the reasons I'd never found the maze as a child. I'd been scared

350

of the woods, and wouldn't have ventured too far in for fear I'd get lost. Micah had preferred running up the mountains, and that had been that.

"Did you design the maze?" I asked, knowing how much Mom had always loved gardening.

She nodded as we trudged through copses of trees, thrust into shadows.

"It was supposed to be the greatest thing ever," she said wistfully. "This feat of topiary. My parents had been friends with the owners of the lodge for as long as I could remember, and Morty had always been kind – letting me follow him around the gardens. Come summer we were out together every day, planting, and planning. He treated me like an adult, and not the child I was when I first played here. He completely understood my love of horticulture, and tried to guide me, went out of his way to teach me what he knew. So when we came across this clearing I had the most spectacular idea..." She tailed off as we got deeper into the woods.

"Building a maze?" I asked. Morty, I knew, had been the previous owner of the lodge, but knowing he'd shared Mom's love of gardening was something new.

Mom nodded. "Not just any maze: a maze that would be a work of art, and almost impossible to navigate. Dead ends, and false laneways. I designed it and we planted it. It took years for it to mature, of course. Morty pretty much left me to my own devices, not really believing I could accomplish it, I think. But I was determined. Years passed and, when I was a teenager, they hired me for real, and I worked the grounds here. It was my dream job, just like it's Isla's. I loved plunging my hands into the fertile soil, helping plants thrive." She lapsed into silence and I reached over to take her hand. I hoped she'd see the gesture as a show of support. I knew how hard this was for her, reliving the past, going back to a time that obviously tormented her still.

After a good twenty-minute hike we suddenly came upon it. I would have missed it if Mom hadn't paused and stared at it, her eyes filling with tears. The area was so overgrown it almost looked like every other part of the woods, except for one tiny difference – the clearing it was sitting in once you got past the outer bank of forestry.

"Why did I have to be so hellbent on making it impossible to navigate? I ask myself that every day."

"What happened, Mom?"

Her hands fell to her sides, and she closed her eyes and craned her neck to the sky. "I still feel her, after all these years I still feel her here." She tapped her heart.

"Who?"

"Tabitha. Little Tabby cat, we called her."

"Was she your daughter?" I held my breath, thinking of the black-and-white grainy pictures, the baby who grew into a toddler. The rocking horse on the front porch.

"No, no, of course not! Is that what you thought?" She looked at me incredulously.

I bit my lip, and shrugged.

"No, Tabby was *their* daughter. But she was my shadow, just like I'd been Morty's all those years ago. She followed me everywhere like a little pup. I should have known when she went missing where she'd be, but I just didn't think."

I grappled with the details but didn't dare interrupt. Mom needed to tell this story at her own pace, so instead I let her talk, let her words wash over me and hoped that through the telling she'd find a way to move forward.

"The lodge was jumping that summer. They needed it too." Her voice sounded almost dreamlike as she recounted her memories. "It had been hard going and they nearly lost Cedarwood so many times before that. But finally, families were swimming and sunbathing by the lake, some were playing croquet on the green lawns, the scent of roses heavy in the air, laughter punctuating the day. Guests were arriving by the carload, and Morty and his wife were checking them in and showing them to suites or chalets."

I could envisage Cedarwood as it would have been back then, a bright summer's day, people dotting the landscape.

The heady feeling of a long hot summer spent with family and friends, and no schedule.

"I remember feeling this sudden sense of dread, even though the sun was shining, the guests were singing, dancing, parading in swimsuits... I couldn't say why, but something just felt off. When Morty realized Tabby wasn't in the kitchen where he'd left her he asked me to find her because it was time for her dance lesson." Mom took a deep breath before pressing on. "So I searched in the usual places, that same feeling of unease creeping over me. When I couldn't find her, I told Morty, and he got the strangest look on his face – fear. His wife, too, was almost frantic. Tabitha was too young to be wandering off alone; she couldn't swim, for one thing. We must have checked the lake a dozen times. Before long the guests were searching alongside us. They recognized the distress on our faces."

I gulped, my heart hammering in my chest at Mom's recall. In my heart I knew something terrible had happened to Tabitha, but I hoped I was wrong. I waited for Mom to continue.

"Then it hit me," she said, her eyes a little wild. "The maze. We'd been at the maze that morning. She'd toddled after me as I hid the scavenger-hunt prizes in its hedgerows. She'd been desperate to know what the little gift boxes contained..." Shaking herself, Mom carried on. "...So I broke into a run, trying all the while to calm myself down. She'd only been missing a few hours, so even if she was lost in the maze she would be safe." Mom took a shuddery breath, tears running in rivulets down her face. "I dashed in, screaming her name, getting lost myself because I was so frantic to find her. I hoisted myself up, and tried to balance on top of the hedges so I could look over the top, and I saw a flash of blue. Her blue dress. I scaled over the side and made my way through the laneways. She was OK, I could see her – she was wearing her little cornflower-blue pinafore, the same one from that morning. I expected to feel relief, but still I had that overwhelming sense of dread."

Mom paused and I wished I could offer her some comfort.

"I got to her." Her voice sounded strangled. "At first it was like she'd fallen asleep, but when I got closer... her tiny neck was at an unnatural angle, and her eyes were open, unblinking. She was dead and it was all my fault. She must have tried to climb up to get out when she reached a dead end, only to fall and break her neck. If I had thought of searching the maze hours earlier we would have found her alive. If I hadn't designed the thing to be so goddamn difficult she might have found her way out. But she was gone. When I picked up her lifeless body and made the arduous journey to her parents, part of me died right there. That walk was the longest of my life and with every step I wished I was dead instead of her, but I was left to deal with what I'd done."

My pulse skidded with shock. I couldn't imagine how Mom had found the strength to walk with the lifeless little girl in her arms. I laid my hand across her arm as tears slid down my cheeks. "But Mom, don't you see, it wasn't your fault? You built a maze that would have drawn tourists to the lodge. You couldn't have foreseen an accident like that would happen."

She wiped at her face, pulling her arm away almost angrily. "It *was* my fault, Clio. I should have known to search for her here. I just wasn't thinking at all. I'd been so worried she was in the lake that I completely forgot about the scavenger-hunt prizes, and how curious she'd been. I should have *known* she'd come here."

I shook my head, but she was so adamant, though I just couldn't see how this could ever be her fault. It was a tragedy, yes, but it had been an accident. "Her parents didn't blame you, though, did they?" I said in a small voice.

Mom hugged herself tight, looking torn. "I don't know. They were in shock, completely and utterly grief-stricken. Morty kept trying to revive her, pressed his mouth against her blue lips and tried to breathe life back into her. His wife was on her knees keening, a primal sound I still hear every night when I try to sleep. Police came, the guests left, and the lodge closed. I couldn't face anyone. I locked myself away, and Bessie says I had a breakdown, not that I remember it really. I spent some time in a psychiatric hospital, but that felt like cheating because the drugs numbed all thought and that wasn't fair to Tabitha.

I had to suffer like she suffered, so eventually I came home. By then, Morty had left. Just walked out the door one night. Clio, their grief shattered their lives and wrenched them apart. Eventually his wife left too. Just abandoned the place. I didn't get to say goodbye. I wouldn't have, probably. I never wanted to see them again, knowing the blame I'd see in their eyes when they looked at me."

I cried with Mom, for all the hurt, all the guilt she felt. The way she'd suffered her whole life for an accident that truly wasn't her fault. Choking back her sobs she turned to me, and said, "Then I met your dad. I didn't want to fall in love, but I did. I definitely didn't want to have children, but then you came along… I was happy, which felt like the worst kind of betrayal. How could I have a child when they'd lost theirs? But I *loved* you, how I loved you the very moment I met you. And then I thought, but what if I lose you too? What if you were snatched away as punishment? It was easier to hold myself back from you, not to tempt fate by showing how I felt. Not giving in to those overwhelming feelings of love."

"Oh, Mom…" I'd never in a million years have guessed it was all as complicated as that. What a waste her life had been, punishing herself, and pushing me away so I wouldn't get taken from her, because she felt she didn't deserve to have a child she loved. I moved to hug her. Her shoulders were wracked with sobs and I stroked her back, hoping to comfort her.

"You have to let the past go, Mom. You can't keep blaming yourself."

She sniffed and nodded. "I know. But it just feels so wrong, like I'm disgracing her memory."

"You've suffered long enough, Mom. No one would begrudge you happiness. *No one.*"

She remained silent and I thought about the Evergreen townsfolk and how well they'd kept her secret. "You realize no one spoke out of turn about you? All the people I asked kept their lips clamped closed because they didn't want you to have to relive it. That says a lot about you, and the way Evergreen locals regard you, Mom. They don't blame you, so maybe it's time you forgave yourself."

She nodded stiffly but didn't speak, and together we turned to stare at the maze, the place that had haunted her for so long. Would she finally forgive herself? Surely she'd lived with this grief for far too long now.

***

"Let's take Scotty for a walk?" Amory asked, interrupting my thoughts, her eyes clouded with concern for me. Since Mom had left I'd been staring out the bay window, watching the snow drift lazily down while I tried to reconcile everything I'd heard. I nodded. A walk would do me good.

"You'd better put his little vest on," I said, glancing at the overexcited puppy, who'd just learned the meaning of 'walk'.

I'd laughed over the last week as packages had arrived for Amory at an endless rate. She'd found an online doggie designer who made everything from coats to t-shirts. I'd have put money on the fact that Scotty's mini wardrobe probably had more designer labels than mine.

"Ah, so you're saying you don't think my puppy purchases were so silly now?" She arched a brow.

I giggled. "Well, I think a doggy jumper is probably wise in the snow… I'm just not sure about the design."

She rolled her eyes. "Doggy denim is hot right now, and how much does it suit the caramel tones of his fur?"

"Oh my God, you're one of the designer doggie moms. How sad for you, Amory." Scotty tried to escape her clutches as she wrestled yet another doggy jumper on him.

"Yeah, I know! How sad am I?" She giggled, not sad in the slightest.

We wound on scarves, and made our way outside, the cold, crisp air stealing the breath from my lungs.

"Have you spoken to Kai today? I didn't see him at breakfast, which is unlike him," she said, wrinkling her brow.

"He was heading to the chalets the last time I saw him, but then Mom came over..." I trailed off, the unspoken words hanging in the air.

"God, that view just never gets old," Amory said, pointing to the snow-covered mountains in the distance, gray, somber skies above filling the silence we'd lapsed into. "It always sort of shocks me when I walk outside and see the sky, rather than a skyscraper. It stuns me for a second, every single time, and then I wonder how I lived so long without a place like Cedarwood in my life. If I had to leave Evergreen, I'd miss it every single day."

Gone was the high-heel-wearing Manhattanite, gone was the girl who'd spend an hour doing her hair every single morning. Cedarwood had gotten under her skin, she'd swapped heels for boots, sleep-ins for morning walks, and straight hair for windblown curls. Life was so much easier here, so natural.

Scotty ran past us, barking at a rabbit who hopped past, easily evading his curiosity.

"So, are you going to tell me what happened with your mom?" Amory asked.

I spent the next hour explaining everything to my best friend, how I'd felt growing up, and what I thought would happen to my mom now the secret was out.

"Golly, goes to show you just never know what someone is really going through," she said, shaking her head.

"I know," I replied with a nod.

Amory hugged herself tight, calling Scotty back from the dense foliage by the lake. "I think you did the right thing, getting her to come out here. To explain it to you in person and face up to the past. Now you can both finally move forward. It's time to focus on the future."

"What about the maze?"

"Ask your mom. Involve her in it. What does she want? Really, you can understand if she wanted it to remain hidden. Maybe you could plant a rose garden there, in memory of the child. Something to honor her, and what happened."

"That's a great idea, Amory. It would be nice to remember Tabitha, not hide away from it any more." I gazed out across the expanse of water, still frozen, waiting for spring to come bringing its thaw. "Maybe it would also give Mom a sense of closure."

"Oh, darling, it definitely would. I mean, look at what your mom's been through, and how she punished herself for so long over a tragic accident. It's so bloody sad. I hope she starts to forgive herself soon."

"Me too." I turned back to my best friend and smiled, feeling the pressure of the secret lift off my shoulders. "Thanks, Amory. It's so nice to be able to talk about it openly now."

We walked in silence for a while before I said, "So, you know we have nothing booked for the next two weeks, and after that we're going to be super-busy the way our bookings and enquiries are going."

"Yeah, and where exactly are you going with this little tidbit?" She stared me down, provoking a laugh. She knew me too well.

"Well, if you wanted to go for a quick vacation, I don't know, to South America…"

358

She swatted me on the arm. "You minx. Threaten to push me over a cliff, you would, just so I'd agree to meet the parents. You know," she said more seriously, "I think I might take you up on that, though, because it does seem really important to Cruz, and I'm a bit of a harridan for saying no before, aren't I?"

"You're not a harridan." I searched her face, so glad to have her here and realizing she was truly a different person to the one who'd arrived a few months ago. It wasn't that she was maturing – she could still be the most childish person I knew – but she stopped to think about other people more, considered their feelings, their wants and needs ahead of her own. While we were busy at the lodge, we also had more time to reflect; the peace and quiet of the place gave you ample time to think about life and love and everything in between. It was shaping Amory in a way I hadn't seen before. Already perfect in my eyes, she was just losing that prickly edge she sometimes showed the world to hide her vulnerability.

"Will you puppysit?" she asked suddenly, shaking me out of my reverie. "When we go to South America? I mean, I'm only going for a week. I absolutely refuse to leave you and Scotty for any longer than that, no matter what Cruz says!"

I smiled. "Of course. Scotty will be fine with me." It would make the lonely nights easier, when they were gone. Kai would be gone by then too… At least I'd have a little ball of fur to curl up with.

Chapter Thirty-Eight

With one day until the party, things ramped up at the lodge. Deliveries were coming thick and fast, and Amory directed everyone with the assiduity of a railway conductor while I was busy tearing my hair out in the office.

"Tim, I totally understand, he wants it perfect – but he has to remember we've had less than a week to make this happen. And we're in *Evergreen*, not exactly a hive of activity where I can step out at any hour for supplies."

He sighed, and I could hear his frustration down the phone. "I know, I know. I don't think he really gets it."

I softened a little. "Look, tomorrow he will be so totally wowed with what we've done, he won't notice the things we didn't do. We're about to start decorating – full Gatsby Roaring Twenties-style – and I promise you, you'll be searching the crowd for F. Scott Fitzgerald himself, that's how amazing it will look."

"Thanks, Clio. I know you've worked miracles to get it done on time and we've kept throwing curveballs. Maybe once this is done we can have that drink?"

"I'd love to catch up with the gang again, Tim..."

"With the gang? Not just us two?"

I thought of Kai, of the fact that ever since I'd told him how I felt he'd somehow managed to avoid me. To be fair, after everything with my mom, I hadn't exactly been looking for him or in the right frame of mind to talk about it all. But still...

360

I sighed and tried to say what I needed to in the clearest way, but I really didn't want to hurt his feelings. "Tim, I'm sorry, but I don't think just the two of us dating is the best decision. Honestly, I think we're more suited to being just friends. I know we used to have something special, but I think you're caught up in the past. Things are different now."

He let out a soft groan. "I had a feeling that was coming," he said. "I wish things weren't different, Clio. But I understand. Maybe there will be someone for me at the party, a girl I can sweep off her feet." He laughed as if he was joking, but part of me thought he was serious. Maybe he was really ready to love again. I hoped he'd find someone sweet and at the same stage in life as he was.

I felt lighter now I'd finally spoken up. It was better that he knew I was only interested in him as a friend. "Well, if you're really interested… your secretary Vanessa seems a little smitten with you." I'd spoken to Vanessa close to a hundred times that week, and she'd always steered the conversation back to Tim, her voice dreamy.

"Vanessa? No, I think you're mistaken. Vanessa doesn't say more than two words to me. We correspond by email even though her office is attached to mine." Love! We really made it hard for ourselves. My matchmaker hat flew on…

"Let's see what some Gatsby sparkle does." I laughed, already wondering how I could maneuver them under some mistletoe.

He laughed. "See you tomorrow, Clio. And thanks again."

Once I hung up, I emailed Vanessa. What? So, the matchmaker instinct was strong in me.

Timothy mentioned how much he's looking forward to dancing with you at the Gatsby party. I hope you have your dancing shoes at the ready…

She replied instantly:

He did?!

I left it at that. Sometimes the only way forward was when someone gave you a little shove.

***

In the ballroom, Isla's face was dusted with glitter, and she sneezed before greeting me with a quick wave. "We're going to be sweeping up gold for the next ten years," she laughed as she tied a bunch of balloons together and put them by the cocktail bar.

Scotty ran underfoot, leaving a trail of debris in his wake. To say he was quite enamored with the decorations was an understatement and none of us wanted to begrudge him his fun.

That was until Scotty munched on one of the feather boas and Micah suggested we put the puppy outside while we finished up.

Amory's eyes flashed and she lifted Scotty to her chest. "You... you MONSTER! It's freezing out and you want me to put a poor defenseless animal outside for the sake of one piddly feather boa?"

"He's got a real fur coat," Micah added unhelpfully. "And a faux-furry jacket to boot."

She narrowed her eyes. "You are truly despicable! When you and Isla have your first child I will remember this, and instead of getting a gold locket for their first lock of hair, you're now getting silver!" She stomped off and it was all I could do not to laugh.

Micah let out a snort. "What the hell!"

I shook my head, "Let's just keep going. I'm sure you'll convince her to go back to a gold locket soon!" I laughed and we continued decorating.

On the table we had vases full of feathers, the tips dipped in gold, and glittery candles, and strings of pearls were draped over the back of each chair. The photo booth was set up in the corner with props: moustaches on sticks, feather boas, black and gold cigarette holders and pearl necklaces.

Micah had convinced Kai to stop the renovations he'd been doing on the chalets to help us decorate and they'd already draped the ceiling in black tulle, which cascaded down elegantly. I'd tried so many times to get his attention lately but he'd been running here and there. Worry gnawed at me – maybe I'd put him in an uncomfortable position by sharing my feelings?

Snapping myself out of any anxiety, I looked at the rest of the room, trying to get my head back in the game. We'd hung various art deco signs saying things like: *Drop it like F Scott*, and *Prohibition ends here*. I was giddy with how great the ballroom looked. It was completely transformed, and you'd never have recognized it from the bridal expo we'd held just over a week ago.

Sailing back into the kitchen, Cruz had everything under control. I could tell by the way he glided around humming, his chef's whites pristine, foodie smells scenting the air. "All OK?" I asked.

"Smashing, *dollface*."

I laughed.

"I'll mind my potatoes then!" I trilled in my best attempt at a flapper accent, and sashayed out. We were on track! This party was going to propel guests back to the Twenties, and who didn't want to spend some time in the jazz era?

We had a few hours until the guests were arriving so I went to find Amory and check she was OK after her spat with poor Micah, who was still confused over how he'd upset her. It was only that Amory had fallen hard for her canine progeny, and her protectiveness for Scotty knew no bounds.

Taking the steps two at a time, I found Amory talking earnestly to Isla halfway up the stairs about how to apply eyeshadow for the smoky-eye effect.

"We're all set, pretty much," I said.

"Why don't we get ready together and I can show Isla how it's done?" said Amory when I caught up.

"Let's! The jazz band is arriving in an hour, and we've got to help Aunt Bessie set up too. So let's get our skates on."

I let them go ahead and watched them giggle like schoolgirls as they ran up the rest of the stairs, Scotty going at double speed to catch them on his little legs. I couldn't wait to transform myself into a flapper.

After a quick shower, I joined the girls in Amory's suite.

"Oh my God, Isla, you look like Clara Bow herself!" She was draped in pearls and had an exotic and intricate feathery headpiece attached, with her hair curled and tucked up. Amory had applied her makeup perfectly – smoky eyes, ruby-red lips.

"Thanks, Clio! I feel like I've dunked my head into wet cement, but the mirror certainly says otherwise."

I laughed, remembering Isla rarely wore makeup and was usually more comfortable wearing work clothes than sequined dresses and heels.

Amory clucked her tongue. "I'm so proud," she joked, and began getting herself ready, including applying false lashes encrusted with diamantes that made her look every inch a Twenties movie starlet.

An hour and a bit later we sparkled and shimmied as we walked downstairs, in a mixture of sequins, beads, and pearls, on a cloud of sultry perfume. They sure knew how to dress to impress back in the jazz era.

Micah was waiting at the bottom of the stairs and held out a hand to Isla, kissing her sweetly on the cheek and murmuring in her ear. Cruz was still in the kitchen so Amory went to show off her Charleston moves to him there. I was about to head out on my pre-party check, but gasped when I saw Kai standing off to the side, a thumb looped in the pocket of his three-piece suit. The wavy-haired athlete had vanished and been replaced with a suave and sophisticated specimen of a man. *Was it hot in here?* His blue eyes shone appreciatively as he gave me a slow once-over.

"It's clear to me now that you were born in the wrong era, Clio…"

"Likewise, mister." We stared into each other's eyes and I wondered why he'd been avoiding me. I wanted to ask him, but Aunt Bessie walked in, arms laden with boxes. Besides, it smacked of desperation, didn't it? Better to pretend all was well, and save my pride.

"There you are, you glamourpuss. Can you take this please?" Aunt Bessie drawled.

Kai, ever the gentleman, stepped forward. "Here, let me take those."

She gave him a saucy eyebrow waggle. "If I was younger…"

"Aunt Bessie!" I said, faux-shocked. She was a flirt from way back when.

"What? He looks good enough to eat."

Laughter burbled from me. "Let's get you set up."

From the boxes Aunt Bessie unloaded a range of donuts, burnished gold and black to suit the theme.

"They're so pretty, Aunt Bessie!" I said, ogling a tray of mini gold-glitter donuts.

"I've got the most amazing cake pops too, done with edible black lacquer, so shiny you can see yourself in them."

We went briskly back to work, setting up her dessert table. Before I knew it, cars were crunching the gravel and our first guests arrived, drawing excited squeals from us all. Amory and I would usually be hosting a party near Times Square, waiting for the ball drop, but here we were, making Cedarwood Lodge the place to be. Even though we were technically working, it felt like a fairy tale come true to be sashaying around the lodge in a flapper dress.

Taking a moment, I watched as everyone got into position. We were getting more organized, my team, like a finely tuned machine, and I beamed with pride.

"Well, everyone. Let's go welcome our guests to the jazz age and show them one hell of a party!" Amory whooped and we swarmed to the entrance.

Amory welcomed guests, checking them off the guest list, while Micah showed them the way and Isla handed them a glass of champagne as they floated past.

Men wore dapper suits and women were dressed flamboyantly. I was impressed people had made such an effort, as it wasn't always the case – but who didn't like the glitz and glamour of another era? The romance, the poetry, the shunning of rules and regulations in the Twenties. It was impossible not to smile at the women speaking huskily, or throwing their heads back, laughing hard, as if they were truly transported to another time.

When Vinnie arrived we fussed and fawned over him and his guest of honor, Mr Whittaker. As soon as they even *thought* about another drink their champagne flutes were refilled. When one of them fumbled with a napkin, another was pressed into his hand. When I sailed past them for the third time, checking everything was going well, both of them were smiling as Amory regaled them with a hilarious story.

The jazz band played the Charleston, and people danced and kicked up their heels. They tangoed and foxtrotted, only stopping to guzzle champagne as though it was water. Even the most sedate of guests was inspired to join the others on the dance floor. The tap of high heels made me smile; this was what I wanted for the lodge – fun, frivolity, *dancing!*

With the party in full swing, the guests' sunny faces and raucous laughter high in the air, I signaled to the girls that it was time to take a breather – safe in the knowledge everything was on track, the skill-hire staff were working well, and everyone was having fun. Tim was wooing his clients and gave me a thumbs-up whenever I dashed past him. Maybe he'd hire Cedarwood every year for parties. The possibilities were endless!

Amory and Isla huddled by a wall, sneaking their first glass of champagne and gossiping about the guests – who had the prettiest dress, and who danced like no one was watching.

"Look how happy they are," Amory said. "This is one of the best parties we've ever done, Clio, and we've done some truly spectacular ones."

"I think so too," I said, grinning as I sent up a silent thank you to F. Scott Fitzgerald and his wife, Zelda, for making the jazz era so fashionable and so much fun to recreate.

Isla sipped her champagne and, as she craned her neck back to sip, a slim necklace she was wearing caught the light. I hadn't noticed it when we were getting ready. It was truly beautiful, a delicate constellation of stars, shimmering and twinkling under the lights.

"What's the symbolism of your necklace, Isla?" I asked. "It's gorgeous! Is it to do with the stars Micah named after you?"

She flushed deep scarlet, bringing out the freckles on her nose. "Umm, yeah. We, ah…" She frantically waved Micah over, who was restocking the champagne behind the bar. When he got to her, they clutched hands, and he searched her face for clues. It must have dawned on him because he nodded. "We were going to wait until the party was finished before we asked you, but…"

"Ask me?" Isla darted a nervous glance up at Micah, and he grinned like the Cheshire Cat. "Oh my God, ask me what?" I had a feeling I knew what it was and goose bumps broke out over my skin in anticipation.

"So, ah… would you and Amory be our wedding planners?"

Amory and I jumped and squealed as quietly as we could. Which under the circumstances was pretty damn loud, but hey, this was the most amazing news! There was nothing quite as romantic as planning a wedding, but to plan the wedding of two of your best friends, well, that was even better.

I grabbed Isla and gave her a hug, "You're getting *married*!" I pulled Micah into the hug, and Amory clasped her hands around the outside and we were one big circle of shrieking joyfulness. I was immediately in the realm of neither here nor there, stuck happily mentally planning their big day... *A winter wedding, the lodge lit up with fairy lights, their special constellation twinkling above, an ice sculpture, white roses, simple yet elegant...*

"You guys... oh, you've made this year end on the highest of notes." I waved Kai over, and Amory dashed to the kitchen to get Cruz, and came back with a bottle of bubbly under one arm and a bewildered Cruz in the other.

"Will you do the honors, Micah?" She handed him the bottle.

The cork popped, and foamy bubbles raced up and over. As flutes were filled, I said, "On behalf of Cedarwood Lodge, and all who inhabit the grand old dame, I'd like to congratulate Micah and Isla on their engagement."

Kai and Cruz shook Micah's hand in turn, slapping him on the back the way men do, and hugged Isla, kissing her on the cheek. Tears welled in my eyes; it felt like the most enchanted moment and I was so thrilled they'd shared it with us tonight of all nights, when magic was in the air and anything could happen.

We clinked glasses and toasted the happy couple. Everyone around me was falling in love and yet I couldn't even get Kai to spend a moment with me without dashing off with some excuse thrown over his shoulder. Maybe I'd always be the wedding planner, never the bride.

One of the waiters bustled over and tapped me. "Ready for the countdown?"

"Is it that time already?" I asked. The night had flown past. It felt like it had only just started and here we were on the cusp of a new year. Time sure did fly when you were having fun.

"Yep, I'll get the mixologist to count it down?"

"Please."

The mixologist had turned out to be seriously popular among the guests – not only could he mix a good gimlet but he laughed and joked with the crowd, making them feel special. And it definitely helped that he was easy on the eye... Amory had chosen well, and I hoped to secure him for every future Cedarwood Lodge event. If we could continue to tempt him out to the wilderness of Evergreen, that was.

"Ready for a new year?" I asked my friends, eventually settling my gaze on Kai. He took my hand and squeezed it, giving me a look loaded with meaning. But what that was exactly, I didn't dare interpret.

The countdown started as everyone paired up and raced outside to the decked area to watch the fireworks. *Ten. Nine. Eight.* We all chorused, a whole group of people together in one moment in time. *Seven. Six. Five. Four. Three.* I felt Kai pull me away from the crowd. *Two.* His arms closed around my waist and all I could do was stare into his eyes. *One.* Cheers rang out as the fireworks lit up the sky in a riot of color. But I didn't see them at all because Kai's lips were pressed firmly against mine, and I felt as if I was floating. Here I was, surrounded by my friends, a deck full of strangers, and Kai exactly where he should be – with me. Did this mean he felt the same, or was it the magic of New Year's Eve rubbing off on him?

The world spun dizzyingly around as the opening to 'Auld Lang Syne' rang out and the guests joined in... this truly was the most magical of moments. That song always made me cry, dammit, and I tried very hard to rein in my emotions, which were scattered like marbles.

Amory came up behind us. Once again interrupting a moment between me and Kai, and completely oblivious to it. "Before we get back to work, let's share our New Year's resolutions," she said, dragging Cruz behind her. "You first, Cruz."

Cruz, the only one not in a suit, still looked handsome in his chef's whites. "I want to find the perfect recipe for beef wellington and I'm willing to put in weeks of practice. Is anyone willing to be my taste tester? I warn you, it's going to be a lot of fun…"

Amory raised a brow. "Oh sorry, darling, but I've signed up to be Aunt Bessie's new taste tester. And I might be a little busy fulfilling my own resolution – to buy every kitten-heeled Jimmy Choo I can get my hands on. It's such a hard life."

"You, Clio?" she said, turning to me.

"I…" I froze as all eyes were on me, worried I'd blurt out something about Kai.

"OK. We'll come back to you. What about you Kai?"

Kai blushed and averted his eyes.

"You two are useless," Amory remarked, turning on her six-inch heels and sauntering off into the crowd as the mixologist gestured for her help. Guests were clinking glasses, and some were locking lips under doorways laced with mistletoe.

Micah and Isla were called away by guests, but Micah paused before he left and whispered to me, "When you know, *you know*." He was referring to his marriage proposal, and I gave him a quick squeeze.

We'd been through a lot, Micah and me. Sometimes we'd been there for each other, and sometimes we hadn't, but now he'd found the perfect girl. One who loved him unconditionally, who didn't take him for granted, who didn't stomp all over his dreams. He'd known she was the one from the moment he saw her, and I'd been there and caught the moment Cupid's arrow had struck his heart. When you know, *you know*, he'd said. And I couldn't help thinking his sentiment applied to me too. Hadn't I known it the first time Kai had jumped from the cab of his truck?

I had recognized him, yet I hadn't met him before, or something primal had happened, because the world had got brighter, music had sounded sweeter, laughter had come quicker, and all of that paled when he wasn't here. And I couldn't let that happen again.

Shuffling on our feet, we tried to talk, but the music had been turned up and I soon found myself pulled back to the party – ensuring everyone's champagne flutes were filled to the brim and bidding farewell to a few guests as they left, slightly wobblier than when they'd arrived. I grinned when I saw Kai get strong-armed into dancing with a foxy seventy-something-year-old who wouldn't take no for answer.

Hours later, the party was winding down; women carried their heels and men had shrugged off their coats. The last partygoers were sitting around drinking the rest of the champagne. The party had been a roaring success but it wasn't quite over yet. By the photo booth Timothy stood with Vanessa, his assistant. They had their heads bent conspiratorially and, before I could avert my eyes, they kissed, and I smiled, glad Tim would find his own happy ever after, because he deserved someone to love. All they'd needed was a very gentle hint and they'd realized... Love was so simple for some.

"Go," Amory said, tapping me on the butt.

"Go where?"

She pointed to where Kai was standing outside on the deck, fairy lights twinkling above him, his hands deep in his pockets. He cut a fine figure standing under the moonlight with soft snowflakes drifting down.

I gave Amory's hand a squeeze and went to him.

Sensing my presence he turned and gave me a heart-melting smile. I smiled back; I couldn't help it – even if Kai was about to break my heart and announce he was off again, being around him just made me feel lighter.

"Clio, I've been heartsick at the thought of leaving..."

I couldn't speak. I just stared at him, my hand tingling in his. Eventually I managed to nod.

"When I wake up," he whispered, "I'm thinking of you. When I sleep you inhabit my dreams. Your smile, your laugh, the way you cry to Bonnie Tyler when you think no one can hear..." He tailed off and a smile crept onto his face.

Oh, God.

"Your ability to burn toast, and blame the toaster, the way people flock to be in your spotlight. I've been so torn about everything, not wanting to appear like the lost soul I was. How do I say how I feel without putting any more pressure on you?"

"What do you mean, Kai?" My breath caught. *What pressure?*

"You know, when I found out I was adopted I ran, took my things, cursed them all and got lost in the biggest country I could find. And now I see that for what it was. Without knowing the truth, without reconciling the past, I wouldn't have found *you*. I would still be in Australia catching waves, and building other people's houses, but missing something I couldn't quite put my finger on."

"So...?" Was this goodbye?

"It was you, Clio. That's what's been missing from my life. And now I see I had to make sense of the past to be able to live for the future. And I hope that future will be with you. Here."

"You're staying at Cedarwood?" My legs were like jelly, but I fought the urge to stumble into his arms. It was all too good to be true. I was sure it was a dream and any minute I'd wake up. But I needed real words this time, real answers, not just the press of his lips against mine.

"If you'll have me. I told my boss I wasn't coming back. Leaving you would be like someone turning off the sun, and I just want you to know, you've changed me, made me whole again, and even if you don't feel the same way, I will always love you for that. For what I know can be..."

"I can't believe you're really going to stay." I grinned, while my heart thrummed so hard I was sure he could hear it.

"For the last month I've been trying to find a building job closer to Evergreen so I could be near you. Just on the off-chance, in case you had the same feelings for me."

"But wasn't it obvious how I felt?" Golly, I was clearly useless at expressing myself to him. "I told you! I kissed you, I made it quite clear, didn't I?"

"Well, there was Tim calling every three minutes, and with your history and all… I wasn't sure if you meant it. And I had to get myself together, first, before I admitted it to you. Then there were my parents, my job. I had to be sure I was in the right space and was making the right choice by *you*, Clio. And if you'd have chosen Tim, then I would have respected that. But the last thing I wanted was to admit how I felt about you and have you tell me you loved someone else. And I had to make peace with who I was, and who I want to be. Which is here, with you, for as long as you'll have me."

"Tim is just a friend, but how did you even know it was an issue?" Before the words left my mouth, I knew.

"Amory," he said, laughing. For once I wouldn't scold her about sharing my secrets. "She told me you weren't interested in Tim like that because you were head over heels in love with me." That minx!

"Head over heels? Well, I guess I am."

My pulse raced, and I wanted to pinch myself to make sure this was real. That the blue-eyed Australian boy in front of me was really staying at the lodge, because he wanted to be with me. I was the girl Amory had dubbed icy heart – but Kai had proven a heart could be thawed, it just took the right person. *It took Kai*. A man who'd managed to sweep me off my feet with his sensitive soul, his zest for life, and his passion. "I hope you stay for ever, Kai."

"I'm not going anywhere, Clio. I promise you that."

He lifted my chin and pulled me in for a swoon-worthy kiss, and while I still felt dizzy with desire for him, I also felt something else, something like hope and the promise of for ever. Right here, in the place we all felt at home.

Epilogue

Fourteen months later.

The sun shone down, training triangles of light on the lush green grass. With respectful faces, we stood huddled by the newly pruned maze.

"Ready?" I asked and gave Mom's hand a squeeze.

"Ready."

Hand in hand we wandered through the entrance. Mom knew her way even after all these years. When we came to the middle, the large square, we stopped short. Mom gasped and covered her face. After a minute she removed her hands, and said, "It's beautiful, Clio."

In the small square clearing at the center of the maze, we'd planted a garden bed, and laid a length of grass. In the middle of the grass patch sat a stone memorial bench with Tabitha's name engraved on a gold plaque.

Mom reached out, ran the pad of her finger along the plaque and said, "I'll never forget you, Tabitha, but today I'm saying goodbye." Her small shoulders shook with the effort of her farewells.

Tabitha was gone but never forgotten. And now Mom could let the past go.

Kai wandered over, a pot of roses in his hand. "Any place in particular?" he gently asked Mom, who pointed to a spot. He dug out the earth, and planted the pretty pale-peach rosebush. Mom had asked for a rose garden, and a rose garden she would have. The maze was a place of solitude for her now, a place to visit and reflect. Her days sitting in her cottage alone were over. She'd moved into one of the chalets, and spent her days with Isla, manicuring the gardens and the grounds – just like she'd always dreamed of doing. The work had made her stronger, in myriad ways, and her cheeks weren't as hollow any more.

Reaching forward I gave her a tight hug, glad to have her back in my life now. And grateful that we had made it through everything to be here today. Not quite the TV mother and daughter I'd pictured, but close enough.

Pulling back she laid a hand on my cheek and smiled. "I'm just going to sit here awhile," she said, shading her eyes from the spring sunshine, which we took as our cue to leave.

As we left the maze behind us, Kai reached out to me. Hand in hand we walked back to the lodge, and took a pitcher of iced tea to the deck. Kai's mom and dad were sleeping off their jetlag in one of the suites upstairs, and I was eager to show them around once they'd napped. They were a lovely couple; I'd spent two weeks last winter with them when we made a flying visit to Sydney, Australia. They'd promised us then that they'd come and visit Cedarwood, and here they were. I was proud of Kai – he was their boy again, and it didn't matter that they were bound only by love, not blood. They were eager to see what Kai did, and where he lived, but I was more nervous about the secret we'd kept from them.

It was getting harder to keep it secret, too, as each day went on and the weather grew warmer. Tonight, we'd surprise them all. Mom and Aunt Bessie were staying for dinner. They'd assembled the world's biggest donut tower to wow Kai's parents. Aunt Bessie was leaving Puft in Mom's capable hands a week later because she was being interviewed for a segment on a cooking show with the potential to have her own show if ratings were good. It was mind-bending that my aunt had set Instagram on fire with her donut pictures. People adored her, worshipped the bubbly woman, and we had a constant stream of visitors at the lodge who came all this way to meet her in person. To know Aunt Bessie was to love her, and I was so proud of her. And Mom too. Mom still struggled being the center of attention in town, but she didn't run and hide any more, just faced it head-on and smiled her way through it, claiming that each day it got a little easier.

Cruz and Amory would also be joining us. They were eager to meet Kai's parents, and eager to show off the newest edition to the family. Scotty the dog now had a sibling, a little fluffball named Hem. Amory worked hard planning parties, and keeping me sane at the lodge just like normal, but on Saturday afternoons she volunteered at the local dog shelter, and it lit her up from the inside out. While party planning would always be her passion, I think the work at the shelter grounded her.

Even Micah and Isla were taking time out of their renovations to the new house they'd just bought and would attend dinner tonight. They worked at the lodge during the day, and spent most nights bashing down walls and then rebuilding them, hoping to get their house finished by summer. I could only imagine how amazing it would look once Isla planted a garden out front and Micah painted the new roof. Their wedding had been a hugely fun night, our bellies had hurt from laughter, and it was obvious how perfect they were for each other. When Micah had serenaded her, there hadn't been a dry eye in the house. I was glad they were taking a night off their renovations tonight, because I wanted them to share in the special moment with us too.

Summer was around the corner and the lodge was completely booked out for the season. We'd soon be run off our feet, which was very exciting – that and the secret we'd managed to keep thrilled me. I only had to keep my mouth clamped closed for a few more hours, and then I could tell my family and my friends. *Finally!* It had been torture not confiding in my best friends, but I figured our parents should all find out at the same time.

Everyone would be together and it would be the perfect time for Kai to brandish the tiniest of hiking boots we could find, and tell our loved ones there was a baby on the way...

When you know, *you know*.

As the sun colored the sky saffron, Kai leaned over and planted a kiss on the soft swell of my belly, and I sent up a thank you to the universe. It was true: coming home had been the best thing I'd ever done...

Read on for an extra short story featuring all of your favourite Cedawood Characters.

Christmas at Cedarwood Lodge

Five years later.

The office door swung open with a bang, bringing with it the sound of Christmas carols and Cruz's dark face. Amory moved quickly to hide the gift she'd only half-wrapped.

"What is it?" I asked. Cruz was usually the epitome of cool, but something bothered him this fine Christmas Eve.

"Have you seen the ham hock?"

I pressed my lips together to stifle the laugh that threatened to escape. *Ham hock?* When no response was forthcoming from me he turned his steely gaze on Amory. "Well?"

She shook her head, innocent eyes wide. Just then a little giggle carried from down the hallway. We did our best to ignore it, knowing quite suddenly where the ham hock had gone.

"What did you need it for exactly?" I asked, buying time. The little giggle was edging closer, bringing with it the cheery notes of 'Have Yourself a Merry Little Christmas'.

"I need the hock for soup; waste not, want not." His words were clipped as they so often were, having given up on me and Amory eons ago when it came to our education in the culinary arts. The only part we were interested in was consuming the delicious dishes – *quality control*; we wanted no part in the making of them.

"Didn't we just eat our body weight in ham?" Amory asked. We'd been feasting on Christmas menus for the month of December in light of our festive season guests.

"Yes," he said, his voice huffy. "And the remnants would make a fine soup. Running a kitchen is all about budgeting and minimizing food waste…"

Amory held up a hand, her eyes getting that particular glaze when Cruz tried to explain his position to her.

Unbeknownst to Cruz, five-year-old Millie appeared, light shining on her blonde head like a halo, the perfect disguise for the little minx she was. In her hand was the vestige of the ham hock, or at least that's what it appeared to be to my untrained eye. Either that or she'd been excavating the garden for dinosaur bones again, but perhaps not in such snowy weather. You never could tell with Millie, though.

Cruz sighed and scrubbed a hand over his face. "It was Millie again, wasn't it? And she's behind me, isn't she?"

Millie let her giggles spill out, and we soon followed suit. "Yes," I said, lips twitching. She wore a bright-red Christmas onesie whose padded feet helped her sashay about undetected.

The tension left Cruz's face and he turned to the small child. "Ah," he said, taking the hock from her hand. "I should've known you'd be the culprit." His voice softened. Millie had stolen the hearts of everyone at the lodge, despite her rascally nature. "Who were you saving this time?"

"The doggies," she said in her cherubic voice. "Amory helped me."

Amory let out a gasp and said, "I most certainly did not." And then made shushing gestures to Millie behind Cruz's back. Those two were partners in crime and it warmed my heart, even though Millie often gave her so-called confidante up to save herself.

Cruz just shook his head. "At this rate we'll go bankrupt but the menagerie will be plump enough to live through the winter."

We had amassed a number of stray animals at the lodge. Dogs, and cats, and once a pony, which I had spirited away to a friend's farm before Millie could lay claim. Amory took the dogs home at night, but during the day they roamed the gardens, or snuggled by the fire, being secretly fed by these two conspirators.

"Amory told me no one likes ham soup," Millie continued, getting her godmother well and truly in trouble.

Cruz turned slowly to Amory. "Did she now?" Amory's mouth opened and closed while Millie just grinned, like the Cheshire Cat.

"She did." Millie shrugged her shoulders, as if such trivial things bored her. "Can we open the presents now?"

"Not yet." Millie's face fell.

"Maybe I can sneak you one or two later," Amory said. "How about we go grab a snack while Cruz isn't looking? Some of those Santa-shaped gingerbread men…?"

Millie squealed.

"I'm right here, you know," Cruz said, but smiled. He loved feeding people, and secretly delighted that none of his cookies ever made it through a day. There were plenty of hands snatching from the cookie jar.

For someone who didn't want children of her own, Amory sure didn't mind spending time with them. It was a godsend really. She was the fun aunt, the one who got up to mischief with Millie, or cuddled and crooned to baby Brooklyn when my eyes were popping out of my head from lack of sleep.

Motherhood had been my greatest achievement to date, but I hadn't been prepared for how much strength it sapped. Brooklyn was only three months old and had trouble settling. Then I'd have Millie up with the sparrows. Luckily I had plenty of hands at the lodge, so I could duck off for a nap when my brain turned to mush from fatigue.

The trio left the room, hands entwined, Millie negotiating for more cookies.

Alone, I kept up with wrapping the gifts, smiling when I came to ones I'd bought earlier in the year when I was fueled with pregnancy hormones. I really don't know what I'd been thinking. Why would I have bought Kai a compass? The man read the stars, the moon, the sun, the wind... Still, I'd managed to get it all done and the children's presents too, which were hidden upstairs in the attic. Millie had hunted high and low for them, but she had no idea there even was an attic. She hadn't clued on yet the little cord dangling down was the access point.

Kai wandered in, his cheeks red from exertion. I hastily covered his present with the bright-red foil. "Been wandering up the mountain?" I asked.

"It was lonely without you."

I stood and kissed him hard on the lips, tasting the fresh mountain air and his particular Kai loveliness. My heart did somersaults and I wondered if the effect he had on me would ever fade. It was still as strong as ever, but more solid now, more real. "My mountain-climbing days are numbered," I said. "Until I've slept a good eight hours in a row." Well, that was my excuse, anyway. He still dragged me out for midnight yoga over the summertime, and I'd fallen in love with the way it made me feel. Now I did it of my own free will, but cloistered inside, where it was warm in the winter.

I put my cheek against his chest, the thrumming of his heart almost enough to lull me to sleep. It still seemed like a dream, our fairy-tale romance, the fact we'd made a little family together, built up a thriving business and kept our love alive despite long hours and sleepless nights. Unlike my previous relationships, things just gelled with Kai. The more life got hectic, the more I felt his support. When I was stressed or overworked he sensed it and made me climb that godforsaken mountain. And when I noticed the same in him, I made him take time for himself. To wander, to go be with nature, to go get lost in that way of his he so yearned for. Eventually, he'd acquiesce, and take his truck and go find some waves, somewhere where it was warmer, somewhere far from here.

I guess we found that balance, and learned to intuit what the other needed. His parents were coming soon, to stay for the winter. I worried they'd freeze with their Australian bodies, so used to heat and sun, but they assured me they'd acclimatize quickly, climbing mountains if need be to keep warm. Not hard to see where Kai inherited his love of hiking from then... I loved Kai's parents. They were laid-back and easy-going, and all the adoption business had been squared away. It still came up every now and then, but there was no bitterness any more, just a sense of wonder at what might have been.

There was a knock on the door. I pulled myself away from Kai. Dazed from his proximity.

"Sorry to disturb you two lovebirds," Micah said with his impish grin. "But Aunt Bessie is here. Says she wants to make an early start on dinner."

I checked my watch. It was barely eight in the morning. "That's Aunt Bessie. I'll call Mom."

I buzzed Mom's extension and she said she'd come right over.

"Where's Isla?"

Micah shrugged. "In town, doing some last-minute Christmas shopping, I imagine. She won't be long."

Isla's parents couldn't make it this Christmas, so she was all set to fly out to them the day after Christmas for the week.

"As long as she's not working." When winter set in and snow began to fall there wasn't much need for a landscaper, so Isla helped out with the guest activities. She relished the work, and I often had to tell her to turn in for the day, so caught up was she with sorting dance lessons, or art classes, that she lost track of time.

"I've hidden her work file, so she can't."

I smiled at the knowledge. Isla didn't have an *off* button and it was easy to work too hard at the lodge because there was always something that needed doing. "Good, she needs a proper break."

He nodded. "I keep telling her."

"Maybe she should take a few weeks over Christmas?" I said, mentally trying to rearrange staff, and who'd step in for her. Isla needed time to recharge her batteries and she would only do that if she wasn't here.

"You tell her then. She won't like it." And she wouldn't. That was the problem. Isla loved the lodge as much as I did.

"Yoooo hoooo," a voice rang out.

"Aunt Bessie, we're in here!"

My aunt sauntered into the room, her bleached-blonde hair curled to perfection, her face made up. I kissed her heavily rouged cheek, her flashing candy-cane earrings making me blink. "Merry Christmas," she said.

"Merry Christmas, Aunt Bessie!" I darted a glance over my shoulder, hoping she couldn't see her present. I'd found her the sweetest silver bracelet with little donut charms, perfect for the woman who'd taken the humble donut to the next level. In the years since she'd embraced Instagram she'd become something of a social media sensation, which had led to her being invited on to a plethora of mid-morning TV shows to do baking demonstrations, and now she had her very own cooking show. Filming wrapped in November so she was back at Puft, plying her wares and sharing all sorts of celebrity gossip with her goggle-eyed customers. But she was still the same old Aunt Bessie, a breath of fresh air and fun to boot.

"Where's Anabelle?"

"Mom's on her way," I said as she took Micah into her arms, swishing him from side to side as if he were a little boy and not a full-grown man.

Just then the baby monitor rustled to life with the cries of Brooklyn. "Oh, my baby is awake," Aunt Bessie said, grinning. "I guess that means you get to unload the car, and I'll sort that precious little bundle out?"

Aunt Bessie loved my kids like they were her own grandbabies. She was the veritable baby whisperer when it came to Brooklyn, and when all else failed I called on Aunt Bessie to come and help if I couldn't get her to settle. "I was going to bath her."

"Leave it to me. Has she got some gorgeous little Christmas outfit?"

I grinned. "Of course. She's Santa's little helper, didn't you know?"

She clapped her hands and rushed off toward the stairs.

***

That afternoon we had a full house. With everyone present we finally let Millie decorate the tree in the front salon. We had other Christmas trees scattered around the lodge, but they were professionally adorned by Amory, and more for the enjoyment of the guests. This one was all Millie's and she'd made all sorts of garlands for it, including strings of popcorn she and Amory had laced that morning.

"Now, Mama?" she asked.

I kissed the top of her head. Her hair smelled like apples and innocence and I felt a fierce tug in my heart. How I loved her. "Now," I agreed, and she shrieked and grabbed her grandma's hand. Mom smiled, and bent over the box with Millie, discussing the pros and cons of putting the tinsel on first or last.

While they were occupied, I ambled to the kitchen and checked in on Aunt Bessie, who was helping Cruz with the Christmas Eve dinner prep.

Amory must've smelled something on offer and crept up behind me. "I hope you're making gingerbread coffee to go with those," she said, pointing to the tray of Santa gingerbread men.

"Aren't we banned?"

Our last attempt to make eggnog had resulted in carnage. At least for the eggs involved. How exactly did one separate the yolk from the white? We didn't think it mattered, but clearly it did. Cruz bemoaned the fate of so many eggs, and banished us with a stiff warning never to attempt cooking again.

"Technically. But this is just a snack, and you can't mess up coffee. That's the one gift you do have."

Aunt Bessie shooed us out. "Come on, you two, you'll set fire to something, or turn the oven off by mistake. Get out and we'll make you some gingerbread coffee, yeah?" Baby Brooklyn was snug in her capsule, smiling and gurgling at Aunt Bessie's voice. I gave her a kiss. She looked adorable in her little Santa's helper suit complete with Santa hat. "I better feed the munchkin," I said, taking the warm bundle. "We'll be in the front salon then. Out of harm's way."

Amory snatched the tray of biscuits when Cruz had his back turned and we stole out of there like the thieves we were. I settled Brooklyn for her feed, while Millie and Mom heaped the poor fir tree with baubles of red, green and gold, as she bent Mom's ear about everything she'd done that day, an exhausting list by the sounds of it. My little girl reminded me of me and Micah, and the fun we'd had on the grounds of the lodge growing up. So many places to explore and mischief to get up to.

Amory sat next to me, munching on a gingerbread man. Her wedding ring flashed under the Christmas lights, reminding me of their wedding. Well, their elopement actually. A few years back they'd announced breezily they were off to Vegas to get married, simple as that, as if they were talking about a weekend getaway. In typical Amory style she'd been married to the man she loved, wearing a flame-red dress, with just her, Cruz, and a witness they'd paid ten bucks.

"What's that look you're wearing there?" she said, squinting at me.

"What look?"

"You're all misty-eyed…"

"Am I?" I laughed and dashed at my eyes. Weddings… I loved them no matter what scale they were on. "I was thinking of your elopement, actually, and how radiant you were coming home."

The fire crackled behind as she contemplated. "It was perfect for us," she said, her voice softening. While Amory was all bravado and brisk efficiency when it came to Cruz, she was almost shy about revealing her feelings. Eloping had been the right choice for them. It did make me wonder, as a wedding planner myself, if I'd ever get to walk down the aisle. I guess Kai and I had done things backwards: built up the business, had the babies. Did we really need a certificate to prove our love? Probably not in his eyes, but in mine, it was all about the celebration of that love. About sharing that precious moment with people who made your life complete. Still, we didn't discuss it. But I often imagined my own wedding, what I'd wear, how we'd decorate the chapel, what on earth I'd say in my vows that would be enough to describe my love for him…

"What is it about Christmas that brings all this to the fore?" she asked. "You know, the memories, the love, all that soppiness."

I laughed. "It's the time of year to reflect, and hope and dream."

"You'd look amazing in a backless gown," she said, waggling a brow. Golly, the girl knew me so well, she could read my mind.

"Why, thank you," I said, pretending not to understand. "But it's a little cold for that."

"Oh, please, you know what I'm talking about. Don't make me open Pinterest."

I colored. So, I'd been adding pins to my dream-wedding board? I *was* a wedding planner!

Isla wandered in, and our talk fell silent. "Take a seat," I said, smiling. In the years she'd worked at the lodge, she'd grown even more beautiful with her fire-red hair, and willowy frame. But it was more than looks alone, it was an inner confidence she'd found that made her so striking.

"My shopping is finally done and just in the nick of time. Who wants to help me wrap them?"

I let out a groan. "I vote Amory."

Amory surveyed her nails, which had little Christmas trees painstakingly painted on. "I can be swayed with champagne," she said. Isla's eyes brightened. "Deal! Oh, I got Micah the cutest gift! It's a sketch of our wedding day, you know the picture under the arbor?" We nodded. "That one, in charcoal. It's the prettiest thing."

"I love that picture of you two," I said, remembering it in detail, the way they only had eyes for each other.

"What picture?" Micah said, wandering in and holding his hands to the fire.

"Nothing," Amory said, quickly.

"You three look guilty as sin."

"Micah," Amory said in dulcet tones. "It's Christmas. Can't a girl have some secrets at Christmas without getting the third degree?"

"Yeah," I said. "Geez, Micah. Let there be some surprises, please."

He colored. "When you three confer like that, it usually means trouble."

I scoffed. "I hardly think that's the case." Poor Micah, he was right. We made a formidable team and it often led to trouble, at least where Micah was concerned. We'd cooked up crazy ideas for the lodge over the years: Halloween parties, Teddy Bears' picnics, all sorts of things where we made Micah be the ghost, the bear, even the Easter bunny once. Not to mention all the girls' movie nights we'd subjected him to when he couldn't think of an excuse quick enough. In this case, however, it was innocent, but I didn't blame him for being suspicious.

Kai came in and took a contented Brooklyn from me. Usually she'd be fussing, but it was like she knew Aunt Bessie was in the house, so was being the prefect baby. It was nice to relax, knowing she was settled.

"These ladies are up to something, Kai. I just know it."

Kai raised a brow. "There's an adult-sized Santa suit in the cupboard, is that it?"

I kept my laughter in check, knowing there was no such thing. "Kai, that was a secret!"

Micah's mouth fell open. "Oh, God, please don't tell me you've organized some kind of Cedarwood Lodge Christmas Pageant or something, and I'm riding on a float."

Dammit, I wished I'd thought of that. Before I could say anything to Amory, she'd taken her phone out and was making a note about it. Great minds and all that.

Aunt Bessie sashayed in with a tray of gingerbread coffees, the spicy, nutty scent peppering the air. "Get these down, would you, so we can crack open the champagne already."

We each took a mug, and Millie had her own gingerbread milkshake, topped with whipped cream and the most enormous chocolate donut. "That'll ruin her dinner, Aunt Bessie," I said, picturing Millie dosed up on all that sugar, careening around the lodge.

"Hush now, who called the fun police? It's Christmas, last time I checked."

I shook my head ruefully. There was no winning when it came to Aunt Bessie and her donuts.

***

"Urgh," said Amory clutching her tummy. "How are we supposed eat a proper meal? I'm still full from afternoon tea."

Sure enough, like she did every year, Aunt Bessie had doled out some pre-feast snacks, so we'd managed to polish off piles of her latest creations, donuts in every shape and flavor you could imagine, some with candyfloss, others filled with luscious chocolate ganache. Mom had baked a pumpkin chiffon pie which had been demolished too. She'd come so far with her cooking over the years, and had also put on some much-needed weight. That haunted look she'd worn for so long was gone, and it made me smile just looking at her.

"Too bad," I said, feeling decidedly sleepy myself. "We have to feast and feast we will." I pulled my best friend up by the hand, the cat jumping from her lap, but the dogs near her feet snoring away, oblivious.

"Mom," I said, entering the warmth of the kitchen. "We'll set the table, yeah? Do you need help with anything else?"

She looked down her specs at me, and wiped her hands on her reindeer apron. "Set the table, and light the candles, and we'll be ready in five. Millie needs her face washed, she got into the gravy."

"*The gravy?*" That child was a bottomless pit.

"She loves it."

I called to her as Amory and I went into the dining room to prepare the table. Our color theme this year was silver and white and as much bling as we could find. It suited the winter wonderland feel the lodge had at this time of year.

"Yeah?" Millie said, poking her little blonde head around the door. To my surprise she was dressed in her Christmas outfit, a frilly green dress, with matching headband, and her face was clean, her hair neatly held back.

"Aw, you look beautiful," I said, snatching her up for a hug. "Very festive."

"Daddy made me take a bath." She rolled her deep-blue eyes.

"You probably had gravy from head to toe."

"Yeah. Can we open the presents now?"

"Soon." I kissed her cheek as she wiggled to get down.

Each year we handed out presents to one another on Christmas Eve as had become tradition. On Christmas Day our friends would visit their own families, and we'd go to Aunt Bessie's to repeat the festivities. Millie knew she was in for a treat and couldn't contain herself.

"How soon?"

Kai snuck in dressed in a black-knit sweater and denim jeans. He looked every inch a Vermonter these days, and less like a nomadic yogi. Golly, the guy took my breath away. "My little cherub can't wait another moment for a present!" He scooped her up and rained kisses over her face.

"I can't, not another minute! I've waited all day-y-y-y-y."

The rest of the gang took up places at the table, Aunt Bessie and Cruz dashing in and out with heavenly scented dishes, my mouth watering despite what I'd eaten that day.

"Give that child a gift!" Aunt Bessie cried out. "We'll be another few minutes at least."

Amory bent to the tree and took a candy-cane-wrapped box. "For you," she said, kissing the tip of her nose. We exchanged a smile as Millie dashed the paper off in seconds, and let out a squeal. "Ice skates!" She kicked off her ballet flats and went to put them on.

"No, no," I said, laughing. "You can't wear them inside! After lunch tomorrow, Daddy and I will take you skating on the lake."

"Tomorrow?" her voice pitched. "That's for ever away!"

Kids! Time moved so much slower for them.

Amory bent and helped Millie put her ballet flats back on. "How about I get here bright and early and take you? Once you've opened up all of the gifts Santa brings you…"

Mollified, she beamed. "Yes!"

I knew Amory had matching skates, and they'd look a picture zooming around the ice hand in hand.

Millie opened the rest of her gifts, while we finished setting the table.

Amory winked and took fidgety Brooklyn from her capsule. There were presents for the baby too, Christmas books made from felt, and a rocking horse from Micah.

We sat down to eat, Mom and Aunt Bessie fussing with the placement of dishes, while I poured champagne for the table, and sparkling apple juice for Millie.

"A toast," I said, as everyone took their places. "To another wonderful year at the lodge with the greatest family and friends anyone could have."

We stood and clinked glasses, laughing as we tried to edge around each other's outstretched arms. Just then Millie piped up. "Oh, yeah, I almost forgot," she said, lifting her finger. "Mom, Daddy has this big sparkly ring for you in his pocket..." Before she could say any more Kai clamped a hand over her mouth.

Everyone froze.

"I forget just how good those little ears are," Kai said, gently tugging Millie's earlobe.

Again the room fell silent. It could be a dress ring, an eternity ring, a pendant even, I told myself. It might *not* have been an engagement ring... I'd almost gotten used to the fact I'd planned the most glamourous weddings, yet had never walked down the aisle myself. We were busy, then we had the children and were even busier. And we loved each other, which was all that mattered, right?

But still, my heart pumped with hope.

"Well," Kai said, taking my hand. "This wasn't exactly how I planned this." And then he dropped to one knee. "Clio, will you marry me?"

I blinked back happy tears, but I was lost for words. Until Amory coughed and motioned for me to respond. Oh, right! "Yes, my answer is yes!"

While I knew Kai loved me with his whole heart, I was a wedding and event planner, dammit, and I knew we'd have the most wonderful wedding that ever was. The wedding I'd been dreaming of since I was a young girl. And we'd have it right here, at Cedarwood Lodge, where I first clapped eyes on the man of my dreams...

Acknowledgements

For my cousin, Tracy Farr. The coolest, funniest girl there ever was! Thanks for supporting my writing from day one onwards. It means the world to me.

And Liesel Lou, my sweet, caring, compassionate sister-in-law who is also a massive support for me and my writing. Love you lots.

And finally heartfelt thanks to Victoria Oundjian and Hannah Smith, editors extraordinaire who encouraged me when I thought I couldn't do it, promised me wine at the end of the tunnel, and most of all believed in me! You make every story sparkle and I love working with you both.

ONE PLACE. MANY STORIES

Bold, innovative and
empowering publishing.

FOLLOW US ON:

@HQStories